Lydia M. Millard

Nepenthe

A novel

Lydia M. Millard

Nepenthe
A novel

ISBN/EAN: 9783337000707

Printed in Europe, USA, Canada, Australia, Japan

Cover: Foto ©Andreas Hilbeck / pixelio.de

More available books at **www.hansebooks.com**

NEPENTHE.

A Novel.

BY THE AUTHOR OF "OLIE."

> "We get no good
> By being ungenerous, even to a book,
> And calculating profits—so much help
> By so much reading. It is rather when
> We gloriously forget ourselves, and plunge
> Soul-forward, headlong, into a book's profound,
> Impassioned for its beauty and salt of truth.—
> 'Tis then we get the right good from a book."
> BROWNING.

New-York:

CARLETON, PUBLISHER, 413 BROADWAY.

M DCCC LXIV.

TO

CLAUDIUS B. PEASE,

WHOSE KINDNESS SOOTHED, WHOSE CONSTANCY CHEERED,

WHOSE DEVOTION SUSTAINED,

TILL ITS LATEST HOUR,

THE LIFE OF OUR GENTLE ANNIE,

WATCHING SO TENDERLY THROUGH THE NIGHT OF ANGUISH,

TILL ITS RADIANT DAWN,

THIS BOOK

Is Affectionately and Gratefully Dedicated.

CONTENTS.

CHAPTER	PAGE
I.—Mr. Douglass finds a document not in his line.	9
II.—Prudence Potter's Discoveries—The Doctor's Comments	14
III.—Mr. Trap Holds Forth and comes to a Climax.	24
IV.—Mr. Stuart's Affairs suddenly close up	28
V.—Mrs. John Pridefit's Murmurs, Perambulations, Charities	35
VI.—Mrs. John Pridefit in the Dark.	46
VII.—Mrs. Pridefit's Indignation and Consternation	51
VIII.—Mrs. Pridefit takes a Course consistent with Personal Convenience and Pecuniary Liabilities.	55
IX.—A Chapter with Some Preaching in it.	65
X.—Dr. Wendon's Self-Denial	73
XI.—The Midnight Visitor.	83
XII.—Dr. Wendon's Dream.	87
XIII.—Excitement in a Parlor Up Town	86
XIV.—The Wendons talk about the Opera.	109
XV.—Impulses—The Arrest	112
XVI.—Fifth House in the block For Sale—Inquire of John Trap	122
XVII.—The Mountain Ride.	131
XVIII.—Carleyn at Work.	147
XIX.—The Convenient Crack—Dr. Bachune's Wisdom—Orthodoxy—White Cravats and Puritans	158
XX.—Carleyn's Tiger in a Trap.	171
XXI.—Nepenthe on Exhibition	181
XXII.—Madame Future	189
XXIII.—Carleyn's Journal	191
XXIV.—A bit of Philosophy about Husbands	196

CONTENTS.

CHAPTER	PAGE
XXV.—Nepenthe Writes	200
XXVI.—Carleyn's Conceit	204
XXVII.—Love, Jealousy and Rivalry	209
XXVIII.—Nepenthe refuses a Self-Made Man and Worthy Husband	220
XXIX.—The Music Book Open at the Wrong Place	230
XXX.—Mr. Nicholson resolves to be Intellectual	247
XXXI.—Disclosures	252
XXXII.—Darkness Without—Light Within	258
XXXIII.—Prudence Potter's New Discoveries	262
XXXIV—The New Private in Company G	267
XXXV.—Among the Missing	270
XXXVI.—Baconian Philosophy Illustrated in a Literal Way	276
XXXVII.—Carleyn's Ideal	284
XXXVIII.—The Heart at Midsummer—From the Life	288
XXXIX.—Astrognosia	296
XL.—Mr. John Pridefit goes to the Wedding	302
XLI.—The Return—The Surprise	305
XLII.—Mystery Cleared Up	307
XLIII.—What the Critics Say	315
XLIV.—Compatibility	321

NEPEN'THE.

CHAPTER I.

MR. DOUGLASS FINDS A DOCUMENT NOT IN HIS LINE.

> "Life's like a ship in constant motion,
>   Sometimes high and sometimes low;
> And we all must brave the ocean,
>   Whatsoever winds may blow."

"IF you will walk two blocks from Mr. Elden's, then turn up a narrow street, the third door from the corner, on the right hand side, you will see an old-fashioned house, with a green front door, and on the door an old-fashioned plate; inscribed upon its brightly-polished surface in plain large letters, is the simple word—

'STUART.' "

"Are you sure that is the Stewart I want?" said Douglass.

"I think so—it is the only one I know of in the vicinity."

Mr. Douglass was a small, shrewd, busy, practical man; he hurried on in pursuit of the old house with the green door, when a paper partly torn and folded, lying upon the edge of the walk, attracted his attention; fearing some of his valuable law-papers might have escaped from his capacious pocket, he stooped and picked it up. It proved to be the fragment of an old letter, written in a lady's hand, defaced and torn by exposure to wind and rain. The first legible sentence began with the words, "my heart." Yes, yes, thought Douglass, every thing *begins* with the heart—but it ends in "lands, tenements, and hereditaments."

Mr. Douglass adjusts his spectacles and reads on—"My heart, like too many human hearts, has one big joy in it—and like too many more human hearts, it has one big sorrow in it. Were it not for the sorrow, I might be too happy. Every day I see something new and delightful in this precious joy, yet each night my pillow is wet with tears at the remembrance of this my ever-living mysterious sorrow—a sorrow I cannot reveal to all"—here the letter was torn and soiled, and only a fragment remained legible.

Mr. Douglass adjusts his spectacles and reads on—" You know how romantic I used to be about large dark eyes and long heavy lashes. I have now just such eyes and lashes in the face of a cherub child I call my own—the lashes are like dark curtains fringing their lids, and the eyes are an exact image of eyes that will haunt me forever—they are brilliant and soft, expressive yet mild, winning yet resolute; sometimes I think I see around her perfectly moulded young head, a kind of halo of glory. In happier days I should have called her Aureola, that beautiful name given by the old painters to the crown of glory around the heads of their saints and martyrs; but now, I cannot call her any such radiant name, my life is too dark—every hour for months, has sent up its prayer, that this shadow may be removed, and one day in the agony of my supplication, as my tears fell on her curl vailed face I gave her the name Nepen the, praying that like the magic potion of the old Greek and Roman poets, she might make me forget my sorrows and misfortunes.

"This little joy-cup I hold in my hand so carefully, so anxiously. If she sleeps, I fear she may never wake; and if she is ill, I fear she may die; if she is out of my sight a moment, I tremble lest some one take her from me, and she return to me no more.

"Until my Nepenthe came, this old house seemed like a prison—I could not write you before;—how could I with the weight of this great sorrow pressing heavily upon me?—I have now much business to attend to. I wish when a girl I had learned a little of law; I am now finding the difference between law and equity—in equity, I am entitled to a large fortune, but in law, strict law, I don't know how matters will end, but here comes Mr. Trap to see about that mortgage, so I can only add the hope, that my little darling may be as good and as happy as you were when I first saw you in that dear little school under the shade of the old elms where we passed together happy hours of our light-hearted childhood."

" There—that is all there is of it," said Mr. Douglass, folding up the paper, " we have such windy days lately, I suppose it must have blown out of somebody's window. Sorrow! sorrow! If these women lose a lap-dog, or freeze a rose-bush they call it *sorrow*, if they are in trouble they write a letter, if they are in deeper trouble they add a postscript; if Mary should see this, how she would puzzle and sympathize over it. I'll drop this in her box of literary curiosities," thought he, as he passed rapidly up street.

As he approached the old house with a green door, a delicate looking woman stepped over the threshold, and called gently, " Nepenthe, Nepenthe ; come here, Nepenthe."

"I wonder if there's more than one Nepenthe in the world," thought Mr. Douglass, in his practical way, as a bright-eyed child suddenly appeared from behind a corner, and passed quickly into the house.

As he entered the house, a queer, haggard-looking woman stood near the door, glancing back stealthily yet earnestly. Her careless worn garments, manifested no extreme poverty, only indifference to dress and manners. She had walked so far that morning, without observing any thing, it was strange she should stop so near that particular house, and look up into that man's face with such an eager, curious expression. Her nose was long and prominent, her eyes deep set, yet full and piercing. As he entered the door, she muttered between her half-closed teeth, " Yes, he *is* a lawyer." She paused a moment longer as the door closed, and then passed on with a hesitating step, muttering again as she tapped her forehead with her left hand in an emphatic, violent manner. " Yes, he must be a lawyer." Bright-eyed children, dignified men, beautiful women passed by, but she heeded them not, her eyes looked ever forward, as if seeking something in the distance.

A strange looking woman, whispered some who passed her, as she walked on as in a dream, without moving to the right or left to accommodate any passing pedestrian. At length, starting as if seized and propelled by some sudden impulse, she walked on with a hurried step, as if bent on accomplishing something of immediate consequence, and passed out of sight.

Five minutes after, a boy rang violently Mrs. Stuart's door bell, and asked if there was a lawyer there? that a gentleman in Bleecker street wished to see him immediately on business of great importance. He handed Mr. Douglass a name written on a slip of paper.

R. T. RIVINGTON,
126 Bleecker street.

"Rivington, Rivington," said Douglass, "why, yes, that is my old friend Rivington; he has returned from Cuba. I'm afraid he wants me to draw up his will,—he looked like a ghost when he went away."

After some rapid walking, and long impatient riding, Mr. Douglass was soon at the door of the house mentioned on the paper. "Is Mr. Rivington within?" he inquired, almost out of breath after his hurry.

"No sir, there's no such person here, nor is there, as I know on, in the neighborhood," said an old lady who opened the door and looked at him crossly over her spectacles.

"That is what I call a complete sell," said Mr. Douglass, frowning his heavy eyebrows. "I'll tell that boy to go to thunder, the lying rascal—there's some design in all this. But I'll hurry back, I'll not be foiled by this scamp. When was a Douglass ever foiled?" Mr. Douglass put his foot down determinedly and resolutely, looking at his watch and exclaiming, "This paper *shall* be signed, and signed in time if I have to fly for it. I'd like to get one sight of that young rascal, wouldn't I blow him up? I'd put him through," said he, as puffing and blowing, and frequently exclaiming, "Thunder and Mars," the deities mentioned on all extraordinarily provoking occasions, he actually *ran* to the house with the green door, exclaiming all out of breath, "Sign, madam, sign, only sign; there's just half an hour. I'll be at the City Hall in time if you sign immediately."

"A fine form, handsome eyes, yet careworn face," thought Mr. Douglass, wiping his spectacles, as the lady, plainly dressed in black, bent over the document he had requested her to sign and wrote in a firm legible hand, "CAROLINE STUART."

There was nothing unusual in her manner, only a quiet

tear dropped on the end of the word Stuart and blurred
the " T " a little.

Mr. Douglass was soon walking back and forth in his office,
" I paid about fifteen dollars costs," said he, " that must come
out of these scamps, they'll swear to all sorts of things. I
hate to pile up a big bill of costs, I always have to slide
down on it if I do. I'll make about fifty dollars out of this
Stuart operation—it is an extra case," thought he, as he
walked back and forth, " 'tis an extra case, worth fifty
dollars. I'll get wifey a green silk dress, green suits her
complexion best, and twenty dollars I'll spend in ducking
and diving at Coney Island. Then there's that suit of Mor-
gan's, it has been on the calendar long enough, I hope it'll
come on next week."

Mr. Douglass always walked back and forth when any
important matter absorbed his attention; the more he
thought, the faster he walked. When a young man his
maiden aunt often preached to him about " saving his steps,"
and " saving the carpet," but he walked at home, he walked
at school, he walked at college, North College, north section ;
he walked the office, he walked his wife nervous, he walked
his boots thin—all his opinions were literally walked out.
He stopped a moment to give an advisory shake of the head
to the boy who sat before a desk strewn with paper, most
demurely copying writs—he was ever prompt, correct and
exact when Mr. Douglass' shrewd face dawned on his expectant vision—but no deponent hath ever said how many
papers he *did not* serve at the right time, or how many small
bills he collected on his own account.

Mr. Douglass brushed his hair, caressed his whiskers, and
glanced at the calendar—the calendar was full of Mr. Douglass : his thoughts were all available ; could such a test have
been applied they would have had a regular *metallic ring*—
it was always *quid pro quo, quid pro quo ;* he was the party
of the first part, and Mrs. Douglass party of the second part,
and both these petitioners daily prayed in their hearts, if
not with their lips, that the house in Fifth Avenue might
soon be bought, furnished and occupied by Richard Douglass
and Ellen his wife.

He was saving his ideality, he owned and acknowledged,
for the aforesaid house. Now he seated himself by his
desk, quite tired after his his up-town journeying, and

commenced stuffing his pigeon holes with sundry documents, collected during his morning tour, or left on his table while absent.

Unless for business purposes, he was no close observer of autographs or searcher of mysteries; and this afternoon he had a will to execute, a title to finish, and some money to let out on bond and mortage, so he thought no more of an old picked-up letter which by some strange coincidence had fallen from out his other papers and was lying beside the one just signed " Caroline Stuart."

CHAPTER II.

PRUDENCE POTTER'S DISCOVERIES—THE DOCTOR'S COMMENTS

> "Through the closed blinds the setting sun
>   Poured in a dusty beam,
> Like the celestial ladder seen
>   By Jacob in his dream."

NEPENTHE's eleventh birthday came; the old house looked older still, the door-plate still bright, the shadow of the maple swept gracefully over the stones without. The shadow of a great sorrow rested within; far above the maple boughs, rolled the gloomy clouds; down through the waving green shone the gentle stars.

The house was of faded brick—no marble front attracted carriages or callers. Now and then a rag-picker's establishment passed leisurely by. The house looked neglected, slats and shutters were broken, and the paint was worn off the door, all the wealthy people had moved up town. In that narrow, dull street, one cool autumnal morning, walked an old lady who was carried by there a child the day the house was finished. Accustomed for fifty years to daily walks in the green fields about her country home, where nearest neighbors were half a mile distant, this visit to her city cousins was no trifling event in her hitherto eventless life.

It was a long way hither, and now the hoarded savings of years had paid her journey's expense. She must see all to be seen, know all to be known. She might never come again—she had so long watched the growth of each tree in the old apple-orchard and the coming and departure of each venturesome fly in the old perpetually scoured kitchen.

She could better canvass particulars, than comprehend generals ; she was no lion-hunter, no star gazer, no searcher of chief attractions ; she revelled in minute details. Her favorite theme was *exercise*, upon it she theorized and practiced. She always walked dàily as far as the old elm tree in the conntry, but since coming to the city, while riding one afternoon in an omnibus she had lost her money so carefully tied in her silk handkerchief, so that her subsequent expeditions were on foot. But one day, led by curiosity to join a pedestrian crowd in a procession to the Tombs, she had lost her old pocket-book and her new spectacles from her pocket, and ever since that much lamented catastrophe she only walked a short distance from home. One morning, tired of looking down into her cousin's little yard, on the weakly grape-vine, and closely-cut yellow gra-s, she started out for a tramp. "Dear me!" thought she, "if I only had my new spectacles," as she paused before the old green door, to be quite sure from the closely curtained and silent looking windows, that no eye was observing her curiosity, she spelled the letters, "S, T, U, A, R, T—Stuart—nothing but Stuart. Couldn't they afford silver enough for the whole name ? Is it Doctor, Captain, or Squire ? James Jones married a daughter of one Mrs. Stuart. I wonder if she is any kin to this Stuart. I'll find out some time, and tell her, *I know Mrs. Squire Jones ;* my cousin's brother's wife, called on her once, but she never returned the call! It may be the same family, they have a large circulation of relatives in the States."

The old lady had three rules for action :

Never to go out in the rain.

To be always ready for her meals,

And to get her money's worth.

After many walks, she concluded there were no gentlemen about the house, therefore no name but Stuart. This conclusion was satisfactorily established in a most natural way. When looking down from her cousin's third-story window into the rear of the old brick house through her new spectacles one Monday morning and examining the clothes on the line, a favorite amusement of hers ; she could tell which were bleached, which unbleached, which new and which patched, and how many sheets there were in the wash, "No men, no children," said she, as she put in her head and drew off her spectacles.

One day as she passed she saw a doctor's gig before the green door. The door-plate was not as brightly polished as usual, the Autumn leaves not brushed from the walk, and the pot of violets always set under the open window was not to be seen—somebody must be sick, and she had lived in that street two whole months, and not known who it was, nor what was the matter—she must call and see that afternoon, going home first to dinner—it was now twelve, by the old clock on the brown church on the corner—but it rained that afternoon, and it rained for three days, and so her curiosity waited.

Morning came again, and the sun shone through folded curtains into Mrs. Stuart's room. It lingered upon her pillow, as she turned uneasily after a restless night. In her sleep she had murmured faintly, "Must I drink this bitter cup "—when all alone she drew from under her pillow the letter brought by the postman the day previous. Holding it in her trembling hand she read once more, the most brief, the most cruel letter a strong man can write to a frail suffering and helpless woman.

Another day passed and the invalid was a little better. The violent pain in her head was soothed, she could sleep longer. "I have nothing now but this poor child to live for," thought she, "It is my duty to live. I must try to trust."

She had awaked but recently from the delirium of fever, she could not think long on any subject, but texts of Scripture, and snatches of old hymns passed pleasantly through her mind, as if some angel having charge, was giving her famishing spirit morsels of comfort, as she could bear them. "Up to the hills for strength," seemed singing itself along the chords of her soul, and her crushed spirit was becoming wondrous hale and brave, as it climbed on eagle's wings those sunny hills.

While her thoughts were soaring upward for strength and consolation, a tall form closely shawled and bonnetted, holding tightly a green umbrella, emerged from her " cousin's " house, and passed quickly up the street, and paused at the green door. Looking up she exclaimed—

"There—isn't that providential, the door is open on a crack, I will go in quietly as I would call on an old neighbor at home ; knocking always disturbs sick people ;" pushing the door open and seeing no one, she walked as rapidly up stairs as her new creaking shoes would allow, and stopping before the door of the room whose closely curtained window had so long attracted her attention, she gave three successive knocks with her umbrella handle, to save stretching her new silk gloves—and was answered by a feeble "come in."

Going up to the bedside with a preliminary throat cleaning, she exclaimed—

"You are sick, ain't you ? very sick ?"

"Yes. I have been ill some time."

"You are more poorly than I thought for ; I saw the doctor's gig before the door, and I thought it was heathenish not to come and see you—but I didn't know how dreadful poorly you was. My name is Miss Prudence Potter ; I'm used to sick folks. My family died of consumption. I took care of all of them. When I first went to take care of brother Simon, he looked about as you do, he lived *two months* after that. How long have you been so dreadful miserable ?"

"I have been confined to my room about three months," said Mrs. Stuart.

"Three months," said Miss Prudence ; "no wonder you're wasted to a shadder. Did you inherit consumption from your father or mother ?"

"From neither," said Mrs. Stuart faintly.

"Did you catch cold and get it ? I suppose the doctor calls your disease consumption ; you look consumptive ; your nails are hooked over, people always have consumption when their nails are hooked. Then you are very thin— there are great holes in your cheeks, and I, dare say you would look worse if you were sitting up."

"My physcian says my lungs are not diseased. I believe he thinks they are sensitive ; but with care I may recover."

"These doctors don't know much more than we do. They are not sure," said Miss Prudence. "People used to live a great deal longer than they do now, and they didu't have much to do with doctors either. Have you ever lost any brother or sister ?"

" Yes, one of yellow fever," said Mrs. Stuart.

" How long since he died ?"

" About a year," said Mrs. Stuart.

" Where was he buried ?"

" In New Orleans, where he died."

" New Orleans ?" said Miss Prudence. " *Buried in New Orleans !* in the ground ?"

" We have not yet ascertained," said Mrs. Stuart.

" I hope not in the ground," said Miss Prudence, " for I have been told you can't dig any where there without soon coming to water—they say coffins are often found floating about the streets. I wouldn't have a friend buried there for any thing; I should never have any peace or comfort. It's heathenish to bury a body so."

Miss Prudence didn't see that Mrs. Stuart's pale face was growing paler, but after some more talk about New Orleans, burials, etc., she suddenly took from under her shawl a little cup, covered with a white paper. " I have brought you some currant jelly of my own make, from country currants, fresh and nice ; I thought perhaps you would relish it. I didn't know as you could afford such things. You can keep the cup carefully for it belongs to a nice set of chany, my mother's wedding set. If you should need a watcher, I'll come and sit up with you any time except Saturday nights ; that child looks young and inexperienced—she don't know much about nursing ; I could give her a few valuable hints, I know so much about consumption. But don't be discouraged, I've seen people look as bad as you do, and live along quite a spell. ' While there's life there's hope.' If your feet should swell, (they often do in the last stages,) they should be bandaged ; I'll come and bandage them, and you mustn't see much company, it's very bad for you."

Miss Prudence had risen, and once more approached the bed, exclaiming, " Why, what makes your hair so grey ? you look as if you might be young," when Nepenthe came in, and, starting as if surprised to see a strange face, placed a bottle on the mantlepiece. Child as she was, she noticed her mother's pale face, and wished the stranger would go down stairs or somewhere else, and let her mother rest. But looking down significantly on Nepenthe, as such faces only can smile on a child, the old lady's critical eyes spied the newly-arrived bottle, and she exclaimed emphatically, " Is that *real Port wine?*" going up to the shelf.

" It is," said Nepenthe.

" I've no faith in wine, nor no kind of spirituous liquors," said Miss Prudence Potter, " it never did our family any good—I never derived any benefit from it. It costs a good deal, too," said she, looking expressively around the room, as if in their apparently moderate circumstances, it was a useless and foolish expenditure. " My cousin Susan was carried through a severe fit of illness without it. I used of a morning to beat up a raw egg in a clean saucer, with a small tea-spoon and put in a leetle grain of sugar, about as much as you put on the end of a knife, and give it to her between meals ; it is the best *to*-nike you can take ; and the wine may make you deli-rious, too. How much is this a bottle ?" said she, taking it up in her hands, and examining it as if with a microscopic eye.

The clock struck twelve very conveniently just then, so she waited not for an answer to her last question.

Just as Nepenthe opened the street door for her egress, Miss Prudence turned and said in a loud voice, " Your mother looks poorly, *very* poorly. I shouldn't be surprised if she didn't last long. Did your father die of consumption ?" (determined to be sure of this fact.)

" I don't know, ma'am."

" What was the nature of his disease ?" persevered Miss Prudence, thinking, as many others do, she could get all the particulars by catechising the child closely.

" I don't know as he is dead."

" Not dead," thought Miss Prudence on her way home, " where on earth can the man be ?"

Soon the doctor came and Nepenthe went to prepare her mother's dinner. There were oysters to be slightly cooked and poured over crackers.

" How is this ?" said the doctor examining the patient's pulse, " more fever—cheeks little flushed, temperature of the room about right—rest well last night ?"

" Yes, better than usual," said Mrs. Stewart.

" Pulse too quick," said the doctor, shaking his head. " Pulse too quick—eaten any thing stimulating ?"

"No, nothing but oysters."

"Oysters can't hurt you—we must expect changes—can't be better every day—we all have our ups and downs. I'll leave you some lupulin pills, and drop in again this evening. You must get some sleep. You mustn't think about any thing. Lie still and count black sheep, or the leaves on the wall."

"How is this?" said the doctor, as he met Nepenthe in the hall—"any mental agitation?"

"She had a call while I was out; an old lady walked in up stairs and staid a good while; that might have excited her. I'm afraid mother heard what she said in the hall, she spoke so loud, she said mother wouldn't last long"

"She calls herself Miss Prudence Potter," said the doctor. "She ought to be called Miss *Impudence* Potter. I'll not have her going around visiting my patients, telling them how miserable and dreadfully poorly they look; she'll give more fever in ten minutes, than I can cure in a month. I'd like to feel *her* pulse and tell her she needs a change of air and quiet, and I'd have her keep *her* room a month or so. She goes round like a raven, croaking, croaking in every sensitive ear. I won't have it. Look at that sunshine, stealing in that house over there, brightening everything that's dark—so it should be with those who visit the sick, they should make every thing brighter. Your mother will get well yet. But she must have nothing to excite her; any great excitement will place her beyond the reach of my aid. I tell you *this*, child, though you are young, *very* young—yet you can understand me."

As the doctor left, he said to himself, "That woman has suffered so much, and is prostrated by long illness, one little trouble—one more care might—*yes*, it *might*.

"What's the use of aggravating the world so?" he went on soliloquising, as he drove to the door of his next patient, "if you *do* meet a man as thin as a rail, and pale as a ghost, don't *tell* him he is thin; if he is as white as a sheet, don't tell him he looks miserable, don't tell him you shouldn't have known him, he's changed so—he'll go home and grow thinner and paler, and worry himself sick.

"All these croakers that go around with their long wise faces telling people how poorly, miserable and pale they look —I'd like to shut them up a while in Sing Sing—they had better *sing-sing* than *croak-croak*—there is a wonderful connection between health and happiness, convalescence and cheerfulness. That was very true, that translation from Friederich von Somebody—he knew something, if he did live way back in the seventeenth century.

> " ' Joy and temperance and repose
> Slam the door on the doctor's nose.' "

Miss Prudence Potter was seated at the dinner table, before a cup of strong black tea, unmitigated by sugar or cream—she could not be persuaded to taste of that poisonous city milk, and the sugar was so mixed with flour, there was no sweetness in it. " I told you, Priscilla," stirring the spoon in her cup, " l would find out who was sick in that house ; I don't believe in being so ignorant of your neighbors. How are you going to love your neighbors as yourself, if you don't know who they are. I think it is heathenish. I made a call there this morning," said she, smiling—and *such a smile!* Every muscle of her face was screwed up to make that perpetual smile. I verily believe she would smile even at a chicken if she stumbled over one on the walk. It was a geometrical smile with an infinite series of grins. I have often wondered if she really had that smile when she was all alone, whether she went to bed with it and woke up with it.

Far more agreeable is the stern frown of a dignified man or the thoughtful glance a of true-hearted woman than this live-forever smile of one who at heart cares not if you are living or dead, yet she will smile and smile as she just touches your hand and says, " I hope you are well."

Such eternal smiles are only caricatures of those sunny flashes, the play of the best feelings and kindest thoughts as they ripple up from the clear depths of an innocent heart —only a stereotyped plate with which every look, tone, and word of a shallow heart is issued.

She would look at you up and down, and then across, measuring with sharp eye your latitude and longitude, wondering about the probable cost of your dress, as she looked over her spectacles to inquire how you were getting on, seeming to say, " I could tell you a *much better* plan than the one you are pursuing—I could save a great deal, if I could manage for you."

With no idea of etiquette, she went *right at* a subject, handling it with shovel, tongs or poker, using the nearest weapon. She never skirmished around ideas with plausible words. If she had never seen you before, she would walk right up to you, and if you had on a good-shaped collar ask you for a pattern of *that collar*. It was amusing to see her approach all classes with so much assurance ;—there was no hinting *her* down, if she came to ask the price of your new carpet. All dignity, reserve, elegance and hauteur were wasted on her. "My pedigree is as good as anybody's," she would say, "my father was deacon in parson William's church, and my grandfather was a Baptist minister." Were her royal majesty the Queen Victoria to appear in full suit she would probably walk up before her to shake hands, saying, "How do you do, Victoria? I hope you are well."

"That Mrs. Stuart is an examplarous woman," she said, as she took up her ball of mixed yarn, and began setting up a stocking for cousin "Susan's intended"—"but I wonder what she had that basket by her bed for. When she turned her head to cough, I tried to raise the lid a little with my umbrella handle, and I could just see a whole row of little stuffed Quakers, with real bonnets on, like the one Rachel Strong had on when she came back from yearly meeting. I wanted to take one in my hand, to see what they were made of, but I thought I'd wait a spell. I forgot to ask about them, when that child came in ; she had such a queer name, it put the Quakers all out of my head. I never heard such a name. Why, Priscilla, you might guess all through the spelling book, and you wouldn't guess it. I've looked all through the Bible and can't find it, though I suppose it is somewhere in the Old Testament among those strange Jewish names. If Mrs. Stuart warnt so examplarous I should think it was some heathenish name ; but it can't be, for she's a professor, and I'm sure there's names enough, without going to forrin parts for one. Nepenthe, Nepenthe—I'll ask her next time what part of the Old Testament she found that in, but I would like to know what those stuffed Quakers were for," said she again as she smiled to herself and went on with her knitting. There was a slight variation in that smile a half an hour afterwards, when Bridget actually brought up from the ironing, her "span clean, bran new" handkerchief scorched in one corner where Levi Longman had designed with indelible ink the wreath of flowers inclosing her name. "Oh

dear !" she said dropping a stitch in her knitting. "Pru
dence did look so beautifully written in a round hand, and
now it is as yellow as saffron dye, it might as well be old as
the hills. I wish it had been my old silk one."

There she sat in her cousin Priscilla's best room, you could
see her smile and hear the click of her needles making their
rows of decades as she said to herself what she had written
in her copy-book years ago—

"Never less alone than when alone."

On the page before she had written and copied well in
her head—

"My mind to me a kingdom is."

What a mind! what a kingdom! what an independent
monarchy! an absolute sovereignty!

She always, if possible, spoke in set phrases which she
had used faithfully the last thirty years. If you knew her
well you could quite accurately guess her probable exclamation "in sundry times and divers manners;" that is, given a
set of circumstances, you could guess her corollaries and
conclusions. She was not one of those who sit down and
grieve and sigh over words thoughtlessly spoken or deeds
wrongly done, wondering what she "did that for," while
her pride was writhing and torturing itself on the hot coals
of regret. She always did her best—"Who could do
more."

In every affliction, dispensation, accident, the climax and
quietus of all her sentimental, ideal, and pathetic flights,
was this line—also written in her copy-book.

"What can't be cured must be endured."

Oh, Miss Prudence, how delightful it must be to feel
that you always look well, always talk well, always think
well, always manage well, that however weak, foolish, and
wrong everybody else is, you are right.

CHAPTER III.

MR. TRAP HOLDS FORTH AND COMES TO A CLIMAX.

"Logic forever!
That beats my grandmother, and she was clever."

"This lawyer, you know, could talk, if you please,
Till the man in the moon would allow 'twas all cheese."
OLIVER WENDELL HOLMES.

MRS. TRAP was very restless, very—first, she took the evening paper and tried to read, then she went to the window and looked out, and finally, taking that best of all sedatives, her knitting, she seated herself in her rocking-chair, occasionally glancing at Mr. Trap—who, with his hands full of papers, bills, and receipts, sat doing them up in separate packages.

"Mr. Trap," said she, suddenly dropping a stitch in her knitting, "Mr. Trap, are you really going to foreclose Mrs. Stuart's mortgage ?"

"It is my intention to do so ," said Mr. Trap, dryly.

"But, Mr. Trap, is it right to deprive a widow of her shelter, particularly in her delicate health, when a little money paid down would save her a home, and perhaps keep her alive ?"

"Right, right, madam, you're always preaching about right—what do you know about business affairs ? I shall do nothing contrary to law. You do very well, madam, in your own sphere, but you nor any other woman know anything about business matters—what do you know about law ? Law is law. I invited you, Mrs. Trap, to take charge of this establishment, to rule in the kitchen and preside in the parlor—of my shirts, collars, clothes, and food, you have the arrangement, the control, but you are not to interfere with my business matters. I have made up my mind to be rich, cost what it may. Law is law." Mrs. Trap sighed, and mentally said, " Yes, law is law, and equity is equity." " Money does every thing," continued Mr. Trap, " money does every thing; no matter how good you are, no matter how wise you are, who can do without money? Money only gives power, gives position, and position is every thing, Mrs. Trap. There are men in this city, courted and flattered, bowed to and fawned around, who if they were poor to-morrow, would not be tolerated in any decent society. Might makes right, and money is might. If women ruled affairs I wonder how our agricultural and commerical interests would prosper, or our government officials be paid ; how many profitable investments made." Mr. Trap paused to take breath, and Mrs. Trap said mildly, " Remember the sermon, my dear, last Sabbath morning's sermon, 'The love of money is the root of all evil.' "

" Yes, yes," said he, " I could preach another from just as true a text, money is the root of all good. What good or goods can you get without it, 'tis not only the root of good, but the tree, and the branches and flowers—food, clothes, houses, lands, every thing. I will be a rich man before I die. In this city, we must make all the clear gain we can. I got this house by just such another operation. What a lawyer you'd make, madam! If we'd get along fast in the world, we must put people through, put 'em through. These ministers—why, they think just as much of money as we do—and they get it easy enough, too. If they can get a fat salary in a more fashionable church, they preach a farewell sermon to their beloved flock, and off they go, as they say, ' to do more good in an enlarged sphere of usefulness.' I'm going to enlarge my sphere of usefulness, Mrs. Trap! I heard the Rev. Dr. Smoothers say the other day that proprietorship is inherent in man's nature. ' God made some to be above others.'

" You talk about Providence opening a door. I tell you you've got to open fortune's door yourself, or you may stand outside and freeze forever. I wonder if you had a note to pay at three o'clock to-morrow, if this bank of Providence would cash it. Put your bills in that bank of Providence, or that famous bank of Faith either, you'll neither get principal nor interest. There is a pretty heavy discount on that bank. Then where's your certified check? The bank of Providence pays in bills of faith, hope and charity. These are all shinplasters when you want hard dollars ; their value on demand, situate lying and being in the moon.

There's no paying teller in that bank; you may put in and put in, and yet never get any thing out. What kind of a legal tender would humility constitute? You've had so much laid up in that bank of Providence for years—you ought to be pretty rich now, Mrs. Trap.

"If I should ever fail, my assets would be in western lands. I'll fail for about half a million. I shall pay you over, madam, as the favorite creditor, about thirty thousand for good advice and services rendered, and then you can support me, you know.

"The land for which I paid three dollars an acre last year, I can sell for eight hundred now. This Stuart operation is a real streak of luck. Is Mrs. Stuart one of the silk stocking gentry? Is she the French china of humanity that she shouldn't be put through according to law?

"There's too much of this Presbyterian cant; this ortho-doxy, tight as a drum, now in the world. You women jump at conclusions, you make a 'twill do of every thing "—'twill do, was Mr. Trap's favorite phrase when he wished to ex-press the height of inefficiency. "I shall keep my mascu line prerogative, I shall get all the lands, tenements, and hereditaments: I can, if all the women in creation keep up an infernal charivari in my ears;" charivari was the only French word Mr. Trap knew, and it was a mystery to Mrs. Trap how he learned that. Mr. Trap looked over his spec-tacles, as if his wife's arguments were annihilated by this chef d'œvre of logic—this last sounding, flourishing, com-plimentary climax.

He sat in his chair and thus silently soliloquized:

"I am glad I dissolved the partnership with that squeam-ish Douglass, he never would jump into a case unless he could be up to his eyes in honesty. This double refined outrageous honesty is all perfect popcockery."

He sat about five minutes looking over some old accounts of the firm of Douglass & Trap.

It disturbed the dignity of his masculine prerogative, to speak so soon again after his recent powerful remarks. But he did speak, for he wanted to see something in that day's "law reports."

"Did the carrier come this morning? Where in thunder is that paper?"

"He didn't come this morning," said Mrs. Trap in a low mild voice.

"Didn't come! Well I want to see him to-morrow morning. Do you understand? and tell him if he can't bring my paper earlier, I shall stop it. The lazy scamp goes moping along puffing his cigar—gets here about ten o'clock with the outrageous lie 'that the steamer hadn't got in yet.' I'll stop the paper, and if you don't blow him up, I will."

Mr. Trap believed firmly in the gunpowder suasion—if the cook was slow and careless, "blow her up," "breathe the breath of life into her." If the biscuits are burned, or a goblet broken, "Why don't you blow her up?" So fond was he of blowing people up, he might well be appointed to construct and take the directing of a powerful magazine to blow up all the evils in the country. Commander-in-chief of the gunpowder army, as if evil—solid, substantial, heavy as it is, if blown up, wouldn't come down larger, more solid, heavier than ever.

If we could get some kind of philosophic glass, and take a good look at Mr. Trap's conscience, 'twould be made of something like gutta percha, it would stretch the whole length and width of a Blackstone, and wouldn't be able to take in these minor decisions, such as the ten statutes once promulged on tables of another kind of stone by a Hebrew law-giver. The golden rule he used to say was nothing but jeweller's gold, and only plated at that—he never found it of any weight in the scales of equal justice. His rule was never to do any thing for any body, unless he was well paid for it.

Mr. Trap was not always so cross, but he had been beaten that afternoon in a game of chequers. He never would own that he could be beaten in any game. He used to keep a few chequers stowed away under his coat sleeve, ready to drop down in the most desirable places, when his opponent's back was turned. But this afternoon his defeat was owing to some "disturbing cause." Then he had rolled ten pins, and been beaten in that, too—he declared this was because the boy didn't set them up right, though the party of the second part demurred from that opinion.

Then the truth must come out. He had lost a case in the Superior Court, because, as he said, the witnesses didn't swear to enough.

Mrs. Trap had *her* burden to bear, so had the carrier—up till half-past eleven at night, up at one the next morning, walking fifteen zigzag miles that day, up all night on Saturday.   So he toils, while the grumbler sleeps on his soft pillow, and if his paper is not by his plate at breakfast to greet his sleepy eyes, there echoes in trumpet tones through the dining room, " Stop that paper.   I will not encourage such laziness."

" Ah !" said the carrier, one morning, as he carried along his head ache and his bundle, through wind, rain, and sleet, " poverty is not a crime, but it's terrible onconvenient."

I wonder if he of all men couldn't agree with Southey about the road of life, " There is a good deal of amusement on the road, but, after all, one wants to be at rest."

Rest, rest, rest—there's no rest for mortal burden carriers on the rough road of life.

Chiming high up in the great tower of humanity, is the yearning, soothing, unquiet refrain—rest, rest, rest.

Rest, rest, rest, tolls the starlit clock on the stairs of time.

Higher up in the eternal dome, strikes forever the immortal horologe, rest, rest, rest.

———

CHAPTER IV.

MRS. STUART'S AFFAIRS SUDDENLY CLOSE UP. .

" Weep for the voiceless, who have known
    The cross without the crown of glory !
Not where Leucadian breezes sweep
O'er Sappho's memory-haunted billow.
But where the glistening night dews weep
On nameless sorrow's churchyard pillow.

" O, hearts that break and give no sign
    Save whitening lips and fading tresses,
Till Death pours out his cordial wine
Slow-dropped from Misery's crushing presses,
If singing breath or echoing chord
To every hidden pang were given,
What endless melodies were poured,
As sad as earth, as sweet as heaven !"

JUST a month after the conversation in our last chapter, Mrs. Trap took up the morning paper ; as men say women always do, she looked first at the marriages and deaths.

The paper fell from her hands, and she uttered an exclamation of surprise, followed by a long sigh.

" Poor Mrs. Stuart is dead," said she to Mr. Trap, who was looking over his "Revised Statutes." Mrs. Trap took up the paper again, and re-read, as if to be sure it really was " Mrs. Caroline Stuart."

" Ah ! is she !" said he, rising suddenly. " I thought she was one of those kind of people that never would die. I'll have a title that'll do for any State in the Union ; there's almost as many changes in this case, as there is in the nine bells. I've a pretty good legal claim to hang on to. I won't let them kick out of the traces ; we'll want unanimity and concentration. Smith'll be as mad as a March hare. I'll finish up this matter ; now we'll advertise. There's nobody to interfere, we can put that thing right through," and he whispered to himself as he went out of the door, " Mrs. Elliott is sure of a fortune now, but I'll make her pay me well for it."

Mrs. Trap sighed again, as he closed the door. " Yes," said she, " Mrs. Stuart was literally put through the world ; but she's passed into the possession of a house not made with hands. I'm glad there's no mortgage to foreclose up there ; the title to that inheritance is certain, and well secured. But there'll be a pretty heavy judgment entered up there. I wonder who'll pay the costs."

Mrs. Trap went around the house, polishing mahogany, arranging drawers, and dusting out the parlors, as she always did when her heart was heavy ; she went about singing with a trembling, mournful voice, stopping every now and then, to wipe away a tear that would come :

> " When I can read my title clear,
>   To mansions in the skies ;
> I'll bid farewell to every fear,
>   And wipe my weeping eyes
>
> " Let cares like a wild deluge come,
>   Let storms of sorrow fall,
> So I but safely reach my home,
>   My God, my Heaven, my All.
>
> " There I shall bathe my weary soul
>   In seas of heavenly rest,
> And not a wave of trouble roll
>   Across my peaceful breast."

This dear old hymn, like a nightingale in the great heart of humanity, has lulled many a weary soul to rest. Mrs. Stuart, the night before her death, sat up supported by pillows, and in a clear voice of unearthly sweetness, sung it unfalteringly through. How the worn spirit gathers at times, wondrous strength as it throws off its earth mantle, to plunge in the swelling tide of the dark river.

While Mrs. Trap is singing her sorrow to sleep, like a sobbing child, Miss Prudence acts ; she deliberately attires herself for another walk to the old brick house. She gets out from the closet the straw hat with the green ribbon, the high-crowned cap with a frill all around, her brown shawl, and the grey bag. She never went out without her "riticule," she said, with her two handkerchiefs, one of silk and the other of linen, to be kept round the snuff box filled with choice Maccaboy. The shawl when taken off, was carefully folded in the same folds it had when purchased eight years ago. This was her invariable promenade costume.

"We must all die," said she to Nepenthe as she entered the deserted chamber. "Your mother was sick so long, it didn't take you by surprise ; I suppose you were ready for it ; her sickness must have been a great expense. I was afraid she might last all winter, and it would have cost a great deal—but I always thought if she'd had Doctor Brown, *he* might have helped her. Cousin Priscilla says she ought to have been taken out in the fresh air often, and not kept confined in bed all the time. I dare say you didn't know it, but it was the worst thing you could have done. If *I* had had the care of her, I'd had her walking all around long ago ; but you'd better sweep out this room, some folks might be coming in, and it don't look very tidy, and I'll take that pot of Johnny-jumpers home out of your way. I guess cousin Priscilla has room for 'em. I suppose you'll leave here soon, and want to sell off some things. There's that shawl of your mother's, it is old fashioned now, and a little faded—'tisn't worth much, but I'd take it for three shillings to accommodate you ; plain modest colors do very well for me. I'll give as much as any one for it," said she, smiling, and attempting to make her voice more persuasive, for she really wanted the shawl.

"I cannot sell mother's shawl," said Nepenthe with quivering lips.

"Well, well," said Miss Prudence rising, "you'll see the day when you'll be willing to take a friend's advice." Without formal adieus, she disappeared, emphatically closing the door behind her.

"Pride and poverty," exclaimed Miss Prudence, as she entered her cousin's door, "always together. There's that child as proud as a queen, and my word for it, she's as poor as a church mouse, and think of all the wine they've bought that's no use now. I went there to give her some advice, to help her, but I got my labor for my pains; then she wouldn't even give me those Johnny-jump-ups, to bring to the children; and to think of the interest I've taken in her mother, too; she is going to put them on the grave, as if any body could be any better off under ground, with flowers growing by their tombstone. It's heathenish!"

"I wish, oh, I wish," sobbed Nepenthe as she knelt by the bed that lonely night, "I wish I could stay here always and have every thing just as she left it."

At last she went to the window, as she had done for weeks, to close the shutters, she could hear the moaning night-wind as the black clouds moved gloomily over the sky. Only one star could be seen, and that was soon covered—"The last star has gone out," sobbed Nepenthe as she rested her aching head on the table—she raised her head at last, and opened her mother's bible, and read this verse which met her eye—

"I am the root and offspring of David, the bright and the morning star."

Then she turned over the leaves, and read on the first page in her mother's hand written with a pencil—

"The path of the just is as the shining light, that shineth more and more unto the perfect day."

Nepenthe read it over and over—and as long as she lived, these words would come every day to her mind; she lived long enough to know there is nothing on earth that grows brighter and brighter but this shining path of the just.

Mr. Trap passed rapidly down the street that evening, to the office of Mr. Douglass. Mr. Douglass was in his office writing all the evening; it was something unusual for him.

"Douglass," said he, "you may put on your list of houses to rent, Mrs. Stuart's—possession given immediately—we'll have that thing put right through. It has happened right after all ; it is a good time to rent houses now. We'll say nothing about there having been a death in the house, for some people are so superstitious.

As Mr. Trap was on his way home, a tall, stern looking woman, with hollow eyes and prominent n se, came in most unceremoniously, upon Nepenthe's tearful silence.

"Child," said she, "don't sit here so long crying ; you can never bring the dead back. There's worse off than you are—why, you might be dead yourself. Lie down on that bed and sleep ; I'll watch to-night. There's no use crying your strength away—you'll need it enough yet."

Nepenthe sat motionless with grief, but with wide open staring eyes.

The woman looked astonished at the still, resolute child, keeping her sleepless vigil by her dead mother—she looked, and then walked quietly out, muttering.

In half an hour she returned with a plate and a cup, saying, "I shouldn't wonder, child, if you'd eaten nothing to-day ; here is a roll and a cup of tea—try them, they'll do you good."

Nepenthe sobbed again ; she had bought rolls last week for her mother's breakfast. She shook her head mournfully.

"Then drink this tea. It will do you good. It would please your mother," added the woman, in an imperative tone. Half frightened, and really thirsty, Nepenthe drank half the cup of tea, and soon sunk into in a deep, quiet slumber.

Holding up a little bottle, which she drew from her pocket, the woman exclaimed, "Well, that's done me good service —there's no fear now." She turned and walked to the bed where the dead lay, and with a pitiless look, she muttered, "She's gone at last." She gazed at the pale face, with an expression of intense curiosity, as if closely scanning the form and expression of the still features. "And she was so beautiful once, they said. She is gone, and I am here. there's grey in her hair, and she is young too, and he must have loved her—I wish, I wish," and the woman clenched her hands, and then pressing her forehead closely, as if forcing back some wild, deadly thought, she said, "I wish she never, never had been born—and then what might I have been."

She walked back and forth an hour, and then, placing the light on the bureau, she cautiously opened the upper drawer, and first looking back to see if she had disturbed the sleeping child, examined carefully each drawer.

She found in one corner of the lowest a box containing an old package tied up with faded blue ribbon—she turned over some of the papers, as if seeking for something, and nodding her head as if satisfied, she read them all, and then tied them up very carefully, all but one paper, and putting the package in the pocket which she wore tied round her waist, under the skirt of her dress; this one paper she hid in the folds of her waist, which was buttoned up to her chin. She replaced the articles in the bureau, putting up each thing as she found it; then gazing again at the dead woman, she took from her pocket a small knife, and cut from the neck a little locket, hidden under the folds of the night-dress. Holding it tightly in one hand, and half covering it, with the other, she kissed it over and over again passionately, and tried to stifle the great sobs that would struggle for utterance. She looked wistfully at a diamond ring, glistening on the emaciated left hand, and shook her head, saying, "Not that! no, not that!" She gazed at the locket again and again, till an expression of quiet tenderness stole over her face, but forcing it back, she looked up and a superstitious fear came over her, till she thought she saw a smile on the cold lips.

"Mother," said a low voice, "Mother, come here." The woman looked uneasily around, but the child had only spoken in her sleep—the sleeper woke not, and noiselessly the woman stole away; and as the midnight moon shone down full on her resolute face, there were great tears rolling down those wan cheeks—tears that had been frozen up for thirteen weary years.

Only the next afternoon a head was stretched out of an attic window in the next block, and a voice exclaimed, "Look quick, Bridget, there comes a funeral."

"Why no, Margaret! that's not a funeral—there's only a coffin in a wagon, and a girl sitting by it. See, there are no carriages. Well!" added she, emphatically, "as long as I live I'll not have such a funeral as that."

The mother and child were taking their last journey together, they were going through beautiful Greenwood, for the undertaker had received·orders, in a letter enclosing money and directions, to bury the dead in that spot.

Had Nepenthe raised her head, as she came out of the gate, she might have seen the tall form of the watcher, as she stood near the door of the nearest marble shop, muttering, " Well, she is dead, she is buried. It is as well, after al'. There isn't room enough in this world for her and for me. The air choked me, while she breathed it. But there goes the undertaker," she added in a whisper. " Yes, yes, he may well be called undertaker, for he takes us all under."

The woman had a card in her hand, it was—

" Trap, Fogg & Craft."

" Well," said she, going on her way, " I've business enough for them now."

Though Mrs. Stuart had been some time ill, her death was sudden and unexpected ; so much so, that there was a *post mortem* examination. She was heard to exclaim the morning of her death, that her " heart was breaking." The examination proved the correctness of her feelings.

The tremendous propulsion of the blood, consequent upon some violent nervous shock forced the powerful muscular tissues asunder, and life was at an end. Her heart had literally burst open.

Some months after Mrs. Stuart's death a stranger passing through one of the sylvan dells in beautiful Greenwood, stopped to read this one word plainly carved upon a new marble slab over a not yet grass-grown grave—

"Caroline."

A lady elegantly dressed, stood a long time by the grave, one pleasant morning, gazing intently at the simple inscription ; she turned away, saying to herself, " She can never be identified, from that stone or its inscription. No man shall know where Caroline Stuart sleeps 'after life's fitful fever.' She shall sleep well and undisturbed."

The lady was too much absorbed in thought, to notice that a card had fallen from her half open card case, and was lying on the ground. An old gentleman passing by a few moments after, picked up and read—

"Mrs. Clara Elliott,

"*Fifth Avenue.*

"*Thursdays.*"

With scornful eye, firm step, and haughty bearing, the lady passed out of the portals of Greenwood, and took her seat by the side of a beautiful child, who was waiting in a carriage outside for her mother. The beautiful child was a perfect copy of the beautiful woman.

There was a gentleman in the carriage, and no one who had once seen him could mistake him for anybody else. It was Mr. John Trap, smiling and talking in his low tones, as plausible as ever.

CHAPTER V.

MRS. JOHN PRIDEFIT'S MURMURS, PERAMBULATIONS, CHARITIES.

"If I have money, I buy books; if I have any left, I buy food and clothes."　　　　　　　　　　　　　　　　　　　ERASMUS.

Mrs. John Pridefit was trying to decide whether a Tyrian purple, or a gay plaid ribbon would look the best on her new spring bonnet.

She sat quietly thinking, it was very still outside—nothing but the oyster man's most melancholy cry, prolonged and doleful, broke the unusual stillness of the night. "That man's oysters must have a solemn taste," thought she, as laying down the ribbon, and rocking impatiently back and forth, she broke out into an emphatic "Oh! dear! ho, hum!"

"What is the matter, my dear?" said Mr. Pridefit looking up from his evening paper, which he had been reading about ten minutes, "is your neuralgia worse?"

"I do wish," said Mrs. Pridefit, "that for one month at least, there could be no newspapers."

Every woman finds out after marriage, that a man's first love was his newspaper.

"Mr. Pridefit, you read when you are sick, you read when you are well, you read before breakfast and after breakfast, you read at dinner, you read in the cars. I'd like to know when can I find you without a paper; every mortal man must have a paper in his hat, or in his vest or coat pocket; and the moment he sits down, there is his paper, like a shadow before him. You're always waiting for the last of the Tribunes, the newest Herald or the latest Times. I'd like to see the last of these Tribunes, and I wish some final Herald would announce that the dull Times were over, and that the last of Tribunes was about to appear. You say it is in the way of business, to keep up with affairs—there are things of local interest, and general importance, national politics, latest intelligence by telegraph, market, elections, commercial affairs, bank dividends, public needs, quack medicines, police reports, of all things these police reports. Michael kills Patrick one day, and then the next day, some other Patrick kills Michael. Then there's a supplement to the Times, a journal extra, which men must say they've read, of course. Handsome books with fashion-plates or stories, are so much more attractive to look at than this endless black and white. Then they don't litter up the house so. The week you were away, John, I thought it was a pity for the paper to come every day, and no body to read it— so one rainy morning, I resolved to read one all through for once, and find out what was this wonderful charm. I read every thing, even to the general markets. I can't see for my life, how whiskey was quiet yesterday, and steady to-day; that Timothy was firm I understand; (that must mean Timothy Titus, he's the firmest man in town I ever saw,) and that tallow was flat, that is why the candles run down so in the kitchen last night. I can see how sugar is quiet with a downward tendency—but how rice is more animated, and cotton dull—how Scotch pig is quiet, I can't tell. It must be an uncommonly taciturn pig, and then how does Marsh dry Caloric for three dollars and fifty cents? I don't understand these general markets. I can't go into a car, but my ears are stunned with the bedlam cries of noisy urchins screeching out, 'Eagle, one cent,' 'Morning Herald,' or 'Herald,' or 'Weekly Tribune.' Won't these newspapers

ever get out of fashion?   Why, yesterday morning when I
rode down with you, John, you actually had three sticking
out of your pocket, and were reading one besides.   You
never said a word to me the whole way, and I kept nudging
you to look at Miss Gouge's new brown bonnet.   A fan is a
good thing for a lady to flirt behind, and a paper is useful in
one way to a gentleman.   When you are riding home at
night, tired, and get nicely fixed in a good seat, if you are
deeply absorbed in some leading article in the paper before
you, why, you need not see every lady who is standing up
in the car, glancing round for some gentleman's seat!   I
have seen such unconscious gentlemen.   It is a great deal
of trouble to see all the Irish girls with big baskets, and the
fat colored women with their bundles! and the old ladies
with their bags ; then, when you are not reading the paper
in the evening, you are off attending some ' board meeting.'
I wonder what good all these board meetings do ; so far as I
can find out, they might as well be so many boards laid together, for any *practical* purpose.   Why, men can't do anything for an object, but they must have a committee to draw up
resolutions about it, and then a committee to discuss the resolutions ; and then to consummate their wise plans, they get
up these board meetings ! and form, perhaps, some charitable association just to have great dinners occasionally, and
see their names in the paper.   If you go to them with any
application for some individual's relief, they'll be sure to
say that that particular case doesn't come within their organ-
ization."

"Well, Mrs. Pridefit," said her husband, resignedly laying down his paper, " you shall have a hearing ; you can be
the reporter for the evening."

Mrs. Pridefit had been rocking restlessly back and forth,
as if anxious to reveal some newly-gathered information.
" Where do you think I've been to-day, John ?" said she.

" At Stewart's or Madame Flummery's, looking at fashions."

"No such thing, John, I've not looked at a bonnet, a
shawl, or a dress ; but I never walked so much in a day in
my life.   I went up Broadway and down Broadway, and
across Broadway, and around Broadway ; through the ave-
nues and over the squares.   I visited all the Intelligence
Offices, the Bible House, and the Home for the Friendless.

I looked in the Times and the Herald at 'the wants;'
climbed up back stairs in the Bowery, and explored base-
ments in Madison and Pearl streets.   I've seen English,
Scotch, German and Irish of all ages, sizes and descriptions.
None suited me. All were respectable, and could do all kinds
of work ; and accustomed to have ten dollars a month, but
they would come to me for eight.   Passing up Eighth avenue, I saw some fine sugar almonds in a small toy shop."

" Of course," said Mr. Pridefit, knowing her failing in
that line, " you laid in a quantity."

" Yes, there's a pound to keep you good natured while you
listen," said she, handing him a small package.

Sugar almonds were the only thing in the confectioner's
line Mr. Pridefit cared any thing about.

" Well, well !" said Mr. Pridefit, looking wistfully at the
evening paper which had fresh news from England, lying
on the table before him—" What have the almonds got to do
with the girl ?"

" You always talk like a lawyer, John.   You want me to
state the bare facts of the case, just as if I were a witness
on the stand, and you cross-questioning me.   You've been
away all day.   I think you might have a few moment's
patience for once, and let me tell my story according to the
best of my knowledge, information and belief."

" Well, go on and state your case, and swear to it, too,
if you've a mind to."

" As I was turning to go out of the shop," said Mrs.
Pridefit, I happened to see on one of the shelves, some of
those comical little Quaker pin-cushions, like the one you
saw on Mrs. Trap's dressing table, which you admired so
much.   That was the first I ever saw, and I've wanted one
ever since.   There were only three left.   The woman said
the last basket came in last week, and she couldn't get any
more, as the lady who made them had died a few days
since.   While I was deciding which one to take, the one
with white, drab, or black bonnet, a woman came in.

" ' Susan,' said the toy woman, ' have you found a place
for the girl yet ?'

" ' No,' replied the woman, ' she's a nice girl, and willing
though she is small, and she grieves so much after her
mother.   She was in a swoon-like most of the time for a
week after she died.   Her mother was an industrious smart

woman, and she made hundreds of those Quakers for me to sell. She sat up in bed as long as she could hold up her head and sew. I didn't think she would die so suddenly. She was gone just in a minute, as if somebody had killed her. If I hadn't had so many troubles of my own, I should have seen her oftener; but with the children and William to worry me, I did not do much for her; but I wish I had carried her a little nourishment that morning she died, it might have comforted her to think some body thought of her; but it can't be helped now,' (and the woman whispered so low I could hardly hear her; but you know I have uncommon good ears, John.) 'William carried on so that morning, I didn't know what I was about. I had to hide the children for fear he would kill them. He don't get drunk so often as he used to; but when he *is* drunk, he goes on like a crazy man. I have to bear the brunt of it myself, to keep him off of the children:' and as the woman turned her head, I could see a fresh bruise on her forehead. 'But,' continued the woman, 'I took the girl home with me— what else could I do? There was no one belonging to her any where around, as I know of, and I couldn't let her starve. I've kept her two weeks, and it does the children good to have her around—she acts like a little angel dropped down. I'd keep her until somebody claimed her, if I had to work my fingers off to do it—but William has carried on so since she came, I'm afraid he will kill her if I keep her; but she don't cost *him* any thing, for he never brings a cent to the house—he drinks up all his earnings and most of mine, too. Oh, dear!' and the woman actually sobbed. 'I do believe I could do a little good in the world if my husband would let me.'

"'Susan,' said Nellie, for the toy woman's name was Nellie, as they went out together into a little room next to the store, 'people used to call you smart, but now all the smart I can see, is you take your husband's part.'

"'I was sure,' said Susan, 'when I was a girl, that if *I* ever had a husband, he would kindly love, fondly cherish, and tenderly protect me, I would make him as happy as I could, by kind words, and soothing and sharing his troubles and bearing with his faults. His honor, reputation, and even his mistakes, should be safe in my hands. I see his faults as plainly as you do, but I believe it is a wife's sacred duty not to speak of her husband's faults, not to reprove or chide them before others. I may have done wrong in alluding to them, even to you, but I shouldn't if you hadn't seen him at all times and didn't know about it yourself. But if I could hide every fault from human eyes I would. I feel more grieved and disgraced by any error of his, than if I had been doing wrong myself. I would willingly die if my death could restore him to his original manly dignity and integrity. I loved him once—that love is a broken dream—like a plucked, withered rosebud, it lies in my heart; the stem is broken, but if you should tear my heart out, you couldn't uproot the old love—the love lies bleeding. There'll be no more beautiful flowers, no delightful perfume, but the root is there, down deep in the heart. Marriage is a fearful partnership; if one party fails to fulfill his obligations, the responsibility still rests on the other, 'for better or for worse.' The beautiful bridal wreath may fade away in a martyr's crown of thorns; it may prove only an asphodel on the heart's early grave, or a sweet amaranth in constancy's sunshine.'

" ' Yes, yes,' said Nelly, breaking in and interrupting Susan, ' but I don't like to see a delicate and beautiful moss rose planted right out in the middle of the dusty street, and left alone to battle with wind and storm, or for the foot of passing scorn to tread upon, when it might have filled a whole arbor with fragrance, or twined around some manly heart of oak. But I suppose that's what you call poetical, and I don't feel poetical; I feel in sober earnest.'

" ' I have given my heart once,' said Susan, ' and I can never take it back. It may burn, or starve, or freeze, but it must bide life's storm.'

" ' Susan, sister Susan,' said Nelly, ' I wouldn't live with that man another day. I'd see myself in Greenland before I'd slave myself to death for a good-for-nothing drunken husband.'

" ' I took him for better or worse,' said Susan, as solemn as if she was preaching, ' and I will stand by him till the last. I must not cross his will, when I can help it. The girl must have a place. I believe she's got the same grace in her heart her mother had before her. Any body to see her would know she was a little Christian. She'll bear any thing God puts upon her. She goes by herself and reads

that little Bible her mother gave her until my heart aches.
But in this world we can't all stop for feelings—we've got
to live. I've laid awake night after night thinking about it,
but she's got to go, and to-morrow ;—that I promised William to-day, when he caught up that stick of wood and gave
me this bruise—my head aches so I have been dizzy ever
since—but it is hard to know what is right, sometimes.'

" ' Yes,' said the toy woman, 'if you have a good-for-nothing
husband to order you around. I'd pitch him down stairs,
or I'd let him fall down any how some dark night, instead of
breaking my back helping the drunken scamp up. I'd find
out what was right and I'd do it, too. Why, Susan, you've
saved his useless life many times when he might just as well
and a great deal better been run over or drowned. I'd
leave him to Providence and himself a while, instead of
watching him as careful as if he were all diamonds and gold.'

" ' No drunkard shall inherit the kingdom of Heaven,'
said Susan, slowly and with a kind of choked voice. ' I
could not see him die so.—And then I took him for better
or for worse.'

" ' I'd give him worse,' said Nelly, indignantly, ' if I
should see him abuse you. I'd give him a good mauling with
poker or broomstick. Why should he have all the better
and you all the worse. You carry to a wonderful extent
your ideas of love's divine self-abnegation. Why, you had
as fine offers as any girl in the land. There's not a man in the
world too good for you. Judge Corlette has never married
or loved since you refused him. You are only twenty-eight
years old, with your grey hair, pale face and thin cheeks,
your hands browned from toil and exposure. I never saw
such a hand as yours was once. Bensonio copied it as a
model hand,' and the toy woman talked till the tears ran down
her cheeks—' why, if a man had married you, and carried
you all the way through this world and not let you walked
at all we girls wouldn't have thought it too much, he'd only
been carrying an angel. I never was a lady, I never was delicate, beautiful and refined, I was made for work, and endurance, and it suits me, but you, mother always thought nothing good enough for you.'

" ' That is all over now,' said Susan mournfully, coming
out into the shop again. I must get a place for the girl to-
day.' Just then, John," continued Mrs. Pridefit, "I happened

to think what Charity Gouge said about getting so much more out of a young girl than an old one, so I just sent for that girl and engaged her to come to-morrow."

"What's her name?" said Mr. Pridefit. "Bridget? They are all Bridgets."

"No, John; why don't you pay attention? Didn't I tell you she wasn't an Irish girl? Her name is Nepenthe—Nepenthe Stuart. It is a pity she has such an unusual name."

"Nepenthe, Nepenthe," said Mr. Pridefit. "I wonder how the girl got that name. That is rather an uncommon name, but I suppose you'll like it, you'll think it stylish,—you like every thing stylish; and," he added, in a kind of undertone, "I hope you'll forget all your old troubles now with Nepenthe in the kitchen."

Mrs. Pridefit looked puzzled as she said "Why, you know, John, I never wanted a stylish girl." She didn't quite understand her husband's last remark. She thought he was quizzing her, so she pretended not to notice it.

"John," said Mrs. Pridefit the next night, after Nepenthe had been installed in her new post a day—Mr. Pridefit was just closing his eyes—"John," said she, "I think I have done well this time. Nepenthe is a willing girl; she'll do many things a large girl wouldn't. She'll never answer back. Then she's never lived out, and she never says she's tired, and goes muttering round the house. She has no precedents to establish, no "cousins," to come and visit her. I don't believe she has a relative in the country, and that's worth every thing. I'm sure I don't care how many mothers they have in Ireland. You know Bridget wasn't accustomed to do this, and wouldn't do that. New Year's day she had as many calls as I had. I'll begin with Nepenthe and not favor her; she shan't burn much kindling wood, waste so much soap, and give away so much tea, as Bridget did. I found bundles of tea, sugar, and coffee, hidden away in her carpet-bag, and she always saved the best ear of corn, and the sweet-bread of veal in the oven for herself. This Nepenthe'll black your boots for you, too, I guess, John."

"What wages do you give her?"

"I sha'n't pay her any thing now. I'm going to clothe her, you know. I can fix up the old things I have got for her."

"Well," said John, sleepily, "I hope we'll hear no more about girls; it is an awful stale subject of conversation."

"John !" said Mrs. Pridefit, waking up her husband who was just getting into a man's profound slumber, "I'd tell you something else, if I thought you wouldn't laugh at, or scold me ; however, I guess I'll keep it to myself."

Mr. Pridefit promised to listen without reproof, ridicule or exhortation ; so Mrs. Pridefit went on.

"I saw that elegant Mrs. Elliott to-day—I'd give anything to go to one of her receptions—and I met Mrs. Brown (you know I have not seen her since she lived in Fifth avenue, in that splendid house, they say it is a perfect palace,) well, she treated me cordially as ever—invited me to co-operate with her in a little deed of charity. Of course I was willing to write Mrs. John Pridefit's name under Mrs. Theophilus Brown's. It is policy for you and I both, John, to be a little benevolent. Then who knows but you may get all Mr. Brown's business yet ; he'd be a first rate client. I mean to cultivate Mrs. Brown's acquaintance. Are you asleep, John ? Do you hear ?"

"Yes, yes. I hear—go on."

"A poor woman called on Mrs. Brown for some money She had a large family—the father had died suddenly, and they had no means to buy a shroud or coffin. We concluded we would buy a coffin ourselves and send it there, and not furnish means as we first intended. Some time after sending the coffin, we called to see the afflicted family. We knocked, and after some moving about in the room, we were admitted. We saw the man in the coffin, looking not much emaciated, probably on account of his sudden death. We only stopped a few moments. Just as we left the house, Mrs. Brown missed her elegant mouchoir, so we went back to the house and walked in quietly without knocking, and there the man sat in his coffin with Mrs. Brown's mouchoir in his hands !"

"'Tisn't every body that can afford to have his coffin laid in beforehand," said Mr. Pridefit. "I hope it suited him. How much did you contribute towards this most charitable purpose, Jane ?"

"Five dollars," said Mrs. Pridefit, deliberately, "I could not do less. Mrs. Brown was so very liberal, she furnished the shroud, too. I don't know how much money she gave—

she thought I would give about eight dollars. *She* gave her
' services ' you know."

" Services !" said Mr. Pridefit, contemptuously.

" John, you needn't laugh about services. I know you
think there are no services but lawyer's that ought to bring
money. I wonder how you'd get along without services."

" But, Mrs. Pridefit, *my* services are very different from
Mrs. Brown's."

" Yes, I suppose they are. *You* sit in your office and
talk half an hour to a man about some case of distress warrant, and ask him ten dollars for it, and Mrs. Brown will
talk all day long about some case of real distress, and get
nothing for it—that's the difference ; and then she walks
miles and miles. She said to-day she was tired out, and to-
morrow she's going all around again, to get subscriptions, to
get up a fair to pay off the church debt."

" Yes, I know, and wants you to make a lot of ice creams
and jellies. She'll give her services."

" You know, John, every body must do something for the
demands of charity. I am sure I am very economical. I
save all I can. I shall make that set of sable do this winter, and for this fall I had no new bonnet."

" Ah ! yes !" said John, laughing, " but you sent your
last year's bonnet to Madame Flummery's. She gave it only a professional twitch, a professional glance, put in inside
fixins and strings, and sends me in her bill of eight dollars,
when the whole extra fixings wouldn't cost two. She values
her services highly, you see."

" Well, John, I only paid six dollars for all the material
for my new morning dress."

" Yes, that was reasonable ; but your dress-maker sent
me in her bill, yesterday ; a bill of eight dollars for her services in making it. But I suppose she furnished the sewing
silk as you always say, and that must be French silk, too.
I can't see but Mrs. Douglas's dresses fit just as handsome-
ly, and she makes them herself."

" John, you men don't know any thing about these matters. It s every thing to have a French fit, and Madam
Fixeria says my figure is so stylish it ought to have the
best fit, and you know, John, you pay thirty-six dollars a
dozen for your shirts, and they can't cost any thing like
that. You care so much about the fit, and twenty dollars

for that Imperial Dictionary—that was really extravagant.
Twenty dollars would buy so many nice little things for my
etagére.   Why, Webster's dictionary was good enough for
my mother, and it is good enough for me.   I should never
think of paying so much for a book.   There are ever so
many things I should think of buying before I bought that—
and then, ten precious dollars for those dull quarterlies,
with those long-winded articles about assimilation of law, or
Prophetical Literature or Tithe Impropriation, or India
Traditions, or Chineese Aphorisms, or some subject or
place no body cares any thing about."

"Well," said Mr. Pridefit, without noticing his wife's
sage criticisims, " I hope you won't give any thing more in
charity without going to see for yourself.   It was a dastard-
ly imposition, and although that man escaped the grave, he
ought to be consigned to the Tombs in earnest."

Next door to Mrs. Pridefit lived two single ladies.

"Didn't I tell you?" said Miss Susan Simpson to Maria,
(Susan was the elder, and the spokesman for the two,) " that
Mrs. Pridefit would cut off that girl's curls, and she has, all
those beautiful ringlets ; she has bobbed them off close, and
see, her feet can almost walk about in Mrs. Pridefit's gaiters.   I say it is a sin and a shame," added Miss Simpson,
shaking her head emphatically, "I'd like to give her a piece
of my mind."

"I think you'd find she had mind enough of her own, if
you should undertake to give her a piece of yours," said
Maria, quietly.

Susan and Maria got along finely together—one always
kept cool when the other was out of patience.   "And do
you know," added Maria, " that Mrs. Pridefit told Mrs.
Venner yesterday, that the doctor had advised her to take
more exercise for her health—she should keep but one girl
for a while, and do a little sweeping herself, though Mr.
Pridefit was much opposed to it.   But I know how it is.
Mr. Pridefit bought lots of Mr. Trap way up in Fifth avenue,
expecting to sell soon at great advance.   Hard times came,
and he couldn't sell—I know he's had to rake and scrape to
pay for those lots, and Mr. Trap waits for no body, so
they are obliged to economize. They came over here, Mrs.
Pridefit says, because it was pleasanter ; but you know,
Maria, it was because it was cheaper."

" Yes, all for appearances," said Miss Maria, dropping off to sleep.

Venus looked down clear and bright, out from the cold sky, through the uncurtained windows of Mrs. Pridefit's attic ; furnished with a broken bowl, a cracked pitcher, and the shattered remains of an ancient looking-glass, and a table with three trembling legs. The night wind whistled through the broken window pane over the old feather bed which lay on the miserably corded bedstead, covered by a single, faded, tattered spread, ornamented with little tufts of escaping cotton.

As Nepenthe repeated, " Our Father who art in Heaven" —there was her mother's Bible open on the table—and there —clear and bright as ever, on the first page were the words, " The path of the just is as the shining light, that shineth more and more unto the perfect day," that glorious truth mounted like a sky lark into that lonely comfortless attic, and was singing its consolation song as Nepenthe closed her weary eyes with—" Now I lay me down to sleep," the first rays of the shining light were dawning in her soul. The mild stars looked serenely down on that young head, nestled on the single straw pillow, the glossy brown hair waved on a cheek, not yet paled by want.

" Mother ! mother !" broke out from the slightly parted lips as she started uneasily in her sleep.

Sleep calmly, Nepenthe, on thy hard pillow. One better than thou was cradled in a manger. Let the mild stars keep watch, and "*He* will give His angels charge concerning thee."

CHAPTER VI.

MRS. JOHN PRIDEFIT IN THE DARK.

" Oh, charming realm of Nothingness,
Which Nowhere can be found.
While Nothing grandly reigns supreme
O'er Nobody around !"

MRS. JOHN PRIDEFIT was in fine spirits. She had purchased that day, an elegant coiffure, mouchoir, and brocade. They were all bargains—she had saved enough on these articles to pay for the poor man's coffin. It was evening— Mr. Pridefit had gone out to draw up a will for a sick man.

Mrs. Pridefit sat with her satin slippers resting on the register—on her lap lay a mouchoir fragrant with millefleurs, and the last new novel was open in her hand. She had drawn up the table—adjusted the shade over the gas—carefully arranged the folds in her dress, and fixed herself for a good comfortable evening.

She was becoming deeply interested in the plot, and weeping over the pathetic passages, when the letters began to look uncertain and dim—the room to grow dark, and in a minute more, perfectly dark. Groping her way to the bell, she soon summoned Nepenthe, whose dishes were yet un-washed, to the rescue.

"Nepenthe, you ought to keep the metre covered with a flannel blanket—you have put me to a very great inconveni-ence by your carelessness."

"I did cover it, ma'am," said Nepenthe, timidly.

"You thought you did," said Mrs. Pridefit, sternly. "Now bring me some sort of a light immediately—the lamp you use in the kitchen will do."

Nepenthe soon returned with a large junk bottle, from which arose a dripping tallow candle.

"I am sorry, ma'am," said she, "but Mr. Pridefit broke the lamp the other evening in the cellar."

"Well, well," said Mrs. Pridéfit, "you must have cracked it then, you are so careless"—(looking dismally at the new luminary, shedding a ghastly light on rosewood, velvet, and brocatel.) "You saw Mr. Pridefit fix the metre the other night—you can put in a little alcohol, as he did."

Half stumbling over the enormous rat which guarded the entrance, by the aid of a duplicate bottle luminary, Nepen-the found the way into the cellar, and without shutting off the gas, commenced operations to illuminate Mrs. Pridefit's parlor; knowing as much about gas and gas metres as she did of the climate, soil and productions of Liberia.

Into the first orifice she opened, she poured the alcohol, while some of the gas escaping communicating with the blaze of the candle, which holding at least a precarious posi-tion in the old bottle, had fallen forward into the valve.

"Fire! fire!" shrieked Nepenthe, at the top of her voice, and in such terrified tones, that even the immovable Mrs. Pridefit hurried down stairs as quickly as possible.

Shutting off the gas, she poured over the metre and Nepenthe the contents of a pail of water, which erst her delicate hands could never have lifted.

" How could you be so stupid ?" said she, in angry tones. " Didn't you know enough to shut off the gas before putting in the alcohol ? You have done quite enough for one night —you have half frightened me to death—you can put up the alcohol, and wipe the floor "—and Mrs. Pridefit sailed away up into her sepulchral-looking parlor, illuminated by the poorest and darkest of tallow candles—such as she only allowed in her kitchen.

" Stupid thing," thought she, " I'll never let John go away again until I am sure of a light—then the Rev. Dr. Smoothers may call this evening ; and how dull and common every thing will look, with nothing but this old candle. My new picture and this dress would light up so well. I declare I'd like to pound her. No light in the hall, either! How provoking !

Poor Nepenthe was walking the floor and ringing her hands, both of which were badly burned. Poor child, it was her first blister. She knew not that a little sweet oil from the castor, could have eased so soon her agony, and so she walked up and down the kitchen floor the whole evening, moaning with pain.

Mr. Pridefit came home late, cold and tired, and bewildered with perplexing suits, claims and counter-claims. Nepenthe's swollen eyes and hand bound up in an old handkerchief, attracted his attention. As a matter of policy, Mrs. Pridefit was induced by her husband to bind up with sweet oil and cotton, the poor blistered hand.

" Didn't I tell you, John," said Mrs. Pridefit, as she was hunting up some cotton, " to get a dry metre ? If you had taken my advice, all this trouble would have been saved. I wish you would pay some attention to my wishes. What should I do if Dr. Smoothers were to call now? He is so fastidious and refined. He said he would certainly call this week, and there's only one more evening this week when he will be at liberty. It looks as if we were nobody and nobody lived here."

There was a great hubbub in Mrs. Pridefit's house for a week or two. She had kept dinging at Mr. Pridefit, until he had promised to have all the modern " conveniences" introduced. So up stairs and down, everything was remodelled.

Nepenthe was just getting able to use her hands again, when Mrs. Pridefit went into the kitchen one morning to give her directions. "That's the hot water, and that's the cold," said she, putting her hand first on one faucet and then on the other, "and there is the boiler. There is a pump, from which the boiler is supplied. Up in the bath room is a tank; when that is full of water there is no danger, but if the tank is empty, and you should use up the hot water in the boiler, the boiler would burst."

"Yes, ma'am," said Nepenthe, timidly.

"Now, every morning," continued Mrs. Pridefit, "you must pump plenty of water up into the tank, and that will last you all day. I am going out this morning, and you can stand here by the sink and scour all these tins," and Mrs. Pridefit piled up pails, pans, and tin-ware of all sizes and description, all sadly in need of polishing.

The hours moved slowly along—pints, quarts, and two-quarts, pails, funnels, and graters, were all assuming unwonted brilliancy as they lay on the table awaiting Mrs. Pridefit's arrival. "Only one large pail more to scour," thought Nepenthe, as she bent her head over, and tried to remove the cover, which was pressed down very tight.

There was a sudden whizz and report, and then, over neck, shoulder and arm, came the hot water, as Nepenthe rushed frightened back, while the angry water hissing and sissing, burst over the floor.

"Oh!" said Mrs. Pridefit, coming in just then, for she had taken the key of the front basement door with her and had come in very quietly, as she thought to find what the girl was about, she might be up stairs rummaging. "Oh!" said she, shaking Nepenthe fiercely, "you've burst the boiler. There's fifty more dollars gone. This is the way you abuse my kindness. Out of my sight, you good-for-nothing creature; you ought to be in prison." Seizing poker and tongs Mrs. Pridefit, then rushed to the range and with all the skill, energy, and rapidity of which she was capable, poked and scraped and raked the fire out, dashing on cold water to extinguish the last lingering glowing coals. "Up stairs with you! Out of my sight, girl!" said she, giving Nepenthe another push out into the hall.

With face flushed with fatigue, vexation and excitement, Mrs. Pridefit hurriedly ascended the stairs to assume some costume better fitted for removing the water from the kitchen floor, when a new and still more startling sight presented itself to her excited vision.

The bath-room was nearly flooded with water. The basin was full and overflowing; towels, soaps and sponges, were swimming upon its swelling surface. Pomades, pumice stone and tooth powder were floating out into the hall, about to make their democratic way down Mrs. Pridefit's new Wilton stair carpet.

No wonder the the tank was empty and the boiler dry. There was a faucet turned and the water must have been running off a long time, and the unwelcome truth forced itself upon Mrs. Pridefit's unwilling conviction that she herself had left the faucet turned, and carelessly forgotten to shut it off. The fault was hers, and hers alone. But after once making a charge, she would never apologize, never retract—it was not her nature. She tried to say to herself, that the girl might have looked, or examined, or prevented the catastrophe in some way, though she had positively ordered her not to leave the kitchen until she returned.

John Pridefit never knew why or how the boiler burst —but he *did* know that he himself had that identical morning pumped the tank full, fearing the possibility of some accident. Three weeks of lonely, suffering days and painful nights, passed on. Though still sore and tender, Nepenthe began to use the lame arm and delicate hand. There was no boiler in the kitchen yet, and the pump was out of order, and though the weather was severely cold the big stone was moved off of the cistern in the yard and all the water used in Mrs. Pridefit's kitchen had to be drawn up from this open cistern, by a pail attached to a rope.

Mrs. Pridefit began to feel that six shillings a dozen was an enormous price to pay for putting washing out, and when Monday morning came again, she thought Nepenthe could do it if she tried; so Nepenthe's little benumbed hands had drawn up five pails of water when the rope broke, and down went the pail.

"Oh, dear me! dear me!" cried the frightened Nepenthe, "'tis Mrs. Pridefit's new pail, with the gilt band on. What shall I do? What shall I do?" bending down and looking over into the cistern, and then came that fearful cramp she had so often in her right shoulder, ever since it was scalded.

The wind blew violently, there was almost a hurricane ; the next morning's newspapers reports told of high houses unroofed, tall trees prostrated and even persons thrown down by violence. There were two columns in the next morning's Herald filled with damages from the gale in different parts of the country.

CHAPTER VII.

MRS. PRIDEFIT'S INDIGNATION AND CONSTERNATION.

> "He who for all hast found a spot,
>   Wind, waves, and tempest dread,
> Will find a place, oh, doubt it not!
> Thy foot can likewise tread."
>
> GERHART.

SUSAN was the oracle of the two sisters Simpson, and Maria never expressed an opinion, without ending by saying—"Shouldn't you think so, Susan ?"

Seated in her pet corner by her back chamber window, in her comfortable rocking chair, Miss Susan was reading the twenty-fifth chapter of Matthew from her mother's old Bible, and had just finished the twenty-fifth verse—"I was a stranger, and ye took me in,"—when she paused suddenly, and exclaimed,

"Hark! Maria, hark !   Isn't that a child's voice I hear ? Hark! I've heard it twice."

"I guess not," said Maria, who was a little deaf.   "It must be rags, or lemons, or soap fat."

"No! no!   There it is again!" said Miss Susan, throwing up the sash.   "It is in Mrs. Pridefit's back yard.   Quick! quick, Maria!   See that old bonnet on the snow by the cistern!"

Miss Susan Simpson, though a lover of ease, could move quickly enough when occasion required, and tearing a board from the fence, she and Maria were soon in Mrs. Pridefit's yard.

A little hand was holding tight the edge of a loose stone which projected over the cistern.   There were no more screams—the poor child was too much exhausted.

"Keep hold of me, Maria," said Susan, seeing the little hand relaxing its grasp. "We must pull her up."

Miss Susan's form was of masculine proportions, tall and muscular. With superhuman strength, she rescued the half-frozen, terrified child from her perilous position, and finding Mrs. Pridefit out on some morning expedition, carried the almost senseless girl into her own house, and laid her on her own bed.

"There, Susan Simpson," said she, while rubbing the girl's cold limbs. "You've done one good deed now, if you never did in your life before."

Nepenthe was speechless for half an hour. It was an hour of rubbing and stimulating, before she was able to move. Her limbs were partly frozen, and she would not have lived many minutes longer in the water.

About an hour later, Mrs. Pridefit stood at her door, ringing with all her might. She was getting quite impatient, though well protected from the cold by her mantilla, muff, and cuffs of Russian sable. "I declare I shall perish," thought she, "if I stand here much longer. What can Nepenthe be about? I'll give her *one* good shaking when I get hold of her."

"Let her ring a little," said Miss Maria.

Down the stone steps at last, she impatiently flew to the basement door, where her succession of emphatic thumps waked no spirit from within, but burst open the thumb of her tightly-fitting new white kid. "The girl must be asleep," she exclaimed. "I'll give her one good shaking when I get hold of her, for keeping me waiting till I am tired to death. I shall have the neuralgia a month after this. It'll surely go to my heart now."

"Let her knock a little," said Miss Maria, peeping out of her front window. "It will do her good. She'd no business to set that young thing drawing water out of the cistern with that old rotten piece of rope, too, while she herself is all rigged up skylarking around town."

Five minutes more, and Miss Simpson's Bridget, who'd had all her Irish sympathy enlisted in the tragedy, opened Mrs. Pridefit's front door, and told her, with true Irish pathos, the whole story.

It was very provoking to Mrs. Pridefit that her neighbors

had interfered thus with her affairs, yet under the circumstances, they could hardly be blamed.

"Tell Nepenthe I wish her to come home," said she, dignifiedly to Bridget.

"Indade, ma'am," said Bridget, "an shure she's not been
after spaking the whole blissed hour."

This was an emergency for which Mrs. Pridefit was not
prepared, and she had invited the Rev. Dr. Smoothers to tea
that very afternoon.

Taking it for granted that the Misses Simpsons had done
what was necessary for the present, Mrs. Pridefit allowed
herself a few minutes' soliloquy : "Nepenthe had got so
she was doing quite well—she wasn't so quick as some, but
she was active, and learning to do quite well. What if she
should be sick, there would be a doctor's bill, a good round
one, too. Then she half frightened me to death, most setting the house on fire the other night, and now to cap the
climax she has drowned herself, and my new pail, too,
(dear me ! how many pails I've lost.)　Just to think of Mrs.
John Pridefit's turning nurse and getting a new girl. Why,
dear me ! it's one o'clock already, and I told Dr. Smoothers
to come early, and I'm sure I can never wait on my own
table. Perhaps Nepenthe'll get along well enough—I suppose she's scared a little, but that won't kill her, and she
may be a little deceitful, and try to make the ladies believe
she is seriously hurt."

Mrs. Pridefit had always found cards of great use in any
sudden emergency; they could express sincere regret, if she
desired not to accept any invitation ; they could take the
place of many civilities—and it was often said of her when
in wealthier circumstances, that when she could not attend
church, she sent her card to the sexton and had it laid on
the altar—but here was *one* instance where cards would be
of little use. She could not exchange calls with the Simpsons, those parvenu, plebeian, common people. Should she
go now, it would be the beginning of civilities. She would
rather receive and acknowledge a favor or kindness, from
any quarter than "those Simpsons," she had so long ignored
that vulgarly descended, vulgarly connected family. Then
their father, she had understood, was nothing but a *retail
grocer*.

The next morning Mrs. Pridefit lectured Nepenthe about

her stupidity and carelessness in falling and thus ruining her only valuable dress, but these lectures could not quiet the pain Nepenthe felt. When she tried to stand erect, she could not move without the most acute pain. Mrs. Pridefit said, "Perhaps she might have sprained her shoulder." She applied some Mustang liniment, judging from its usefulness when applied to horses that it might be of equal benefit to Nepenthe. The third day Nepenthe was still more ill. She tried hard to stand erect and seem well, but she had apparently lost the use of her left arm, and the left collar bone was inflamed, and the wounded integument was swollen. Some course must be taken consistent with their personal convenience and pecuniary liabilities.

"You might have known, John," said Mrs. Pridefit, "that that old rope would break. I told you it was not strong enough for that careless girl to use. Who knows but this may lead to rheumatism, that is, inflammatory rheumatism ? Who knows but it is catching ?" and she looked disconsolately at her right hand, as she said dolefully, " here I've two big warts, I caught at the industrial school, the day I went with Mrs. Brown. I had to take hold of the hand of one of those ragged young ones. I wish I knew how to get rid of them —they do look shocking on a lady's hand. If Mrs. Brown had Nepenthe she would feed her fat on the milk of human kindness, and wrap her up in the garments of holiness, bandage and poultice her, and make toast and gruel for her to resuscitate her constitution. I can't waste my sympathies on beggar children—if you begin there's no end to it. I believe as Dr. Smoothers says, ' God meant there should be classes in society.' The best way, if you know a girl is getting sick, is to get rid of her before she gets down sick. It's not politic to be caught with a pauper on your hands—and me left with my neuralgia, too—but we could not help this any way, John."

The next morning Mr. Pridefit was walking in the yard. He stooped to pull up a weed, growing by the cistern, and as he stooped he saw a penknife with the blade open, and a piece of rope lay near it. He brought the rope and the knife into the house. " Jane," said he, to Mrs. Pridefit, " was this a piece of that rope I fastened to the pail ?"

" Yes," said she, taking it and examining it, " yes, it was a piece of the clothes line with that very knot on the end "

' 'Tis strange," said Mr. Pridefit, "that it should have broken with only the weight of that pail.   It is quite a strong piece of rope"—and after a moment's pause he added, " Whose knife is this ?   I found it by the cistern.

" 'Tis a good knife," said John.   " It is very strange ; it was close to our cistern ; it looks like a lady's knife—just see, on one corner of the blade are the initials ' H. S. T.' "

CHAPTER VIII.

MRS. PRIDEFIT TAKES A COURSE CONSISTENT WITH PERSONAL CONVENIENCE AND PECUNIARY LIABILITIES.

> "Long the old nurse bent her gaze
> On the God illumined face ;
> Marvelling at its wondrous brightness ;
> Marvelling at its fearful whiteness ;
> Why, amid her deep divining
> Did she shudder at the shining
>   Of that smile
> On her lips, and in the eyes,
> Looking up with strange surprise ?
> Why, in terror, turn her head ?"

IT was Monday again, and windy, dusty, cloudy—nobody would call on Mrs. Pridefit, certainly such a morning. She had washed her own dishes in her leg-of-mutton sleeves, slip-shod slippers and curl-papers. She was completely exhausted—she would get the morning paper and rest awhile on the lounge in the drawing-room.

There lay her velvet coiffure, and her new robe de chambre with cherry facings—her satin slippers, ready to be put on at a moment's warning—they were all so stylish and becoming,—she would just peep out of the door and see if that carrier had brought the paper , but there was not the paper—there was the elegant Mrs. Theophilus Brown alighting from her carriage, radiant in smiles, satin, and velvet. There was no chance for retreat.

After her smiling recognition, the leg-of-mutton sleeves, fearful sack, and frightful curl papers, had to escort the elegant Mrs. Brown into the undusted parlor, whose wide open staring shutters gave to Mrs. Pridefit's toilet a full eclaircissement.   Mr. Pridefit was always tearing the shutters open. Why do gentlemen like so much light? If a room does happen to be undusted, and a dress not quite *à la mode*, or even *en deshabille*, up go the windows, and out go the shutters.

"Is there any one like a man for letting the cat out of the bag? Why must they have every thing so light?" thought Mrs. Pridefit, as she tried to talk blandly, and smile agreeably, and bend her head gracefully.

Mrs. Brown's stay was short. She wanted assistance in making out a subscription for enlarging the Rev. Dr. Smoothers' already large library. Mrs. Pridefit couldn't refuse, so down went ten precious dollars under Miss Simpson's five.

She smilingly bowed out Mrs. Brown, and then frowningly returned, and looked in her full length mirror at the other end of the parlor. There stood Mrs. John Pridefit without collar, without coiffure, without adornment. She would have given ten dollars more to have Mrs. Brown seen her in her new robe de chambre, or rather not to have seen her in that "horrid dress." It was all owing to that careless girl, who ought to have been well and in her place.

Mrs. Pridefit was one of those people, who, when in trouble, reproach the nearest, perhaps the most innocent cause. Pride was the strongest element in her nature— this pride was piqued, and she hated Nepenthe.

If you've had a sleeplesss night, reader, with a sick child or a toothache, and you get up in the morning feeling like letting every thing go for once, and Bridget seems to feel like it, too; if it is the only day in the annals of your house-keeping, when the furnace fire goes out, the parlor is not dusted, your dress *en deshabille*, you sit down with a formidable basket of inevitable mending or a most bewitching book; maybe Bridget has taken it into her head to slip off and get married, or go and see some cousin, all the fires unaccountably go out. Then, surely, some high bred, elegant, fastidious caller comes in her carriage to make you her annual fashionable call, and you so distracted in your deshabille and cold dusty parlor, only heighten the contrast of her self-possessed blandness. You can think of nothing suitable to say, and after looking critically around, and saying a few elegant nothings, your caller gracefully makes her exit, and says to her dear friend at home, that Mrs. ———— has grown old and negligent since her marriage—she's not a nice housekeeper. Her circumstances must be very limited judging from her plain dress and cold parlor. Or if you are literary, it may be because you are a blue, you are so negligent,—and then at last in comes Bridget who has really greatly aggravated your embarrassment by her sudden absence. "She has just been out at the corner to see her cousin "—if you don't scold, it is because you are very good natured.

Reader, before you condemn Mrs. Pridefit for her undignified and foolish impatience, think of the many times when you have been excited, angry, or unreasonable, for some equally trivial cause—something of which you are afterwards heartily ashamed.

When we are sailing off on the high tide of self esteem, self respect, conscious of our all sufficiency to meet all life's little and great ills, some foolish breeze of circumstance, little and weak, will lash up the spirit till it frets and fumes and irritates itself into a kind of madness, foaming with sudden rage, and writhing with impetuous pain.

Let the kind voices of our good old grandmothers still echo in our ears, " Handsome is that handsome does." This voice is an uncertain response for the modern world. The world says, practically, " Handsome is that handsome seems." The first bow of deference will be paid to the agreeable exterior, which is the first passport to the stranger's eye and hand of welcome. It is an instinct of the warm heart, an impulse of the refined mind to make house, furniture, and dress, beautiful and symmetrical. We associate beauty with Heaven itself.

Our ideas of upward climbing and onward advance are of rising to something more beautiful and perfect, and paradise wouldn't be paradise to us if in our beautiful imaginings there were no starry crowns, pearly gates, and golden harps. There is even a kind of beauty in perfect order. Simple and plain beautiful arrangements and elegant adornments, are sought for eagerly by all cultivated human eyes. We turn wearily from a hard granite hill, with its wondrous trinity of quartz, feldspar and mica, to gaze admiringly on the beautiful prairie, bouqueted with sapphire cups and ruby bells.

When Mrs. Pridefit descended the kitchen stairs, after

looking into her truth-telling mirror, there was in her face an expression which may be summed up in one dark word —Retribution.

Giving Nepenthe another lecture on past offences, Mrs. Pridefit was soon transformed into an elegantly-dressed lady in promenade costume, and on her way—whither? By the aid of the directory she was soon in the office of a physician, and after some preliminary and plausible preamble, she said, " I will be much obliged to you, doctor, if you will inform me of the requisite preliminaries to getting her admitted. I am exceedingly sensitive, and my health is extremely delicate, my servants very inefficient, and I wish to consummate some arrangement as soon as possible."

" When did the accident occur, madam ?" said the doctor.

" Day before yesterday, sir."

" Then it will be necessary for you to procure the services of a physician, and get his certificate as to the nature of the accident, and the suitability of the patient for the institution. If you had taken her directly to the hospital on the day of the accident no certificate from a physician would have been necessary. But as it is you will be under the necessity of procuring a certificate from some respectable physician, which certificate you must present to the Commissioner or Superintendent of the Alms House, at the Rotunda in the Park, entrance Chambers street, and he will give you another certificate which will entitle her to admission."

" What do you charge per visit, doctor ?"

" Well, seeing the patient is a poor little orphan, I will visit her and make out a certificate for two dollars."

" Very well, doctor, you will please call at my house immediately."

" I will be there in two hours, madam."

(Mrs. Pridefit makes her exit.)

" Good morning, doctor."

" Good morning, madam."

Mrs. Pridefit on her way home soliloquizes : " What a fool John Pridefit was that he did not know enough to have that little brat sent to the hospital on the day of the accident, and thus saved the payment of an exorbitant doctor's fee. Is't possible ? Two dollars ! Who ever heard of such an outrageous charge ? The doctor has no conscience

—he is a real old extortioner. I wish he could pitch into a cistern himself.''

Some hours after, passing up through the main entrance, through hall after hall, and room after room, lined on each side with rows of cot beds, upon which in all attitudes were suffering invalids, Dr. Guncther came to the surgical ward in the rear building, where were a group of students receiving medical instruction from an old surgeon. The nurse announced the arrival of a new patient in the ward.

" Well, my little girl, what is the matter with you ?''

" Mrs. Pridefit thinks, she says, that I have some of my bones broken or out of joint.''

Surgeon—" Nurse, remove the patient's dress from the left arm and chest.''

" Stand up, my little girl. Ah! gentlemen, there is a language in that patient's attitude and in the deformity of the injured part that tells you distinctly and unequivocably the nature of the accident. What is it, gentlemen ?''

Several voices respond : " A compound fracture of the left clavicle, sir.''

" You are right, gentlemen—this is a compound fracture of the clavicle. No trouble in the diagnosis. It is a compound oblique fracture of the clavicle—and notwithstanding the amount of tumefaction which exists in the parts, our diagnosis is about as easy as if it were made upon the dry skeleton. The wound is a lacerated one, passing directly up over the left breast and clavicle, with which it slightly communicates at the fracture. You perceive, gentlemen, that motion from before or backwards can only be performed with the greatest difficulty and suffering, and the patient is rendered incapable of performing rotary motions with the arm. The great pain produced by the weight of the arm stretching the injured parts, causes the patient to incline her body to the affected side. The support thus given to the arm by the inclination of the body, generally alleviates the pain. By tracing along the upper surface of the bone, you will detect a depression at the point of fracture, and by grasping the two fragments with the fingers of each hand and moving their broken surfaces on each other, you will find the crepitus very perceptible. You will observe that by thus moving her shoulder upwards, backwards and outwards, that I reduce the fragments to their natural position with the greatest facility. Now gentlemen, the indications of treatment in this case are to retain the arm and shoulder in the position in which I now hold them, and with your assistance we will proceed to apply apparatus for that purpose."

After an application of a healing and emollient nature, Nepenthe was bandaged with long strips of muslin passing these rollers over each shoulder, and crossing them in the form of a figure eight, acting in a manner similar to an ordinary shoulder brace.

Hanging over her little bed a board bearing her name, age, birth-place, date of admission and name of injury, the old surgeon and his disciples passed into another ward.

"Dr. Gunether tells me," said Mrs. Brown to Mrs. Pridefit, whom she happened to meet while shopping, "that one of the patients at the hospital is one you sent there."

"Yes," said Mrs. Pridefit, blushing, "it is rather a painful topic to me. The other day I found a poor penniless orphan girl who had no home. My heart would not permit me to refuse her a temporary asylum beneath my roof. I brought her home with the intention to protect and watch over her as a parent until I found some good religious family, willing to adopt her ; but the other day while I was absent for a little exercise, in the exuberance of her sportiveness, while playing around the cistern, she stumbled over its margin, and was only prevented from drowning by a projecting stick of timber which fortunately caught into her dress by means of a spike driven in its extremity. After watching her with intense solicitude and finding my own health failing, and my neuralgia being so much worse—the doctor was afraid it might go to the heart—Mr. Pridefit and myself concluded that she ought to have the close watching and careful and constant attention of old and experienced nurses usually found at the hospitals. I am exceedingly sensitive—my health is extremely delicate, and my servants uncommonly inefficient. This is a trial, but as Dr. Smoothers says, ' We are often called upon to make great sacrifices in the path of duty.' "

Mrs. Pridefit wiped her eyes with her new embroidered mouchoir, and bowing gracefully bade Mrs. Brown good morning.

"I feel so relieved, John," said Mrs. Pridefit that evening when Mr. Pridefit came home, " now Nepenthe is off our hands. I wish I never had brought her here. It makes my neuralgia so much worse to think about hospitals," said she, sitting down to finish some embroidery.

By Nepenthe's bed that night, sat a strange-looking woman —that gaunt form, those hollow eyes, those muttering lips— she turned uneasily on her pillow; was it a dream? No! no! she had seen her once—she was the watcher by her dead mother. Did this strange woman always come to sit by the dead? would she die too?

No, it was only a nurse at the hospital, and Nepenthe fell into an unquiet, feverish sleep.

"It is the twenty-fourth to-day, and to-morrow will be the twenty-fifth," said the nurse, as she stood gazing at the sleeping Nepenthe. "Yes, to-morrow will be the twenty-fifth." The morning dawned; it was the twenty-fifth; well might the old nurse at the hospital remember it.

"It is the twenty-fifth to-day—it is your birthday," said Dr. Gunether to his little nephew. "You may go where you like. This is your day. We'll examine all the balls, tops and marbles in the city if you like."

"And can I go where you do, uncle?"

"Yes, and what will you do first?"

"Let's take a walk in Broadway."

Dr. Gunether had so often paced with weary feet this crowded thoroughfare—he preferred a walk in some quiet street where he might go along leisurely without taxing his attention in steering straight. But Broadway sights and Broadway sounds, omnibusses, hand organs, shows of toys and confectionery, bright windows and gaily dressed ladies, all attracted Frank's curious eye, and as each new bright object attracted his attention the boy kept giving an extra tug at his uncle's coat.

They were soon at the florist's, where japonicas, helio-tropes, roses, and pansies bloomed in elegant profusion. A bouquet of rare flowers was Frank's first birthday gift.

"Uncle, now take me to the hospital," he said, "I want to see where you go every day."

Clinging close to his uncle's coat, the child passed the portal of the building, and was soon by the row of little cot beds, upon one of which Nepenthe was lying, and her pale suffering face attracted his quick eye. While his uncle was convers-ing with one of the attendant physicians, Frank stole away from his side and laid the flowers on her pillow. His uncle called him at that moment without waiting to observe his movements. Frank followed him, trying hard to keep up with his uncle's quick step and look back at Nepenthe.

As the massive door closed behind them, Frank drew a long breath once more, as he said with a tearful eye, " Has she no father, no mother, Uncle ? Who kisses her good-night, and what is her name ?"

" Nepenthe."

" Isn't it a pretty name, Uncle ?"

" Just like his mother," thought the doctor, " always looking after pale faces. I'm afraid he will never do for a doctor—he is too tender-hearted. It is true enough the boy's heart will often take its mother's fine stamp ; he might be a poet, author, artist. He is uncommonly sensitive for so young a boy. I thought he valued those flowers too highly to dis-pose of them so quickly."

The strange-looking nurse watched the child as he laid the flowers on Nepenthe's pillow, and said not a word, but, bringing a tumbler of fresh water, placed them carefully on a shelf in sight of Nepenthe, muttering between her half-closed lips, " It costs me nothing—it costs me nothing."

A shrinking, painful feeling, an anxious dread, seized Nepenthe, as she gazed on the unknown but remembered watcher. But the heliotropes, rose buds and japonicas brightened up the gloom of the hospital. She slept and dreamed of the violets under the window of the old brick house, and now blooming on a grave in a Green-wood dell. She turned and awoke. There were those eyes still looking so cold and unfeeling.

" The Stuart hair, 'tis the Stuart eyes," the woman muttered, contemptuously and bitterly, " but she has an ugly name, and it is well she has no pretty name, with the life she has before her.—What will you have, child ?" said she, harshly, as she came suddenly and stood by the bed, drawing the sheet over the hot hands of the feverish patient with an almost choking closeness.

The next week Mrs. Pridefit was again at Stewart's. There was a new assortment of chené silks and she was looking them over. She heard a voice in the next room say to another lady, " Mrs. Pridefit and I do not exchange visits : she does not move in our circle. Pridefit is a respectable lawyer, I believe, and I get small subscriptions from her occasionally ; every little helps. When our church was first organized I called on her. The church was small then, and we wished to draw in all the new comers. She is a weak-minded woman ; and flutters in every new fashion that comes out, and if she were really high-bred or well-bred I could not make a friend of her. She must lead her husband a merry kind of life."

Mrs. Pridefit bought no dress that day—and that night she was so quiet and yet so cross, Mr. Pridefit thought she must have a severe attack of neuralgia.

I cannot tell you why, reader, because I do not know, but Nepenthe Stuart was in a few days removed from that hospital to another, and that other not half as comfortable. Behind her pillow was a window—one of the panes was broken, and through the broken pane the wind blew roughly in on the pale cheek of the sufferer. Her fare was miserable, she was much neglected, and many an occasional visitor at the hospital has said, "How can the child get well there ?"

CHAPTER IX.

A CHAPTER WITH SOME "PREACHING" IN IT.

> "I hurry up heaven's viewless stairs,
> And casting off life's weary cares,
> Open the pearly gates of prayer."
>
> ALAN.

> "And some fell among thorns.
> "And other fell on good ground, and sprang up and bore fruit an
> hundred fold." LUKE VIII. 7, 8.

"Dr. Wenden," said Mr. Douglass on their way to church one Sabbath morning, "I should think you would have the blues all the time ; you see the saddest sights of humanity—wounds, bruises, agonies and broken limbs. I couldn't have the nerve to be a physician."

"Get used to it—get used to it," said the doctor.

"Yes, but every terrible scene must make a wound in the spirit, and there'll be the scar—there's the scar."

"Have to get used to it, Richard, have to get used to it. When I first commenced practice, I took to heart every broken limb I saw. If I lost a patient, I felt as if I were going to my own funeral; and every interesting destitute child, I was for taking home, feeding and clothing. Had I followed my early professional impulses, I should have had five hundred in my house to provide for. There are few things done in this world half as well as we think we could do them ourselves; the hungry starve, the sick are neglected, the convalescent hopelessly put back by harsh and indifferent treatment. When I first came from the country, and walked through the streets of the city, I was inexpressibly pained and exceeedingly shocked at the sight of the first pale, half-starved ragged baby, held in the emaciated arms of its wan-faced ragged mother, and in those thin pauper hands I dropped a half eagle, and passed on, wondering greatly that such a case of forlorn destitution should have stood at that corner so long, empty handed, ragged and hungry, while velvet and diamonds passed by unmoved; but as I walked on, I saw ragged mothers and white faced wailing infants at every corner—and now I find these sad visions are a part of the daily city programme, which every body expects to see as they pass along. We even think them impudent for standing and shocking our delicate and cultivated 'vision with their unsightly pauperdom. Only a little kindness would do so much; I would say to myself, and sigh as I theorized about elegant schemes for ameliorating the condition of the race. If I only could get up a phalanstery where all could have equal right and privilege to enjoy life, liberty and happiness. But with a great part of the world, life is half death, liberty half servitude, and the pursuit of happiness only a struggle for to-day's bread and to-morrow's clothes. If some body would, if people would do something, why the world might be set up on its heels and go on right; but I am not people, I am only one man with more wants of my own than I can gratify, so now I meet with interesting cases all the time— but I say to myself there's wrong all around that I can't help. I'll try and mend the broken legs—then they must walk for themselves. I row them over the river of health—they must help themselves up the bank though it is steep enough —the road of life is rough to all of us. We walk it till our feet are sore and bleeding. Struggle, struggle, struggle, rich and poor climbing for something. If you stoop to pick up the weak behind you, one loses one's own footing—who'll pick us up. I go home, put on my slippers and don't think about patients—but I must confess there's one little patient at the hospital who has unusually excited my sympathies. For three long months she has been an example of patience. If there ever was a waif on the world's wide sea, she is one—she has a child's innocent helplessness, and a woman's patient self-control—but we must walk faster; the bells are tolling, and we have half a mile yet to walk—we might stop at Dr. Elgood's, but I prefer going on ; I feel more at home in my own pew. I like to sit in the same seat in church. I am so driven round during the week, I like a few nodes in my orbit through which I may pass, and recognize something quietly familiar. Last Sabbath morning, that agent from Constantinople refreshed our imaginations with a whole chapter of statistics, relieved by a few bald, bare, dry facts. If I had had his rare opportunity for gathering information, I I think I could have got up something without bearing so much on the dates. If I only preached once a year to a congregation, I'd try and write one wonderful sermon that wouldn't keep them yawning two hours, and looking at their watches. When the sermon was half through, Mr. John Trap got up and walked out, an exceedingly rude thing for a man to do. In the afternoon we had a sermon about ' those who go down to the sea in ships.' I saw Trap slip a sixpence into the box. That's a pretty close Trap ! and we all had an opportunity of giving. These precious opportunities are coming pretty often and we have to put something in the box, it looks so if we don't—if I don't go any other Sunday, I am sure to go when the agents preach. Wouldn't it be a good plan, Richard, to have an agent for the relief of hard-working doctors and bewildered lawyers ? We might as well have help as the destitute heathen in Farther India. If we give them more light and they still sin, they sin against more light, and their condemnation will be greater. ' That law written in their hearts ' often puzzles me. Are these myriads of people with souls as precious as our own, and having no Bible, are they all hopelessly lost ? We may talk about the utter. selfishness of that man who prayed—

> "God bless me and my wife,
> My son John and his wife,
> Us four and no more.
> *Amen.*

It is the unuttered prayer of half the world. Do we not all therefore practically pray? It's a great deal to discharge one's duties as a husband, father, doctor. If I do this well, how can I do more in this age when we begin housekeeping in the style in which distinguished men lived in the zenith of their prosperity fifty years ago. How are we to meet expenses, pay debts, live generously, give bountifully, walk successfully with men, and humbly before God. If each man would take care of himself and family, the world would wag on well enough, but we have to help some poor stick or other, all the time, or else we are called selfish, and close, and heartless. As to disinterested benevolence, if there is such a thing, it is a century plant, blooming in the heart of humanity once in a hundred years. *I* can't find it, and I see human nature in its every day and natural face. I saw a half starved beggar child, the other morning on a door step, sharing its last crust with another stranger beggar child ; that was the only shadow of a type of it I could find. I've about made up my mind, I've seen so much selfishness, that I shall take good care of myself, and get as healthy, wealthy, and wise as I can."

"You can't attend church often, doctor," said Mr. Douglass, " you skillful physicians have few days of rest."

" Yes, I am often professionally engaged, or professionally tired, and many a Sabbath morning the sofa is the best church for me, and as for Dr. Smoothers, he is so often perched up on the frozen heights of theological speculation, or soaring off in some transcendental balloon, overlooking or examining some barren field of conjecture, that he surrounds me with a metaphysical fog, or drags me through a perpetual swamp, as he rings the changes on his infinite series of doctrines. There's no knowing on what wild ocean we'll land if follow him in his thought balloon over the sea of conjecture, and his tone I really dread. I can't see why a man speaking to men from behind a pulpit should talk in a different tone than from behind a chair or table. As somebody who once heard Dr. Smoothers said, there is the same key note at the begining of each sentence, the same monotonous level through the middle, be the middle long or short, the never-failing dactyl and spondee at the end, and so on until seventeenthly. ' A few words more, and I've done,' and off he starts again on the track of monotones for half an hour longer. He reminds me of one of those little electro-magnetic railcars going round and round on the top of a table, and never getting any where. No accident of feeling, no sense of danger, ever occurs on that track. A thought must be incarnate, have a shape, form, dress, before we give it a reserved seat in the private box of our heart. I like this pictorial preaching, illustrated by familiar images, planted with flowers, studded with stars, where thoughts marshalled on the mind, costumed and vivid, move before the rolled-up curtain of the soul like a bright panorama. Such sermons take us by the hand and talk with us, and years after they'll come again in some lonely hour, and pass in full review. In the open cage of memory such bright winged thoughts nestle and perch ; at early morn and still twilight they'll come out like musical birds, and hover and warble in the drooping branches of the shaded soul, singing their matin and vesper hymns, chanting their midnight mass for the repose of the unquiet spirit."

" Yes," said Richard, " long elaborate essays, dull learned disquisitions, dry profound researches (not of human life, but of Hebrew lore,) are all in keeping with those old pictures of ministers in square frames, white cravats, Bible open exactly in front, and exactly in the middle of the Bible, fore-finger raised, so that the observer could see, and know and feel in the top of his bump of reverence, that that is a minister. Modern hurried and worried humanity is not always sitting erect in pews, docilely waiting to be admonished by the fore-fingers of men in angular framed notions, in immaculate cravats."

" No," said the doctor, " the police walking about the ecclesiastical walls, *may* do a vast amount of good, these metropolitan soul police in citizen's dress, taking us by the hand and helping us safe across the muddy, crowded thoroughfare of evil. Why should they stand in life's picture-gallery, a series of moveless portraits: In God's great Academy of Design they are living artists, moulding our rough-hewn souls into God's great pattern. Why keep those souls idly rolling over vague conjectures like balls of clay, till we gather not even the moss of veneration or the form of worship. We each of us think in some particular favorite avenue. Into that familiar avenue a spiritual guide may come, walking on before, and not standing at the locked portals of the soul, ringing gently, and waiting politely to enter at the front door of thought, but stealing through some by-lane or side path, into the soul's cozy sitting room or climbing the winding back stairs of feeling, into the attic of the heart, where are laid away musty bundles of old hopes and old opinions which need to be rummaged and overhauled, well assorted, and laid open for careful inspection and repairing."

"Dr. Smoothers," said Douglass, "airs once a week the nice sets of doctrines in his own head, beating them, and turning them over on the line of his sermon, just as the housekeeper beats and airs her furs, to keep out the moths. These good strong doctrines will last long enough without airing them so often. Of all things deliver me from these doctrinal preachers. Crossing the long bridge of forms, why not ford the stream of feeling, stoop under the gate of sympathy, and steal in at the citadel and take by storm of powerful eloquence, 'the sin beleaguered soul.' I don't know why," continued Richard, "religion must be so gloomily represented. We get the idea that it's a good thing for Sundays, for sick beds, and for the superannuated. If all these christians are really bound for the port of peace, why don't the light of the shining shore break on their faces? This solemn cant, serious drawl, sanctimonious look, if spiritual, was never imparted from the bright spirit-land, never borrowed from a heaven of bliss. Last Sabbath we had a sermon from the text, 'Blessed are the merciful, for they shall obtain mercy'—there goes John Trap; he might preach from the text, 'Blessed are they that take care of themselves, for they shall be taken care of.' "

"I must tell you the anecdote of an elderly Scotch woman I read this morning," said the doctor. "The Scotch woman gave her son the newspaper to read aloud. The only reading he had been in the habit of hearing was at the parish kirk. He began to read as he had heard the minister read. The good woman was shocked at the boy's profanity, and, giving him a box on the ear, exclaimed, 'What! dost thou read the newspaper with the Bible twang!' I know much of this professed religion is mere '*Bible twang*.' I can't see that Christians live any different from other people. They are just as anxious about the world, and just as absorbed in its cares. They all prate about self-denial, but there's hardly one of them knows what it means. They load their persons and houses with luxuries, and if they happen to have a few loose pence left they give them to some beggar to get rid of him. To increase their reputation they head some long subscription list with a respectable sum, and pinch some household charity a little closer to make up for it, so ministers often smooth over the points in their discourses. If they do lay the sermon out plain and clear, they line and wad it afterwards with the cotton of plausibility. A minister must have clear ideas in his own head before he can make them clear to others. And then they do poetize so exquisitely about self-denial. I don't see any of it. But here we are at the church door, but the hymn has been sung, and the sermon commenced. I hear a strange voice in the pulpit, but I'm used to being late."

In a clear, solemn tone they heard, as they entered the church, "Self-denial, self-denial—no man enters Heaven without that; from every land, however remote, there is one straight road to Heaven, the one bridge over which all we emigrants to that better country must pass—the safe suspension bridge over the selfish rapids of this tempestuous life is self-denial. Plant yourself on it once and you may hold direct communication with Heaven. The bridge spans the eternal shore. Self-denial is the one line underlying the waves of life, reaching over the plateau of principle, connecting remote friends, aye, and distant enemies. Form this line of life, it may break once through some tempest of passion, some undercurrent of feeling, the spirit's bark may drift off on some selfish tide, the chain may part, but it shall triumph at last, and out pass miles of arguments, and oceans of theories.

"Cozily you sit in life's easy chair, and bolt and bar and curtain the chamber of your heart lest some mendicant pity creep in, or starving sympathy ask alms. Poor silk-worm soul, crawling on softest medallion, garlanded with ruby and emerald, you're weaving there, shut up so closely, your heart shrouds. The good within you is dying out. You may be good husbands and fathers, models of professional skill and business talent. These are praiseworthy—excellent. But each of these duties is in itself remunerative in money or happiness.

"These give you no pass to the celestial kingdom—you shall never plant your foot on the eternal shore, without this self-denial.

"To be honest, honorable, successful is not all of life. Is not the body more than meat, the soul more than raiment?

"Keep not your stinted self-denial, a sickly hot-house plant, under glass in the conservatory of your souls, where you go on sunshiny days to take a look; or a gold fish in a small globe to move round and round, and never move on. It must live with you—inspire you week long and life through.

"Cultivate self-denial—you will not relish it at first, tho taste is not natural. Cultivate it; it will be a delightful luxury yet—the calisthenics of daily self-denial will keep the soul warmer than if wrapt in a thousand luxuries. Folded in the ermine mantle of self-esteem, you may look out and shiver as you think of this cold hard self-denial. So December night is cold and cheerless, go forth and brave it, and the bright far off stars, will shine down cheeringly. Aurora may fold around you her glorious lights. Selfish monks cloistered in the convents of your hearts—no starlight of love, no sunshine of conscience, no smile of God can kindle your spirit's sky roofed over with the sheet-iron of selfishness. Come out under the clear sky of duty open doored to God. Close closeted with self through time's refracting misty medium, objects look large and bright that are tame and common place after all. Come out and get a glimpse of the upper air where high in the everlasting zenith, truth and duty, shine full orbed and radiant.

"Let not pride come between you and the humblest duty. Pride, pride, pride, poor mortal that can't go with you to Heaven. 'Tis a heavy armor for the frail spirit to bear, it may drag you down.

"This poor body you are glorifying, cherishing, maguifying, beautifying, is only an old tenement house wearing away; the keepers of the house are trembling, the windows are darkening, the panes broken, the shutters swinging, the wheel is breaking at the cistern—you are stuffing the windows with rags of self-rightcousuess—they can't keep out the winds of remorse; you yourself, your lease expired, must soon move out of it. God grant you may move up out of it, into the purer air and more delightful locality of the celestial city, on the heights celestial, near the broad avenue of perfect bliss.

"In life's frail hammock, on trouble's stormy pillow, over the rough billows of care, rocked by a Father's hand, sing this sweet lullaby to your tired soul—

 "'Within this body pent,
  Afar from thee I roam,
 And nightly pitch my moving tent,
  A day's march nearer home.'

"How the great heart of the city throbs with starving agony. Do something for somebody, by hand, or purse, or prayer—the next wave in the tide of life may wash you up —wrecked on the shore. Plant yourself like a flower in the heart of poverty, lean your head for sympathy on sorrow's stony pillow—hard by is some unseen Jacob's ladder where nightly angels troop.

"You may have wealth, and fame, or noble ancestors. What are rank, position, nobility ? Are *they* fetters to bind, barriers to close the full heart's outgushing tide of blessing ? We are all children of one Great Father in Heaven. If we do good, there is no promotion in the celestial army to which we may not aspire—we may be kings among peers. There is no musty mortal word exclusive in the archives of Paradise. Once laid on the earth pillow, once passed the last billow, there will be no circles but stars, no laws but love, no haughty airs those airs of upper Palestine. Worshippers of grace, grace in form, manner, surroundings—thirsters for glory, know you not, there soundeth out in richest melody, this beacon promise, echoing evermore in the ears of grace-lovers and glory-seekers—'The Lord our God will give grace and glory to them that walk uprightly.'

"You are following the bent of your own wishes, the promptings of strong ambition. 'Hark! struggling soul, hear you not those strong head winds of avarice and pride that are blowing off the immortal shore ?'

"Let not your soul sit idly looking out of its windows and waiting for vagabond thoughts, ever strolling by and prating away the hours.

"The bark of the soul is full of such passengers, crowding its cabin, deck, and steerage ; wasting its energies which should be employed in fitting out for life's voyage, with a crew of hardy principles.

"Let conscience watch at the wheel of life, safely steering the spirit bark along the coast of danger, off the dark shore of error, through rough rocks and sandy bars, and shallow channels of temptation, lest, worn out and wasted, the dismantled soul be stranded—lost off the eternal shore in sight of the safe harbor of the port of peace, all hopes on board missing. Once leave the current of right, once dashed against the sharp rocks of temptations you may whirl in the eddies of remorse forever. Spring the leak of one fatal error, down the dark depths the soul will sink, lost! lost, lost. Then what will it profit a man if he gain the golden freight of this vast world and lose his own soul ?"

Prof. Henry had an abrupt way of closing, yet it impressed the last thought on the hearer's mind, and left him usually trembling at the door of conscience—at that door the sermon closed.

Said Richard, as he passed on homeward by the doctor's side, " He seems to me like a man who has waded through a sea of sorrow and reached the shore of peace, and found there his baptism of eloquence. He has a very earnest manner, and most solemn yet winning voice. Ministers talk too often as if ' orthodoxy meant my doxy,' as Dean Swift says. But I do like his doxy—I wish from my heart it was my doxy. I like to hear a man say what he feels and believes, even though I don't agree with him in sentiment."

The congregation moved on—Mrs. Pridefit said, " It was a very nice sermon, but not as pretty as Dr. Smoothers, nor was his prayer as splendid, nor his toilet as exquisite. He didn't look at all stylish, and then he didn't wear a gown, and Dr. Smoothers' gown was so becoming to him ! I don't like him as well as Dr. Smoothers," said she, " he is so abrupt. But I was so glad Mr. Trap was there, it was just the kind of sermon for him. I wonder if the professor didn't have him in his eyes when he wrote it—he is so selfish and miserly. He got it this morning. He hardly ever goes to church, but his wife's brother is there on a visit and *he* is a great church goer ; probably he got him out. I don't think the man has ever been confirmed. He always reads the service, though."

" He's pretty well *confirmed*, now," said Mr. Pridefit dryly, " and as to services, the only service he cares for is the lawyer's liturgy, ' service rendered.' "

" Perhaps his conscience may have been touched," said Mrs. Pridefit.

" There's been too much game caught in that Trap ever to be sprung by any force of eloquence. Peace of conscience is a kind of ' satisfaction piece' he cares nothing about."

If every heart chord that morning touched could have turned into audible melody, what a miserere of penitence, what a diapason of joy would have struggled out and swelled upward on the still air. If every tear that morning shed were impearled, how radiant with pearls the pale brow of the speaker.

Miss Susan Simpson walked on with a quick, nervous walk —she threw off her hat, cloak and victoriue, and exclaimed, " That was a real gospel sermon. How much better we'd all be if ministers never talked without saying something, and stopped when they got through. What are we two old maids living for—just to take care of ourselves, like two silk worms trying to make each day our home warmer, pleasanter. I think we'd better call it Cocoon place. If we should die to-day people would say, ' Those old maids Simpsons are dead. I wonder who's sorry. Who'll get the property now those old maids are gone?' That self-denial bridge— why, I've never put my foot on it yet."

" Well, if you don't get to Heaven, what'll become of Mrs. Pridefit? She's a member of the church."

" The church isn't responsible for its members. If you and I get on the other side of the dark river it will be no comfort to find fashionable professors there with us. Mrs. Pridefit is naturally ugly; she must struggle hard to cross the grain, to be decently good. We should do right just as constantly as if our names were written on church books. She is a very susceptible woman, not exactly a hypocrite, though she really feels solemn in church. I have seen the tears roll down her face when something affecting was said. Then on Monday she'd be blowing up servants, scolding the dress-maker, and putting her whole soul, mind, and strength, in finishing the myriads of tucks in her new silk dress, and bewailing over that neuralgia of hers. She has streaks of good—sometimes she'll attend morning prayers for a week, and express great gratitude for the privilege of coming, and then that's the last you'll see of her for a year. She may come to preparatory lecture—every body goes to that. We have our own life lease and an annual debt of gratitude to answer for. Just three years ago to-day, Mary died. Her last words were 'Susan, live for God.' You used to say the hobby she rode was self-denial—she talked about it so often. If it was a hobby, I believe now like a chariot of fire it bore her straight to Heaven—she crossed the self-denial bridge. What if I should die; my fit epitaph would be, 'Here lies one who took the best care of herself, rose early, dressed well, and retired late daily for fifty years, and died in affluence.' I am too old to be loved, but I do want to be remembered here, and remembered when Christ comes to his kingdom. There are no old maids there—we shall all be young, immortally young—nor lonely nor solitary there ; there will be an innumerable company," and Susan wept, as if the sermon broke up the depths of her long closed heart. She looked at sister Mary's portrait, that sweet, patient face, and exclaimed, " I'll walk over every paving stone in this city until I find where Mrs. Pridefit has hidden that poor child. I have dreamed about her often since I felt her little hand clinging to that icy cistern. Mrs. Pridefit says she is out in the country recruiting, but I don't believe a word of it."

Miss Charity Gouge said in her precise way to Mrs. Edwards, as they walked along together, " It was the right sermon for the times. She hoped it would raise the standard of piety. Christians hadn't come up to the gospel standard yet. Zion was in a very low state."

The tall woman with the long nose and hollow eyes moved along behind the crowd of church-goers muttering to herself, " Yes, yes, let him *preach*. I believe in practice. I would tear him out of the pulpit if I could," she added with suppressed rage.

John Trap did groan in his sleep that night. Mrs. Trap hoped the sermon might have made some impression. He tossed about restlessly as if his mind was disturbed, but at last he muttered in some exciting dream, " Put him through. Put him through."

It was a problem that kept her awake many a night—how she could bring up John Trap, Jr., now only four years old, to be an honest, just, equitable man—more than all, a Christian. The little fellow walked in the light of his father's example. He imitated his look, tone, manner, and only that morning came to his mother, saying, " Mother, that Aleck

Stevens is a scamp. He ought to be put through. When I get to be a big man, I'll put him through."

John Trap sat in his room writing three names—he was getting out some new cards. Those three men for shrewdness, skill, and cunning could not be surpassed in the country. Trap was a good office lawyer, Fogg a sage counsellor, and Craft a skillful pleader. Reader, I wish I could introduce them to you—" Mr. John Trap, Mr. Serenus Fogg, and Mr. Savage Craft. Whoever takes their card and gives them his business will have all his affairs put through."

" I have taken good care of Dr. Wendon long enough," said the doctor, as he walked slowly home, his eyes fastened on the ground. " I must do something for some body."

" I'd like a more aristocratic-looking minister," said Mrs. Elliot, as she passed along. " Dr. Smoothers makes such splendid prayers."

There was a poor lonely French gentleman in Mrs. Edwards' boarding-house who was trying to learn our language. He went to church and somehow understood much of the pure English of Prof. Henry's sermon. It deeply impressed him, and that night he knelt by his bedside and offered this simple and eloquent prayer :

" O, Dieu, donnez moi des paroles non de celles qui flattent les oreilles, et qui font louer les discours, mais de celles qui penetrent les coeurs, et qui captivent l'entendment."

CHAPTER X.

DR. WENDON'S SELF DENIAL.

" Place at thy lattice a flower, and ne'er
  Will it let an evil thought enter there ;
  Bear on thy bosom a posy, and lo,
  Wherever thou goest will angels go."
  RUCKERT.

" Two miles would cover all wherein I have a part,
  But all the great blue heaven could never fill my heart."
  VICTOR HUGO.

" WALTER was clear carried away with that sermon," soliloquized Mrs. Wendon, on Monday morning as she sat by her window grouping some flowers for a vase on a little table before her. "When Dr. Smoothers preaches, Walter generally takes a good nap—he never knows much about the sermon ; but he repeated almost the whole of this after he came home. The text was nothing uncommon—Dr. Smoothers preached from the very same text about a year ago ; but he made a very elaborate thing of it; he is the most elegant sentence-maker I ever heard. I never think of the ideas when I hear him ; I only watch the stately march of words, as they move along grander and higher, like an army of golden clouds. He'd be a very good man if he were converted, for it don't seem to me he was ever converted, though I wouldn't like to speak such a thing out. Mrs. Pridefit says his preaching is very elevating, but it seems to me if a lawyer in court should wander so from the evidence, or so desert his client's cause, the judge would stop him and tell him *that* had nothing to do with the case. He couldn't convince an intelligent jury by such a style of speaking. I imagine, though I never was in court but once in my life, that if a minister would address his congregation as if they were all jurors waiting to decide from his pleading, whether they were guilty sinners or not, he would be more successful. I wonder if half the clergymen try as hard to win a soul to Christ, as a cunning, clever lawyer does to win his case. I heard a celebrated lawyer once talk to a jury, and I verily thought he could make them believe, if he chose, that a cat had six feet, and he'd make them almost see the cat, and hear it purr. It is horrible for a man talking to dying men to spend an hour in wreathing words with graceful flowers, and decking thoughts with tinsel stars. I never could go to Dr. Smoothers for advice or prayers ; I'd as soon go to a star to warm myself—but there comes Walter—I hope he has not brought any body home to dine, for Bridget has one of her nervous attacks, and little dinner we'll have to-day of her getting—and I have cut my finger so badly, cutting that tough baker's bread, holding it up to my waist. I can do nothing with it —every time I try to use it the wound opens again."

Mrs. Wendon left the window to put some more geranium in her bouquet. The doctor stole quietly in by the back door, went softly into the parlor, and then came up stairs.

"Minnie," said he, rubbing his hands together, while his eyes sparkled rather mischievously, " I've got a present for you—I laid it on the sofa in the parlor—it must be carefully handled, as it is delicately made, and I think very pretty. I thought it would amuse you sometimes when I am gone, and you are all alone. I hope you can keep it always, no matter what the fashion is. I think the style will always be good, it is one of those things that improve as you keep it—indeed, I think I shall always like it."

" 'Tis a new piano," thought Mrs. Wendon, rising, and eagerly going towards the door. "Walter is always getting me some pleasant surprise. I'm sure, he has such exquisite taste, I'll like whatever he gets."

She went down stairs, and paused a moment before opening the door, wondering what it could be ; and then with the eager impetuosity of a child, pushed the door open, and there were a pair of beautiful, bright young eyes gazing timidly up into her face, and a graceful young form, startled as a timid fawn when she met Mrs. Wendon's gaze—while a blush of bright crimson suffused the pale cheek.

Mrs. Wendon looked at the lovely apparition, and smiled as she went up to the sofa, and sat down by her side. It was a cold October day—she removed the shawl from the shoulders of the young girl, and taking her hand, drew her to the register. Her hands were cold, and her eyes had a weary look, as if the child had just recovered from a long illness.

Having seated her in a low rocking-chair by the register, she asked no questions to embarrass the young stranger, only, "What is your name, child ?"

"Nepenthe," said the girl, in a low voice, "Nepenthe Stuart."

"Were you named for any one."

"I don't know," said the child, "it was the name my mother gave me."

"Have you no mother, my dear ?" said Mrs. Wendon, tenderly.

"No," said she, bursting into tears. The new face, the new place, the kind words, the excitement of leaving the hospital while still an invalid, were too much, and any allusion to her mother always overcame her.

"I will be your mother, child," said Mrs. Wendon, throwing her arms around her. "You shall be my dear child—you shall be mine as long as I live," and she kissed the pale forehead, the quivering lips, and drawing back the curls from her face, wiped away the tears.

Just then the doctor peeped in at the door and called out—

"Minnie, are we to have any dinner to-day ?—the cook has gone aloft, and the brandy-bottle is empty."

We leave Mrs. Wendon to burn her fingers broiling the steak, and toast her face browning the bread, and we'll talk a little about the doctor.

There was a pleased benevolent look in the doctor's face as he stood by Nepenthe's bedside that morning at the hospital with his new purpose radiant in his eyes. But the nurse, as he left the door, whispered something in his ear which did not change his purpose, but made its accomplishment a far greater act of self-denial. The whisper haunted him, as with a heavy heart, he bore the lonely Nepenthe to his home, and for long months wherever her smile rested, there was the shadow of this dark whisper. The doctor went back to the hospital to ask one more question of the nurse, but she had suddenly disappeared. He returned disappointed, and sat quietly thinking, and then he suddenly exclaimed—

"Minnie, we must get Nepenthe well first, before we set her about any thing ; till then, she may be my page and your cup bearer. Homeless young girls in story books all get to be governesses. What else can an educated poor woman do ? I saw once a very sharp review on a new work, and the point of the critic's sarcasm was aimed at the fact that the heroine was a school-teacher, but this resort to teaching is no more common in books than in real life. ' Wanted—a situation,' is written on many a fair young face. I'm glad there is a world where people can live, and breathe, and move, without struggling for a situation."

While the doctor and his wife were talking that evening, Nepenthe had fallen asleep. Haunted so long by a living, watching ghost, her rest had been troubled, her waking anxious, the sheet was drawn tightly over her face, "Mother, mother," she called out wildly, as if in a nightmare sleep.

"Poor child ! Perhaps her mother was the only friend she ever had," said Mrs. Wendon, tenderly, drawing away the sheet, and gently moving her head.

"Too true," thought the doctor, though he said nothing, for that whisper came in his mind, and that troubled look in his face.

"How proud and fond her mother would be of her," said Mrs. Wendou, "and how pretty she looks in that new blue merino. I have bought her a blue silk and a blue de laine, and the inside trimmings and strings of her bonnet are blue. I am glad blue is so becoming to her, it is a color of which I never get tired. The loveliest of human faces, the most graceful of human forms, look more lovely and charming in blue. It is a color that will never be out of style. Magenta, Solferino and cerise, visible black and invisible green, immaculate white and imperial purple will rival it in vain Each coming spring, as long as blue violets open their eyes, or blue forget-me-nots close their starry petals, the fairest blonde will choose its etherial folds, and the sparkling brunette will adopt its deeper hues. In every festive hour, some first stars of fashion will be adorned with blue. The King of Kings has adopted it for His full-dress evening color ; every magnificent gathering of stars, every resplendent reception of courtiers around His throne, are robed in radiant blue. The illustrious Creator, and magnificent Patron of Art, Author and Artist, has made it the color laureate. His golden psalm of night, His grand proem of creation, His illuminated manuscript, His brilliant vignette, His Bible of the Ages, is electrotyped in blue, bound in celestial ultramarine. I suppose it is true, because every body quotes it so often, that beauty unadorned is adorned the most, but I think beautiful hair looks more beautiful, smooth and glossy when becomingly arranged, complexion and eyes grow fairer and brighter, when the person is tastefully dressed. The best artist hangs his picture in a good light, with a handsome frame, and near some object to heighten its tone or soften its coloring. The charm of many agreeable forms and faces is in the affluence and elegance in which they are set like gems—put them in a log house, in a plain coarse dress, the beauty might be gone. Surrounding happy and fortunate circumstances give a strange charm to many— see them elsewhere, in ordinary and uncongenial circumstances, the illusion is gone. Every good-looking person well dressed, is at times pretty. If people would only adopt the fashion that becomes them, without trying to shine and appear in every extreme and new style, how much better they might look."

" Nepenthe doesn't seem like a jewel in a new setting," said the doctor, when she had been with them several months. " She acts as if accustomed to all the refinements of life."

" I like to watch her," said Mrs. Wendon ; " she stands and looks at pictures as if entranced, she listens so absorbed if I play any pathetic air, and she arranges flowers with exquisite taste. The other day I saw her with a bunch of roses in her hands, crying as if her heart would break. I did not disturb her. She came in an hour afterwards perfectly composed—and that picture of the dying mother in the library, I had to put away, she seemed to be so fascinated with it, and was so agitated as she gazed at it. There's another thing that seemed strange to me : when I arranged Nepenthe's room, I put that little Quaker pin cushion on her bureau. I thought it would please the child's fancy. There were pins up and down the skirt like buttons. She had it in her hands once when I went in the room, and was crying. She put the cushion down as I came in, and then she asked me if I would let her lay it away in her drawer. ' Why,' said I, ' not let it be on the bureau, and use the pins when you want them ? It is only a pin cushion.' ' I would rather let them be as they are,' said she, quietly. I wondered at this strange wish of the child, and since then I found the cushion laid carefully away in her drawer ; not a pin was touched."

" She has very strong feelings," said the doctor, " and some early associations may still be very fresh in her mind "

" Walter," said Mrs. Wendon, laying her hand on the doctor's arm, " I think the child may prove an angel to us both. She has almost made you perfection in my eyes, and I have had many feelings since she came I never had before. If I disliked at first the idea of you bringing home a hospital patient about whom we knew nothing, she has cured me long ago of all these feelings. I believe when we do any thing for pity's sake, joy is brighter, sorrow lighter, duty clearer, and all through life's mingled tide, is an undercurrent of melody."

" Minnie," said the doctor, suddenly, after writing the

name in a new Bible he had been getting for Nepenthe, "don't you think Nepenthe rather a long, positive name for a child? Can't we make some contraction of the word?"

"Did you hear Levi Longman ask me when we were in the country," said Mrs. Wendon, "why you call me Minnie? 'Why,' said I, 'Mr. Longman, don't you think it a pretty name?' 'I never like contractions,' said he. 'I was always thankful I had a name that could not be trifled with.'"

"Nobody would think of contracting him or his name either," said the doctor, with a curious twinkle in his eye, "he would keep stiff and starched, in the folds nature gave him; but then there isn't much nature about him—he is one of those human petrifactions washed up on the shore of creation and furnished with the fossil remains of some antediluvian heart. No matter how warm the day is he cools me when he looks at me. I really believe, as Dr. Holmes says, he would reprove his kitten, if he found her playing with her tail, for useless experiments and idling time, and for undue lightness of manner. I would like to look into his school; his scholars must have their mouths fixed for saying 'prisms and prunes' all day."

"Then those children in the family where we boarded all had such long names," said Mrs. Wendon. "James Richard Henry, etc., and no matter how young the youngster was, the whole of his long name was distinctly uttered every time he was addressed."

"I would not give my child an ugly name if all my ancestors way back to Adam had them," said the doctor. "In my grandfather's family there were three brothers—Jonah Jonathan, Abiathar Benajah and Nehemiah Nicodemus. I wonder why my sister Mary wasn't called Mehitabel Jerusalem. The name is the first association we connect with an unknown individual. Think of an artist getting along well under the name of Job Smith. People are so fastidious about names that musical characters go off to Italy and come back celebrities with some new suffix to old names or an entire new cognomen. Had Jenny Lind been Peggy Snooks, we would not have liked her quite as well. Think of Peggy Snooks Polkas, Peggy Snooks bonnets. The name never would have been the rage. You may say fudge! Minnie, but you must acknowledge it to be true. All the Carolines are Carries now—Janes Jennies, and Minervas Minnies," he added laughing. " But see that child—look out of the window, she is arranging a most beautiful boquet."

"Doctor! John says Mrs. Cherrytree has broken her limb on the railroad," said Margaret, coming up the basement stairs as Dr. Wendon stood in the hall putting on his overcoat.

John Trap has heard of Mrs. Cherrytree's misfortunes, and has gone around to get Cherrytree to sue the company for damages, for six thousand dollars.

"Mrs. Cherrytree has a fortune in her own right, so she will probably recover heavy damages," thought the doctor. " If she were a poor washerwoman two hundred dollars would be enough. Trap will get a large fee, and so he will get a big verdict. He'll talk to the 'intelligent jury' until he makes them believe anything. He is as cunning as a fox."

As the doctor drove hastily around the corner, he saw John Trap and the hollow-eyed, long-nosed nurse of the hospital crossing a street together. They seemed to be in earnest conversation, and she handed Mr. Trap just as they passsed out of the doctor's sight, a small roll of bills. She was looking really quite angry, and almost cross. They seemed on very familiar terms. " I kept back the letters," said the woman in a low tone, " and so the property could not be redeemed."

" The Stuart estate is worth a fortune now," thought Trap, though he said nothing, but looked all at once pleased and satisfied with his shrewdness and success. "Mrs. Elliott shall pay me two thousand for my services for her."

CHAPTER XI.

THE MIDNIGHT VISITOR.

"While powers unjust and guilt prevail,
Stone I would be, and sleep I hail.
To see or feel would each be woe ;
Oh ! wake me not, and whisper low."
MICHAEL ANGELO.

NEPENTHE had been at Mrs. Wendon's about a year when Mrs. Wendon's cook was ill—quite ill. It was the recurrence of some constitutional malady. She asked leave of absence a week—meanwhile, one as competent as herself should supply her place.

The request was granted—the new cook was installed. Nepenthe went down one day to get something in the kitchen—it was only the day after the new cook came. She was tall and thin, with brown false hair parted low over her forehead. She wore a closely fitting cap with a plain border. She looked very cross at Nepenthe, and muttered something as she stole back quietly up stairs, as if escaping the presence of a disagreeable object.

The next evening, Mrs. Wendon had a severe headache. Nepenthe remembered having seen the camphor in the cook's room on the table. It was about nine o'clock; the cook had retired early. Nepenthe walked softly up into the room, her cap was hung on a nail at the foot of the bed, on the table was the patch of brown hair, and on the bed lay the cook, fast asleep. A lock of heavy black hair had escaped through her nightcap, and hung in a half curl over her face. The hair was long, fine, black and glossy. The forehead was high and white.

"Why," thought Nepenthe, "does she wear that ugly patch of faded brown hair, when her own is so full and black and her forehead so white and high ?"

She walked softly to the table, took the camphor, and stole out, shuddering as if she had seen a ghost. Mrs.

Sharp, as the cook called herself, was taciturn and peculiar, yet respectful to the doctor and his wife.

One day Mrs. Wendon was ill. Nepenthe wished with her own hands to make some oat-meal gruel. Mrs. Sharp turned as she saw her standing by the range stirring the meal, and looked at her with a fierce look, saying something in an undertone about *her* not being mistress of the house— she worked in a kitchen once.

Nepenthe was timid, and was really afraid of this harsh woman, who seemed to have taken a strange dislike to her. She breathed more freely as she went up stairs again, glad to escape from the region where the new cook reigned.

She said nothing to the doctor about the cook's strange manner—he might be angry and scold and send the woman away, she might seek some revenge, she evidently had a great dislike to her—it was best not to trouble the doctor with these little annoyances, it would end soon, when the old cook came back. Nepenthe, though young, acted with remarkable prudence. She had learned patience and consideration at her mother's sick bed. That mother's patient endurance of suffering had made an indelible impression upon her, and given a cast and tone to the whole of her future life.

As in every house, there are days when everything seems to go wrong—the bread will burn, the milk sour, the fire go out, or the cake be heavy—so at Mrs. Wendon's things went wrong the whole week, as if an evil genius presided over the establishment.

As the doctor drew up his face when he tasted the muddy coffee one morning, " It takes a week for a new girl to get used to a strange house," said Mrs. Wendon, apologetically, " and my not having been about has made it harder for her," but yet that night she wrote a letter to a friend of hers, a young housekeeper like herself, and pathetically described her troubles. We make this extract from the letter, though she will hardly justify us in publishing one of her letters:

" I left the care of the lower regions yesterday to bells and speaking tubes, till a peculiar odor ascending into the upper regions, prompted my speedy descent about noon. I found my new tea-kettle high and dry on the red hot range, the potatoes roasting in the bottom of the pot, whence issued clouds of angry gas, hissing and sissing. Bridget was in the yard talking with Bridget next door. My new keeler, for which I paid so many second hand clothes last week, had been hastily washed and put on the range to dry clean. Bridget says she 'always generally' fills the kettle full of water, and as for the keeler, she only just put it there. One of my new goblets lay on the table in sundry fragments—that, she said, had been broken 'this long time' —though I am quite sure it was on the breakfast table in a good state of preservation. The elegant glass pitcher given me by mother when I was first married had been left out on the stone steps for the milk-man to fill. When filled, some wandering tabby in taking a drink had upset it, and the handle was broken. In the centre of the bottom of the keeler was a suspicious-looking dark spot, which will probably soon need a tuft of rags to fill an incipient perforation, and the next week she'll be coming and saying with a bland smile, ' If you plase, ma'am, will you be so good as to get a new keeler, for it lakes. Sure it was very poor tin ; folks says them old clothes women allays generally gives poor tin, ma'am, and we want a new tub, too.' Sure enough, the tub had split its sides for want of hoops, and lost its foundation for want of water. I can't make Bridget understand that a tub is an aquatic animal, and must have water. The tub lies in the cellar, its different sides hopelessly severed, for two of them had been burned that morning for kindling—' it was so convanient '—now we have the tubs set, I suppose we won't have that trouble. The clothes are all washed and ironed, but not thoroughly aired, and she has put them on the beds damp. Nepenthe has taken a violent cold, which resulted in a violent attack of influenza.''

We take this little account from something she wrote herself long afterwards. Says Nepenthe : " I lay wrapped in a pile of bed clothes one night, as I thought, fast asleep. It was about midnight when I was certain my door opened, and some one walked softly in, and yet I thought I was dreaming. Nearer she came to the bed—there was a bowl of flax-seed tea on a little table by the bed, and lemons cut up in it. I heard the rustling of a paper, as if the tea was slightly stirred, and yet I dared not open my eyes. Spell bound I lay, almost afraid to breathe. I thought I was in a horrid nightmare. I could neither scream nor stir. I knew I heard the click of a spoon in the bowl of tea. I moved as I felt a handkerchief over my face and some strong odor almost choking me. A dog barked under my window—I never heard a dog near the house at night before. I started, and I know some one stole hurriedly out. It was a cloudy night, but the moon looked out suddenly from the clouds and shone full through the open shutter on my bed. I could just see through the crack of the open door a kind of dark shadow moving along through the hall. The shadow was taller than Mrs. Wendon. It was not a man—I have a sure feeling it was not. The clock in the hall struck the hour of twelve. It had never been wound up to strike since I came to Dr. Wendon's. I had never heard it strike before. I know not how it happened to strike that night. By some strange phenomenon of dreams, the bark of the dog may have awaked me and caused the dream. I have since thought it might have been an optical illusion, but yet I can still hear, when I lie awake at night and think of it, the rustling of that paper—the click of that spoon.

"I have a vague remembrance as if the shadow had the cook's long black hair. When I think of ghosts I think of her. She might have come in to see how I was sleeping, to taste of the tea, to sweeten it, to see if I were really ill—but it would be very strange and unusual for her to show any interest in me. I threw away the tea the next morning. The cook left the next day—did she not like my awaking or did she not know it? When, and why, and wherefore, was that mysterious visitant? Since that night, I sleep with my door locked, and I always shiver when I hear a dog bark at midnight. It was not a dream—I am sure it was not—for the next morning there was a little piece of white paper, which had been folded like a paper for powder, by the bowl on the table. There was nothing in it. I threw it into the fire. This dream, vision, apparition—whatever it was—I never told. We have impressions, foolish yet fixed —we may be in false or real danger, but the wisest and strongest have often a little superstition. Then nature has a dread of the supernatural, and I would walk miles to get out of the way of that cook, never to see her more. I would rather such an eye as hers would never rest on my face. I looked out of my bed-room through the half-closed shutters the next morning as I saw her walking off rapidly, and I felt really glad that I should see her no more."

For weeks while Nepenthe slept in that room, night after night in succession she was visited by this same figure walking through the room at midnight.

Some would ascribe this to supernatural causes, or to the activity of the imagination. A scientific physician has said this kind of spectral illusion is always the renewal of actual impressions made on the sensorium. It is, he says, a peculiar disease of the internal optical apparatus, the effect of which is to produce a repetition or an imitation of former impressions.

CHAPTER XII.

DR. WENDON'S DREAM.

" One of those passing, rainbow dreams :
  Half light, half shade, which Fancy's beams
  Paint on the fleeting mists that roll.
  In trance or slumber round the soul."

" We can dream more in a minute than we can act in a day "
RANT.

" IT is foolish to talk of dreams," said Dr. Wendon, one morning, when Nepenthe had been with them some time, " but I had a dream last night, and as I dreamed it the night before, too, it made so vivid an impresssion I could hardly convince myself when I first awoke that it was nothing but a dream. It was as if I had seen a panoramic painting unrolled before me. I thought I sat on a lonely rock by the ocean, and above me were radiant clouds. It seemed early in the morning—before sunrise. Suddenly the clouds over my head parted, and a glorious form with shining wings descended, approached me, and gave me a half-open bud with snowy petals edged with ruby. As he handed me the bud, a delicious fragrance perfumed the air about me. 'Take this,' said the angel, ' watch it carefully till it blooms : years shall pass, it will be planted in another's garden, when rough winds will blow upon it, but it will become more beautiful and fragrant than ever.' I turned suddenly, and standing almost close to me by the rock was a form, all black—not black like a negro, but black as charcoal. He had in his hand, a huge ball of fire ; he looked so ugly I thought he must be the devil. I looked down, and I could see one cloven foot. He reached forth to take the flower from my hand. I shivered with fright, and tried to utter the name of Christ. I thought if I could only utter the name of Christ I could keep my flower, but some night-mare spell seemed on me. Suddenly the whole sky was black. I could see nothing. I could hear the waves dashing against the rock, and a great storm coming on. It seemed dark for a long, long time ;—my flower was gone. Then the scene changed. I was in Italy—there were groves, and fountains, and vines, and such a clear sapphire sky ; I sat by a fountain ; I could feel the cool winds on my face. I looked up, the angel was by my side again : —' The flower you reared is fresh and beautiful,' said he, ' and some one will pay a great price for it.' Again the scene changed. I was in my own land once more ; I walked by an artist's studio ; I looked up at the window and there was my flower in a golden vase, more beautiful than ever.

"The dream is no sphinx, no poetic myth, no mystery or riddle I cannot solve. Some little Daniel walking about my heart tells my kingly reason that the dream and interpretation are one. I will not waste my time or puzzle my brains with settling the question whether coming events ever do cast their shadows before them on the shore of dreamland ; whether real deeds and words are ever thus foreshadowed. I *did* have the dream ; but it is the first dream I ever had that I repeated to any one, and it made a vivid impression. My dream seemed to think, and feel, and imagine, and reason all at once. It is photographed on my soul, and who shall dare to say that the picture may not be reproduced hereafter on life's unfolding canvass. Dreams are only the chaos of our thoughts, but out of the world's first chaos came living light, and solid land. Out of the ark of sleep, dreams may glide over the future, and, like the dove, bring back olive-leaf tokens of subsiding billows and cleared up skies, bidding the heart safely go forth on life's rainbow spanned pilgrimage.

"Nepenthe is my flower, and who knows some one yet may pay a great price for her, if now she is carefully culti-

vated and kindly watched. How I would like to educate
her myself, but I've no time in my absorbing profession.
She has read some history and poetry, writes well, has a
sweet voice, gentle manners and warm heart. But she must
have a systematic and thorough instruction in some school.
I believe with Jean Paul Ritcher, ' L'Education doit mettre,
au jour l'. idéal de l' indindu.' There is a circular Mr.
Brown handed me last evening. He says it is a fine school.
I'll read a little to give you some idea of it.

" ' The admirable location of the Institute, magnitude,
adaptation and beauty of the edifice, the arrangements which
have been made for thorough systems of instruction, &c.' "
—the doctor skips over a little and reads on—" ' Its large
patronage, ample means enable the trustees to avail themselves of all the educational improvements of the day, and it
is believed that this Institute can furnish facilities for a
thorough female education, at least, equal to any in the city.'
Here is a long string," said the doctor, " about ' resources,
quietness, beauty, and healthfulness.' I insist upon it,
Nepenthe mustn't learn more than six histories at once.
Miss Kate Howard came home from school the other day
with American History, Natural History, Modern History,
History of Literature, History of England, History of
France, and all these she was actually studying. I want
Nepenthe to spell well ; as for me, I have no eye for spelling. I could read Latin long before I could spell correctly.
I never can remember whether there is a double p in
opportunity, a double l in immortality, or how many s's there
are in possession. I can't think whether the e or i comes
first in piece or niece, and just as I get a few words right
side up with care in my head, out comes Mr. Webster with
a new dictionary, bobbing off venerable consonants and
shortening ancient syllables sacred in the memory of the
oldest inhabitant's spelling-books from time immemorial.
That word theatre, with its illustrious Latin and Greek
origin, I am told is descended from the theatrum family on one
side, and the theatron family on the other, and yet it is
changed now to theater, so that it is almost impossible to
trace its ancient descent, or find its old coat of arms. If I
belonged to the theatre family I should think it a disgrace.
Among the old·Greeks and Romans it is said that the
theatre family was thought a great deal of, but now even

a venerable Greek wouldn't recognize the name. I have a
scientific friend, who was educated at Oxford—he has the
noblest of hearts, and wisest of heads—he is quite indignant
about this changing illustrious names. Besides, an *r* looks
more elegant and classic, before an *e* than after one. I don't
believe in taking a word out of its patrician classic attic, and
putting it under cover of modern dictionary, with such a new
plebeian face you wouldn't know it.   If anything is entitled
to unchanging respect it is a word that has lived in the best
families of words for years.   There are so many of these
old fossilized words dug up and new-fangled over that my
bad spelling is becoming a chronic difficulty ; it is chronic
and constitutional.   I call it spellingetis ; no pathy or
catholicon can cure it. To look in the dictionary is the
only polychrest I know of.   When I write anything important
I peep into that, but it is a great trouble always to have a
dictionary by your side.

"But, Minnie, suppose we send Nepenthe to Madame
Largadoo's, she is all the rage ; she will teach, so the magazine states, ethnology, embroidery, philosophy, natural and
moral, geology, anthropology, scripture exegesis, music,
vocal and instrumental, the languages, French, Italian,
German, Spanish, dancing and christian evidences ; all for
four hundred dollars a year, invariably in advance ; extras
not included.   Wouldn't Nepenthe make a Largadoovian
paragon ?   A young friend of mine lately engaged as a
governess in an illiterate family, and the anxious mother
told her at first she wanted her to teach the children every
kind of manners.   I wonder if Madame Largadoo couldn't
teach every kind of manners.   The rule for her school, as a
French author says, is, ' Be handsome, be polite, people see
you, be gentle, submissive, cure no evils, conceal them, people hear you, change not, only disguise.'   We have professors to study a flea, to classify a gnat, to distinguish a cat
from a rose tree ; but where is the sublime and hidden
being ? where are the moral sense, reason, conscience developed ? Such a school as Madame Largadoo's makes all
alike, knocks off all the salient points of character till there
is not a nuance of character, not a finesse of feeling left.
Madame Largadoo thinks it a greater sin to eat a pie with a
knife, than to tell a lie.   There is not a Largodoovian grad-

uate any where, that would dare to touch a knife to her pie
on any account, not even to manage a countrywoman's tough
buttermilk crust. The girls all write their letters in Largodoovian hand ; superscription, contents, adieus, au revoirs,
all just alike. You can tell a Largodoovian epistle any
where. The scholars come out at sixteen with assurance enough to stare out of countenance half a dozen gentlemen, as they flirt their fans, ogle and serpentine through the
world.

" But Nepenthe must be well educated—you remember,
Minnie, how the chariots of the gods are represented in
mythology as drawn by peacocks. To condemn Nepenthe
to a life of drudgery, would be like harnessing a bird of
Paradise to some Liliputian chariot, to draw sand or earth
around the same barren circle for years. Nepenthe is a
flower in the casement of our hearts—she has shone and
sunned there for months. I mean that no barren rock of
circumstance, no gnarled stump of duty shall bend her out
of her native course, and keep her thoughts trailing on the
ground. There are everywhere half-starved minds, living on
stray drops of kindness, and occasional dews of knowledge,
struggling up through all the strata of difficulties, and blos-
soming at last in beautiful perfection. Yet they sometimes
lament bitterly through life the want of early culture—
greater still they might have been had they had early correct training. We all have some defect in education, or
character, we lean ever to some ruling fault or error, like
the leaning tower on the banks of the Arno—it is a marvel
we stand so long, so erect while we incline so far from the
true centre of spiritual gravity. There's not a being of
whom somebody doesn't say, ' Well, she has her peculiarities.'

" Did you get those violets I ordered for Nepenthe ?
She seems so fond of flowers. The violet is my favorite
flower. In my grandmother's garden I never heard of pansies, but there were plenty of violets. I could pick all day
and still find an inexhaustible supply ; they grew lovingly
together, like country hearts ; not in circumscribed patches
of solitary rows, as in city gardens, planted at conventional
distances, with only three or four flowers in a patch.
They might well be called ' touch-me-nots.' ' Hithertos,' I
call them. They can never creep out of their green par-

quettes with box all around. If anything ought to be left to its own sweet impulses, it is a violet. We can't change the faces of the flowers, the patterns of their velvet crowns, or the shape of their purple robes ; they will keep the primitive style in which God fashioned them, only wearing sometimes, when highly cultivated, a more double skirt, or a deeper fringe, or a rosier blush. We can't alter their faces, so we change their names. We might as well call a violet ' Mary-meek-eyes,' with its downcast head and up-turned face as to give one that mocking name ' Johnny-jumper.' I sent home three roots of tropiola, too, it is much thought of in the modern couservatories, with its velvet dress. I do believe it is only the old nasturtium we used to know so well in the country, where· it lingered by our doorstep or climbed up into the low windows. It has come to the city and changed its name. I don't think, if there is any difference its city dress is half so pretty as its old rustic garb ; it looks paler and out of spirits. But a Fifth avenue violet, though surrounded by wordly influences, sends up, just as pure as ever, its velvet prayer to Heaven."

" Violets," said Mrs. Wendon, " are like God's great re-hearsals. His soft prelude of silent melody in Nature's green orchestra, before He comes out with the full floral an-them, the grand philharmonic of the season. Some flowers seem to have a soul, so spiritual are their sweet faces and fragrant breath ; and who knows but this year's violet is some violet soul of last year waked from its bed ?"

" If Nepenthe were my own child I should call her violet," said the doctor, and then he was suddenly silent, as if dis-turbed by some uneasy thought. He went to the window to fasten the shutter, which was blown back and forth by the wind, and exclaimed, as he looked out, " There ! there she is again." Seizing his hat, he rushed out of the house. He was gone about an hour. He came back, judging from his ab-sent and dissatisfied manner, disappointed in the object of his search.

He sat quietly thinking for some time, and then broke out with an abrupt, half-impatient exclamation, not original, but always true.

" This is a strange world, Minnie. Only an hour ago I felt in quite an elevated mood, thinking of flowers and you and Nepenthe. When I was out I passed a flour and pro-

vision store, and just next it was a large book and stationery
establishment. I could not help thinking how closely our
physical wants were allied to our ideal needs. No matter
how bright our quiet, happiest day-dreams, some clamorous
want always rudely wakes us out of them. In the daily
journal of our lives, as in the daily papers, many of the inside columns, the long pages, are taken up with the list of
' wanted.' I wish I could follow the bent of my own preference, and do that which I like best and enjoy most, but I
read in every morning herald from my heart so many wants,
and I must tug away so patiently to earn them, and I can't
cross a ferry, or ride in a car, or walk down street without
hearing some thing of wants, and money is the key note on
which every note is pitched; it is buying or selling, borrowing or loaning ; you can see it in almost every man's eye,
you can hear it on his tongue. Even if you do not know
him, there's a golden link of sympathy between you and every mortal you meet. I have sometimes a great and sublime contempt for this money, as if it were beneath a moment's thought or care. There are so many things nobler,
better, higher, and then again, I long for it, for the power it
gives, the influence it sways, the sorrow it banishes, brain,
will, talent, generosity, and all God's good gifts are so often
cramped, fettered, crushed by the want of it. I hear men
say, I don't care any thing for money, but I don't believe it.
Only a small, contemptible string of common cord may bind
together, for our handling and owning, books and flowers,
diamonds and pearls, and all precious and charming things,
and money is the contemptible, yet indispensible cord that
gathers and binds, for our grasping and using, the treasures
we most highly prize. If you despise money, just live one
day without two shillings, find yourself suddenly without
even five cents to pay stage fare when you are three miles
from home, among strangers, and very weary, and you have
to walk the whole tiresome distance for want of it. I did so
the day my pocket-book was stolen, and I emptied my pockets two or three times, to be quite sure there was no lingering, lonely five cents left. But look at that child, Minnie,"
said the doctor, suddenly looking out of the window, " how
well Nepenthe looks since her visit in the country. She is
just crossing the street, and her step is light and graceful.
I wish we all could have stayed longer at that old farm

house. I have no attachment to this building. I only know it by the number on the door, unless I see your face at the window when I come home. It is just like all the other houses—it is the fifth house in the block. There is a good deal of individuality displayed in dress. I don't see why there shouldn't be in the exterior of a house. I want something besides a printed directory to point out the place of my residence. I like some railing, or wing, or tree, or shrub a little unlike my neighbor's, some peg on which to hang an association. I want one tree of my own, not one of a stiff row, but either so luxuriant or crooked that I should know it. I could tolerate even a luxuriant cabbage or gaudy sun-flower. Nepenthe says these rows of houses remind her of the little wooden houses that come in boxes for children to play with, with six trees to stand in front, with little round green bunches for foliage. These trees in front of our door are all just so high, large, round and green. They look prim, stiff, and prudish, as if afraid to rise a little higher and meet the kiss of some caressing breeze or catch the low whisper of a frolicsome zephyr. I get tired of hearing people ask, Do you live in the fourth, fifth, or tenth house in the block? Block—block—how I hate the word block. It is a very good name for such a set of houses that have about as much expression as a block. We have to go into the country every summer to get our souls chiselled out of these blocks. I am one of the doctors and you one of the ladies in this block. We lose all our individuality in this brick-rowed city. I'd rather spend an hour in the forest, listening to the weird music of the hymning leaves than hear a whole year of Broadway sounds. I hope I shall live long enough to have some trees of my own. If I were in the country, I would never cut down a tree,"—and the doctor opened a book and read, " He loved old trees, and used to say, ' Never cut down a tree for fashion's sake, for the tree has its roots in the earth, which the fashion has not.' " —GRATTAN.

"But it stands in the way of the tree."—GRATTAN'S FRIEND.

" You mistake ; it is the house that stands in the way of it; if either be cut down, let it be the house."—GRATTAN.

Closing the book, the doctor said with a sigh, " That vine-covered, flower-adorned, and tree-surrounded cottage in the country looms up before me in such dim and distant perspective, if I wait to carn it, I fear I shall be too old to enjoy it. I must invest—the truth is, Minnie, I *have* invested in some thing which has paid large dividends for many years. I have put six thousand dollars in a mining enterprise.

"After careful calculations, shrewd financiers prophesy, I shall make at least seventy-five per cent. My money will work while I sleep. Mr. James thinks I'll clear three thousand the first year. I will invest one thousand of the profits in bond and mortgage for Nepenthe's benefit. Bond and mortgage is the safest kind of investment."

"Take care you do not burn your fingers in this coal speculation," said his wife, laughing and shaking her head.

"Oh, no," said the docter. "This enterprise is a rare chance for making money—but there goes Mr. Mellin—do you know I have lost my practice in all the Mellin family through Trap's influence? He is a rascal, but I can't see what possible grudge he can have against me."

We leave Dr. Wendon a year with his mining operations, but we put down his first reports from the mines.

"With the present arrangements, there is a clear profit of forty-one cents, in full working order. They yield fifty tons a day, and with additional expenditures named, can be made to reach at least one hundred tons a day, Sundays excepted. The engines and all the fixtures are new, operating since August last, and if we were disposed to push things, would draw up one hundred and twenty tons a day. Six hundred dollars will be wanted in January next."

We drop the curtain for two years on the mining operations, and leave Nepenthe awhile at school—a schoolgirl's history is of little interest to strangers.

Dr. Wendon had built, in imagination, his charming cottage in the country—he had planned a tour of Europe—he would do so much for Nepenthe. She should have the advantages of society, of travel, of lessons from the best foreign artists—her future should be as bright as her childhood had been dark. Each day in moments of leisure, and each night in dreams, he added one more beautiful turret to this Chateau d'Espagne.

He couldn't keep from congratulating himself, and telling

others, how glad he was he invested in this fortunate coal
enterprise.   So sanguine was he of his success, that he
would have been perfectly candid in advising any person to
invest their surplus in this promising speculation, but that
word speculation always reminds one of risk ; he called it
enterprise.   He practised his profession faithfully and constantly, while he was saving up daily in the bank of his imagination, piles of shining dollars.

CHAPTER XIII.

EXCITEMENT IN A PARLOR UP TOWN.

" Two ears and one mouth thou hast ;
　Dost thou of this complain ?
Thou much must hear, but must
　But little tell again."

RÜCKERT.

ONE could hear nearly all the interjections in the grammar,
had they listened at the key hole of a small parlor up town
one Wednesday evening.   "The dear knows !" the " do
tells," and the " you don't says," made a perfect jargon to
masculine ears.

What could so raise those carefully cultivated voices so
far abone the conventional pitch ?

" What's all this about, girls ?" said a voice in a clear
masculine baritone sounding through the crack of the
door.

" Why, Fred, it is the most wonderful thing you ever
heard of, most unaccountable," said his sister Kate.   " You
know that large house on the corner we passed the other
day ?"

" Kate," said Fred, " I wish you wouldn't begin everything with ' you know.'   I counted all the ' you knows ' in
one of your sentences yesterday, and there were actually
five."

" Fred, I wish you wouldn't bother me so much about my
talking," said Kate, as she turned dignifiedly round to Mrs.
Edwards, and went on with her story.   " The family live
in the fifth house in the block."

"A ring was heard at the street door one afternoon, and the girl went. There stood a man wrapped up in a cloak."

"Approved brigand style," exclaimed Fred, laughing.

"Don't bother me, Fred," said Kate, really vexed. "He was wrapped up in a cloak, with his hat drawn over his eyes."

"Yes, that's just it; slouched hat and intense black eyes," interrupted Fred again.

Paying no attention to Fred, Kate went on. "Only one of the servants was in. The man asked if the doctor was at home? She said, no. He then inquired if his wife was in? The girl replied, no. The man then turned as if to go, when there was a loud rap at the basement door.

"Probably Bridget was expecting her beau that night, for she left the front door open, and went down in haste to see who was there. It was a boy with a basket of apples. She stayed to chat with the boy and put up the apples, and coming back up stairs, closed the front door, and went up to her sleeping-room on the fourth story, to beautify, preparing for the expected visitor, with whom she had been 'keeping company' so long. It is now thought that the man improved the occasion of her temporary absence to slip into the library at the end of the hall, and then into the extension room in the rear of the parlor. There was a young lady in the front parlor who was singing,

'Life let us cherish,
While yet the taper glows;
And the fresh flowrets
Pluck, ere they close.'

As she finished the last line, the wind came in through the open shutters, and blew off one of the music pages from the piano. She stooped to pick it up, when a bullet whizzed through the air, and lodged in the wall directly in front of her—a bullet intended for her, and which would have killed her had she remained a moment longer in her erect position. A breath of wind had literally saved her. Isn't there a line of poetry somewhere about 'A breath can prostrate and a breath can save?' But whatever was his design, the assassin fled."

"You are quite poetical, Kate," said Fred, in a complimentary tone; "you quote so accurately, you might get up a verse of your own sometimes. If I were a relative of the young lady's, I would ferret out the mystery. There is some wild love or deadly hate about it." Here he paused, and then added, " I have a slight recollection of something occurring away back "——

Fred stopped suddenly, as if broaching a forbidden subject.

" Do tell us !" exclaimed two ladies at once, with all the eagerness of curiosity. " What do you know about away back ?"

" O nothing," replied Fred, quietly. " I have no right to reveal that which I must unavoidably find out in my profession. We shouldn't abuse fiduciary relations—those impromptu disclosures, often so unwillingly made. But really, ladies, I have no disclosures to make. I had once a few suspicions from a few stray facts ; and unsettled and vague as they now are, I would trouble or trust no one to help me keep such secrets."

" As for me," said Kate, " all secrets are a burden ; and isn't it provoking, that the very condition of a secret is often the keeping it forever from the knowledge of the very person to whom of all others you would most like to tell it ? I like to surprise, excite or amuse people with unexpected or startling news. Somehow it does give us a little extra importance in our own eyes, to have some wonderful secret confided to us—to be the only person beside the narrator that knows it. We promise never to tell anybody as long as we live ; but then people will guess sometimes, and guess right—and we must blush, dodge, lie, or keep silence. Some people have such a way of pumping about a thing, you really feel rude if you evade their queries, and they'll get everything out of you. But these very ones will never tell you anything of their affairs, never allow in any way any of their secrets to escape them. It is rather mortifying to have every bundle of secrets in your head overhauled and inspected, while you remain utterly in the dark about their concerns. I declare I believe if it was only right to lie, I'd like to try it occasionally, and say I don't know, right up and down. There's Charity Gouge ; she begins at you with one of her ' Do you really think so and so ?' when she knows you *don't* think, you *know* all about it—and she's the last person in the world I would choose for a confidant."

" There's no place in your head, Kate, for a secret," said

Fred, laughingly; " you remind me of the little Irish Jim I saw in the old farm house, where I was laid up two days last summer. We had a terrible thunder-storm one night— every board in the old house rattled. The wind, and the rain, and the shaking of the house, altogether, aroused Jim from his sound sleep in the sky parlor of the establishment. When the next crash came, Jim could stay no longer in his snug corner, but hurried down stairs in his dishabille into the old farmer's bed-room, exclaiming, all out of breath with fright, ' It's started—it's started !' looking as wild as his rough erect hair and big eyes could make him. And when you get a secret, Kate, I'm sure of one thing—' It's started.' "

" That must be where I stopped the summer before last," said Kate, not noticing his remark. " They had a little factotum 'Jim. It was a careless habit of mine, throwing water out of the window, but they had so few conveniences in their sleeping rooms, I really couldn't help it sometimes. I emptied a pitcher of water out of the window one day, just when the Irish girl came out and stood in the back door. She had just asked Jim, who happened to be standing under my window, ' Will it be afther being a wet day, Jim ?' ' I don't think it will be wet,' said he, turning up his big eyes towards the zenith, as the most authentic source of information ; when the entire contents of my pitcher fell on his broad, upturned face. ' I beg your pardon, sir,' said I, hearing his sudden scream, and seeing the unexpected effect of my cascade upon his clean coat and collar. His momentary vexation cooled off, he was so delighted with the extra politeness of my apology. To be called *sir* for the first time, elevated him in his own estimation a foot higher in the scale of masculine existence."

" If you tell a woman a story," said Fred, " she will instantly think of another like it to tell, and so wander off from the subject. It is surprising what wandering minds women have."

" Fred," said Kate, not noticing his remark, " you find out to-day who that young lady was that was fired at yesterday."

" The house up town," said Fred, looking very wise, " was Dr. Wendon's ; the young lady was his ward, or protegée, or adopted daughter, or whatever she is, Miss Nepenthe Stuart ; and I saw the bullet, the piano, the doctor, the Bridget, and the young lady herself this morning; so you see it is a well authenticated fact. Moreover, the boy with the apples was part of the plan. He told the girl that her cousin George was waiting around the corner, in a great hurry to see her, so the door was actually left open by the girl for at least five minutes."

"Fred," said Kate, "you ought to be ashamed of yourself, pretending ignorance all this time, when you knew so much about it."

"Maybe it is an old love affair," said one of the ladies.

"They say the girl never had any love affair, or any avowal of love."

"Well, she might have injured somebody."

"No, she has not an enemy in the world, that she knows of," said Fred, "she is young, amiable and on good terms with every body she knows; neither is she an heiress; her death could be of no known advantage to any living person."

While these ladies were continuing their conversation, another group were gathered in the parlor up town. It was Dr. Wendon, Mrs. Wendon, and Nepenthe.

Nepenthe sat on one corner of the sofa away from the window, the shutters were tightly closed; Dr. Wendon was walking back and forth, and occasionally stopping and talking in a kind of hurried, excited way; he was really exasperated, and spoke in rather an impetuous manner though he tried to assume an air of unconcern.

"Well," said he, "there is the bullet, and there is the hole, and here is Nepenthe as white as a sheet. I would like to sift to the bottom of this matter. I can't get any more out of Bridget. She says she 'always generally keeps the door fastened,' she 'always generally stays close to the house, she always generally is very careful.' One thing I know, I'll ship her, if she leaves that door open again. These villains always generally come and go like shadows. I wish I did know something about this thing." Nepenthe evidently had some enemy; but, we very well know, not of her own making.

"There is something, we may be sure, depending upon her life. The ball was fired by a person standing about here," he added stepping back a few paces in a line with the piano. "There is no getting any more out of Bridget; she says the man was tall, but not so very tall ; fat, but not so very fat ; old, but not so very old ; he might be young—she couldn't tell. There's no accident in this it was all designed and plannned, and pretty well carried out," said the doctor.

"I shall always keep that page of music, for it saved my life," said Nepenthe.

"Well," said the doctor, "I've had this house pretty well secured to-day with iron, brass, and plated chain bolts, safe night latches and bolts, secret sash fastenings and shut-ter bars and secret bolts. I'll have my double barreled pis-tol at the head of my bed, and I've engaged two private watchmen to watch my house."

"I can't sleep to-night," said Mrs. Wendon, as she retired early to rest. "I can't sleep, though the house is all locked and fastened up. Did you see that man's nose flattening against the window pane only night before last as you went to shut the bliads ? I dreamed about it, and every time I opened my eyes I could see that face."

"The professional burglar can get in any where if he is determined to. But this man was no mere burglar. My watch lay on the table near where he stood, and he could easily have taken it if he chose," said the doctor.

"If I am excited or frightened at night," said Mrs. Wen-don, "I imagine all sorts of things, and remember all the stories of murders, ghosts and robberies I have ever heard. I tremble at every noise—There ! do you hear that ?" she said suddenly, as she turned to the doctor, and whispered as she heard some noise in the lower part of the house.

"'Tis only a big rat knocking down something in the cel-lar," said her husband. But what a strange propensity there is, thought he, to talk and think over tales of ghosts, murders, and mysteries, just as we are about to retire, until we are almost afraid to look into each other's frightened faces. How the forgotten facts of a long veiled mystery loom up in the night—how the clairvoyant soul walks all night on the dangerous battlements of terror and mystery— and when morning comes, she laughs at the fears she has summoned !

Nepenthe's room now is next to the doctor's, her door is bolted and locked, her windows closely fastened. She has rolled up by the door two trunks, and near the edge of the top of the upper one she has placed the big dinner bell, so that if the door is at all moved or shaken, the bell will fall, and awaken all the surrounding sleepers. She lays awake a long, long time, and at last she sleeps, but it is a disturbed nightmare sleep—and at midnight she could see a figure once more walking through her room and standing by her bed ; but the figure was no longer a woman—it wore a man's slouched hat.

As Mrs. Wendon lies awake one night, talking to the doctor, she says,

" No state of mind is more rapidly developed than the emotion of fear. It soon gets to be all eyes, all ears, all brain. While Fear patrols through the soul, a sleepless, vigilant sentinel, every other power seems dumb and quiet. All are vulnerable to Fear's alarms at some point. When she springs the soul's loud watchman's rattle, she calls to her aid Dread, Terror and Fright, the active, alert police of soul. Every body is afraid of something. I believe there is one little space in every man's mind where may be written ' coward.' Every one is at times troubled, tempted, or tortured, harrassed, harrowed or haunted by some constitutional or chronic fear, which takes to him the shape of moral ghost, mental ghost, spiritual ghost, nervous ghost, legal ghost, or hereditary ghost—and the boldest, when confronted with this shape or shade, says to himself, ' I am afraid.' The greatest, strongest, bravest soul has a morbid dread, a chronic fear of something—he calls it dislike, but he knows it is fear."

" We often find ourselves," said the doctor, " talking to ourselves as if we were two distinct beings. We argue, reason, and persuade—promise and retract the promise, decide and undecide—we are sure of something, then doubt it altogether."

" Yes," said Mrs. Wendon, " bold young Faith and grim old Fear, like two stout champions, seek each to gain the field of soul, and master the other. Fear gives Faith such a sound drubbing we begin to doubt every thing, and we wonder whether even the great reel of Eternity will ever wind up clear and smooth the great snarl of facts and fancies in which we find ourselves so strangely, sadly entangled—and then all at once, as Faith stands up triumphant under the cloudless blue sky of soul, pressing her conquering foot on the maimed Titan Fear—then we sail along through truth and duty's sea so sublimely, that daylight, moonlight and sunlight gleam and flash, brighten and illumine each passing hour."

Mrs. Wendon had talked so long about these things that she could not sleep. She lay awake a whole hour trying to settle in her mind some doubtful thoughts of powers seen and unseen, influences real and spiritual. She was so wide awake, every sense seemed doubly active, every sound doubly loud. The clock on the mantle struck one; the old clock in the hall struck one; and then the front door bell rang once. She awoke the doctor, who waited to answer the summons till the bell should ring again. But there was no more ringing that night. The next night it rang again at just one o'clock. The doctor went to the door; no one was there. He looked up and down the long silent street; he could see in the clear soft moonlight no retreating shadow, nor hear any lingering footfall. He latched and locked the door, walked half way up stairs, and the bell rang again; a little louder and quicker, once, twice, thrice. He hurried back to the door, annoyed at the impertinent persistency of the invisible bell ringer. But no one was there, nor was any one hidden under the steps near the basement door. He came in again, turned his face to the stairs, and the bell rang three times more, louder than ever.

He looked out. No one was visible. He stepped out on the sidewalk, looked up and down and under the steps, and in the little front yards of the houses next door. Then he examined the bell handle carefully, to see if possibly the invisible bell ringer hadn't fastened to it some cord by which it could be rung while he was secreted in some house near. But no such cord, hand or person could be detected. Baffled, puzzled, irritated, excited, he closed the door again, latching, locking and bolting it, saying to himself, "Let them ring all night; I'll not open that door again." * Then there was a sudden, loud and quick succession of rings, as he began to re-ascend the stairs; and there was no pause, no cessation, until he reached the head of the stairs, where stood Mrs. Wendon, peeping through the crack of her nearly closed door, waiting in mute suspense for the doctor's re-appearance with some solution of the mystery.

The bell had at last roused Bridget from her profound slumbers in the third story. She was on her knees praying to the Virgin. She was sure it was Mrs. Fedurell's spirit ringing the bell.

Mrs. Fedurell had lived three doors below them, she was an intimate friend of Mrs. Wendon's, and a refined and gifted woman, who had died only last week of consumption.

Bridget really believed that she, now in Heaven, and of course more elevated and refined in her spiritual state, could stoop to descend to the earth, and go around ringing her old neighbor's bells.

But Bridget was sure it was Mrs. Fedurell's ghost, and at last as she gained courage to look through the shutters, she was sure she saw a light, and something like a white object standing motionless in the moonlight.

Even Mrs. Wendon, with her cooler head and better judgment, began to connect something a little supernatural or mysterious with this unaccountable ringing, commencing both nights at the ghostly hour of one.

The mystery continued for three weeks. Each night about midnight, the bell would ring. Every nap was interrupted, every dream disturbed, and one good night's sleep impossible.

No matter how weary or sleepy the doctor or his wife or Nepenthe might be, their slumber must be rudely broken.

Bridget soon notified Mrs. Wendon that she must go next Tuesday when her month was up, she couldn't stay in such a place.

Bridget had informed all of her dear particular friends, among whom was every Catharine, Bridget and Margaret in the neighborhood, of the reason of her leaving. She had told them in vivid, graphic colors, of the nightly bell ringing—the light and the ghost.

Mrs. Wendon began to think it would be difficult for her to secure any more good help, as all the girls in the neighborhood looked up at the house and whispered to each other as they passed it, as if it were really haunted.

The thing began to be intolerable, as the boys began to say as they passed—"Did you know that house was haunted?"

Bridget said that the dogs stood before the house, and stared, and barked, and howled at night, when the bell rang.

One old lady in the neighborhood thought that the ghosts of some people who had once lived there had come back to disturb the house, and that each of these gaunt, strange looking dogs, was a howling medium for these unfortunate unhappy ghosts.

Mrs. Wendon began to imagine that everybody looked up strangely at the house and peered curiously into the windows as they passed. A story of a haunted house had always been to her the most foolish and ignorant of super-stitions; yet as that ringing continued, she wanted to move out of the place, the noise, notoriety and gossip were becom-so intolerable; but the doctor didn't like to be rung out of his own door in that summary style, and be condoled with forever after, as a fugitive from a haunted house. So one day he persuaded Cæsar, a trusty colored man, a servant of one of his friends, to come and watch his door for him a few nights, promising to pay him liberally.

Cæsar declared that nothing could frighten him; neither ghost, goblins nor the devil—for, said he, " Lor bress me, Massa, how can de debbel hurt poor black man who neber done nuffin wrong."

The doctor retired, having great confidence in the courage of the new detective.

Cæsar watched faithfully, inside and out, now with the door a little open, and then with it closed.

He listened for the least noise, and suddenly, about one, the bell rang once. Cæsar was startled : then it rang twice— he did grow a little more startled. He seized the door and opened it; the bell rang still, but as he looked at the bell handle it did not move. Ring, ring, ring, it went again; but the bell handle never moved at all. Just then, as if by some bodily agitation, the door was thrown wide open, and as the lamp light on the other side of the street, interrupted by the large limbs of the trees swaying backwards and forwards, sent into the hall behind him a host of trooping shadows, to Cæsar's excited fancy they were a band of fearful ghosts.

Without stopping to look longer behind him, he started and ran, turning neither to the right or left, chased by a big black barking dog, who deemed it his duty to run because he saw some one else running. A policeman, thinking the bareheaded, flying Cæsar an escaping burglar, joined in the pursuit, till Cæsar, just as he came to the corner where he must cross to reach his master's house, tripped and fell over the curb-stone, bathing eyes, mouth and nose, in the puddle of muddy water, which was meandering along the gutter. Without pausing to brush the mud from his broadcloth, he ran on faster than ever, out-distancing the pursuing police-man and dog—and rushing into his master's basement door, which happened to be open, as Dinah and Rose had had some company pretty late that night, and they were just kissing their fond adieus by the open door :

" Cæsar has had a spree, Cæsar has had a spree," said Dinah, as the gaslight fell full on Cæsar's bold, bare head and soiled coat and dirty face, " Cæsar has had a spree."

But he hurried by her, not minding her bantering, nor stopping until he found himself in his own bed, and covered up his head with the welcome and familiar bed-clothes.

His master's grave inquiries the next morning about his suspicious plight the night before only got from him the brief answer. "Haunted house, Massa; haunted house."

Dr. Wendon was awake, and hearing no more opening and shutting of the front door, though the bell kept on ring-ing, he went softly down stairs to see how investigations were progressing ; but no Cæsar was there. The door was wide open and there lay on the upper stone step Cæsar's old hat : and in spite of everything, the words came into the doc-tor's mind, " I come to bury Cæsar ; not to praise him."

His inquiries of Cæsar the next day about his last night's adventures met with no answer. He could get nothing out of him, only he could see he had been in some way thoroughly frightened.

The next night Patrick, a bold, smart, stout young Irish-man, who had worked a great deal for Dr. Wendon, offered to keep watch.. He said he had seen ghosts in the " ould counthry," and he wasn't afraid of any spirits. He took his post by the door, having in his pocket a bottle of fourth proof, from which occasionally he refreshed himself by tak-ing copious draughts. At one o'clock the bell rang. Pat-rick looked. The bell-handle didn't stir, but the wire twitched back and forth violently.

" By jabers," said the Irishman, " who is afraid of yer murtherin' noise ?" and stooping down, he tried to seize hold of the lower part of the wire ; but he suddenly fell back on the floor, shaking the house as he fell. The spirits within and the spirits without had conquered the redoubtable Patrick.

As Dr. Wendon rushed down stairs, Patrick said, in a hoarse, terrified whisper, " I am kilt !   I am kilt ! The murtherin' ghosts have shook me all to pieces intirely !"

Dr. Wendon, as the bell rang again, noticed the lower part of the wire twitching violently, and by some sudden instinct or inspiration, he said, " 'Tis rung from below. Some one is in the cellar. I'll stop that performance.''

He seized his pistol, while his wife took hold of his arm, begging him not to go down in the cellar, as she was afraid to stay up stairs without him, and afraid to follow him into the lower regions. But Dr. Wendon was in that fast, fierce, and furious state of mind, that nothing could keep him back. He was ready to face a troop of ghosts, a den of lions, or a legion of devils, rather than be foiled, puzzled, baffled, tormented longer.

With a lamp in one hand, and his pistol in the other, he entered the deep, dark, dismal cellar, where for a moment the most profound silence reigned ;—and there before his eyes were three formidable members of a well-known band of burglars and housebreakers. No law had yet been made or enforced powerful enough to detect, imprison, punish or banish these merciless, successful, daring burglars, always armed to the teeth.

The Doctor stood motionless, his pistol powerless in his hand, as he faced the villains, whose name is a public and private terror. But he did not fire his pistol, first, because it might alarm his wife : second, because the weapon didn't seem adequate to the occasion.

No—the Doctor didn't raise his pistol to destroy those three —*rats*, because he might need it more at some other time, though they had dared to interrupt his midnight slumbers by dancing on his bell-wire, and hanging by their teeth from the wire, so as to produce those vibrations—highly gratifying to them, as their first concert, as they were a family so fond of music.

By mere accident, on the first night, while one of their number was engineering across the beams, he chanced to touch the bell-wire once, and hearing the ring, was a little alarmed ; but seeing no harm come of it, they had all, night after night, commenced a concert in earnest, quite delighted

at their repeated successful performances, little dreaming
of the thrilling effect upon the audience up stairs.

"To-night is their grand carnival," thought the doctor,
as he went back up stairs, and finally succeeded in helping
Patrick out of "the haunted house."

Mrs. Wendon, meantime, sat crouching in a corner up
stairs, afraid to stir, and afraid the doctor might never come
back, as she heard nothing of him and no more of the bell-
ringing. As he returned, at last, alone, unarmed, and unharmed, with a curious smile on his face, and as he saw her
so pale, motionless and terrified, he burst out into a merry,
ringing laugh, and laughed away as if he would never stop,
while she sat there, half frightened to death. Finally she
began to cry, thinking the doctor had lost his reason from
some sudden shock, or fright, or he wouldn't stand there
laughing like a fool, while she sat mute, with a face white
as any ghost.

"Don't—don't laugh so, Walter!" she said, bursting into
tears again.

Ten minutes after, had you stood at the key-hole of that
door, you might have heard two voices mingling in convul-
sive, merry laughter, as the door-bell rang on thirty times
more that night. The doctor called that night forever after
"The benefit night of the Rodent family."

Bridget was still on her knees, praying. She still believed she saw and heard the mysterious, ghostly bell-ringer.
Tired out at last, she covered her head with the bed-clothes
and fell asleep, about four o'clock, and dreamed of the
ghostly light shining in her room.

The mystery was at last explained, but Cæsar always insisted upon it that he saw a troop of ghosts in the hall, and
Patrick never would give it up but that it was a ghostly
shock he received when he fell on the floor in the hall, and
even the doctor admitted that it was probably the effect of
some spiritual influence—the spirits had something to do
with it.

In the morning, when Bridget told the doctor all about
the wonderful light, and described vividly and graphically
the white shadowy ghost which she saw under the window,
he told her that it was not one white ghost, but three black
ones ; and that he saw them in the cellar, ringing the bell.

"Faith," said she, with a sudden wise look and a surprised stare, " I was sure the Evil One had something to do with it ;" and she went off very slowly down into the cellar to get her coal and kindling-wood, fearfully afraid of encountering the " three black ghosts in the cellar."

CHAPTER XIV.

THE WENDONS TALK ABOUT THE OPERA.

"Make love in tropes, in bombast break his heart, -
In turn and simile resign his breath,
And rhyme and quibble in the pains of death."—TICKELL.

MRS. WENDON sees that the doctor is growing pale, careworn, depressed. She can imagine no adequate cause. His practice is increasing and successful, his professional position high. She fears he is injuring himself by close confinement. Change and recreation, even a little pleasurable excitement, might do him good. She urges him to go occasionally to places of amusement—they have not been to an opera in a long time. It might please Nepenthe—she has never been, and she needs change, too ; something to divert her thoughts from the recent mysterious attempt on her life. She is now old enough to enjoy and appreciate fine music. So she talks to the doctor one morning, as he rises from the table, leaving his untasted coffee and neglected omelet.

He is not musically gifted or musically appreciative. He laughs a little about this foolish worship of imported prima donnas, but promises to go that evening on Nepenthe's account, not on his own—he is getting on well enough.

Mrs. Wendon reads from the morning Herald " The farewell Concert of Madame Geztimer, who is in opera again. It is not her farewell, after all. She is giving us four nights of opera, and charming nights they are, too. We have never heard finer music—a different opera each night—or seen larger or more fashionable audiences. Her little season is a decided success."

" How did you like the opera last night ?" said Mrs. Wendon to Nepenthe the next morning.

" I am no judge of music, and then I took my novitiate in

opera going last night," said Nepenthe. " You understand all those scientific trills, rolls and quavers of which I am so ignorant. I sat last evening nearly three hours. The singing was wonderful. I might practice all the hours of three lives, and I never could sing one of those trilling, warbling, soaring, flying, swelling, vanishing strains. Yet no mortal, in exquisite joy or overwhelming grief, warbles like that. Joy is an outburst—a gush—not an elaborate flourish. Loving, fighting, heart-aching, heart-breaking, were all wonderfully sung.

" Think in real life of contending armies of real men, with real swords, standing and patiently waiting for a man to sing out a petition for some captive's release. Such artistic grief is never seen—such sudden terror or joy is never sung out. The singing is wonderful, but I am continually drawing the startling contrast between operatic representation and the real deeds of real people."

" I cannot even work myself up into a pity for a woman," says the doctor, coming up just then, " who sings out her broken heart in such elaborate strains ; and if a lover makes his avowal in the same artistic melody, I always feel like saying, ' If you love her, why don't you walk up or kneel down and say so like a human man, and not stand there singing your heart out like an amateur ?' I know you go to the opera to hear the fine singing, and see the wonderful power of music to express every variety of feeling and action. The heart's best feelings are never in full dress ; this idea of giving love and regret the full toilet they get in operatic scenes, is to me unnatural. The charm of tragedy is in making one, for the time, feel that the characters are real. These groans and sighs and battles and deaths are all well sung, but if I were very angry with a man I don't think I should stand up before him and sing at him.

" The thing I dislike most is this operatic death. Young and beautiful women will sing their disappointed love, their failing health, their aching, loving, breaking heart, with pale face, dishevelled hair, and white shadowy garments— coughing, gasping, trembling, fainting with the airy breath of fleeting song. We listen to the last musical sigh, we catch the faint echo of the last warble, till the last low life note dies on the hushed lips ; and then, a moment after, re surrectionized from the song-death, the singer comes out and moves off the stage, brightly smiling, pleasantly bowing, and gracefully picking up showers of falling flowers. The farce comes so soon after the death tragedy.

" I think the death scene should be the last act of life— when the last curtain falls. I don't like this make-believe failing and dying. I may speak professionally. Wasn't it horrible, when the cholera was raging in Paris, the people were amusing themselves in the theatre in acting death by the cholera in all its fearful stages and mortal agonies ?"

" But did you hear the squeaking tenor ? Why will people insist on playing the part ot which they know nothing ?"

" I believe it is the way with most of us," said Mrs. Wendon. " We are all apt to think we can do some one thing well, in which we are really deficient. The very faults we have, so glaring in the eyes of others, we think are only respectable, comfortable, decent peculiarities, rather becoming than otherwise."

" But how in the world are we ever going to know what we are, or what we can do ?" said the doctor.

" Every man I have well known," said Mrs. Wendon, " is sure he can do something quite well, of which he really knows nothing. One man is very deaf—so deaf we all have to scream out our questions and answers when talking with him ; he says he isn't much deaf after all, he can hear most as well as anybody if we only speak distinctly. My old aunt Jane is quite sure she can see without her spectacles, almost as well as ever—she only wears them to rest her eyes -—but she is almost as blind as a bat. Her husband thinks he is a very young looking man, as smart as most young folks, and can do more work in a day now than any young man ; yet he is nearly a cripple, has a trembling voice, tottering step, and is almost toothless. One gentleman who wrote the dullest essays I ever heard, said he thought he could do one thing well—that was, write essays. He made the remark to his wife, and I overheard him. She was the homeliest woman I ever knew, and she said to me once when we were talking about looks, she was ' always thankful for one thing—that she was made at least good-looking.' A lady once brought me some poetry of her own composition to get my opinion of it. It was about cold stars, fair flowers, and pale moons. She said it was always easy for her to write poetry—she never had to fix it over ; it always came right. She would string words together of all sizes, shapes and accents, and if there was a jingle at the end it was poetry."

As Nepenthe went out of the room, the doctor said,

"How Nepenthe has changed! She is quite young to think so originally and speak so frankly about something she has seen and heard but once—but she has a wonderful ear for music. I have engaged Signor Venini to give her instruction. He is an incomparable artist, and she has already an exquisite touch; but those Scotch songs she sings charmingly. I think she has the sweetest voice I ever heard—it is sweet as a lute, rich as a harp, soft as a flute; why, Minnie, if we had searched the world over, we couldn't have found a more gifted soul or affectionate heart."

CHAPTER XV.

IMPULSES—THE ARREST.

"One thread of kindness draws more than a hundred yoke of oxen."
TUSCAN PROVERB.

"Edel sey der Mensch,
Hülfreich und gut."
GOETHE.

"THERE are some things I never told you, Minnie," said the doctor one morning. "When I took Nepenthe from the hospital the nurse whispered to me that she was of low family and doubtful origin. I wouldn't prejudice you, so I kept it to myself. I believe with a French author, that all our first benevolent impulses are good, generous, heroic—reflection weakens and kills them. The soul first speaks, and the language is that of love and virtue: the intellect reasons afterwards, and its reasonings are more favorable to matter than the soul.

"I was told when I took Nepenthe from the hospital, that I was acting solely from impulse, and that impulse was a very imprudent guide; but I have done nothing kind or generous in my life without yielding to the promptings of some noble impulse. There is more good crushed in the bud by resisting good impulses, than evil prematurely done by acting too suddenly upon them. There isn't much danger of our ever being too good, too kind, or too generous.

"Many a wrinkle of care you can smooth out clear and beautiful, if you seize upon the impulse while it is warm and fresh, and press life's rough seams down. How much happier and more benevolent would I have been, had I always acted promptly upon my first, best, warmest feelings, without arguing and reasoning, and wondering whether after all it would be best—would it pay, was it prudent, expedient?"

"These noble impulses," said Mrs. Wendon, "are like the little Artesian wells I used to see in California—an invisible hand penetrates the troubled strata of the soil, till from its depths upwells a fountain pure and sparkling, invigorating the whole valley of the soul. One of these Artesian impulses jetting out, may freshen and beautify hundreds of drooping thoughts and withering hopes."

"Yes," said the doctor, "impulses are the first stamps from the mint of thought, clearest and deepest, the most durable on the leaves of the unfolding soul, like the figures on the first sheets of our quires of cream-laid paper; and the original pictures of great masters, clearer and bolder than the weak after copies and feeble imitations, they flow spontaneously from the creative soul, and are not mechanically struck off on steel or wood.

"Impulse is the great artist of the soul's studio; with marvellous dash and sweep of hand, she sketches the outlines of great deeds for us to execute through our lives full lengths, those beautiful pictures of genial kindness and cordial benevolence, which illustrate the long story of our dull common lives, are engraven by her skilful hand."

I beg your pardon, reader, for keeping you standing spiritual, hat in hand, so long in the vestibule of my story, listening to the doctor's talk about impulse, but poor impulse is so often berated and abused, censured and maligned, as a wrong-doer and mischief-maker, I always wait patiently and thankfully when I hear her praised or truly valued.

"The greatest things we do," added the doctor, "we feel stirred up as by some oracular voice within to do suddenly and successfully. Nepenthe is a child of impulse, and I believe she had a refined, accomplished, and virtuous mother.

If a man is ever so great and good, and his wife ignorant or commonplace, you rarely find the child above mediocrity in appearance, taste or talent. People say so much about great men not having distinguished children ; they forget that inferiority and mediocrity may be traced to an inferior or commonplace mother. Nepenthe's gifts and graces were not acquired from recent associations, but are evidently entailed by nature and improved by very early, correct, and careful training. Her father may have been low, dishonorble, cruel—there might have been a mock marriage, or some thing of that sort. I have no means of finding out, but Nepenthe's mother could hardly have been guilty of an ignoble action, and yet I have some information which almost proves she was unfortunate and imprudent. I wish I could solve the mystery about Nepenthe's earliest history. I knew I should love her," said the doctor, as he arose and walked back and forth, " but I didn't mean to draw her quite so close to my heart, but she is now very dear, and I would like to take this one young life and cheer and strengthen it all through. I can do more good by watching this young, bright soul, moving on to its zenith without a chilling tempest or obscuring cloud, than by throwing miscellaneous crumbs of kindness to every passing beggared soul, whose destiny is cut in stone, whose happiness is hopeless. To take a life despised, circumscribed, care-encumbered, and make it happy, would give me more sublime delight than all the Io Pæans of transient fame."

Nepenthe had been sent to the post-office, but it had commenced raining, and she came back for an umbrella just in time to overhear the remark about her father.

" My mother, my gentle mother, has any one reproached *her ?*" thought she. " I know she was good and noble, but why did she never mention my father's name ? Why weep so when she received any letters ? Does Dr. Wendon fear to love me ? Does he attach disgrace to my name ? Is this why he so often sighs when he speaks to me so kindly ?"

While the doctor is out that afternoon, Mrs. Wendon looks over his wardrobe. The black vest has a rip in the pocket. She empties the pocket to mend it, and there falls out a folded paper, part of a printed document, which, with a pardonable curiosity, she reads, and learns the probable cause of the doctor's late absorbed and troubled manner.

She finds also a written note in the corner of the pocket with
severe threats of immediate arrest. Her honored, high-
minded husband arrested for fraud, for breach of contract!

This letter of Dr. Wendon's she reads with surprise and
alarm.

"DEAR SIR :—I write this communication to prevent any
additional loss to you, and to suggest by what means that
loss can be repaired. I understood you to say that you
would be content if your securities were restored. You declared to me if these securities were not replaced, you
would proceed against me, 1st—civilly at common law ; 2nd
—criminally, by a police warrant for false pretences; 3rd—
ecclesiastically, by presenting the case to my pastor ; 4th—
domestically, by communications with my wife ; and 5th—by
securing the publication of the matters between us in the
periodical of a person whom you suppose to be my bitter
enemy.

" You know very well that a threat is the weapon of a
woman, and that bluster and bravado are the tactics of a ruf-
fian. From your position, from your education, from your
association in youth with British officers, and in maturer
years with the finest minds, I cannot interpret any thing
said or done by you in that direction. Your object is to
get back your money, instead of adding to your losses. Putting me in prison would not do that. Prejudicing me in the
estimation of a minister would not do that, especially as he
has no ecclesiastical control over me. Communicating with
my wife would not do that, and as she has never injured
you, there can be no adequate cause for such a step."

The rest of this document had been torn off and destroyed,
so Mrs. Wendon could read no more. Her husband did not
come home that night, but sent her a note, saying that he
had left town suddenly on business, and would be home on
Saturday. Saturday came, and he came not, and Monday
and Tuesday passed away.

Late on Wednesday evening he came, tired, a little lame,
and with one hand bound up and a bruised head.

" I have had some trouble in the mines," said he, as he
sat down weary in his easy chair. " There was a riot
among the workmen. They laid it to the agent, but I think
some thing else was at the bottom of it. They didn't act
like men ; they acted like fiends. That poor little colored

boy, Thomas, who has made himself so useful to me, they rushed upon him without the least provocation and inhumanly murdered him, dashing out his brains on the road ; they threw volleys of stones until every window-pane was shattered in fragments. I was the object of their personal fury and violence, but I escaped with only a bruised head and lame hand. I'll be over it in a day or two," said he, cheerfully, as he saw how troubled his wife looked. " It was all quiet when I came away. There is a large guard of soldiers there now. The ringleaders are arrested. I had a store there that they destroyed ; they have carried off or destroyed all the coal stored there ; they tore up part of the railroad track ; they seemed to have some grudge against every person in any way connected with the mines."

Mrs. Wendon said no more about the mines ; but after supper, as they sat together on the sofa, she said, " I really felt afraid, during the presence of that epidemic last summer, that you might be taken away, and the world would be so desolate without you ;"—and then, rising suddenly and putting her arms round his neck and kissing him, first on one cheek, then on lips, eyes, check and forehead, she exclaimed, " You dear old bear "—as she frequently called him, as she put her hands on his face, one on one side and one on the other ; then, turning his head upwards towards her, " You dear old bear, you are locking up something in this head away from me ; and do you know I accidentally found the key of your secret in your pocket the other morning ? There was a rip in your black vest, and to mend it well I first emptied the pocket, and I saw a printed document there giving W. W. Wendon's name considerable prominence. Now, Walter," said she, in a cheerful voice, " don't let any pecuniary matter prey so heavily upon your spirits. You told me *I* was your fortune, when you married me, and nothing can really impoverish us while we have each other. You need not explain, though you said nothing to me about it. Your motives were the purest and best. It would weary and annoy you to repeat them now. Never mind about that portion of my fortune you have lost ; but listen, here is something I was just reading when you came in : ' What a prodigious science is that which can say to man, If thou dost such a thing, such a thing will happen to thee. Then again, The reaction of riches is poverty of the soul, and bodily infirmities. Prosperity has its root in man himself: it is the want of his being, the product of his intelligence, the link of society, the right of labor.' You acted as you thought best, and don't be troubled about that three thousand of mine. You have learned experience in this speculation. In the matter of investing there is nothing like experience, and there is no great good acquired without some risk; but I don't see how you failed in this coal-mine speculation, after all."

"Failure," said the doctor, drawing a long breath, "is common with all speculations where one looks for large profits; but in this particular instance I wonder now since I can be so frank with you, that I could not have foreseen the result. You know that in all mines—whether of gold, silver, lead, iron or coal, that you may strike a vein of inferior quality: just so it was in this instance. I had raked and scraped all the money together I could get by borrowing and mortgaging, and when I could get no more money by these means I induced others to invest their money in the mines also. We set the miners at work. After mining a few tons, which sold well in the market the workmen struck for higher wages. We refused till their starvation and our own want of means compelled us on both sides to compromise the matter by paying a little more, and when we got them to work again winter came on and the canal stopped: no more coal could go to market till spring. We kept the miners at work, however, getting out several thousand tons; but navigation opened unusually late, the spring came, and when we sent a cargo to market we found to our surprise that the coal was of an inferior quality: we had struck a poor vein, and whether the men and their dependants had known of it or not, they certainly were interested in not disclosing the fact to us; but if we could not sell the coal we certainly could not pay the men; and then they resorted to the law—for by the law they had a lien upon the mine for their wages, which we would be obliged to discharge, or stop further proceedings—but how could we do this?—for borrowing, and mortgaging, and persuading others to invest, were all at an end. There is when I passed my sleepless nights, and here is where I was swamped," said the doctor, rising up and walking rapidly back and forth. "I can now clearly see, in the light of my past experience, that one must not go into a speculation without having under his control three times the amount of means which it will probably require to carry it out, and then he must not be in haste to get the profits and become rich out of it all at once—he will only be swamped, just as I have been ; and it will take all my earnings for the next year or two to pay off debts. But my integrity, Minnie—that was my crown, my glory, and my pride. I have never had an enemy until this coal operation, and now Mr. Janes is doing all he can in every possible way ; because, thinking it a very desirable speculation, I persuaded him, after referring him to others who knew more than I did about the matter, to invest with me in the enterprise. Mr. Trap is his lawyer ; he will stoop to any thing to get money. He boasts of never having lost a case ; he'd sell his soul for twenty-five dollars. He'd probably get along without a soul as well as with one. He is a sneaking, rascally fellow, and his partners are equal to him ; there's not a more rascally firm in the city than Trap, Fogg & Craft. There's one thing aggravating about it, the enterprize failed at a time when it was yielding more and better coal than it had done and boats could not be had to take it away fast enough. I have sent on for mining operations at first over five thousand dollars ; I paid on the colliery property over sixteen hundred dollars, I have sent on for mining operations and for purchase money over eight thousand dollars. I would have paid more and succeeded at last, but there was no more money to be had. I know now very well that closed canals, strikes, faults, fire damps are incidental to all mining operations in that region, and no human sagacity can either foresee or prevent them. He who would succeed at last must carry sail enough to outweather such obstacles.

"I believe coal-mining to be really an adventure. Once I thought certain rules were to be followed, certain indications would be positively sure, certain results inevitaby gained. But I have made the matter a profound study, and puzzled and bewildered my brains with formations and variations—lamination and stratification — identification and generalization, crystallization and complication, until my deepest calculation and clearest examination, end in perturbation and consternation.

"I agree with Lesley, the topographical geologist, that theories of identification, however correct, will be set at naught by unaccountable and invisible misdemeanors of fact. Sand rocks will slide into shales, conglomerates become fine sands, favorite coal conceal itself under a degraded type, never-to-be-mistaken limestone disappear, or some new calcareous layer intrude itself among previously pure clay beds. There'll be metamorphoses of rocks, hidden rolls, increased and even reversed dips, strata thrown over on their backs, down throws and up throws, and oblique dislocations of crust. In some places, the whole operation of mining is a perpetual experiment, no one knowing what an hour may bring forth, nor the wisest able to fix a certain value on an acre, a bed, or a gangway. Like a magician among his uneasy spirits, the coal hunter must be forever on his guard against surprises of all kinds, and expect his embarrassments, conjectures and discoveries to begin anew at every fresh location. When beds are crushed together, folded up, turned over, and every hillside shows rocks dipping a different way, the problem becomes of enormous difficulty, and I am not to blame for this great disappointment. I have made up my mind I will do nothing rashly, nothing I should regret in another world. I have no wish to revenge.

"If a man wrong me, hereafter, remorse will haunt him. In a short time we shall all stand before the judgment seat. I may be the prey of slander. I shall do nothing but stand against the wall and defend myself. It is pretty hard for one man to stand up and keep off howling enemies, making threats of prison and disgrace—perilling life, liberty, and estate."

"Well, judge, I told you that man was a scoundrel."

"What man?" asked the judge.

"Why, the doctor whom I arrested the other day," replied the policeman.

"That doctor, man or what not, is all the same to me—has demanded examination in the complaint against him. I suppose he is fool enough to think I will discharge him, but I have made up my mind not to be bothered with these long winded examinations any longer. They are taking the examination before the clerk, and I shall decide of course there was probable cause for the arrest, and send the whole thing down to the Grand Jury."

"You are a trump, Judge," said the policeman. "Always knew you were death on scoundrels."

"Between you and me, Jim, you know I always deal out ample justice to every one who is brought up here—man, woman or child, I don't care who."

Yes, he had often dealt out ample justice, as he called it, and it had been whispered about that a little consultation with him beforehand, and possibly a bribe, no one knew how often had made innocent men the victims of his indiscrimination and recklessness. Every time a Judge takes a bribe, the State totters to its lowest foundations, as if shaken by an earthquake. A good Judge is almost the sole prop of the State; for a good Judge mirrors forth in his opinions not the passions, nor the prejudice, nor the caprice of the people, but only their Laws as expressed in their constitutions and in all their legislative enactments.

The policeman complacently took his leave of His Honor. He had been bribed by some one of the complainant's friends, to use his influence, (that meant bribe,) with the Justice, against Dr. Wendon. He boasted of having great influence with that official in assisting him to come to the right (?) conclusion.

I said the policeman had been bribed, and I have intimated that the Judge was, too, but I cannot prove it. It may be hard always to prove a Judas to be a Judas; for who sees him when he takes a bribe, or who can follow him through all that dark labyrinth, wherein he has betrayed justice.

While Jim goes off to his beat, Mr. Janes goes in Mr. Trap's office to get him to put the doctor through.

Mr. Trap was peculiarly happy in making his clients believe that everything he did for them professionally, was the best that could be done in the premises. Sometimes in the rush and hurry of a city practice, some case would be overlooked and quite forgotten, but Mr. Trap's anxious client would turn up in due course of time to remind him of it. But no matter if the case had gone over from time to time, or had got out of court entirely, Mr. Trap could expatiate largely upon the advantage accruing from such delay in the discovery of new testimony, which must decide the case in favor of his client, or the benefit of some new decision, which was about to be made, and which would make every thing all right.

Of course the client was quite delighted with the delusion that he should surely win at last, and that the law's delays were after all, most wise dispensations of justice, and Mr. Trap, and so the credulous client would go away rejoicing, while Mr. Trap would turn upon his heel saying to himself, " Well! so long as he's satisfied, that's enough."

" What became of Doctor Wendon's speculation ?" said one lady to another, as they were walking down street some three months after the conversation in Mr. Trap's office.

" Oh, it was a dead loss, and the lawyers made it out a case of fraud. It was a time of great panic, great scarcity of money, and many really believed the doctor guilty of fraudulent intent. Janes persecuted him relentlessly, actuated by pure revenge because he had lost himself. He said he would persecute the doctor to the last extent of the law, if only to punish him. Of course he knew he could get nothing. The doctor really was imprisoned. He was, I believe, a most upright man. I don't know as he is out of prison yet. I don't know all about the matter. It was a tedious law suit. I couldn't tell about it if I should try. Law is dull enough, except to parties concerned. But I believe the doctor is one of the most honest and honorable of men, and Mr. Janes had most false accounts of the transaction put in the daily papers. If I had been the doctor, I'd sued him for slander."

Late one evening Nepenthe Stuart sat alone in her room, reading a little note brought by a boy to the door, and this brief warning was all it contained.

" Do not leave the house for ten days. Your life is in danger. SUSAN."

It was nearly midnight, and Mrs. Trap sat up waiting for her husband. He was unusually late. He sat in his office, looking over some papers, and the tall, dark woman sat in front of him, looking over some papers also. Neither spoke for half an hour, until the woman broke the silence at last, and only one thing she said.

" We'll keep him in prison as long as we can, and gold shall pay you, Mr. Trap, plenty of gold."

CHAPTER XVI.

FIFTH HOUSE IN THE BLOCK FOR SALE—INQUIRE OF JOHN TRAP.

> "And the grass that chokes the portal,
> Bends not to the tread of mortal."

THE fifth house in the block was empty, the shutters closed. You could read deserted, in plain letters on the tarnished door-plate, broken shutters, leaf-strewn walk and grass-grown yard. No breath of kindly zephyr cooled the hot, midsummer air long shut up within those brick walls. Wanted, lost, and gone, the three tragedy words of life, mocked you with ghost-voices if you listened at the key-hole, or peered through the neglected shutters, where the lawless sunshine played on the bare walls.

Few noticed the change in the fifth house in the block. One old gentleman, as he passed slowly by, leaning on his cane, said, in an asthmatic whisper, "Some doctor used to live there. How things have changed." On the door was a bill in large letters.

"THIS HOUSE FOR SALE.

Inquire of JOHN TRAP,

No. 16 ——— street."

No eye, no voice, no footstep met you if you climbed the staircase and entered the vacant front chamber. There was only a little empty crib in the corner. There, for six months had little Violet Wendon nestled, as she twined her dimpled arms close around the doctor's neck at earliest dawn. He called her "his peep of day."

"How pleasant the houses in that row," said many a passer-by at nightfall, "when the chandeliers light up, the damask glows rubier in the gas-light, and a crystal polish glistens on the illuminated windows : but out of that block God has chiselled two glorious souls, and placed them in niches in the upper court of His great studio above."

'Tis sad to go away from scenes familiar, and come back only to hear strange voices, and meet new faces. Of all the actors in our little programme, all had changed homes the last year save Prudence Potter, whose eventless history was marked by few new eras. There was no near relative for her to lose but brother Zekiel, and he was married. Their two single lives had paralleled so placidly along for years, she could brook no change, and since his wooing and wedding, a hoighty-toity school-girl, with only a pink and white face to recommend her, she could not go back to the old place and see her hitherto precisely managed household affairs going on at "such loose ends," so she still remains with cousin Priscilla. She has been talking of "going home next week," ever since we first heard of her.

We will find her one Monday morning reading aloud from an old paper she has picked up in the garret, for she has a passion for rummaging and ransacking; possibly, had she been a man, this propensity might have led to some valuable discovery. She read aloud in a precise and hesitating manner, every now and then turning her paper towards the light, for she has just bought glasses number thirty-six instead of fifty-four, and for once, she owns she has made a mistake. She reads all the murders, shocking casualties and disasters by sea and land

She reads at last, devouring every word as surprising intelligence, part of a letter from Dr. Wendon, who was one of the passengers on the wrecked steamer.

" We were driven by the flames back from the quarter-deck, where we had been standing. I let myself down into the sea by a rope, and tried to swim, holding the child ; and my wife was sitting across my shoulder. It was two o'clock in the afternoon ; the gunpowder exploded when we had been some time in the water. I tried to hold my child above the water ; the water from the screw washed over us for some minutes ; first my child was forcibly washed away by the waves out of my arms, and then my wife. I saw them no more. Having lost the rope, I seized a plank that was floating along, and fastened myself to it. I was getting faint and weary when I saw in the distance a vessel. I tried to steer towards it. After nearly three hours I reached it. I remember very little about the fate of the steamer. I was completely exhausted when taken on board the vessel."

It is said, that after the accident, the front lock of the doctor's raven hair was grey. His hair had always been beautiful, black, glossy, matching his eyes. He was really handsome, yet so noble, manly, and digified. He never betrayed any vanity, or consciousness of beauty.

Few strangers met him without exclaiming, "A fine looking man ; one of nature's noblemen."

There were never more beautiful eyes in a human head than Dr. Wendon's. Clear, bright, piercing without being sharp, you might not even remember the outline of his other features, but if you talked with him you only knew you had seen some radiant eyes ; perhaps you could not tell their color. In the evening when animated, you would call them black, in the sunshine hazel.

When a boy he was told so often about his beautiful eyes it would be strange, if he should grow up unconscious of his chief attraction. Then they were such strong eyes ; he had read, late at night, Greek tragedies and closely written manuscripts ; he had used his eyes for hours with microscope and telescope, their power never seemed weakened, never deficient. He would often read some soothing poem when harassed and excited, books had been in the weary hours an unfailing resort. He was enthusiastic about paintings and flowers—then his face was so expressive, his eyes would light up so when in conversation, they were so full of soul and feeling.

At last the auctioneer's hammer sounded its doleful "going, going, gone," knocking down all of Dr. Wendon's household goods.

His young wife and his little Violet, those incarnations of loveliness, had perished by that fearful accident—and months had passed.

One day, when life looked its loveliest, nature was frolicing with zephyrs and kissing the flowers, an Eden glow rested on earth's garden. Far above life's busy stage, folds of sapphire, and amber and gold festooned the draperied clouds. There was a grand floral matinee ; Nature's great dress circle was clad in its gala robes. Whole families of royal carnations and delicate violets, were out in full dress with their green opera cloaks, enchanting the eye as they coquetted with whispering zephyrs. As you watched the airy dance of the butterfly, or listened occasionally to an oriole's soprano, or caught the low strains of the humming bird's contralto, you might, from the depths of a happy heart, chime in your grateful anthem—"how full and how precious ; how sweet the brimming cup of life." Beneath such sunny skies, under waving boughs, one might sit down and re-weave the broken web of happiness, and robe the spirit anew in hope's gayest gossamer.

Dr. Wendon stands by the window, almost bathed in a golden flood of sunshine, and tries to catch some view of the distant spire of a familiar church. The outlines are bold and distinct, yet he sees them not. He places his hands over his eyes, staggers, sighs heavily, and at last there breaks out from the depths of his surcharged heart, that most sorrowful of all sorrowful sounds—a sob, a man's irrepressible, hopeless sob.

He stands up again, erect, still—and waits, and listens, and waits. The door opens, and a man enters—'tis Dr. Cerrier. He walks up and shakes hands, but almost impatiently, Dr. Wendon says, " Give me your opinion, Dr. Cerrier ; I want your final opinion."

The oculist looks, examines, looks again, hesitates, then he says, slowly, " You have amaurosis. The great and protracted exertion of your eyes, the painful circumstances through which you have passed, the severe blow on the eyebrows you recently received, have all produced this result. Yours is one of those rare cases, when a wound on the eyebrows and neighboring frontal region, has caused serious injury. The fracture extends along the thin brittle orbital process of the frontal bone, reaching to the optic nerve, or to the union of the two nerves. I cannot see that in this instance, the blow has affected the vascularity or the transparency of the different textures of the eye.

" The injury did not seem serious at first, but actual blindness will supervene sooner or later ; you must keep up your general health, and be perfectly quiet, avoiding all excitement."

The scientific cause, the scientific possibilities, the scientific probabilities, the scientific words, fell unheeded on those quivering ears.

The epitome of all sorrow was summed up in these simple words, ' I am blind !'

What avails the moving of scientific hands over closed

eyes, the sounding of technical terms in grief-stricken ears ; once enter the realm of blindness, what professional aid or counsel can ease the grief or soothe the malady ?

"It requires a great deal of philosophy to bear these ills of life," said the oculist as he left.

Once more alone, Dr. Wendon sat as if stupefied. "Quiet, quiet, quiet," he repeated at length, slowly and half unconsciously, "when my soul is tossed and troubled on this great sea of sorrow. Philosophy! what philosophy can irradiate the gloom of blindness? Must I, who have restored sight to so many eyes, cease my precious labors— those labors which bring forth rest, rest so sweet after toil ? Must I lay away from my sight the consoling faces of books, the kindly looks of nature ?"

For weeks he planned and thought, and thought and planned to find some way to give vent to his feelings, as he sat in his perpetual twilight, trying to catch glimpses of the fading sun, by the light of his fading vision. He closed the shutters, and sat in gloomy retrospection, trying to think of some way of writing down his thoughts. Clasping his hands in despair, he arose, and walked back and forth, exclaiming "Must my solitary thoughts melt away with hectic, or freeze within me ? Must my soul in this endless nightmare never be able to cry out for help ?"

He bemoans his loss, and at last he writes, in crooked, unsightly lines ; but he writes in that old journal of his. The paper is all blank to him, but the words are burning, as he feels his way along the page, folding and creasing it as he writes, so as to fancy he has some guiding lines : and thus he writes.

"The gate of the eyes is closed, and all the joy-avenues of life are closed at once, and there is a wall around my spirit —it is buried alive, star and sky and green earth are sheeted and shrouded from my vision.

"In the tomb of my heart nature is only an embalmed, coffined mummy. My soul is vaulted in darkness. Every passer by can read on its darkened front, ' Here lies buried the soul of Dr. Wendon, bereaved, beggared, blind. Bound like Prometheus to the rock of darkness, with Memory's vulture preying at my heart, dwelling like Tantalus near the gushing stream of human life, but tasting its bliss no more.'

" Left starless, sunless, moonless, skyless—guided, fed
by attendant hands—O God ! there is no preparation for this
shock of blindness. With what raiment, what food, what
staff, what lantern can the soul provide itself for this dark,
faltering, stumbling, trembling, rough life journey ? Must
I walk forever the silent shore of Memory, watching the
shadowy sails of phantom joy-ships drifting out of sight, or
lost in the gloom of an endless night ?

The sunshine dances no more on the deep sea of thought ;
Memory's torchlight procession moves on as the muffled bell
at the gate of the soul tolls out the departure of light. Retrospection sits at the stern, throwing back its dim light on
the wake of the spirit. Lonely thought keeps up its gloomy
night watch all the long hours of weary years, while the soul
chants its dirge out on life's dreary sea. Alone in the dark I
hear the shuffling feet of worshippers outside, on life's outer
coast echoing around my soul's closed doors and dying
away.

" The inner veil is hung, the soul goes no more out to
meet the responses of earthly oracles—it kneels alone."

No, not alone, poor desolate blind man—for when the
soul is walled up high above the stars by its wall of darkness, through God's great skylight, away up in the top of
the spirit's dome, there streams down clear, radiant light on
the artist soul, as it works alone with its finely carved and
fretted thoughts.

Unseen hands unroll the spirit's canvas beautiful painting and frescoed thoughts, adorn its walls, mosaic truths inlay its floor, till base and battlement, frieze and entablature,
glow with living light—while away back in the spirit's holiest, the Great High Priest kindles on the darkened shrine
His radiant Shekinah.

When orient morn, cloudless noon, and gorgeous sunset
shine no more through the stained windows of the soul, barred and bolted, shuttered forever from cheerful day, celestial stars come out one by one and twinkle in the spirit's
sky, eternal lamps are hung along the soul's vaulted halls,
cheering the depths of its caverned gloom.

When the daylight dies from the spirit, in the hidden
recesses fall celestial dews, and fragrant night-blooming
flowers unfold their snowy petals.

Reader, did you ever sit for a month in the dark. with

shaded eyes, with the fear of blindness like an adumbrated terror ever before you—and have those lonesome, tiresome, doleful words always sounding in your ears from mother, sister, doctor, " You mustn't use your eyes—you mustn't think about any thing " ? Every day somebody comes in to tell you there are many people worse off than you are, many have lost their sight with eyes quite like yours ; you sit and think till you are nothing but thought. Resigned you may be, but never thankful, till unshaded, unveiled, unparasolled, you emerge from prison gloom, and your long blindfold soul looks up into the clear sky again as you sit once more in mother Nature's lap, and read her nursery rhymes semi-colored with stars and vignetted with flowers.

Then never weep, never despond, never falter, you who have strong hands, honest hearts, and clear-seeing eyes, and never pass unmoved the blind man by the wayside. Say to him, in the kind language of the Carthagenian Queen, " Not ignorant of evil, I myself know how to succor the unfortunate."

Days pass on. Dr. Wendon can still tell the daylight from the dark as he sits in that silent room, surrounded by his books, the wreck of his former fortune. There they are, large libraries from floor to ceiling, all around him ; but between him and them, near as they are, is a great gulf of darkness fixed. . Flowers are sent him—tulips, dahlias, elegant, brilliant flowers : he sends them away.

A friend in Europe, not having heard of his misfortune, sent him a magnificent painting. He says with a sigh, "Go, put it up where you please."

One afternoon he sleeps in his chair, and putting out his footsteps on his favorite dog, almost crushed his leg. The frightened animal runs off howling with pain. The doctor never liked a cane ; now he never can walk out without one.

He sits at life's closed keyhole, in the dark, watching for voices. The musical voice once always first to whisper consolation, is hushed ; if those arms could only clasp him in one more tender embrace, he could better sit forever in the dark. He listens as he turns his head at the least sound : he hears only the rough billows dashing against the cold shore of memory : each echo seems a booming minute gun for some joy going down. He says mournfully, " All thy waves and thy billows are going over me—I shall perish in this dark."

He hears not the sweet voice of that only One walking serenely on life's rough billows, " I am the light of life ; if any man hear my voice he shall not walk in darkness, he shall see light. Catch the hem of my radiant robes and you shall walk in light forever." .

Once when he passed along, strangers asked " Who is that gentleman with those fine eyes ?" Now for the first time he goes out, carefully attended by his kind young friend. As he tries so hard to walk along unaided and un-attended, he stumbles against the curb-stone and almost falls. He shudders as he hears some thoughtless, light-hearted maiden exclaim as he passes, " Who is that poor blind man ?" Is he really a blind man ?—no more the cel-ebrated Dr. Wendon, but a poor blind man !

It is so hard for a man once praised and envied, to be the object of pity to a heartless crowd—to be pitied for a hope-less misfortune. A man would rather rule, protect, defend, than be always an object of compassion and care. In a lit-tle trouble, he may fret and fume and annoy others, but in a great sorrow even a wife's pity must be carefully manifested to an unfortunate husband. There are moods in a man's life when he will gloomily bear alone, rather than share some business trouble, mental suffering, or bodily agony.

It was a Sabbath—a sweet, balmy Sabbath—and Mrs. Pridefit, elegantly dressed, is walking home from church.

" What a pity, John," she says daintily, holding up her unsoiled brocade, for the ground is damp, " what a pity that Dr. Wendon is blind ! It has spoiled his beauty. He was such a stylish-looking man. Don't that gray lock on his head look odd ! I would have it dyed if I were in his place."

Miss Prudence Potter overhears something about some doctor's being blind, and she says, with her old peculiar smile, " He couldn't be much of a doctor, if he couldn't keep himself from being blind."

" 'Tis a punishment for his sins," said Miss Charity Gouge, daintily holding up her new green brocade, " 'tis a punish-ment for his sins."

" Punishment for his sins !" said Kate Howard, who was walking by her side. " What great sins has he committed ?"

"Why, he was guilty of fraud," said Miss Charity. "Mr. Trap made it out a clear case of fraud."

"If Mr. Trap proved his guilt," said Kate, "I believe he is innocent, as all sensible people know he is."

"Well," said Miss Charity, "if he is not guilty of fraud, he is not a Christian; and it is a sad thing for a man to get to be of mature years and not be a Christian. This may be the judgment of God that is to lead him to repentance."

"Well," said Kate, "if all the wicked people in the world were made blind, we'd most of us be left in the dark. One of the noblest and best Christians I ever knew, became blind by accident, when a child. I have often guided him up and down Broadway, and I felt in a blaze of spiritual light when walking by his side. He has piloted many an erring soul through the world's moral darkness. There is a shade over his eyes, but his soul 'sits high in its meridian tower,' and dwells forever in that radiant zone where no shadow falls. Yet hidden forever behind life's magic curtain, he throws out his brilliant phantasmagoria of imagery, to the instruction and charm of watching eyes.

"He is a clergyman, and his clarion voice and radiant thoughts have made him the grandest living monument in the land, of the sovereign power of a royal soul over a locked sense. His soul, like a peerless diamond in the dark, ever emits flash after flash of vivid light, kindling in the eye and burning in the heart of admiring crowds. If any man deserves a cordial grasp of the hand, and a fervent God speed, it is this spiritual giant, finding his sightless way to classic founts, and peril's peak, carving his name in Christian hearts, as he safely leaps from hill to hill of faith, across the rolling flood of popularity, and over the dizziest sleepers of the bridge of fame. His laurel crown, though green and beautiful, must be, in his loneliest hours, wreathed with a 'chaplet of thorns.'"

Kate Howard often felt bursts of enthusiasm, but she seldom spoke with as much feeling as on this occasion.

A few of the doctor's old patients, seeing him out pale, blind, and leaning on the arm of his young friend, say, "What a pity Dr. Wendon is so unfortunate! Who'll we have for our doctor now?"

The oculist is walking along with another physician. He too is talking about the blind doctor. He says it is an in-

teresting case of amaurosis—he is glad to have an opportunity for diagnosis—the diagnosis is easier than the progno-
sis. He thinks electricity a wonderful therapeutic agent.

Just behind the corner stands a woman with hollow eyes
and long nose, muttering to herself: "The doctor can't be
of much use to any one now—he might as well be dead too.
The scales of trouble are balanced after all. Rich to-day,
to-morrow poor and blind. That girl will have to shirk for
herself now."

CHAPTER XVII.

THE MOUNTAIN RIDE.

On, on through the long woods the clumsy coach rumbles,
the trees almost meet overhead—but a small patch of blue
can be seen—you could only catch at intervals any glimpse
of the western sky.

The first intimation of the coming storm was a heavy roll
of thunder. Way out of sight of the woods, the western sky
was gathering blackness. As on through the winding road
the stage rumbled, there came all at once a heavy clap of
thunder, and then a flash, lighting up the dark woods with
gloomy grandeur.

"Hurry up, driver, hurry up—most there?" shouted the
fat man in the corner, putting his gray head out of the window as they came out under the open sky, where black heaps
of clouds were piling higher and higher.

"Eight miles yet," said the driver, impatiently.

"Thunder!" exclaimed the fat man again; which exclamation was for once singularly appropriate, for just then a
heavy clap came, and then all was still.

In one corner of the stage sits a lady with straw bonnet
and green ribbon, drab shawl and brown dress, gold-framed
spectacles over her eyes, reticule in her hand. On her lap
is a bandbox, containing her new cap, and in her other hand
her green silk umbrella, as it rains. She has taken off her
shawl and put it on again wrong side out, to keep it from
being soiled. There is a small square paper pasted on the
top of her bandbox, labeled "Miss Prudence Potter." There

is the old smile on her face. She says nothing about the storm, but contents herself with her old consolation, "What can't be cured must be endured."

"Drive on, drive on, don't keep us here," said one of the passengers. Crack, crack went the whip, and on they sped like lightning. Suddenly there was a crash—but this time the crash was not above. Over went the passengers—the stage was upset—one of the wheels was off.

One half-intoxicated man in the corner was the first to slip out. He rolled over, with his head almost crushed by the weight of a fellow-passenger. He drew a long breath, as if struggling out from under something, and exclaimed, with frightened tone and bewildered look, "I say, driver, are we or—up or—or down, or—or where?"

"Great Governor of Egypt!" screamed the fat man from Arkansas, as he stood at last in the doorway of the only house in the vicinity, looking all around, first up at the sky and then at the frightened, dripping passengers, huddling into the one little sitting-room. "Great Governor of Egypt, warn't that a buster, stranger? I came nearer going to the devil that time than I ever did in my life before. That upset and all pretty nearly made a galvanic battery of me—only one side of me don't connect at all," he added, rubbing his right ear, which looked a little red. "That pretty nearly broke the drum of my tym—pan—um. This road must be the road to Jordan, for it's hard enough to travel."

Just then a traveller rode up, a young gentleman in a one horse carriage, evidently to gain a shelter.

"Why, Carleyn, where did you come from?" said a tall man in the corner, as the stranger drove up and entered the door. He had kept silence for five minutes, as if his thoughts had been swallowed up in the storm and fright. His voice was deep, hollow and sepulchral, as if it came up out of some gloomy depths. "Have you been taking this thunder-storm, or has it taken you?" said he to Carleyn. "You always wanted to be out in one good storm. Such a storm shakes up a man's ideas wonderfully. Did you meet our vehicle on the way? I remember that lecture you gave once about the stage before and behind, &c. Well, to-day we are all *before* the stage, and if you came that way, you must have concluded that the stage isn't *well supported* in these parts. We've been on the stage to-day, practicing comedy and tragedy together. We all acted. You might have thought our parts overdrawn—we were pretty well overdrawn, if our parts were not," he added, facetiously. "Anyway the tragi-comedy scene is over, and we've left the stage for some more active profession. We think of making a pedestrian tour to explore the country. But you've come in good time. You can take this young woman here in your buggy. The rest of us are all men folks—we can walk a-foot to Gray's Tavern. There's no resorting to the stage this night, and Bill will have to take the mail on the horse's back."

"I will be happy to take the young lady under my charge," said Mr. Carleyn, removing his hat and bowing politely to the young lady, who sat alone by the window, apparently looking at the bears and lions conspicuously displayed on the blue window shade.

"Carleyn," spoke up the tall man again, "the young woman has a trunk. Can't you fasten it in the boot, if you think there is room?"

"I've no baggage of my own," said Carleyn. "I've room enough. As the storm seems to be over, we'll fasten it in now, with your permission," he added, politely again addressing the young lady.

As Mr. Carleyn lifted so carefully the small trunk into the carriage, he couldn't help seeing on one end the initials "N. S.," and then he couldn't help wondering what the rest of the name was.

There is something mysterious about initials—they leave such a vague field of conjecture. "N. S." Was it Nelly Sinclair, or Nancy Smith, or Naomi Stevens? How many thoughts may huddle into a man's mind while he is fastening up a lady's trunk. "What is the use of guessing, when you've no certain data?" Levi Longman, the new schoolmaster in that district would say, as he always promptly dismissed such foolish, wandering thoughts.

"But who *is* this N. S. ?" thought Carleyn, as he stood a moment buttoning up his traveling coat and glancing up at the door, over which was this new inscription :

<blockquote>
"Cake and beer
Sold here ;
Crackers and cheese,
If you please ;
Walk in, I swear,
And take a chair."
</blockquote>

" Timothy Titus must be getting poetical," thought Carleyn, " to have so much hexameter over his door. He has also two new window-shades in the upper story with larger bears and lions than ever."

Miss Prudence Potter's new spectacles are broken, her bandbox is smashed in, her bonnet-strings are soiled, the front breadth of her dress is torn, two of her new front teeth are broken, the top of her umbrella handle is off, and the strap is off of her trunk. She says nothing as she enters Mrs. Titus' front door, but walks right out into the kitchen, hangs her shawl on the back of an old chair, mourns over her broken teeth and dilapidated spectacles, and mutters indistinctly, as she goes around hunting up some liniment to keep off the rheumatism, " It is heathenish to have such careless drivers. She won't start off again on any journey on Friday. She won't go a step further this night. She'll never get in a stage-coach again. If she once gets home, she will stay there."

Mrs. Titus says there is no unoccupied lodging-room for her in the house, but there is a little wash-house built back in the yard, where a temporary bed can be made. So Miss Prudence consents to " colonize out " that night in the wash-house.

Prudence Potter has one tender chord in her heart, after all. Zekiel's wife is dead, and has left an infant six months old, and she is going home to take care of it, to love it, and, in her rough way, to be its mother. She will probably trot it half the time, and give it catnip tea and Godfrey's cordial, and make it just such a little blue silk hood as she used to wear when a baby.

While the trunk was being put in its new quarters, the young lady looked out of the window, and saw Mr. Carleyn place, very carefully, a flat bundle in the bottom of the carriage. It was not exactly a bundle, but looked more like large sheets of pasteboard laid together.

" We'll have showers all along the road to-day," said he to the tall gentleman who had been assisting him a little. " I mean bush showers. We'll have plenty of bushes to ride through ; there'll be shower baths enough."

" Take this shawl," said Mrs. Titus, who came rushing out of the door with a large plaid shawl ; " you'll need it ; you can bring it when you pass this way again. Our Timo-

thy got a very sore throat the last time he rode through
those high bushes. You must take better care of yourself,
Mr. Carleyn," said she, kindly.

Just then a tall man came up to the door. "I'll make you
acquainted with our new school-master, Mr. Levi Longman,
a cousin of Rachael Longman's, Mr. Carleyn," said Mrs.
Titus.

You might travel a great distance and not find a larger
heart or a larger person than Mrs. Timothy Titus. Her husband was exceedingly long and narrow, approaching seven
feet of longitude. He had a peculiar twist in his walk,
which made him lean forward a little and incline to the right
side ; but Mrs. Timothy always insisted upon it that it was
a good fault for Timothy to incline to the right. She was
exceedingly straight and exceedingly wide. Every year increased her apparent size, while each year Timothy grew
narrower.

While the gentlemen outside are talking about the storm,
the roads, and the stage, Nepenthe, for it was indeed Nepenthe Stuart, sits within, and looks listlessly around as if her
heart was far away. She was not quite alone, for in the
corner sits Mrs. Titus in the rocking-chair, occasionally
looking out to see if the stage from the other direction is
coming.

" There is a sense of light, a sense of emptiness, a sense
of loneliness in this plain room," thought Nepenthe, as her
eyes rested on some thing hanging over the mantel-piece.

" That head was drawn by my boy," said Mrs. Titus, with
a low tone and a moist eye. " It was taken four years ago,
and Mr. Longman says it is very well done."

" How old is your boy ?" said Nepenthe.

" He would have been sixteen the tenth of this month,
had he lived," said Mrs. Titus ; " but won't you come in and
see him ?"

Nepenthe followed her into a little room nicely papered
and carpeted. There were white curtains at the windows
trimmed with neat fringe, and looped with pink muslin
bands.

" That's my boy," said the mother, as she drew aside the
curtain, so that the light fell full on the face of a beautiful
portrait finely executed and elegantly framed ; " that's my

boy. It cost a hundred dollars, but I would not take thousand for it."

" Was his name Ernest ?" said Nepenthe.

" Yes; he was named by a Frenchman who was taken sick some where on the road and brought here. He named him, and every year after he sent him some present. He sent him the last two years pencils, paper, and all kinds of things to draw with. Here they are," said she, taking a key and opening the drawer of a little stand in the corner, " they are just as he left them. I can't bear to touch them," said she, closing the drawer again and locking it as carefully and gently as if a favorite child were asleep within.

The portrait was indeed a rare Milesian face, with the father's black hair and the mother's blue eyes. Such a face as sometimes greets us, surprises and attracts us in some lowly house with mediocrity for its father and unrefined simplicity for its mother. It bore the stamp of genius.

Just then the tall man stepped inside the door, and asked in his deep hollow voice, " Is the young woman ready ?"

As Nepenthe stood in that room a feeling came over her, a half consciousness that she had been there before. The pictures, the window, the table, even Mrs. Titus looked familiar. It seemed as if she had been there before in some dream. She had seen those curtains, the open drawer, the little stand with the Bible on it, and when the tall man came in, she knew what he would say: " Is the young woman ready ?"

Are there not prophetic thoughts hovering like sea-birds over the future sailing on a head like *avaunt coureurs* on a road through which we afterwards travel, and meeting us as we pause on the journey with the greeting " I'm here before you ?"

Nepenthe was soon seated beside Mr. Carleyn in his comfortable carriage. She was so grateful for this unexpected escort, she knew not what to say. She could hardly open her lips to say any thing. That hackneyed " Much obliged to you," or cold " Thank you," which means every thing or nothing; she could not say even that. She broke out abruptly, as we are apt to do after passing through great dangers and finding ourselves safe at last. " You have done me a great kindness, sir," she said, and she was silent.

Were she moulded after the ordinary type of artificial

young ladies, she would have begun a lively conversation ; but no—she was silent.

There are times in all our histories when it is a trial to talk, when we feel willing to endure patiently, to suffer silently, but cannot lift off the burden and talk lightly, cheerfully, and we are unwilling to talk sadly, gloomily, or allow a stranger to guess our sadness. It is a consolation to lock up some thoughts in the safe of the heart secure from any mortal eye.

"That is a musical voice," thought Mr. Carleyn as he said politely, " we are coming now near those high bushes ; lean back in the carriage, throw your veil over your bonnet, as the drops will fall."

" Will it rain again ?" said Nepenthe, half frightened.

" O, no ! But I see you are not used to these impromptu shower baths. This road ought to be better, and these bushes cut down ; but as it is no one's particular business, it is left, and it is very uncomfortable to ride along this way after a heavy shower—but lean back," said he, throwing his big shawl over her shoulders.

True enough, just then there came an actual illustration of his remarks, and in shielding her he received himself the full benefit of the shower. Who was Nepenthe Stuart riding off with alone ? Who this unknown, suddenly appearing before this rude cottage, with fleet horse and comfortable carriage ? Was it safe so to place herself under the charge to an entire stranger and alone ? All the stories of accidents and injuries thus incurred by young ladies carried off into wild woods, rushed through Nepenthe's mind when she looked up into his face, as the tall man so unceremoniously made the offer of her company to Mr. Carleyn. But as she looked into his face, she was sure, that stranger as he was, the law of kindness was written in his heart, the law of politeness written on his lips, the law of honor in his eye. She had so dreaded staying all night in that uncomfortable house, and besides, there was no unoccupied room to be had, so she rode calmly along, sure of safe protection.

Nature is such an informal cicerone, she brings people together so unceremoniously, and they chat cozily with wild flowers, or green leaves, or wayside hills. She introduces us with a flash of lightning, and smiling on us in a beam of sunshine, makes us so well acquainted. If leaves could rehearse to us as well as they can whisper to each other, how many tales could they repeat of confidential chats softly whispered under their friendly shade. Out under the true-hearted sky, before the open face of Nature, the heart will find its way to the lips, and thoughts are severed no longer by conventional distances.

They traveled on till they came to a turn in the road, at which they made a sudden halt. There had been a freshet. The bridge over which passengers had crossed for years had been carried off. The only way was to go back a mile and round the other unfrequented road. The old bush road it was called, and it was only a kind of winding path.

" You will have to ride much further than you expected," said the young man, as a fine blush colored his face. " The other road is pleasant, though unfrequented. It is long and winding, and you may find it tedious. It is more like a path than a road. I am glad we did not reach here at night. I might have urged my horse on without noticing the missing bridge. I am so familiar with this road I quite often drive along here carelessly, if my thoughts are pre-occupied. I often drive along without looking up ; my horse knows the way as well as I do. I sometimes think he goes it blind, too. I have traveled along here when a boy," said he, half sighing as he turned his horse's head and drove back.

There was something in the cool, invigorating mountain air which refreshed and exhilarated Nepenthe. She was young, and until recently had had little care or sorrow for the last four years, yet this ride among the mountains was to her new and delightful. As they passed through the forest they saw one of the tallest trees lying in fragments on the ground, the trunk shivered to splinters, some of which were sticking in the ground some distance off. A gleam of sunshine brightened, just then, mountain, forest, and stream. Nature seemed rejoicing to get back her old pleasant tone and look again.

" How much we are affected by gleams of sunshine," said Nepenthe. Her face brightened up as she looked on the clear sky, the trees, glowing with that beautiful emerald light, the sunshine, leaves on Nature's fair face wet with tears of weeping skies, a golden emerald light, like living, breath-ing, human joy.

"Yes," said Carleyn, "there's something depressing in a long storm, a gloomy sky and shivering leaves."

As the sunshine broke through the branches of some tall trees along which they now rode, it made his own face radiant.

"Nature's moods seem contagious. She plays with our faces, and plays with our hearts." Says Novalis, ' Nature is an Æolian harp ; a musical instrument whose tones again are keys to higher strings in us.'

"The universal character of the law of Nature is universal aptitude, *convenance*," he thought ; the word seemed so expressive in the French convenance, he only half uttered it as Nepenthe whispered it to herself.

Mr. Carleyn, of all things disliked seeming to wish to impart his own superior knowledge to others in common conversation as if to inform them, and for fear they might be ignorant of the French language. She seldom made use of a French word in common conversation.

Nepenthe was pleased that the same word was uttered almost by both at the same time.

Why is it that unsuggested and with no previous communication, two beings will be just about to utter or utter the same thought in the same language—this is a fact in psychology—and it often causes a sensation of great pleasure to two persons.

Mr. Carleyn talked on, and we will listen and interrupt him no more by soliloquizing ; but if we hear others talking, we feel like breaking in and talking too. We fear if we wait, we would lose our idea that is trying to get out, and try the air too.

Did you ever try, reader, to hold fast an idea, waiting for a chance to utter it, fearing if it escaped your memory, it would not come back again ? Isn't it an unpleasant sensation to try to catch and hold fast an idea ? How forgetfulness chases memory around at " hide and seek " behind the curtains of the soul, and then when at last your time comes to speak, the word you were saying over to yourself to try and remember, you can't recall—and you are really vexed at yourself as you say, " Oh ! dear ! I wish I *could* think of it, but it has escaped my mind." The little prompter behind the stage of the heart is a very uncertain character.

But Carleyn talked on as they rode through the most enchanting scenery, and Nature is a good prompter for extempore eloquence. Who said Carleyn ever heard of a man who was puzzled for words or ideas either out in the woods ? " In Nature there is nothing melancholy," says Coleridge, " yet every person of fine feelings, after passing through such a terrific storm as we have to-day, his mind wrought up to the sublime sense of danger, must have felt a touch of sadness in the mingling of danger and security, the vivid flash of lightning, followed by the sweet sunshine of repose. If nature has so many moods, is it a wonder that we are so often stirred with sorrow or thrilled with ecstacy."

Poor Nepenthe, she was not talking of shadows of *might-be's* or of sentimentals. She was sorrowful, though just then in tune with happy nature. She was homeless, and like a " bewildered wanderer she stood, shouting question after question into the sybil cave of Destiny, and receiving no answer but an echo."

" But look yonder," said Carleyn, " do you see that church spire through the trees ? There is a little village where I stayed one tiresome week. I had been out sketching, and, by the merest accident, I sprained my ankle, and was laid up. There is a church, a duck-pond, an academy and a meeting-house. They are the three central points of interest. The duck-pond is a resort for all the children. It is omnibus, hand-organ, museum, everything. The academy is the light of the village. There country fairs, exhibitions, and singing schools come off—and the meeting-house is the rallying place for all. But I was laid up there in the heart of the village—in a house in the principal street ; the sofa, high-backed and hard, on which I was allowed to rest by day, overlooked the street. There was a stupid-looking Dutchman's house in front ; the clatter of machinery disturbed the most pleasant hours of the day, and the incessant barking of dogs broke the repose of night. There were once to redeem the ill looks o f the unsightly building opposite, flourishing trees ; but these were prostrated long since by some wood-loving, not tree-loving Dutchman, the barking of whose dogs was to him more agreeable than the carolling of birds in waving branches. At earliest dawn worn out mules, not yet rested from yesterday's hard toil, dragged by heavy loads of sand or earth. A long procession of these carts and mules, guided by toil-

worn men, whose life was literally given to the earth,
earthy, was the sure harbinger of daybreak. I pitied the
mules, and I pitied the men; for me the necessity of doing
just the same things at the same unvarying moments, with
no alteration, variation, deviation, relaxation, is intolerable
botheration, as a friend of mine would say. That friend
spent one night in that house, and there happened to be
there, or there belonged there, he says, a hundred turkeys,
but he's a little given to hyperbole. They were there for
safe keeping, or taken on execution, *and they did execution*,
gobble, gobble, gobble, all night long. He could not sleep,
and there was also at that time, a piano in the house, waiting to be sold. He was a fine musician, and to still the tumult
of the turkeys, he commenced *executing* on the piano, and the
result was, the much admired turkey waltz, which he
dedicated to me. He made the piano talk, and the imitation
of all the ancestral and juvenile gobblers, is perfect. 'Tis
probably the first piece of music suggested by so *fowl*
means.

"I was there a week, and it seemed the longest week in
my life. I was quite ill for two or three days and unable to
sleep. We had bread pudding every day for dessert and
there were chunks of bread sticking all up in the top of
the pudding. I was to take morphine to produce sleep.
But it had no soothing effect. My nerves were as keenly
awake as if I had taken hasheesh. While under the influence of morphine the nurse came in, looking much taller
and narrower than usual. Her cap frill touched the wall,
her feet the floor, and she held in her hand a huge basin of
bread pudding, with sundry chunks ornamenting the top.
The basin was at least ten feet in circumference, the chunks
of bread, looked liked miniature mountains. 'Know young
man,' said she, authoritatively 'you must swallow this pudding in an hour.' Then I had another vision after this horrible pudding. I must confess I've never liked bread pudding
since.

"Long processions of mules and men, with enormous carts,
kept passing and repassing my bed. The men were giants,
the mules equal to any fossil specimens of antediluvian animals. At these processions I was obliged to look, whether
I would or not. Since then, I never look on these poor
men carrying earth from one spot to another in the sun and

in the rain, in the heat and in the cold, without pity. I wonder if they never tire of their earth-march, and long sometimes to move off into some other path.'

"One would think," said Nepenthe, "that these human clocks, wound up to the same unvarying beat, the live-long year, would break their springs, fold their hands, strike for freedom, or wind up despairingly their earth-march."

"There—there goes Captain Jack now," said Carleyn. "They are all captains in that village. Captain Jack, Captain Sam, and Captain John. And then there's the spot where I fell from my horse. I was glad and sorry I ever stayed there. I was glad, for I met Mr. Selwyn, the kindest friend I ever had—one to whom I owe all my success in life."

"I do love these old evergreens," said Nepenthe, "shut up in the heart of a great city so long. It is delightful to ride through these green fields, and over these wild mountains, and hear the wind rushing through those magnificent pines. Last Sabbath evening, one verse was sung in church while the rain fell in torrents, and the wind blew outside so that the gas just over my head flickered and almost went out. The deep tones of the organ added sublimity to the words.

> " ' Howl, winds of night, your powers combine—
> Without His high behest,
> Ye cannot, in the mountain pine,
> Disturb the sparrow's nest.'

"I have thought of these words since we rode through these woods. The pine and shadowy evergreen seem as the faces of dear old unaccomplished friends."

"Yes," said Mr. Carleyn, "in summer we have our beautiful shade-trees, and we almost forget to prize these quaint old evergreens—they are not brilliant or showy; but when summer friends and summer birds have left us, they are with us still, changeless as ever."

"Yes," said Nepenthe, "in this great drawing-room of trees there are many graceful willows, elegant . maples, and stately poplars; but I am getting a profound respect for these sires of the forest—for when these summer-hangings in the tree drawing-room are down, not like politicians of a month, here they are still, holding audience to the cabinet of the winds, receiving unmoved the most *moving* addresses from Eolus, surely they claim, by nature, the *highest* place

on the emerald throne. The forest king, robed in fur that
no moth can consume, lives through many forest dynasties,
and waves his sceptre to the wooing breezes."

" You," said Mr. Carleyn, " have paid your tribute of respect and admiration to the forest kings ; but look, see that
gorge wood yonder—those ' tall, dark mountains,' looking
down and listening mutely to those rustic serenaders, smiling and frowning on those crystal sheets issuing from the
rough rocks, stereotyped in murmurs, printed in indelible
associations on the brow of nature and the heart of man."

" Yes," said Nepenthe, " I envy them their celebrity,
bound as they are in evergreens, lettered in golden sun-
beams, wept over by dew-drops, puffed by the breezes, and
heralded among the stately trees, living in such close communion, that stirring tidings may spread rapidly through the
forest city."

.. " How can anybody," said Carleyn, " admire more houses,
and stores, and shows, and glittering lamps, when they can
have sun-beams, and dew-drops, birds and trees, wild flowers and waterfalls. I was born among mountains, and the
earth seems to me to be literally and spiritually nearer to
Heaven, among mountainous regions. The thoughts are en-
ticed upward—from valley and plain they ascend the mountain side—the sublime in nature wakes the sublime in us.
If I couldn't see a mountain occasionally, I should tire of
one everlasting level. The greatest men often come from
mountainous regions, and as they approach the last dark
valley, how they long for one look at the old mountains. I
have felt, when leaving a group of mountains where I had
lived for days, like a child going away from an indulgent
home to a boarding-school. I had that choking sensation,
as if I couldn't half breathe—I was expecting to be homesick. Those lower mountains seem like nature's dress-cir-
cle, with reserved seats for best thoughts.

" Nature, high priestess of art, tireless worker in the
studio of time, toils patiently for human needs and human
comforts, planting lovely flowers in the niches of some
lonely rocks, weaving her graceful tapestry, adorned with
cups and bells and wreaths and vines ; but tired at last, she
dashes off hand into one grand ideal impulse, one high flight
of fancy, and makes her chef d'œuvre, one eternal picture,
God's grand cathedral mountain turrets, under whose colos-

sal arch hides the key passing for ages down the grand hie
rarch of nature.

"Many a fervent hope climbs up the mountain minarets,
to the celestial city, purer and holier than some stifled
prayer, struggling up 'through long-drawn aisle and fretted
vault.' I took an old uncle to the city once. He said he
should tire of those long brick rows—and then there was
ne'er a mountain there. The scent of these mountain breezes
lingers round the old leaves of the heart after long years of
absence. Little mountain evergreens keep their freshness
in the heart's herbarium, while we press the dusty highway,
or turn the musty ledger. These mountain memories, like
tented angels, have encamped about my heart, guarding it
from many a temptation for many weary years."

"For years!" uttered Nepenthe—and then, astonished at
her frankness, perhaps presumption, she paused suddenly.

"Yes—I have not lived many years, but I have seen
many a long day when I have sent out my heart like a dove
far and near to find some olive leaf of comfort," said Carleyn.

They stopped the carriage and threw the top back, as they
were now under the shadow of those waving branches where
matin birds were warbling as they looked up at those blue
mountains in the distance.

"I have often," said Carleyn, "when a child, looked up
to that tall mountain yonder, and wished I could climb to
its top. I felt sure if I could only reach the top, I could
touch the golden clouds, and grasp the stars, Heaven seemed
so near. And now, when I see some great object I wish to
attain, it rises up high like a mountain of ambition, mocking
and tempting me to climb. I feel if I could only reach the
summit, I could touch the cloudy skirt of Fame, and grasp
the stars she holds in her hands. Our greatest thoughts
are all like mountains, whose shadowy summits are high up
from the low plain of our common thoughts. If we could
only climb from thought to thought and reach the summit
of our highest soul's peak, looking into Heaven from the top
of our giant thoughts, we could almost scale the clouds and
touch the stars, and bring Heaven down to us. We do not
revere that we tread upon, but we do revere, admire and
worship that for which we have to climb, pant and struggle.
By the window of that little cottage at the foot of the moun-

tain, I have sat on my mother's knee, and said my little prayer :

"'If I should die before I wake,
I pray the Lord my soul to take.'

And I really believed if I *did* die in my sleep, some angel would take me up from that green mountain top to Heaven. I thought there was the gate through which angels walked up and down the mountains of. clouds above, which seemed like the projected shadows of the mountains beneath. My mother loved mountains. I am enthusiastic about them, for in that little cottage at the foot of yonder mountain, one Sabbath evening, my young mother died. It seemed to me, that with transfigured robes, her pure spirit climbed the mountains she loved, till it ascended to walk through the open gates of Paradise.

"I remember my mother's telling me those mountains often called her thoughts up to Heaven. Now she is gone, I associate these mountains with thoughts of Heaven. Her happy spirit, far above me, may now be climbing some lofty spirit range. some sapphire ridge of glory, some golden peak of immortality. Her soul may climb forever, rising higher and higher in exalted perspective of bliss, warbling as it soars from peak to peak of glory, gaining new views of the river of the water of life, winding beneath, and those glistening, pearly. gates, on which the sun never sets.

"Sacred is the memory of mountains, for there, lighted by vestal stars, the great High Priest went up, entering the veil of curtained clouds, baptizing the mountain's brow with the divine tears of sympathizing humanity."

I hope Levi Longman, that inane and buckram individual, so fond of the exact sciences, so indefatigable in calculating the sum of probabilities, will never read the conversation recorded in the foregoing. He would shake his head, shrug his shoulders, frown his eye-brows, and say, "Strange, that two persons, entire strangers, should talk so long about dreams, trees, and mountains." He would call it highfalutin, stilted. Stilted was a favorite word of his. But it is a long time since he was young. His imagination was born blind and lame, so he has never taken any flights of fancy. He never dreams, day-dreams nor night-dreams—he always sleeps right through, like a *sensible* man. There is a sign on the front door of Levi's brain, which any one that sees him can read : "To these head-quarters, no admittance except on business."

Levi feels no spiritual shocks of joy or sorrow, sensible to nothing but "positive cuffs and downright hard blows." Levi Longman's and Frank Carleyn's spiritual horizon might stretch on like parellel lines for years, forever, they would never meet or harmonize. Levi was an unexcitable *nil admirari* man—Carleyn had a soul coated with sensibility, on whose surface every passing thought daguerreotyped itself.

Most everybody has solemn and enthusiastic thoughts at times. Frank Carleyn differed from most of us in this—he thought aloud ; and Nepenthe's life had been so real that none but her real thoughts came to her lips.

"Why did Nepenthe Stuart go to the Elliott's ?" said the voice of a lady in close conversation with an old friend, on the deck of a southern steamer, two months after this mountain ride through Titusville road. "She can't be very happy there, for Mary Lamont heard Miss Florence talking with her mother the day after Miss Stuart's arrival. She heard Florence say in her overbearing way, ' I'll know why this Stuart girl is here. I think her presence an intrusion. We have lived here so long interrupted, I don't see why you have brought her here.'

" 'It was not to gratify you that she came,' said Mrs. Elliott. 'I have reasons I do not choose to tell. I cannot be opposed in this matter. I am under obligations of which you know nothing, and of which you never can know.' "

CHAPTER XVIII.

CARLEYN AT WORK.

" The past is very tender at my heart:
Full, as the memory of an ancient friend,
When once again we stand beside his grave,
Raking amongst old papers thrown in haste
'Mid useless lumber, unawares I came
On a forgotten poem of my youth.
I went aside and read each faded page,
Warm with dead passion, sweet with buried Junes,
Filled with the light of suns that are no more.
I stood like one who finds a golden tress
Given by loving hands no more on earth,
And starts, beholding how the dust of years,
Which dims all else, has never touched its light.'

THERE was no light from the world around. Down through the sky-light above, it shone clear and pure. None but the stars looked in, where art and the artist held high communion. Weary feet grew tired as they climbed—but the long flight of steps once ascended, they found fair and bright thoughts resting there, which had climbed far higher ideal flights

Night and day toiled the artist to bring out on canvass in the face God had made, the soul he had so mysteriously half hidden, half revealed.

There was one picture on the easel nearly finished. To the rapt artist, that one picture seemed the whole world, as he added the last touches, and stood back and gazed, and gazed again. " It is done, and well done," said he. " I have succeeded. I will call it Dawn—the expression of that face has dawned upon my soul like some radiant mountain sunrise."

He held his hand on his tired forehead, and gazed again. Not often did he thus dwell in the land of the ideal, and this was his first ideal. He had painted week in and week out, the portraits of dull living faces, for money, winning fame, and fame's golden reward. He wished he was never obliged to handle money, he always dreaded to ask for it, when his labors were finished. His soul was so peopled and crowded with beautiful visions, he longed to paint them —but this one picture is the only idea he could now afford leisure to take. He would not sell it for any sum. He couldn't tell why he painted it, only the lovely face seemed ever looking in at the door of his soul, pleading with earnest eyes, " Paint me—am I not beautiful ?"

" This may be the dawn of my future fame," thought he ; " it is better finished than any of my old pictures. Let me put it where the first morning light will dawn upon it."

" Come," said Douglass, one morning, as he met his friend Selwyn, " let's go in and look at Carleyn's studio. If he has no one sitting with him, we'll look around. He's a fine fellow—I'd like you to know him."

" I don't care to visit any more studios," said Selwyn, dejectedly ; " I have recently visited the picture gallery of Dresden, which is a perfect palace and paradise of art. There are more than twenty-two hundred pictures, and none of them are inferior. There is one known all over America by plates, but I wish you could see it there in the original. It is Raphael's Madonna. I think this picture must affect any man, if he were not a clod. It represents the Virgin Mary as ascending to Heaven with the child in her arms ; one of the Popes and St. Barbara at her feet, and beneath, two angelic children. The faces of these children and St. Barbara are very beautiful, but the power of the picture is in the soaring, in the majesty ascending form of the Virgin. It stands by itself, in a room set apart for it alone. As I entered the door, the picture came over me like a spell.

" Beautiful as are all the other paintings, the transition to this is abrupt and great. I have seen demi-gods of Phidias. I have visited galleries of Venice, Genoa, and Florence. I have looked at French copies and Italian originals and American imitations. I take no interest in anything now. I wish to form no new acquaintances "—but as he saw how disappointed his friend looked, he added, " I will go if you wish it, if the artist is a friend of yours."

Reader, have you never seated yourself in the morning for a good, quiet, comfortable day at home, when some sudden impulse or persuasion has led you, half against your will and wishes, to start out and go into some out of the way place ? You go and you meet—'tis the merest accident, you say—you meet and almost push by him in the crowd, a dear old friend, the node of whose eccentric life-orbit chances to be that one day in that particular spot such a greeting and such a meeting. " Why, where did *you* come from ?" you each exclaim. " *You* are the last person I expected to see here." You sit down together, talk over old times, deaths and marriages of mutual friends. You hear so much news, such strange things have happened, the day wears away, and it is four o'clock before you know it. With a cheerful " God bless you," you part, and every little bud of memory has had a fresh sprinkling of sympathy, and holds up its dewy head like a violet after a shower, perfuming the whole heart. So your life streams part again, and you old friends meet no more, and no white sails on life's wide sea shall ever speak return to you. Such a glad surprise to Carleyn was Mr. Selwyn's sudden entrance into his studio.

As Mr. Selwyn walked around the room, he said, "My likes are not artistic. I am no amateur, yet I think I have some idea of a good portrait. Were I an artist, I would always send portraits of handsome subjects to public exhibitions. People are apt to think more of a handsome picture than a very correct one. They will pass by admirably executed portraits of plain faces, and linger before some handsome picture with glossy hair, brilliant eyes, and ruby lips. For myself, I am often more interested in a plain face than a mere handsome one. A fine expression flashes more wonderfully over plain features. Every face that shows the soul best, gets to be handsome to us. I have heard many an eloquent man speak who had a most awkward physiognomy. I have listened until the highest admiration for such powers of mind revealed by pen and tongue so associated the soul with the face, and the face with the soul, that the individual, in spite of long nose, large mouth, dull eyes, looked well. ' I wouldn't alter that face if I could,' I say. I like its individuality. The lips are ennobled by the words they utter, the eyes beautified by the soul they reveal. There are people so good and noble, in spite of plain features, we call them fine looking. Handsome homely people they are. There is a queer, quaint, striking contrast between these roughly-moulded features and the strong, beautiful, soul-light flashing over them."

"It is amusing to see," said Carleyn, "how the mass of people are influenced in the same way. If a man is great, gifted and popular, they will be sure to see something peculiarly interesting in the way his hair grows around his forehead, or in the glance of his eye, or the curve of his eyebrow, and the very young ladies will even find some thing so interesting in the tie of his cravat. Few ever call an acknowledged great man homely. They'll see some thing striking about him. If he is awkward, it is scholarly; if absent minded, reflective; if conceited, dignified; till, by-and-by, we all get thinking every thing he says sounds well and he always looks well. But in a picture you can't so express the full power of symmetrical mind over homely features; as you can feel and see it when a face lives, moves and speaks. I like that crayon portrait. A crayon portrait has a rare charm of its own. The effect is decidedly unity, a concentration of soul in the face; with no vivid coloring to heighten effect, no glowing drapery, nothing to divert the artist's attention from his one purpose—the correct outline and the true expression. A fine crayon drawing seems more, to me, like the shadow of the soul than any other kind of portrait, giving a faint conception of the look of those white-robed ones with whom we never associate glowing drapery or vivid coloring."

"There is a picture," said Carleyn, "I have just had sent back to retouch. It is a portrait of Mrs. John Pridefit. I did my best, but did not satisfy the sitter. She really wants it more beautiful, yet her friends say it flatters her now. She says the eyes are too sharp, the lips too thin, but the fault is in her face, not in the picture. A lady often wants to have her own features taken as a kind of background, and then have it filled up and beautified with all kinds of ideal hues, and glows, and lines. It is very difficult for me to take the portraits of people I dislike. I am afraid I don't really do them justice. This Mrs. Pridefit fusses and prims so much, it is difficult to give her the 'fine expression, she says she wants. Some seem to think I keep a box of fine expressions to put on my portraits just as they put on smiles when they go into their parlors to receive callers."

"A picture," said Selwyn, "often looks better than the original. It is almost always handsomer or homelier. I can't see why ladies want their portrait to looks better than they really do. It is so mortifying to hear people say of one's portrait, ' It is a very handsome picture, but it looks a great deal better than she does,'—but sometimes I have noticed in daguerreotypes people look pretty who never look pretty any where else. Mrs. Pridefit says she always makes good photographs."

" The face of every true woman wears, at times, a beautiful expression," said Carleyn. " I want to come in contact with the soul, to watch the face in its various soul moods, to see it in its thoughtful, tearful, or mirthful moments. I like even to know its history, for the most important events of a life have and leave their traces on the face ; and if you watch it long and see it often, you can read the outline of the life's history, the noble epic of some heroic or weather-beaten soul carved in wrinkles, translated in patient smiles, emphasized with sighs, and margined with tears.

" We love our friends for their souls, and if I know the sitter well, I can bring out the best expression—the expression worn when thinking kind thoughts alone, or genially communing with others. How different every friend we have looks when we come to know him well, from what he did when we first saw him ; it is almost like two faces—the way he looked when we first saw him, and the familiar expression we get to know so well at last. We can hardly close our eyes and recall that first look. We saw only the outline of the features, the color of his hair and eyes, but now we know how he talks, smiles, looks. He always does so and so, he has his way of smiling, that makes him so unlike any body else. Often we say, ' I thought him homely at first, but now he looks handsome to me.' To get this natural and familiar expression is the artist's aim—for this look the soul will wear when the body is cast aside."

" We don't know how we look ourselves," said Douglass. " We look in the glass, but who ever has on his best, most natural expression, when toileting before a mirror ? I can't help it, but I sometimes think I'd like to come out of myself for once, and be in some corner, and see myself sitting in another corner opposite me—I'd like to know for once, how I really do look. Sometimes I think I am quite a decent-looking man, and then again I am positive I am intolerably ugly, and if I were a woman, I'd always wear a veil."

"But the veiled gentlemen," said Carleyn, "would not be as interesting or romantic an object as the veiled lady. We gentlemen must come right out on all occasions with our plain, unveiled, unadorned face, without the advantage of one of those pretty, little, fine, soft, elaborate black lace veils, through which modifying medium so many women look so very fair and fascinating.

"It is a very pretty drapery, too, a kind of shade through which they can quietly look out on the world though the world can't fully gaze at them."

"I rather like a veil; there is an air of refinement about it."

"I suppose Mrs. Carleyn will always wear a veil," said Douglass, laughing.

"Certainly," said Carleyn, smiling. "No rude sun, or sharp wind, must spoil *her* beautiful complexion," and he thought, though he didn't say so, "how pleasant it would be to say some time, 'this is my wife's veil.' But I don't mean," he added, aloud, "one of those great, thick, blue, long veils, through which all ladies look alike, and it is impossible to know who they are."

"An artist's profession is an anxious one," said Carleyn. "No matter how many portraits he executes, each must be as satisfactory to the new sitter, as well executed, as if it were the picture on which the artist's name and fame depended. That one picture will be a gratification or disappointment to some family; wherever it goes, it may be the only representative in that locality of the artist's name—the single picture giving its individual verdict of his genius. Stranger judges will say he paints well or ill, as that picture fails or suits; and then all the beauty of some face may be its expression, and such a face may be one of those never at rest, we never think of its being still; and if we paint a stationary smile, it will look like a grin; if we leave it off, then the mouth will be unnatural, prim and sober."

"To catch one of these animated smiles, is about as easy as to daguerrotype a shooting star or falling tear; and then the sides of some faces are not alike. That portrait I painted yesterday, I had to take each side of the face by itself; they were most as different as two faces.

"I must confess I feel discouraged sometimes, when I think that after a few years, all my portraits will be cracked and defaced in some garret. They'll be tattered and torn, soiled and defaced, in the attic style after all.

"Old sofas and chairs are used somewhere, but old portraits almost always go up garret. So here I stand and paint for posterity's garrets. Isn't it a dubious immortality? If I wrote a wonderful book of poems, that would always keep in fashion."

Mr. Selwyn looked at the different pictures, and then stopped as if riveted to one spot, spell-bound, before one painting.

"Is that a portrait, sir?" said he, turning suddenly and addressing Carleyn, with some new emotion struggling in his eye.

"I call it an ideal," said Carleyn. "I have just finished it. Perhaps the expression of the face dawned upon me once in a thunder-storm, on a wild country road, in an old house. I *call* it an ideal, and yet the expression flashed upon me from that face. One of the first portraits I took, was in that same old house. It was that of a beautiful youth, Earnest Titus. I have been asked many a time to send it to the Academy, but the mother will never part with it a day. She spends hours in that little room sitting beside it."

"Would you sell that picture?" said Mr. Selwyn.

"I prefer to keep it. It is more valuable to me than it can be to another," said Carleyn.

"Will you paint a miniature on ivory just like it, and get that expression, only make the hair a little darker, and the lips not quite so full? That is a beautiful name, *dawn*. If I were to paint anything," he thought gloomily, "I should call it midnight."

More gloomy than ever looked Mr. Selwyn as he walked homeward with his friend who tried to rally him.

"Stop thinking of that gloomy subject; divert your thoughts," said Mr. Douglass. "Court sleep; you are too young; life has yet much for your enjoyment; too much to give up to gloomy reflections; you'll wear yourself out thinking. Act, enjoy, use the present, forget the past."

"You bid me travel," said Selwyn, " to gaze on land and sea, and moon and sky, commune with nature, revel in art.

I have travelled. I went last year to Milan, and then to Genoa, and thence to Leghorn, Pisa and Rome.

" Genoa is famous among the Italian cities for the number and splendor of its palaces and so has received the title of 'The Superb,' for the Italians have a pretty way of giving their chief cities some descriptive title. In Leghorn, which was the next place at which I stopped, there is not much to see besides straw hats, glass, paper and soap. There are about as many things of interest there as there are snakes in Ireland—that is, none at all. It is rather strange, too, for most every Italian city, even when small, has either a fine cathedral or some fine work of art. I went to Pisa to see the cathedral and the famous leaning tower, over which, when a school-boy studying geography, I wondered so much, and over which Galileo made the old churchmen wonder when he performed from it his experiments with falling bodies. But I couldn't begin to tell you all I saw in Rome. Three civilizations, an Etruscan, Roman and Christian, have conspired to make it the most interesting city in the world. The number and grandeur of the relics of old Rome surpass anything I had imagined. Whatever the Romans built, they built grand, massive and solid, as if they were fully per-suaded that Rome was to be the Eternal City. Had no bar-baric violence overthrown and demolished them, hundreds of her structures would stand to-day more perfect than the Pantheon, and even now, many an old column and arch stands as solid, and presses the ground as firmly as when first erected. Everywhere you turn yourself, you will see some old ruin lifting its head picturesquely against the sky. It is a long, fatiguing walk to go through all the rooms and see the enormous treasures, works of antique art, which have been found and preserved in the Capitol and the Vatican. Nor in point of art does modern Rome fail to rival the ancient in interest. She is crowded with the miracles of the great master. I wish, if you never have, you would read Haw-thorne's book, called Transformation. As far it goes, it is an excellent, accurate description of Rome. Most of his criticisms seem to me superb. Hilda's tower has verily a local habitation and a name, for I have seen it, but whether any such being as Hilda ever inhabited it, I cannot say. I made two long visits at Rome. I stayed some hours for sev-eral days in the museum at Naples, where are the articles found during the excavation of Herculaneum and Pompeii. We had a splendid day and a fine party for making the ascent of Vesuvius. Many persons came back disappointed, because even in quiet weather the smoke is blown about so one can scarcely see anything. We had a favorable day, and I enjoyed the excursion immensely. One gets so little idea of a real live crater from books. One must see the monster, to have any faint conception of the lava fields and enormous, bellowing, smoking crater. I felt as if I were on some other planet, they were so different from anything I had ever seen. I had some singular sensations at Pompeii, for here is a veritable old Roman city with streets, houses, temples, gates, fountains, baths, tombs, mosaic paintings, laid bare to the sun, so you tread where its inhabitants trod two thousand years ago. I saw many of the articles there found and preserved, in the museum at Naples. I had a charming ride at Sorrento, just across the bay from Naples. We plucked the fresh fruit from the trees of the beautiful orange groves, and visited a little island, near where was a grotto and some water with a peculiar bluish lustre. I was at Rome during the ceremonies of the Holy Week. They are the most imposing in all the pompous ritual of the Romish church. On Easter Sunday, when the Pope elevated the host, and all the long line of splendid military in St. Peters and all good Catholics went down as by one accord on their knees, and adored in a silence broken at length by a beautiful burst of silver trumpets, the scene was quite imposing. The washing and kissing of the Apostles' feet by the Pope was a mere form, for they were already as clean as water could make them. Not so with the washing of the pilgrim's feet, for they were dirtier than mud. Italy lies behind me like a rich dream, for nature has made it a paradise in loveliness, and art has beautified from Venice to Sicily a land she could not save.

" Florence is the most delightful of Italian cities to me, certainly it is the loveliest. It is in the midst of a lovely valley, the most charmingly verdant spot I ever saw ; with every varying shade of green, from the light of the olive, to the dark of the pine. Of the pictures in the galleries at Dresden, Rome and Florence, you can believe every thing that you hear, for they are absolutely wonderful. It would

seem impossible that so much great and varied expression
ever could be transferred to canvas.

"There is a statue in Florence of the Venus de Medici,
so famous the world over ; yet I saw standing by my side
some who failed to like it, it seemed to me for no better reason than that it is old and tarnished, and the arms and hands
badly restored. With the exception of these arms and hands,
I have never seen such grace and elegance.

"I had the pleasure of a few moments' talk with Gari-
baldi. I was charmed with his perfect simplicity and un-
affectedness of manner. The people of Italy almost worship
him. I saw where he first entered the Sardinian chambers ;
and as he was going into the building, they crowded about
him with uncontrollable enthusiasm. It is a good thing for
a nation which long oppression has made extremely selfish,
to have one man whom they can genuinely love, who can
draw out from every breast its nobler sympathies."

"But," added Selwyn, coming back. to his own thoughts
again, "I shall travel no more ; wherever I go, I carry an
unhappy, restless traveller with me, my own aching, sor-
rowing, broken heart, whose constant beat seems only like
that of a sleepless 'sentinel, waking me out of every pleasant
dream, calling me back every hour to bitter memories. I
hear every where under life's darkened windows, hung with
crape, this ceaseless beat of my sad sentinel heart. You
tell me not to think, to act, to enjoy. O, Douglass, you
know not my wretchedness. There is a shore for the moor-
ing of the lost voyager's bark, a lull for the direst tempest,
a waning for the silver moon : the raging billow sleeps at
last. At the coming of the morning the bannered clouds
fold their white tents, but thought never folds her wings—
the spirit's bark is never moored. Thought's billowy surges
rise higher as they roll on, but never blend with the ocean
of oblivion. Her strange electric light pales not with de-
clining suns, or waning moons, her throbbings lull not with
lulling tempests. I am weary of life. My poor thought is
a weather-beaten traveller over the stormy past, keeping at
midnight her sleepless guard like a vigil of arms, always
walking among tombs and shadows, and then to sleep only
to awake and find the next morning the same old haunting
trouble rising and going about with you. You who have
never had a trouble, to walk and talk and sleep and dream

with you, know not how Trouble's to-day goes hand in hand with its elder brother of yesterday, walking restlessly the lonely hall of the soul, and when you open your eyes in the morning, and the bright sunshine steals in, there is the 'raven' trouble croaking at your chamber door, 'croaking evermore.' My soul is like a haunted house. Such noises and shrieks and groans and half-hushed voices and raps and wails, startle me at night and torment by day. My life is a burnt-over prairie—the flowers are gone."

Mr. Selwyn walked back and forth gloomily.

"You need change of scene," said Mr. Douglass; "go and spend a few days with me at Niagara."

"I have visited Niagara," said Mr. Selwyn. "If there's a pall within, even beautiful nature will seem only a shadowy procession of slow, mournful pall-bearers to the shrouded heart. My kneeling soul has said its mournful litany under the brow of table rock, beneath earth's great baptismal font, sprinkled with ascending spray, where is shadowed forth in rising clouds, the glory of the Father, Son and Spirit. Long shut up within brick walls, catching but glimpses and patches of the blue sky, it is like walking with God in the cool of the day, to stand so near the presence chamber of the invisible One, and touch the shadowy robes of the great High Priest, bordered with light from yonder gates of pearl, while ascends from liquid voices the grandest voluntary of ages, where God's great thoughts are ever issuing from crystal sheets, with radiant emerald bound."

"How our little griefs," said Douglass, "little cares, little losses, shrink out of sight before these great waters, which have roared on so patiently and sublimely for weary years, while the tide of many a life-stream has gone out and passed away."

"The roar of these great waters," said Selwyn, "never dies away from my spirit. Those solemn voices echo ever with the voices of the night. Louder and deeper than the moaning of the great waterfall, is the wail of my grief at midnight, sobbing out its voluntary, as it ever accumulates from the great lakes of sorrow, rushing on through the sea of trouble, dashing its cold spray of tears along the silent shore of memory, bearing me on to the eddying whirlpool of regret. O," said he bitterly, "if there were only some Ne-

penthe I could press to my lips, and forget the painful past!
If I could turn over the old dark page, and begin a new
life that would not be so haunted with echoes and shadows
and ghosts!"

CHAPTER XIX.

THE CONVENIENT CRACK—DR. BACHUNE'S WISDOM—ORTHO-
DOXY—WHITE CRAVATS—PURITANS.

"Good are the Ethics, I wis; good absolute—not for me, though;
Good too Logic, of course; in itself—but not in fine weather;
Sleep, weary ghosts, be at peace, and abide in your lexicon-limbo;
Sleep, as in lava for ages your Herculanean kindred,
Æschylus, Sophocles, Homer, Herodotus, Pindar, and Plato;
Give to historical subjects a free poetical treatment,
Leaving vocabular ghosts undisturbed in their lexicon-limbo."
ARTHUR HUGH CLOUGH.

"And the Raven, never flitting, still is sitting, still is sitting,
On the pallid bust of Pallas, just above my chamber-door,
And his eyes have all the seeming of a demon that is dreaming,
And the lamplight o'er him streaming, throws his shadow on the floor,
And my soul from out that shadow that lies floating on the floor,
Shall be lifted nevermore."
EDGAR ALLEN POE.

"Thus much would I conceal, that none should know
What secret cause I have for silent woe."
MICHAEL ANGELO.

"I WONDER what is the matter with that man," said Mrs.
Edwards, as Mr. Selwyn went up to his room from breakfast; (Mrs. Edwards kept a boarding-house; she had about
twenty gentleman boarders.) "He pays promptly, has a
valuable library, rare pictures, costly wardrobe, the best
room in the house; he must be wealthy. I keep his room
scrupulously clean, his linen as white and polished as
sugar, salt, spermacetti and gum arabic can make it. I try
to have him feel at home; I don't understand the man; I set
before him omelets done to a charm, cream biscuit, delicious
steak, irresistible coffee, plum pudding, and everything that
bachelors dote on. I don't believe he'd notice it if I put salt
in his tea, instead of sugar—it does beat all! This morning I had such fresh corn bread, hot griddle cakes, warm
biscuit, right before him when he came down late, and he

only ate a few mouthfuls of corn bread, tasted his coffee, and left the table, neglecting all my delicacies. He is the only man I ever saw who didn't care what he had to eat. He treats my steak as if it were chips. He seems to like cold griddle cakes as well as warm, hard eggs as well as soft. I can't tempt him with muffins, maccaronies, ice creams or ices. They are all the same to him; he never eats jellies or preserves. I wonder what the man does like. I opened a jar of preserved strawberries the other evening, just for his tea, and he never tasted them; that Mr. Hogg is a real hog, for he ate the whole of them. I try to get in conversation with him. I start every subject, and I am sure he has no business to worry him. He comes and goes when he likes. Ann says some mornings his bed isn't even tumbled; she believes he sits up all night. He has a dignified way, as if accustomed to respect. I believe he'd be happier if he had a wife; why don't he marry? There are plenty of nice ladies to be had. The ladies were all in the parlor the other evening—we had such fine music, graceful dancing and nice charades; all my other guests were in the parlor." (Mrs. Edwards always call her boarders guests.) "I did all I could to get him in, but he declined, perhaps he's not fond of gaiety—would prefer a quiet domestic life—but oh, how my tooth does ache! I really believe I will have to have it out yet. But that reminds me my room is so damp since the walls were fixed I will have to take the room next to Mr. Selwyn to-night. It is the only unoccupied room in the house."

Mrs. Edwards' tooth kept her awake for hours that night, and as she tossed about in her bed, she could hear Mr. Selwyn pacing back and forth in his room; he had evidently not retired. She got up and went into the wardrobe to hunt for some cotton on which to put a little aconite in the tooth where the nerve was exposed. There was a closet also in Mr. Selwyn's room adjoining hers, a slight crack or a little hole in the wardrobe would reveal to any eye close to it, any object in the adjoining room that chanced to be in that line of vision. She was rummaging quite near the crack to get the cotton, when a heavy sigh arrested her attention, and before she knew it she found her eye quite near the crack. She could see on Mr. Selwyn's round table some old yellow-looking letters, and open on the floor a small trunk.

If one begins to do a thing not quite right, if there *is any mystery* in the matter, there is a fascination in keeping the eye fixed upon the spot, until the mystery is solved. Nothing but the fear of exposure could prevent her now from seeing all she could through that crack.

He took from his trunk a little box and sat down by the centre table (Mrs. Edwards always gave her nice bachelor boarders a centre table,) took from the box a miniature and laid it upon the table. He placed beside it another miniature, looking newer and the setting brighter. He looked at both of them, as if he were reading a book, as Mrs. Edwards said, and then he sat still so long, leaning forward on the table ; his back was turned to her, she thought he had fallen asleep, the gas flickered, the hands of the little clock moved on to twelve, and yet he stirred not; he must be asleep. But I'll catch my death of cold in my tooth standing here so long," thought she. Just then there was a deep sob, a heavy sob. Yes, he actually sobbed. Mrs. Edwards had a woman's heart ; she half reproached herself for looking through that convenient crack. This unexpected demonstration of grief checked for that time her curiosity.

She stepped softly down off her chair, for she had been standing on a chair, and something fell off of one of the shelves. Just as sure as we wish to be very quiet and secret about any thing how often something will happen to cause us to make a great noise. Mrs. Edwards was provoked that she should have made such a noise when she wished to keep so remarkably still. She stooped to pick it up. It was an old Bible. It lay open on the floor. By some sudden impulse she went to the light and looked on the page where she had found it open, and the first verse that met her eye was this, in the fourteenth chapter of Proverbs : "The heart knoweth his own bitterness : and a stranger doth not intermeddle with his joy."

She went softly back to bed, lying awake a long time, catching at intervals, snatches of disturbed sleep, dreaming that her room was full of old letters and miniatures, and she could hear all through her dreams—sob after sob—but after that she was kinder than ever to her new boarder.

Mrs. Edwards had such a passion for piecing bed-quilts,

such lots of red, green, and blue remnants she bought up, to make an infinite series of tulips, rising suns and elaborate roses.

This was her first tulip quilt and she was congratulating herself upon its rapid consummation. That afternoon, as she sat rocking in her chair fitting her tulips, she said in an undertone to herself, "Well, every body has trouble, but things fit together right after all, just like my tulips."

"Yes," thought Kate Howard, as she caught this part of Mrs. Edwards' soliloquy, as she passed through the hall, "Things fit together like her tulips! very true, very true! many events fit together, just as her tulips—stuck on, nobody'd think they even grew together—those leaves and tulips. So it is in life, the right leaves and flowers seldom get together in one heart."

Feelings are like flowers; they ought never to be cut, and measured, and laid down—they ought to *grow*. Just plant a little bud of hope in the heart, and there'll soon be laid all around it some dark, ugly leaves of regret. The heart is nothing but patchwork after all, odds and ends, new and old, light and dark all together, all made of bright remnants left of joys and loves, paid for with heavy cost. I hate this endless patchwork—patching old loves with new friendships. There's too much light and dark stuck together, the poor patched heart'll never wear well long. We try to join the rent seams of feeling, and to make them last we sew them over and over with the threads of habit, until the heart is full of hard, rough ridges. Give me one good comfortable feeling to spread over my heart, to tuck it in warm—it is the best kind of *counterpane* I know of. It is better than a whole basket of calico tulips, waiting for the leaves to be stuck on. When I sleep under a bed covered with such tulips, I always dream of country fairs."

Had Dr. Bachune heard these ladies talking, he would have put on his most classic face, and exclaimed with emphasis " *Nil disputandum de gustibus.*"

Mrs. Edwards laid her tulips together, all arranged nicely, as they were going to be sewed, and looking at them all admiringly, she exclaimed, " I can finish it all on Wednesday, and it shall go on Mr. Selwyn's bed."

Poor Mrs. Edwards little knew how much Mr. Selwyn disliked these Mosaic tulips and aggravated roses, staring at him when he awoke in the morning, always in their full stiff bloom. She had two *inevitable* baskets, as Kate Howard called them. One had an oval top and the other a round one—one for embroidered bands and the other for patches. She had these two resources for her single solitude. It was astonishing how many bands she had embroidered in all sorts of those varied patterns, leaves and flowers with which the initiated are so familiar.

She lays them all away, and begins to dress for dinner. She brushes carefully her glossy hair, puts on the pink and black coiffure and her new black silk dress. She knew well, like most of the rest of the world of ladies, she looked best in black silk. Her eyes were no soft sentimental blue, but a practical hazel blue. She was neat, prudent, patient, genial, and when well dressed, in the soft light of her pleasant parlor, she looked young still, with that peachy glow upon her cheek.

She was quite willing to please her new boarder. She was tired of being always so self-reliant, always at the head. She had long wished for a little home of her own. She would have been glad to have seen her whole regiment of boarders, save this one, moving out at the door, and herself domesticated in some cottage of her own, going and coming when she chose, with no big butcher's and grocer's bills to trouble her, with no uppish Bridgets and saucy Margarets, and lazy Kates to worry and fret her, and then too, she could make such beautiful quilts, she would have so much leisure, and she could work bands enough to trim up every thing so showily. But it would not do for her to sit still and build air castles, and this evening she took more pains than usual with her dress, in spite of her toothache. She was just the woman in case of an emergency, to know what was to be done, and where and when and how to do it.

A gentleman called the next morning for Mr. Selwyn. He hurried off in great haste, leaving his things around the room. Mrs. Edwards took her bunch of keys—she had one she thought would just fit his door. She tried them all, and at last one of them unlocked it, and she slipped in—and there were the two miniatures on the table. She examined both. One seemed about seventeen. It looked as if it were taken long ago, and evidently just put in its bright fresh modern frame.

"Who were these?" thought she. "Not two wives, certainly. Oh! two sisters, may be—yes, two sisters." Both were beautiful, and she began to see a striking resemblance in the two faces, as she held one in her hand by the window, looking at it, when she heard some one coming up stairs. It was his step—he was coming back. She laid the miniature on the table, and hurried into the closet, crouching down behind a large trunk in the corner. He was hunting for something. He took hold of the knob of the closet door, as if to open it. How she trembled! She moved still farther back into the corner, and pressed open a large paper of Scotch snuff that was lying on the floor.

"There—I did get almost caught that time," thought she, as Mr. Selwyn went down stairs again, after putting up his miniatures and locking the box. As his footsteps died away on the stairs, a succession of suppressed sneezes sounded through the hall, as Mrs. Edwards issued from her retreat.

One bureau drawer was left unlocked, which she rummaged. Some very good people will rummage, and they can't seem to help it—they've such inquiring minds. She found a package of sermons, and a part of an old note. She read the note:

"We all regret very much you have given up the ministry—you could do so much good. Your sermon on self-denial made a deep impression on my mind, and it was beneficial to many others. It so impressed Dr. Wendon that it really was the means of his taking a young and destitute orphan girl into his family, and keeping her for years and educating her. Won't you be so kind as to let me have it for a few days, to read to Dr. Wendon, who is now blind and unfortunate."

"I wonder if this note really was directed to Mr. Selwyn?" thought Mrs. Edwards; "the direction and beginning are torn, so I can't find out. I heard a self-denial sermon some years ago, which would have made a Christian of me if I hadn't kept a boarding-house. I had no time then to turn my mind to penitence and conversion. Who was that minister? They called him Professor Henry, but that name wasn't his last name. There were two professors in the seminary of the same name—so they always went by their Christian names. The one they called Professor Henry and the other Professor John."

Mrs. Edwards takes out a sermon from the package, lays it beside a little scrap of paper on the table, written by Mr. Selwyn, a scrap of quotation from some poet. She examined both carefully, and she goes and gets one of her bills he had signed. She knew the curl of the *d's* and the twirl of the *m's* in the name on the bill. He made such queer-looking *d's* she'd know them anywhere—and the hand-writing of the sermon was the same as the little quotation. "Yes, Mr. Selwyn was a minister—these were his sermons. Wasn't it strange!"

She comes out, shuts and locks the door, goes back to her room, with her head full of information—too much for any one woman to keep alone.

"Wasn't it strange!" she said, as she sat in the dining-room, thinking aloud. "But here comes Miss Charity Gouge. I'm afraid she'll ask for the pattern of my quilt and I don't want another just like it anywhere," said she, quickly tucking her tulips in the basket under the table.

"I had an application for a new boarder this morning, Miss Gouge," said she, "a genteel-looking young lady. She looked at the fourth story back room, with sloping windows, the one for twelve shillings a week. She is to furnish her own fuel, light, food—sit in the parlor but little, never take her work there. She says her name is Stuart, Nepenthe Stuart. She may come, yet she said nothing of reference—but I can manage that. I can get along well enough with women, they usually pay. But, Charity, I must tell you about Dr. Bachune, the gentleman we all admired so much. I thought I would never mention his name again. He had the best room in the house at eighteen dollars a week and all the extras ; his boots must be at the door so early, wine always on the table by him. He was so fastidious and delicate that I really told all the waiters to be particularly attentive to him.

"He looked so gentlemanly, so infinitely *above* all pecuniary considerations, when he said that ' money was no object if the room suited.' He had no baggage—that was ' coming on from Philadelphia.' I have found since that people who are always saying that money is of no consequence, have very little of it in their pockets.

"I put his bill under his plate, as I always do at the end of the week. He took breakfast the next morning, was there at luncheon, and I have since heard nothing more from him. He went off with his imaginary baggage, to his imaginary office, paying his imaginary bill. I really never was quite so taken in, he was so gentlemanly, and I never got a cent. Yes, he was a real gentleman in manners, Kate Howard was saying yesterday. He was so very scientific and correct in conversation, it was amusing to see how easily he would rectify the slightest error in statistics, politics or physics. Fiddlesticks! I get out of all manner of patience when I think how fastidious and delicate was his taste, and what a fuss I did make for him. He used to say that he only ate the griddle-cakes as a vehicle for his molasses. Wasn't that rather highfaluten? I heard him ask Mr. Vole one day if he had pursued much the study of hermeneutics? Mr. Vole hesitated, and then said, ' Not much.'

"Kate Howard said—(did you ever see a Kate that wasn't up to every thing ?)—she said, she saw Mr. Vole, after dinner, slyly looking into Webster's Dictionary. He remarked that he wouldn't ' be caught that way again.' I think the doctor said something about mollusc for breakfast, but I won't be sure. You couldn't mention a place, but he could describe it, or a book, but he had read it, or a great personage, with whom he had not been familiar. Kate Howard said, before a book was written he had read it. Indeed he told Kate that she had the face of Eugenie and the form of Victoria. Of course he has seen all the foreign dignitaries. His coat was buttoned up to the chin—a blue coat—and Kate says she thought he hadn't but one collar—he wore it standing up the first three days, and turned down the next four. But you know, Miss Charity, that thinking over vexatious things only makes them worse. I expect to hear his name as long as the house stands. Mr. Vole and two or three others will keep ringing changes on the doctor's name. Only this morning, Mr. Vole says, ' Miss Kate, you look lonesome at your end of the table, without Doctor Bachune.' I suppose the man is boarding around now, waiting for his baggage. I don't like to lose money, but the worst of it is, I don't like to be made a fool of. He used to sit up so stately, and bow so politely, and smile so blandly, and I had him waited on so assiduously.''

" Who's that coming in the door ?" asked Miss Charity.

" That is Mr. Selwyn, the best guest I ever had. He

seems confined to no regular business. He is good pay, and never grumbles. No ink spots on his table spread, or boot marks on his washstand and bedstead, or spot on his carpet. It is a comfort to have such guests. If you want to be a toad under a harrow, keep a boarding-house.

"You should have heard Dr. Bachune talk about æsthetically, esoterically, and exoterically, and pseudo-dipteral architecture, and thaumaturgia. We had some heavy griddle cakes on the table one morning, and Dr. Bachune remarked that ' their specific gravity was too great for their size ; there was a too great condensation of the cellular tissue.' Mr. Vole always pretended he did not know anything when talking with the doctor, and asked him all sorts of questions.

"I heard Mr. Vole say one day that the doctor would amuse himself so often with the careful analysis and diagnosis of the contents of the tea-pot, laid out as a sort of hortus siccus on his plate. ' This leaf, now,' he would say, ' is fuschia. Observe the serrated edges. That's no tea-leaf— positively poisonous. This now again is privet—yes, you may know by the divisions, panicles, that's no tea-leaf.' I don't believe that all this talk was original with him, he probably got it out of some magazine. But he looked the wisest when he talked about the Bible. He said that was ' an old exploded book.' He said that his creed was ' a creed of no creed.' I wonder what sort of a creed that is ? That ' every therefore must have a wherefore.' Of course it must. Who don't know that ? He got that out of ' Pure Reason,' somebody said. I am sure his reason isn't very pure. I wonder if he got that about the Bible's being exploded out of Pure Reason too. Mercy on us! what are we coming to ? I wouldn't give one leaf of my grandmother's Bible for all the new-fangled ideas in his stuffed head. One would think, to hear men talk at my table about the Bible, that it was a mighty queer book. They get all kind of things out of it. Every queer notion they set up, they pretend to prove from the Bible. I am tired of this cant about *orthodoxy*. One would think, if they didn't know what the word meant, that orthodoxy was the name of some terrible villain, that ought to be hanged, drawn and quartered, for some great crimes, committed with, as the lawyers say, malice aforethought.

"We used to think, when I was a child, it was highly respectable to belong to some orthodox church, but now one would think it was disgraceful to be in such regular standing. What a bugaboo they do make about nothing. Even some young preachers that want to be popular, sprinkle their striking sermons with tirades and invectives against this orthodoxy as if the poor thing were to blame for all the sins and mistakes of the whole Christian world. Time will. come, if they say much more about it, when the subject will be tiresome and common and get old-fashioned, and then I hope they'll let it alone. There is such a rage for startling things. A man will say low, common, coarse things about onions and rat-holes just for effect, to excite a laugh. It is my humble opinion that one coarse idea or a single low image in a sermon, will draw the mind off from fifty beautiful or a hundred serious thoughts. We laugh at the most foolish things, or the mere mention of them in the pulpit; things we wouldn't think of laughing at if said in the street or house; they are not really so witty; we only laugh because they are so out of place and grotesque in the pulpit. We laugh, and we can't help it, to see a round-faced, rosy-cheeked three year oldster walk in with his father's hat, spectacles and great coat on. The inclination to laugh is irresistible, yet there's nothing funny in the hat, nothing amusing in the coat, nor anything comical in the boy, but all together are irresistibly laughable. So in the pulpit, the place for dignified manner, solemn and elevated themes, the great contrast between the place and anything trifling, grotesque, or common, may excite mirth. The best of us laugh to see a 'harmless, necessary cat,' or a quiet, respectable mouse move along through the church aisles. I saw an old sexton once take a dog up and carry it out of church in his arms. The effect was very ludicrous. But I wonder why they do make such a hue and cry now about *white cravats*. I don't see how those white cravats can hurt any body. All the objection I have to them is, they are so much trouble to do up. I think they are certainly becoming. If a butcher can wear his apron, a fireman his hat, a student his badge, if a white cravat is worn at court in full dress, why can't a minister wear one in the pulpit? His office is certainly a dignified one, if the man is what he ought to be—and then, what fun they do make of those poor old puritans. What if they were a little stiff and awkward! We make fun of their old coats and hats, their stiff ways and ridiculous notions, their rush candles. We, enjoying the fruits of their sacrifices, sit by our blazing gas lights and make fun of their old candles. With their toil-worn hands they wrought out the garments of our independence, and made the cradle of liberty for us to rock so lazily in, and they did it all well, too, by the feeble light of their despised candles. If some of these good old puritans could stand by my table now, without being seen, and hear all this twaddle about the Bible, wouldn't they cry out chaff! chaff? Common sense has exploded! What a brainless age this is! There's only a weak drop of truth in this great ocean of nonsense! I believe the whole Bible is inspired from Genesis to Revelations. The moment you begin to allow that one little part of the Bible is not inspired, you drop one stitch in your faith. 'Tis like my knitting ; just drop one stitch in this inspiration, and the whole faith begins to unravel. All these smart progress people begin to set up new foundations for themselves, and they get ever so many new stitches out of this unravelled Bible. Some are dropping stitches out of the Bible all the time. They've ravelled it all out, and in making it over they put such a new face on it, ripping and turning and stretching it so, no one would know it. They make it all over like a coat, till it suits every body's style of thinking. Dr. Bachune says John never wrote the book of John. I wonder by what telegraph he got that news. Did he get that out of his pure reason, too? But Kate Howard said it wasn't *his* pure reason ; it was Kant's. We have so much of mixed up reason, I am glad if some body has come out with some *pure* reason. ' Kant's Pure Reason,'—I'd like to read that book. Kate Howard used to make the doctor believe she did not know much, just to have him enlighten her. One day she asked him if all the beautiful young ladies in old times were named Chloe. He asked her why. She said all the love sonnets and poetical eulogies written by poets to women she had seen in the old English readers and cyclopedias were addressed to Chloe. She made him think she believed all the Shetland wool with which she crochets her mats, was obtained from the Shetland pony. ' Ah, indeed,' said he, ' that must be a woolly horse.' Then Dr. Bachune says so much about Locke on the Understanding. I never liked that Locke for one thing he said, he must have *locked* up *his* understanding when he wrote that 'cry-ing shouldn't be *tolerated* among children.'

"But didn't Mr. Selwyn take Dr. Bachune up nicely? He looked like a minister. Dr. Bachune never said a word more about inspiration. How beautifully Mr. Selwyn talked about those exceeding great and precious promises. I did really like that man; he came out so boldly. The doctor blushed up to his hair, and Mr. Vole looked so full, I ex-pected every minute he would burst out laughing. He says it was so pat—that is *his* word—if he likes any thing it is pat. Where do they get all these words? But there's one thing I never want to hear again; that is that three black crow story. Ignorant as I am, I know that by heart. These crows have crowed enough. I should think some committee of geniuses might scare up some thing that would take the place of that crow story. But I must find out about those miniatures. I'll get talking about relations, etc., and I'll get around to it. I'll ask him how many sis-ters he has."

Sure enough, at the tea table she did ask him, and he dignifiedly replied : " I have no sisters, madam."

Some one, I have forgotten who, told me once that Mrs. Edwards was seen much oftener with the Bible in her hand, after she found out that Mr. Selwyn was a minister.

Some how it did get around the table that Mr. Selwyn was a clergyman. Mrs. Edwards couldn't guess how it got out. One night she was alone in the parlor with Kate Howard talking sociably, and after exciting Kate's curiosity to the highest pitch, she did tell her in " the strictest confi-dence " that one of her guests was a clergyman.

This set Kate to guessing, and very soon she guessed Mr. Selwyn, because he was the only one at the table who hadn't at some time criticised clergymen rather sharply.

But first the secret leaked out, then it was out, and then it spread all over. Mrs. Edwards had found out the fact in such a sly way, she was uneasy lest it should get to Mr. Selwyn's ears, and he suspect that she was a prying, inquis-itive, gossiping woman.

She was old enough to have known long ago that secrets are like books and umbrellas—no one will keep them quite as carefully as ourselves ; that by some kind of law, secrets, like magnetic currents, always move in circles ; you never can find the beginning or end of them—that they always spread as they diverge from the centre of information, and the circles if not hyper*bolas*, are hyper*boles*.

It was too good to keep all alone, so Kate Howard only mentioned it to Mr. Vole, and he promised faithfully he wouldn't breathe a word of it ; and if Mrs. Edwards had gone round the circle like the old game of button, button, who's got my button ?—secret, secret, who's got my secret ? —it would be the answer in the play, " next door neighbor."

There was no use in being provoked with Kate Howard ; she had the best intentions and always looked so good-natured, you couldn't be angry with her ; she knew Mr. Vole would never say any thing about it, of course he would never speak of it, she had as much confidence in him as she had in herself.

It rained one afternoon. Four ladies were in the parlor chatting and crocheting, all except Charity Gouge, who was always working muslin bands, or fixing up head-dresses or discussing the morals and manners of the age. They had been whispering some time, when Miss Charity spoke up. " Why don't he preach if he's a minister ? I don't like to see a watchman deserting the walls of Zion," said she in her solemn sentimental drawl, " but perhaps he's married a rich wife, and has the bronchitis, and can't preach. It is strange how these rich wives affect clergymen's throats. I believe they that wait upon the Lord shall renew their strength," said she in a solemn tone.

" It is a pity you didn't try a little of that yourself," said Miss Kate and her eyes twinkled mischievously. " You are always complaining, it might renew your strength."

Miss Charity was always quoting scripture, and she never got it quite right either. She often spoke of that beautiful verse in the Bible about " that bourne from whence no traveller returns."

" Hush," said Kate Howard, putting her finger on her lip, " there comes Mrs. Edwards, and she won't hear a word against Mr. Selwyn, she thinks he is perfection."

" I haven't said any thing I'm ashamed of, nothing but the truth," said Miss Charity sitting up very straight and looking very dignified.

" Yes," said Kate, " but the truth isn't to be spoken out at all times, we needn't tell all we know."

Mr. Vole often said it was too bad to make a gouge out of charity, he was always saying it was cold as charity, when the thermometer was near zero, no matter how much his prudent mother stepped on his toes, he would say it though Charity sat opposite to him at the table and he knew her hearing was remarkably acute.

" Charity can never be to highly prized in this selfish world," he would say, as he recommended her to his young gentleman friends, " you know ' Charity suffereth long and is kind.' "

CHAPTER XX.

CARLEYN'S TIGER IN A TRAP.

Mr. JAMES VOLE is sitting in Mr. Carleyn's studio, waiting for Mr. Carleyn to come in.   He is humming over these lines—

> " I love sweet features ; I will own
>   That I should like myself
> To see my portrait on a wall,
>   Or bust upon a shelf ;
> But nature sometimes makes one up
>   Of such sad odds and ends,
> It really might be quite as well
>   Hushed up among one's friends."

Mr. Vole had never had any likeness taken of himself— but he was an only son and an only child, so his mother said she must have a portrait of James : something might happen, he was always running into danger, he might break his neck yet, she must have a portrait.

So to gratify her, he had consented, and this was his first sitting.   He said " a profile cut in black" would suit better his style of face.

He thought it would prove a tedious business, but Carleyn had a way of making the time pass very agreeably to his sitters, and they were soon busily talking, and Mr. Vole almost forgot that he was sitting for his portrait.

" I heard Mr. Trap say the other evening at the Academy of Design, Mr. Carleyn," said Mr. Vole, " that he took to himself some of the credit of shaping your destiny and fame as a rising young man and artist."

"A rising young man means a great deal in his mouth," said Carleyn, sarcastically. "It is a favorite phrase of his. He used to mean by it, one who by fraud, pettifogging, sly cunning, secret reaching and over-reaching, gained money, lands, tenements and hereditaments ; one who, by putting himself and others through a course of cunning and deceit, climbed up at last to society's golden roof, and counted there, his increasing pile of shining dollars.

"My destiny," he continued with no little feeling, "would be a ragged, shivering, starving, shadowy, cruel destiny if he had shaped it.

"The word shaped should never be abused by lips like his—he never shaped anything. He has knocked out of shape and symmetry every thing his hard hand hath touched.

"My angel mother taught me when a little boy never to say a cross word when a kind one would do, and when angry to count a hundred before I spoke. This rule I tried to keep.

"There is no art so badly learned, so miserably practised, as that of finding fault. There is not one man in a thousand who does it wisely, kindly or well—and he who is full of faults himself is sure to be watching and improving chances for finding fault in others. He anticipates mistakes, and scolds at a wrong before it is done : he is always on the starboard side of life, straining his eyes to watch and scold, and scare and punish the least floating specks of wrong that may be coming towards him, and to crush an insult before its seed is planted ; he's always gathering clouds to get up a storm, when really the sky is quite comfortably clear. Mr. John Trap was my guardian. I went from my mother's kind care and consistent gentle influence, to John Trap's house. I said to myself, boy as I was and ignorant of human nature, Mr. John Trap is a good lawyer, a successful practical man—so he must have good judgment. Mr. Trap is an educated man ; of course he is a gentleman—dignified, consistent, just. Mr. Trap has a fine position and a liberal education—he is therefore a man of character, and I, as a boy, will acquire some character by being under his influence and watching his example ; and I already began to think of him as a type of manly nobility and a model of manly excellence. Moreover he was a person of fine external appearance, I had often thought as I had seen him standing in a crowd.

" I went to live with him. He was at first pleasant, then civil, and then decent; at last the natural man came out, and he acted himself. I looked at him with wonder and astonishment. He often scared me through and through. Sometimes he would lavish his most complimentary epithets upon me, but if I chanced to be out in the evening three minutes later than half past nine, he would blow me all the way up the two pair of stairs, and I could hear his voice in low thunder dying away in faint echoes after I had closed and locked my door.

" If once in two years he had to get up and let me in, for he never would let me take a night key—if the great John Trap were really thus disturbed, he would get into a terrible rage ; he couldn't have been more excited if his wife had been shot, his child stolen, or his personal property carried off by burglars.

" I was scared at first, but at last I learned to despise the man who had so little control over himself. I used to comfort myself with the thought that as I was not his wife or child, my life-lease with him would soon expire.

" He seemed to think these ' little peculiarities' of his all right—only a part of his dignity and greatness, and now he really boasts of shaping my destiny.

" I think he *has* exercised an influence upon my life. I learned while with him to suspect, to mistrust. Let a boy be deceived once, and he will soon lose some of his faith in human nature. His overbearing tyrannical insolence awoke feelings in me which I knew not before that I possessed. All the indignant manhood within me was aroused. I felt at times as if I would like to see him punished by some despotic power for so outraging all sense of honor and justice. I had such a strong dislike of his stormy, passionate manner, that I had a perfect horror myself of ever being in a passion and losing my self-control. He would seize upon some little mistake or accident, and scold, and scold about it, in every possible shape of scolding ; and if at last the individual scolded defended himself, he would reprove him for getting so excited about such little things. He was always sticking pins into his friends, and then abusing them for feeling so nervous and hurt, and making such a fuss.

" If there was any cross in you, he knew how to bring it out. The cat was more quiet, and hid away from his coming feet. Little John Trap hushed his play and sat quietly in the corner, and Mrs. Trap went fidgetting around for fear some of those little accidents so often occurring ' in the best regulated families,' might disturb John's always ruffled mood, and bring down his thundering anathemas about ' confounded carelessness,' and ' shocking forgetfulness,' showering right and left his complimentary epithets of rascal, scoundrel, villain, scamp, sneak and fool.

" He used to go through the house with a spiritual hammer, hunting out the least corners in character, and knocking them off with sundry flourishes, while he himself is hard all over ; he himself is all corners, and cannot pass through any circle of people without hitting somebody's views, unless they dodge him. He is not a man—he is an animated hammer ; but if anybody suspect him, accuse him, insult him in the least infinitesimal degree—if they show any spunk to him, why he can't tolerate their impudence. He'll put them through—he'll give them a thump and a blow, a curse and a growl. He has a patent right to be ugly—a copyright secured from his father the Devil, as somebody wickedly said. If any of his servants chanced to follow their own inclinations—treat themselves to a little ease, comfort, or pleasure, if they showed any spirit, he would growl and curse, so incensed he would get. Who has a right to be ugly but he ? He never forgets an injury or indignity done to his infallible ugliness—and if a man's conduct don't suit him, how he wishes he could give him a kick or a few shakes.

" If there were a few more such traps sprung in this lower world, we wouldn't have to go to the Ravels for representation of Pandemonium. When his wife married him, she put her conscience in purgatory. To keep him well out of growling, she must be all the time in that intermediate state between right and wrong. If he does come home and find a peg out, or an accident happened, it is all because the girl has not been blown up enough—he'd like to put her through a course of sprouts. His stentorian voice is enough to arouse the dead, and he thinks his voice far preferable to a hundred bells or speaking tubes. If he calls, poor old Bridget's dry bones must quickly stir, or he'll give her a loud essay on slowness. He tells her often her memory is about as long as her nose. He says half a dozen times a day, she is a fool. He always says, if she does not come when he calls, that she is counting her beads or saying her prayers. He was born with the idea that, of course, people ought to know what's what, and to do it, and not make a ' 'twill do' of every thing.

"I wish there was a law against this finding fault, except under certain limitations and restrictions ; for instance : no harsh fault finding more than ten times a day by the same person. I wish there was some clause in the constitution, by which these pounding, thumping, aggravating, irritating, blowing up, knocking down, rocky characters, could be put on spiritual limits.

"Little impulsive, angry children, can be spanked and shut up, and punished in sundry ways, but these grown up human tigers are lawlessly at large, trampling down green leaves of sympathy, crushing fragrant flowers in woman's heart; insulting and ruthlessly killing with their caustic words, and fierce red-hot invectives, all the freshness and beauty of innocent and light-hearted childhood.

"Mr. Trap actually expects his child to be vastly more self-controlled, better behaved, milder, quieter than he, with his mature reason, and enlightened judgment ever is. Why, if John Trap comes home in one of his tiger moods, the child is actually afraid to say boo. I have seen the child after one of his father's unnatural shakes, look up with appealing tearful eyes to some invisible Help—as if to say, 'I never heard of such things in the land from whence I came,' and Mrs. Trap goes around all day and every day, with an ache in her heart. 'Oh, dear !' she whispers as she kneels at night by his little bed ; 'Oh, dear, my boy—my bright beautiful boy can never be a christian if he watches and imitates his earthly father.'

"Her life is a martyr's—the child is her child—and that tiger is her husband, a queer kind of a guardian he is, to love, cherish, protect a child precocious in mind, in heart— and a woman, all heart, sensibility and refinement, and then she thinks how a few brief years ago, he sat by her side, an importunate, ardent lover, with his soft low words, so skill- fully modulated ; and he would like her still as much as he with his fierce nature can like, if she would let him be as ugly as he chooses to his child and dependants. What is it to her how he treats others, if he uses *her* well.

"Two years I lived at his house, and I wouldn't trust a cat in his hands, even a ' harmless, necessary ' cat.

"Mr. Douglass is a lawyer, too, but he is the soul of honor. I would rather be Mr. Douglass's cat than Mr. Trap's wife, and I would far rather be a parish mouse than John Trap's child.

"I lived with him two years, and now I would be choked if I had to breathe the same air with him. I never knew a man before, that I wanted to cage up in iron bars until he would promise in the presence of witnesses, to be good and keep the peace. I have seen him when angry, look at his wife as if he would swallow her; and his child, as if he would annihilate him.

"When he gets enraged, the least thing excites him. I believe he would face a whole regiment of angels, and tell them to go to thunder. If I see a man get in a rage once, I never like him as well afterwards; but if he gets in a rage habitually, I haven't a shadow of respect for him.

"If you will come into my studio alone some time, I will show you the portrait of Mr. Trap in one of these stormy moods. I call it Tiger. I wouldn't have him see it for any thing. Dawn is my ideal of sweetness and gentleness, but Tiger is the opposite node of humanity, its lowest ebb of depravity. I think the two pictures a startling contrast. Were a stranger to see the portrait of Trap, I should call it to him *Midnight*, but I always think of it as Tiger, a human tiger.

"All the little property left by my mother in Mr. Trap's hands I lost. He pretended he had charges against my father's estate for law services. He presented a long bill of costs; it took all the property to cancel it, but I shouldn't like him any better as a man if he had made me a present of several thousands, instead of explaining away my little all —to which I believe I was justly entitled

"When he talks of sympathy, I always feel as if the word was abused. I have heard it reported that in Nova Zembla and in Greenland men's words are frozen in the air, and are never heard until a thaw. I am sure in the congealing atmosphere of John Trap's soul, words of sympathy are *always frozen*, and are never heard, unless in some January thaw, when they fall on the ear cold, chilling and disagreable, and never steal on the heart in gentle, genial April benedictions.

"While studying law Mr. Trap taught school. Over the door was printed in large letters, 'English and Classical school.' Those who lived near could frequently hear suppressed cries, sobs and moans. It was Trap's habit to beat with a rattan the hand of any boy who missed four answers in geography. The reverberations of the heavy blows could be distinctly heard in the neighboring houses, and the sound was occasionally varied by the sharp tones of Trap's coarse voice. One of his scholars is a man now. I finished his portrait last week, and he can't mention Trap's name with calmness. He said he knew his geography perfectly in the morning when he left home, but so poor was his memory, and so great his dread of Trap's rattan, he was sure to miss. He dreaded going to school. He said some of the boys looked on in shuddering sympathy, and others acquired coarseness of feeling and brutality as they watched this human tiger as he cudgelled some mother's carefully reared and ingenuous boy. What taste for knowledge such a man inspires! What true nobility of character fosters. This old scholar of Trap's says if Trap went to Heaven, he was sure he never wanted to go there; and the very name of school is hateful to him since he first attended Trap's English and Classical school. I often wish I could find some Nepenthe to enable me to forget all those weary, unhappy hours of my life at Trap's.

"But what is to become of all these fault-finding John Traps in Heaven, if any of them ever squeeze in there? They may find some little claim to steal in by. If they get in Heaven, it seems as if they would need a little extension-room done off on purpose for them. If I had known only such men as John Trap, I should think the world a very wicked world—but I have seen and known Douglass and Selwyn. Douglass is a conscientious lawyer. There is need enough for more such—and Mrs. John Trap is a real Christian. What a match that was! There was a terrible loss in that wedding. Mrs. Trap would make any upright and reasonable man happy, but ice and sunshine might as well be wedded as Mr. John Trap and she. What does make such scamps get such lovely wives?"

"I met an old lady the other night," said Mr. Vole, "who

told me she had helped you in your early career. She thought you took a different turn while with her. She was glad things had shaped around so that you have made out well after all."

"I know who that old lady is," said Carleyn, with a mischievous twinkle in his eye. "She is always talking about things '*shaping round*.' She wears green ribbon on her bonnet, carries a reticule, always looks over her spectacles, and says, 'I hope you are well.' She always smiles, and such a smile I never saw on any other face. Her name is Miss Prudence Potter. I used to called her Aunt Prudence when I went to school to her in the country. She taught me to pronounce every syllable in Con-stan-ti-no-ple distinctly, to dot all my *i's* and cross every *t*, repeat verbatim, 'the busy bee,' and 'unfading hope,' and 'full many a flower,' and write without blot in my copy-book, 'many men of many minds, many birds of many kinds.' Proverbs innumerable fell from her lips. She tried to make me repeat without pausing or stammering, the whole shorter catechism, as she kept me standing on a crack, till I wished the catechism had been *shorter*. She had an odd way of explaining the Bible. She used to say to us little boys she wanted to make us understand the plan of salvation. She was always talking about that.

"She had an old blue pitcher with a long established crack in the handle and a piece out of the end of the spout. One day when we had school up stairs, while the school-room below was being fixed, she sent me for some water. I started with this pitcher in my hands. I stepped on a stone at the top stair, and slipped all the way down stairs, landing at the bottom with bruised shoulders and aching side, almost breaking my neck, but with unharmed pitcher. Miss Prudence, hearing the noise, came out and screamed at the top of the stairs, 'Mercy, Frank! *have you* broken THAT PITCH-ER ?' 'No,' said I, 'but *I wish I had.*' Whenever I think of the terrible risk of that contemptible old pitcher, I give an indignant grunt, and still I say '*but I wish I had.*' During my first attempt at picture taking she used to say, 'Now, Frank, don't you think you might better never thought of making pictures ? Don't you think it's kinder foolish for you to try ? I *hope* you'll succeed, but I'm afraid you've mistaken your calling; and then if you are going to do anything in the world to get beforehand, you know it is time for you to set about it.' And then she'd take her knitting and go off to spend the afternoon with aunt Sally, and they would talk me all over, and both sigh and groan over Frank, and shake their wise heads, and wish he might do well, but if he had only taken some *regular* business, or even learned a good trade, he might save up a little and settle down in life, 'Settle down in life!' Isn't that a phrase! 'Settle down!' 'I don't want to settle down,' I used to say, 'I want to rise *higher*,' and when the first picture was done, and well done, the first hand to grasp my own with cordial cheer was a stranger's; while Aunt Prudence still said, 'Well now, Frank, think of all it's cost you! How much time you've taken, and how little bread and butter it has brought you. You might have had a few acres all cleared by this time, and a snug house and a barn on it, and a cow and a pig of your own.'

"But that picture. I couldn't tell her how it cleared away acres of obstacles on my onward path, how the troublesome brushwood, hitherto mountain high around me, burned up and vanished away, and an inward voice, stronger than all Miss Prudence's loudest repetition of 'A bird in the hand is worth two in the bush,'—louder than all her pitiful 'Mercies!' urged me on, and my heart said, 'This is the way, walk ye in it.' I never shall forget Prudence's last advice to me when I left home to come to the city. 'Well,' said she, 'Frank, you are sure of a good living on the farm, you'd better "let well enough alone." ' 'O, said I, 'Aunt Prudence,

> 'The better never should grow weary,
> But always think of better and fulfill it.'

> 'High, inaccessible, let all my life
> Be a continual aiming at that mark.'

" ' Frank,' said she, looking over spectacles and shaking her head, ' you'll find, after fiddling away your time awhile, that this poetry, like love, is all *fol de-rol.*'

" But," said Carlcyn, " I have been successful beyond my highest expectations. Orders have come to me from all quarters. But if you'll come in to-morrow, I'll show you my tiger—a 'Tiger in a Trap.' "

What a jubilee there would be if all the fault-finders could be banished for one year! What bounding hearts and beating pulses! What elastic steps—what sunshiny homes—what active Bridgets! How the doctor's shadow on the hearthstone would grow small by degrees, and the nurse's attentions beautifully less. What a fall there would be in the price of pills and powders, blisters and plasters! Wouldn't the little folks have a grand time for once—talk and laugh as loud as they want, without being interrupted, at each new burst of fun, with " Johnny, I'm surprised!" Wouldn't they play stage-coach and rail-road with the chairs, build houses with old books, hunt up unmolested all the old strings to play horse with? Wouldn't they laugh right out, even at the table, if they felt very funny? And if any great pleasure excited them, wouldn't they hop around enthusiastically, and tell about it, without anybody's exclaiming, " Don't holler so, Johnny—we are not all deaf!" and have always to be told " that little children should be seen and not heard." These little boys are kicked and cuffed around because they are only boys, and if they stand still to see what is going on, they are told they are always getting in the way.

Trouble kills, yes it kills, it stabs, it pierces! Many mortal headaches are brought on by finding fault—many a disease, baffling the doctor's skill, many a valuable life ended, many a heart broken, many a widow shrouded in weeds, many an orphan wandering motherless, through finding fault. Yet who ever heard of its doing anybody any good? Who knows how full of sorrow the heart already is? Who knows if their finding fault may not add the overflowing drop?

Hath ever human chronicle recorded one consumptive cured, one headache soothed, heart healed, hope brightened, life lengthened, or criminal reformed, by finding fault?

'Tis poison, sure and slow, administered in homeopathic doses, hour by hour, to suffering, jaded humanity, the effect stealing like small doses of arsenic in the framework of the heart, and making life intolerable.

Many a person can do nothing but find fault. It is a habit—a passion; but when the last mortal lips are sealed, the last mortal eyes closed, the last heart stilled, may those divine lips say to many a scolded, stricken, yet redeemed spirit, " Neither do I condemn thee, go and sin no more."

How can we kneel at the eternal throne, and ask forgiveness for our ceaseless sinning, if we cannot utter, from humble hearts, that most beautiful of all petitions, "Forgive us our trespasses, as we forgive those who trespass against us." While we harshly chide another for little faults, can we not read this startling thesis on the door of conscience, "For if ye forgive not men their trespasses, neither will your Heavenly Father forgive you your trespasses."

CHAPTER XXII.

NEPENTHE ON EXHIBITION.

"Oh la belle, la noble destinee d'avancer toujours vers la perfection, sans rencontrer jamais le terme de ses progres."—ANCILLON.

EVERYBODY went to the Academy of Design that year, and so of course Miss Charity Gouge went. She was growing very near-sighted. She was armed with eye-glass, bouquet and curls, and looked as well as she could in her youthful pink hat and stylish velvet mantilla. She always wore white kids, and if possible a green dress. She had a green moire antique, a green brocade, a green cashmere robed, everything was green to suit her taste.

Mr. Vole said, "Charity always looked green. Everybody knew you couldn't see much of charity out in the world, so it couldn't be used to the ways of society."

Mr. Vole was always punning—he couldn't help it. Many of his puns were very good and bright. Nobody who knew him could help liking him. Nobody ever got angry with him.

Miss Charity, Miss Kate Howard, and Mrs. Edwards were standing before one picture.

Since Selwyn's visit to the studio, Carleyn had painted another ideal, more beautiful than Dawn. No description of ours can do it justice. One must stand before it to feel the magic of its beauty, and breathe the spell of its loveliness. It was the gem of the Academy, and everybody stopped before it, as if enchanted. The picture was in the first gallery, and was marked "Nepenthe, No. 126. F. E. Carleyn, A."

It was the graceful figure of a maiden. All but the face

seemed shrouded in a misty veil. The tearless eyes looked
forward as if in eager expectation into the clear blue sky,
mantling with the first blush of sunrise. In her right hand
she held a goblet, sparkling with diamonds. A radiant
aureola crowns the brow of the maiden, while around the
brim of the goblet play wreathing circles of dazzling light.
The robe is girded by a rainbow, and a rainbow spans the
aureola over her head. She stands on the shore of a raging
sea, yet the turf beneath her feet is sown with emeralds and
enamelled with hearts' ease, and before her rests in innocence a snowy dove ; behind her, are mountains of angry
clouds, which her left hand, slight and delicate as it seems,
presses back ; beneath the clouds rolls and rages a stormy
sea, dashing its angry waves against the trail of her robe,
whose folds in front are bordered with amaranthine light.
She seems forgetful of the angry clouds and raging sea, as
she gazes intently into the sunlight beyond, while from the
ruby scroll around the goblet, flash in crimson and carmine
glory the letters of the magic word, " Nepenthe."

You couldn't catch Miss Gouge in any ignorance. If she
didn't know what a thing meant, she would put on a wise
face, and keep very silent, and go home and look in the Dictionary, or find out in some other sly way. She never
would ask any one to enlighten her ignorance. But Kate
Howard stood looking at the picture, and at the name on the
scroll, with a puzzled expression in her face, as if she knew,
and yet she didn't know what was the real design of the
artist. Mr. Vole came up and stood before the picture, and
she turned and said,

"Mr. Vole, who is Nepenthe ? Was there ever such a
person ? The picture is all sunshine and beauty *before*, and
shadow and storm *behind*. It means something—I'm sure
I don't know, I'm such a little dunce."

" Nepenthe is a remarkable and expressive word—most
comprehensive, most significant," said Mr. Vole, standing
as erect as possible, straightening his collar, adjusting his
cravat, and clearing his throat, and imitating exactly Doctor
Bachune's wise manner and labored enunciation. " Nepenthe is a Greek word, or rather a compound of two Greek
words, *ne*, not, and *penthos*, grief. There is a kind of magic
potion, mentioned by Greek and Roman poets, which was
supposed to make persons forget their sorrows and misfor-

tunes. We moderns," he added, with another throat-clearing, " we moderns use it figuratively, to express a remedy."

" A second Daniel, a second Daniel," said Kate, laughing, " much obliged to you, doctor, you have very lucidly enlightened the fathomless profundity of my incomparably opaque ignorance. I was partially aware that it was something resembling forgetfulness, but I cherished only au adumbrant idea of the real intent of the meaning of the artist's design, in the uniquely original and mysteriously marvellous conception. How much more significant the word Nepenthe than Lethe—

> By whose bright water's magic stream,
> I oft would rest and gladly dream,
> That blest oblivion's pall were cast,
> O'er all my sad and troubled past.

But I'd rather have one quaff of this Nepenthe, than the whole river of Lethe. I could drink Nepenthe and count over my old joys. Very few of us would like to forget all the past.

> For while our thoughts we backward cast,
> We'd grateful be for joy-gemmed past.

Kate knew Mr. Vole never puzzled his head much about the Greek of a thing, and she guessed he'd been asking somebody some questions; but assuming his natural tone again he said, " The picture is really full of meaning; that goblet containing the Nepenthe is made of diamonds, and scrolled with ruby, because these are the most precious of stones, and Nepenthe would be the most valued of potions could we obtain it. The most highly prized varieties of ruby are the crimson and carmine, so you notice these shades in the scroll. The figure stands on the turf enamelled with heart's ease, and the dove is in front, to show that when sorrows and sins are forgotten, our souls might rest in heart's ease and innocence, while our life would be girdled and spanned over by the rainbow promise, that sorrow should overwhelm us no more, and with tearless eyes as we hold this precious cup we could ever be looking out for the sunrise of dawning hopes and the culminating of rising joy, while as with the touch of a light hand we could press behind us billows and clouds."

" I wish, Miss Kate," said Mr. Vole, sadly, " some of this

old Greek poetry were true. I'd give my right arm," he added, " for one good drink of this Nepenthe. Then my sins and troubles would be in the circle of perpetual occultation ; and my spirits would be as far from the pole of depression as any true elevating joy is now above my life's horizon. My past sorrows form a circle of ·perpetual apparition. They are ghosts, spectres, visible spirits."

" Why, Mr. Vole," said Kate, suddenly, " I thought you never had any sober thoughts."

" I do sometimes," said he, " when I read some poem or see a picture like this. I've been here every day for a week to look at this picture. I never had a sober thought in my head until I heard a sermon on self-denial, some years ago, and I will candidly say there hasn't been a day since, that it hasn't come into my mind. It was a sermon by Prof. Henry."

" I don't see much in *that* picture," said Miss Gouge, looking up to them as they were talking. " Who is Carleyn ? I never heard of him before ; he can't be much of an artist of any note."

" I heard of him," said Mrs. Edwards, " where I first saw you, Miss Gouge, in that little village, where we spent the summer, 'twas twelve years ago last June. I remember a friend of yours telling me that evening we were together, at a party where they had such a gay time, that you had just come of age, and you were going to travel. Who'd think it was so long since then—and Mrs. Edwards was there with me then, and you and he danced together, and young Carleyn, he was a mere boy then, said you were the belle of the evening.

" Frank I think his mother called him, was then a boy of fourteen. He was handsome and diffident. He made a good deal of talk in the neighborhood even then. I never saw finer eyes, and his hair was black and glossy—he had a pale face. I've often thought that some souls get into the wrong bodies, bodies that were never made for them, but Carleyn's soul and body were made for each other, they fit nicely ; some clergyman said of him, when he was about nineteen, he was too handsome to be a Christian, but that was a foolish speech I think.

" His father tried to make a farmer of him, but the boy would steal off after flowers, or sit down on the river's bank and watch the shadows of the trees in the water. He would make a picture of every pretty thing he saw, and they say there was not a chip on his father's farm that had not a face or eyes, nose, or mouth on it. He couldn't make a farmer of him because he wouldn't stick to it, so he sent him off to make him a clerk—but before he knew it, he'd be taking pictures of his fellow clerks all over the ledger. His employer sent word to his father that the boy's mind was evidently not on that business ; so Frank came home again and they tried to make a tailor of him, but that wouldn't do.

"One day his father called him to go on an errand, but he was nowhere to be found—so he went up softly into Frank's room, and there was Frank finishing off his mother's portrait. It was really a wonderful likeness, though done with rough materials. The surprised father went down stairs and into his field again, and never said a word—but it wasn't long before he had *his* portrait taken.

"His mother died when he was quite young, in that little cottage at the foot of the mountain. I remember just how it looked when I used to ride by, and stop at Timothy Titus's, and that was long before Ernest Titus died.

"If Frank's mother could only have lived to have known of her son's celebrity ; but she knew before he died that he would surely be an artist, and she helped him all she could. Before she died he had sent a painting on to some exhibition, and he got a prize for it. She knew he would succeed, and she taught him early to fear God. He is said to be as conscientious as he is gifted, which is a rare thing in these days.

"'Tis a false notion which people have, that genius must be erratic ; but it is too true that many of this class are not practical Christians. Yet it is a great mistake to say that devoted piety is not found combined with great ability. I know it is a rare combination, and I acknowledge great reverence for a man who is a true Christian, and great and gifted too. If a man becomes distinguished, he is too apt to be so conceited that it sticks out all over him."

"This picture," said Kate Howard, "is unlike anything in the whole exhibition. Carleyn says it is the only picture he has taken which suits him at all, and he really couldn't have had a better name for it. If it were the face of a real woman, she might feel highly complimented on becoming so celebrated—and if it is an ideal, it does seem as if he must have caught the expression from some living face."

"I never shall forget," said Mrs. Edwards, "how that proud Mrs. Pridefit treated Carleyn's mother when she was in the country—as if she was of no account. Mrs. Pridefit was full of her high notions, and now she has had her portrait taken by Carleyn, and is rather proud of it too."

"Yes," said Kate, "I have heard that Mrs. Pridefit quite ignored that little unpretending Mrs. Carleyn, while in the country."

"Now that he has become a celebrated artist all the girls are setting their caps for him," said Mrs. Edwards. "Florence Elliott is really in love with him."

"Hush!" whispered Kate, with her finger on her lip— "there he is now, and that is Florence Elliott by his side. She always has a bevy of gentlemen around her. I have seen him here three times this week."

"I don't see anything very beautiful about *her*," said Miss Gouge, opening as wide as possible her very small eyes and raising her glass. "Her eyes are too large. I never admired her style of beauty—it is unfeminine."

"All the gentlemen admire her," said Kate, mischievously.

"There isn't one gentlemen in a hundred who is any judge of female beauty," said Charity.

"Well," said Kate, "I hope Mr. Carleyn will suit himself. If he likes Miss Elliott, I'm satisfied. You don't often find a couple where both are equally agreeable. You'll often see a man that is cross as a bear, and a woman gentle as an angel. Carleyn would certainly make a good husband. His friends seem to like him as well as the world. There are many prizes in life's lottery, and some people are always drawing them. Florence Elliott may be one of these fortunate ones.

"I have heard that she has said she never failed in any thing she undertook—but no match suits everybody. But who is that tall, hollow-eyed woman looking so steadily at that picture? She looks as if some new idea had dawned upon her mind—and she is muttering, too : do look at her! don't she look queer? She is the only plainly dressed woman here."

"Oh. she is nobody," said Miss Charity Gouge, going on

with the conversation. " I am sure I don't want Carleyn
myself. I never would marry a genius; but as he is a professor, and has in the eyes of the world set his heart on divine things, and renounced its pomps and vanities, he must
of course seek first the kingdom of heaven. I don't see
how his conscience or Christian vows can ever allow him to
marry such a light-minded, frivolous girl as that conceited,
intolerable Florence Elliott."

" Such men often do marry those who are not professing
Christians," said Kate mischievously, " and for myself, I
would rather live with some agreeable sinners, as you call
them, than some crabbed Christians."

" The directions of the Bible are very explicit on that
point," said Miss Charity. " ' Be not conformed to the
world, be not unequally yoked together with unbelievers.'
I have had reason to think much on this subject from my
own experience, but I am thankful that grace enabled me to
keep firm."

Kate smiled—she was thinking of what Mr. Vole said
about the gentlemen always trying to get rid of the demands
of charity.

" But do see that impudent beggar woman," said Miss
Gouge. " She has actually stepped on my dress. Just see
what a horrid spot of mud this is, and every thing spots this
dress—even water. I wish there were some law to keep off
these troublesome beggars; they are so annoying they ought
not to be allowed to go at large. There are so many benevolent associations for their relief, none of them need suffer;
and then they can surely be made comfortable in the poorhouse. For my part I would have no objection to going
there myself, if Providence should see fit to deprive me of
my present resources, and I should be contented in any situation in which He thought proper to place me."

" I couldn't," said Kate frankly; " as I now feel I should
be a most miserable being if I were poor. It does very
well for you, Miss Charity, so richly clad and luxuriously
fed, with plenty of money in the bank to pay to-day's debts,
and buy to-morrow's comforts, to talk about being contented
in poverty. Poverty looks very different to you, as you
look at it with your glass, through draperied windows, from
what it would if you were hungry and barefooted, walking
the streets with no home in prospect but that ' comfortable '

poorhouse. As to the poorhouse, ' distance lends enchantment to the view' of that mansion of contentment, that safe and respectable retreat for homeless paupers—where. if Providence should mark out the way, so many affluent ladies say they should be so grateful and willing to go and be provided for. I know they don't mean it—their aristocratic heads could not, without murmur, pass under those lowly portals.

" I have often wished I could give the world one good shake, just for a week or so, and see these contented millionaires and miserable paupers change places. There would be far more groans and growls in that comfortable poorhouse than you'll hear in any respectable asylum for lunatics in a month."

. " I know," said Miss Charity, " that I have learned with the apostle, ' in whatsoever state I am, to be content.' I don't think poverty the worst evil that can befall one. I know I could follow the leadings of Providence—but most all poverty is brought on by idleness."

" Yes," said Kate, in a low tone, " it is always idleness ; so the rich say as they fold their lazy hands, and lisp out with indolent tongues, ' 'tis nothing but idleness—they deserve it.'

> " Aye ! idleness ! the rich folks never fail
> To find some reason why the poor deserv
> Their miseries."

" Yes," muttered Miss Charity, drawing her mantilla closely around her, and holding more tightly her well-filled purse in which was the whole amount of her last year's annuity in solid gold—" it is astonishing how little we can get along with if we only think so, and these poor people need very little. The real wants of life are very few," thought she, as she entered a large store to purchase a new opera glass—for hers was a little less elegant than the one she had seen Mrs. Elliott have, and she fancied she would like one of that sort. She also purchased a new breakfast set, of jewelry, ear-rings, sleeve buttons and brooch. " How economical I am getting," thought she. as she gathered up the folds of her velvet dress, which was of the heaviest and costliest material.

CHAPTER XXII.

MADAME FUTURE.

FLORENCE ELLIOT reads in the morning paper :

AN ASTONISHING ASTROLOGER—MADAM FUTURE.—This highly gifted lady is the seventh daughter, and was born with a gift to tell the past, present, and future events of life. All who wish a speedy marriage, may call soon and see her invoke the powers of her wonderful science. She will tell you all you wish to know, even your very thoughts, and show you the likeness of your intended husband. She has just returned from Europe, where she had unparalleled success. No charge if not satisfied."

Florence Elliot was soon at the office of the far-famed and learned Madam Future. The room was dimly lighted, and quite heavily draped in black, and the light fell rather on the face of Florence than on the astrologer, gipsy, magician, or whatever she was. She was closely veiled.

"Lady, do you want your fortune told ?" said she, addressing Florence.

" You advertised, and to amuse an idle hour I have come. Curiosity drew me hither. Can you read the future ? Here is my hand," said Florence, as she held out her small, delicate, jewelled hand, and a piece of gold.

" I see nothing in your hand—no destiny—there are not many crosses there," said the woman. " Fortune favors you—you were born rich—you will die rich. You are an only child. You have been, until recently, the only young person living in that house. Your father was killed in battle. Your were born on Southern soil. That accounts for your blood and temperament, as hot as the climate. Only a week ago you stood by the mirror, and you said to yourself, ' I am young and beautiful, my hair is glossy, my eyes are bright, my lashes long and heavy, my form is symmetrical, and my step elastic. But one thing I must have.' With all these charms, you are not happy. I see it in your restless eye, flushed cheek and impatient step. I see it as you walk in the street, and when you promenade Broadway so often at three o'clock. One image sits at your heart— one form hovers in your dreams—one hope is burning in your life, and one fear tortures you lest that hope be not gratified."

She took her glass, looking in it awhile, and muttering. At length she speaks:

"I watched your star: It has been slowly rising, clear and bright, climbing up the western sky. I turn the glass, and far off in the dim distance, I see a little pale star. From the western sky it rises, appears clear and bright, disappears, pales and vanishes. That little star appears again, slowly rises, and follows in your path."

"Tell me, witch, wizard, sybil, whatever you are, is that a star of magnitude? Is it a meteor only to fade, a planet to wander, or will it be a fixed star in my path?"

"What is your path, lady?"

"That is for you to tell," said Florence. "I came not here to reveal, but to learn.".

"The future is always veiled. I can only see it through misty clouds and shadowy outlines. I can see but one obstacle in your path that must be crushed. I cannot tell you now the end—come again, and I will cast your horoscope more fully."

"Have you no charms?" said Florence.

"I have nothing to cause love. Your charms are already all-sufficient, but even these I can heighten. You shall become radiantly beautiful, as beautiful as an artist's dream."

Florence started. Did this strange woman really know that the dream of her life was of an artist?

"No man is insensible to personal beauty," said the woman, going behind a curtain, and bringing out a vial, saying, "This is no love charm, no spell, but this I give you shall heighten your already peerless beauty. I will give it you in minute doses. It is a tonic and alterative—is sometimes given by oriental physicians, and is remarkable for its wonderful influence upon the skin. I call it *Hidri*. It may be swallowed daily for years, and no harm be done. It will give plumpness to the figure, clearness and softness to the skin, beauty and freshness to the complexion. It will improve the breathing, so that steep heights can be easily climbed; it will heighten your charms—your complexion will be clear and blooming, your figure full and round. You must take half a grain two or three times a week, in the morning, fasting, till you get accustomed to it, carefully increasing the dose. You will soon breathe with greater ease, and your voice will have greater compass and flexibility. But once commence it, you must continue the practice through life, and the results are sure and satisfactory. The dose must be adapted to the constitution and habit of body ; but of this I will tell you more hereafter. I myself have taken it for thirty years. I take two grains at each dose.''

Florence looked through a long glass, to see the object she loved best. She was a little frightened and excited, but sure enough, at the other end of the glass there was a picture of Frank Carleyn's face, distinct, vivid, and life-like.

The globe, charms, parchments, hieroglyphics, heavy curtains, dark-looking bottles, the artist's portrait, and the half-veiled face of the woman, bewildered and excited Florence, and she went home in a strange, unhappy mood, more anxious and determined than ever to go again to the consulting office of the far-famed and learned Madame Future.

As Florence passed out, a lady closely-veiled passed in. Her form, and something in her walk seemed familiar to Florence, but the lady seemed anxious to pass out of sight, and escape observation ; and Florence was so desirous of preserving her own incognito, that she dared not to look back at the lady, to guess or wonder if possible who she might be—and yet there was something so familiar about her.

CHAPTER XXIII.

CARLEYN'S JOURNAL—SUBJECT, MATRIMONY.

> " Of all the myriad moods of mind
> That through the soul come thronging,
>   What one is e'er so dear, so kind,
> So beautiful as longing !"—LOWELL.

" BEFORE I marry, I must know a woman thoroughly—so Selwyn tells me. A woman may be bewitching at opera, fête, or ball, but be no soother or sympathizer to come home to when weary. Before an engagement is formed, solemn and binding as any engagement ought to be, the every-day type of a woman's life should be known. How she treats servants, how much respect, consideration, kindness she shows other members of her family—how she consoles the poor and the sick and the unfortunate. Many women get up sets of charms for public levees, soirées and receptions, hops and musicals. Yet a true wife is a diamond, shining brighter in life's daily rough friction—so the old book says. If I only visit a lady when she expects me, I can't find her out—so says my mentor, Selwyn. She can much easier learn *my* taste, habits and disposition. A business or professional man can never quite hush up his faults among his friends. If he is dishonorable, or ill-tempered, some lady will find it out—she may have some brother or friend who can easily hear of his peculiarities. A man in the business world can't be so walled about with conventionalities as to prevent sundry revealings and multifarious disclosures. Somebody will hear somebody say that he is arbitrary, tyrannical, selfish, passionate, dishonest, immoral, or avaricious—if he really is so, it will leak out. The real man is chiselled out in society with strongly marked features. His tailor and his shoemaker, even while the one takes his measure and the other makes a last for his sole, may get some idea of the spiritual dimensions and the shape and cast of his real soul.

" Men's daguerreotypes and portraits often take more easily than women's—their features are usually more strongly marked. So on the canvas of society, many a man's character is clearly drawn and fully revealed, from some rough and truthful sketch, taken by anxious, watching eyes, in his counting-house, office or studio. But a woman shut up in a temple of home apart, is brought out on festal days, decked with flowers and wreathed with smiles, to receive as her right, the incense of praise and flattery. How easy to robe herself with the magic of loveliness, attracting the admiration of man, and piqueing the ambition of rival women. If she be as peerlessly beautiful as Florence Elliott, how many captivated hearts and worshipful knees will bow at her elegant shrine.

" Selwyn keeps talking to me about behind the stage, as if a woman when in company like the figures in show windows was out on exhibition looking her prettiest.

" 'Tis true you find out what the actor is, and what part he takes, and how much he drills for the public, if you get behind the stage. What a pity that in love as in law, the *attachment comes first* and the *judgment afterwards.*

" It is a serious business to get a wife—but I don't mean,

on account of the risk, to live alone always. One does not want oneself always for one's company through all life's long, lonely evenings, and dull, rainy days.

"Let me sketch my ideal of a wife ; but somebody says no man ever marries his ideal ; but then a man is quite apt to have an ideal walking about his soul like a beautiful vision, half shadow, half substance, and it is a comfort to a man to have an ideal wife, even if you never marry her. It does him good to sit by the fire at nightfall, after contact with rough men and dream of her. It is pleasant to sit and think how Mrs. Carleyn would look in a blue silk dress, how she will smile, what she will say, and how she will have my dressing-gown all ready when I come at night. "

Carleyn writes one or two pages more about his ideal wife, and falls asleep. The soft light of the shaded gas lingers upon his open journal, and if you are not out of patience, reader, we will just read over what he has written. 'Tis a page from his heart, and unless we read it while he is asleep, we are quite sure we never will see it.

"My wife must appreciate me for what I am. If I think deeply, feel strongly, study profoundly, talk eloquently, I could never be satisfied with a wife who couldn't judiciously appreciate my highest efforts in tongue, pen or life. Should I have a beautiful thought, and my wife know it not, or knowing care not, or only amiably echo what Frank says is all well and good, because Frank says it, I should soon feel an indifference for her.

"If she be not always reigning queen in the realm of my thoughts, she may silently, quietly, walk there, inhaling the perfume of every flower therein planted, admiring every gem therein set, and know enough of that complicated microcosm, a man's world, if there is a jar to keep quiet, but ever near enough to give sympathy, cheer encouragingly, when the storm cloud mood is over. A footfall disturbs, at times, man's solitary moods, an echo irritates. My ideal wife does not demonstrate over every demonstration I make, but she must know enough to see clearly if I draw correctly, define correctly, or fill out perfectly. She needn't be able to dig with me among Greek and Latin roots, but keep the air around pleasant, the sky bright, so that I may dig more comfortably.

"No glossy hair, no ruby lips, no glowing complexion,
nor even agreeable manners, can supply the demand of long,
lonely, rainy days, anxious nights, business failures, losses,
crosses. I must have a wife with a soul. But how is it,
when I sketch my ideal, it seems like a spiritual crayon portrait. I think of deeds, tones, words, thoughts, feelings, af-
fections, but I give no color to eyes, hair or lips. I think
not of the temple, but of its fair occupant, who ever lingers
around the shrine of my inmost heart.

"But what shape will this ideal take? Who in this wide
world of mortal women is to share the artist's destiny? If
I am to have a wife of my youth, she is now living on the
earth. Love her, and pray for her weal, says the proverb
poet. How can I love her, whom I have not seen? But I
do love my ideal wife most tenderly. She is a picture in
my soul without frame. I'll hang it up in the private gallery of my heart, and look around and see if I can find a
frame to suit it. Such a picture would look well in an elegant frame.

"'Twill be hard to find one ornate and polished enough—
but they say the best souls have often the plainest frames.
What a beautiful frame that Florence Elliott has! Beautiful, polished, elegant. There is hardly a line or hue you
would alter. Nature has made her with faultless frame, and
she seems every day to me more beautiful, and I do like to
look at a beautiful face. It is a pleasure to gaze at Florence
Elliott's peerless loveliness.

"Tossed on the billowy surges of this restless life, the
only earthly rest is the pillowing the aching heart, sea-sick
with life's rolling, foaming motion, on a heart that loves you.
There is not in all the world a heart so plunged in life's
styx, that has not some loophole or crevice, arch or doorway,
skylight or hatchway, where love may not look through,
creep under, steal in, or climb up, or twine around. Some
times he comes like a fluttering bird asking for crumbs.

"We are all, at some time of our lives, Columbus-like,
seeking for this new world of love. We long to plant our
tired feet on this terra firma incognita. As we sail out on
the stream of life, there come floating to us little green
sprigs of sympathy, and some carefully carved memento of
affection. We know that some heart is carving out some

where a home for us, where we may walk in and rest when weary with life's hot heat and heavy burden.

"Who is now fitting a home for my heart?—what hand waiting to clasp mine?—what voice will say, ' for better, for worse ; for richer, for poorer, in sickness, in health.' This is the charm of the tie.

"What life is ever complete without love ? It casts a shadow or sheds a glow over most every history, yet it is often ridiculed.

"We keep love from the young eye ; hide it from the young heart ; yet surer than prophecy, will that very eye and heart sparkle and thrill at *one* love story, silently, quietly, told all to itself alone.

"We tease and ridicule the young if they talk or read of love—educated to show and shine and flirt, but not to love.

"Even he who laughs at love stories, has hidden in his heart, its inmost holy, when the vail is rent aside, an image of something he could thus love.

"Somewhere in the life of every loving and attractive woman, is written a manly name. Could you trace the hidden hieroglyphics of every womanly heart, you would find moss-grown or grass-grown, cypress-wreathed or turf-cover-ed, one dear name. Sometimes it is on the heart's door plate, finely engraven and carefully kept bright. Tears never efface the name. In the quiet Greenwood of many a womanly heart, never called wife, is an enduring marble slab, with this legible inscription, ' Sacred to the Memory of a Lost Love.' Beside it are little tear-watered, faded bunches of violets and bouquets of withered rose-buds, with the old blue ribbon still around them.

"Many a noble gifted man walks his solitary life way, called by the world heartless, insensible, old bachelor, yet within his heart, torn down or vailed, is a womanly shrine, where once, when skies were bluest and life's flowers so fair, he daily brought offerings of the sweet flowers of af-fection.

"There are many marriages without love, and many a sweet sad love story, that never ends in marriage."

Carleyn awakes and lays away his little book, as he re-peats over and over to himself these lines—

> " If I be dear to some one else,
>   Then some one else may have much to fear,
> But if I be dear to some one else,
>   Then I should be to myself more dear."

CHAPTER XXIV.

A BIT OF PHILOSOPHY ABOUT HUSBANDS.

> " Storms, thunders, waves !
> Howl, crash and bellow till you get your fill ;
> Ye sometimes rest ; men never can be still
>   But in their graves."
>   OLIVER WENDELL HOLMES.

" You are weak, Florence, weak," said Mrs. Elliott. " You do not show your usual strength of character ; this Nepenthe is certainly no rival of yours—I have never seen you so much excited ; it really detracts from your beauty, and makes you appear unamiable."

" I do not wish to be amiable," said Florence, haughtily rising up to her full height. " No man will marry me or fancy me for my amiability. I don't like amiable people— stupid people are always amiable. Nepenthe Stuart's attractions in no way compare with mine. In birth, position, education, she is vastly my inferior ; but gifted distinguished men are every day fastening themselves by some strange freak of fancy to unpretending ordinary little women. May it not be possible for an enthusiastic young artist to take some such freak of the head or the heart, and marry unsuitably or rashly.

" Some men like to have all the genius and attractions to themselves. I can imagine a plain woman loving her distinguished husband with a kind of worshipful, grateful love. Some things beside beauty may excite temporary interest. An artful woman may captivate a man, and if once loved, she will soon look beautiful in his eyes. Many a man is thus taken in. Any good-looking woman with winning voice and manners, if artistically dressed, will at times look interesting. And once caught, a man hopes, believes, and endures all.

" Wise men have such foolish wives—profound men get shallow and stupid companions.

"If many a man had walked out blindfolded and married the first woman he met, he might have done better. There is said to be a place made for each person to fill; if a few get into the wrong places, what is to become of the rest? There must be an odd kind of pairing off if the leading ones are mismatched, yet I have always thought Frank Carleyn would want not only a beautiful wife, but an uncommonly beautiful one."

"These geniuses are not the most desirable of husbands, Florence. They're restless, abstracted, peculiar, and they don't make practical husbands. They'll buy meat all fat or all bone, and pay twice as much as any one else for it. They'll forget all kinds of household matters—they know nothing of practical financiering. If they earn money, some how they never get rich."

"I could manage all that," said Florence. "I would rather have a husband that couldn't tell beef from mutton, than one who would be sending roast meat from the table because not brown enough or too brown to suit his lordship, —or indignantly reject a griddle cake because its circumference was not an exact circle ; or one who is always giving essays about the right way of making coffee, bread, sauces and gravies. Marry the best man, and you'll soon find he has some queer little kinks, some eccentric oddity. It may be he can't eat anything spiced with nutmeg, or sweetened with molasses, or flavored with cinnamon,—and then he talks so glowingly of the way his mother used to make pies —fat pies, he calls them—and that apple sauce, if you could only make some like that. He always thinks his mother used to fix up things in some wonderful way, a little better than any other woman can. Put the same dishes on the table now, and they wouldn't taste the same.

"A man forgets that boyish play, chasing ball, hoop and horse, give marvellous appetite, and the tired hungry boy likes, as he can never like again, mother's dinners, soups and sauces.

"Those old green hills, that bordered the valley, where nestled his childhood's home were lofty mountains to his boy-ish eyes—are only little hills now ; so the virtue of those rare dishes so marvellously good was heightened by boyish exercise and boyish fancy.

"But it isn't the eating part that makes all the trouble.

—There's the washing. I've heard on good authority, that a respectable gentleman actually jerked off and threw on the floor, in a paroxysm of anger, his standing ˌcollar, forsooth ˌbecause it was not starched stiff enough to suit his lordship ; and so a man who will boldly face advancing armies, or coolly reply to an insulting antagonist, will be conquered and fretted by one little collar, dust on his overcoat, a speck or a wrinkle on his shirt bosom ; but if the shirt don't fit, O what a calamity—and when will a man own that a home-made shirt ever does fit ?

" They used to ruffle the shirts, but now, one would think to hear them talk, that the shirts ruffled the men—if it don't fit, if there's a wrinkle in the bosom, or it draws on the shoulder, if there's a twist in the sleeve—the button holes are a mile too big, or they're so small he takes his pen-knife and cuts away at them, the neck band is made so tight, and awkward, he'll get the bronchitis, he's had trouble with his throat these two years, because of these awkward shirts, and so he'll fret and fume and fuss and give each morning an elaborate dissertation on all the manifold benefits of good shirt making : if he had time and materials, couldn't he make a shirt that would fit—it only needs a little common sense— 'tis easy enough to see where the trouble is.

" A woman will often bear a little annoyance better than a man ; a man will use such strong adjectives for weak ideas, such large words for small occasions. Most every man has some expletive, with which his impatience effervesces, George, Harry, Thunder, Mars, Good Heavens ! The man scolds his wife, and always calls it making suggestions. If she cries, *she* make demonstrations if—he threaten to skin or thrash his child, impetuously shaking him, as if good could be shaken in or evil be shaken out, he calls it ' salutary discipline.'

" Talk of a woman's being nervous when sick. Why if a man has a headache, it is intolerable. How he groans ! If he has a little fever he is ' burning up.' If he has a cold he thinks he is ' seriously ill.' If called up once in the night, or awake half an hour, why he is rubbing his eyes, and ' broke of his rest,' for a week afterwards. If a little ill, how very blue, uncomfortable and worried he will feel. But Frank Carleyn is no such fussy, fidgetty, man ; he would be reasonable, and too much absorbed in his profession, to

make an idol of his dinner or a pet of his constitution
—I don't believe he'd know or find fault, if you'd set nails
before him for breakfast, but I don't care what he does, or is.
I don't want to analyze his habits or nature. I love him."

"I think you will find, Florence, that if a man does poetize
and philosophize or paint ideals, he'll know when beef is
well done, and beefsteak nicely broiled; and the best of men
may make a wry face at insipid coffee and tough sirloin. A
hungry husband must be fed before he is caressed, entertained or charmed."

Nepenthe Stuart came in just then, so they continued
their conversation in French, supposing of course she was
ignorant of the French language.

"I will not be cut out by that low-born, low-bred girl. I
have never failed in anything I have undertaken," said Florence, in an angry tone.

"Don't get so excited, Florence," said Mrs. Elliott; "we'll
have her married yet. I have praised her up to the skies
to Mr. Nicholson, and she may well be thankful if she can
get such a husband. It is a better fate than she deserves
to have an offer from a man of his great wealth and acknowledged position. It might make her proud and overbearing
to be placed in such an elevated station. It will no doubt
elate her exceedingly, to receive proposals from such a man,
he is really a great catch for any girl. He is very handsome, immensely rich, and growing richer all the time."

"My name shall be Florence Carleyn, or Florence Elliott
till I die," said Florence; "and I will crush every obstacle
that comes in my path, as I crush this fly," said she, as she
pressed her hand on a little fly on the window sill in front
of her; "but we must take care that Nepenthe does not
find out about that legacy. It would make her feel so independent of us and rich husbands too. I hope she'll know
nothing of Mr. Nicholson's hereditary insanity. Neither of
his brothers lived to be forty without being insane, and I
have heard it confidentially stated that his family physician
says he will certainly be insane before he dies, and he may
be at any time. I really think he acts a little queer now,
occasionally. Why once he brought me a rare boquet of
heliotropes, japonicas, and tuberoses, with a small sunflower
in the centre. It looked so queer, and about as suitable as
one of those hod-carriers would, dancing at my next recep-

tion in his working costume. It is the only queer thing I ever saw in Mr. Nicholson—but sometimes there's a strange wild light in his eye. Of course Nepenthe, penniless and dependent, will be glad and thankful for his attentions, but yet she has a will of her own, and I will crush it if I can. I have shown her in every possible way that her presence in the evening in the parlor is disagreeable to me. She shall marry Mr. Nicholson. I never willed a thing but I accomplished it, and mother, you never opposed me. You always taught me that I *might*, I *must* have my way."

CHAPTER XXV.

NEPENTHE WRITES.

What radiant visions glorious lie
Like sunset clouds. piled mountain high ;
O'er thought's great shore sublimely roll
The surging billows of the soul.

On mem'ry's far-receding strand,
Are shells and pearls and sparkling sand ;
Hope's fading sunset stains with gold
The oriel windows of the soul.

NEPENTHE said nothing to any one of those long days and lonely evenings, when to avoid intruding her presence and society upon the haughty Florence, she secluded herself in her room, writing, by herself, early in the morning, and late in the evening.

With no home, lover, friend, she created ideal homes, lovers, friends. When her aching heart was loneliest, hour after hour she talked on paper with these noiseless, invisible friends. Rapidly the pages increased, as the plot sketched and acted out in dream-land was written out in her manuscript. As her thoughts came fast and warm, rising in misty tears, or falling in radiant pearls along the shore of her spirit or washed up from the great gulf of the past, there were none to gather and polish and prize them, till at last, in the sunshine of her spirit, on the white surface of her manuscript, through the double convex-glass of her experience, the camera obscura of the darkened chamber of

her soul exhibited distinctly in their native colors the images
of her beautiful thoughts. The noblest and dearest of her
ideal heroes, turn the glass of her soul as she would, would
take the shape and form, the beauty and expression of Frank
Carleyn. When he first looked upon the pure surface of
her heart, his image was fixed, photographed there forever ;
and every after manly impression struck off from the leaves
of her soul into the leaves of her manuscript, would have
the look of that first impression, exposed to the vapor of
tears, or to joy's feverish heat—the image was always appearing, as if by enchantment.

She wrote to occupy busy thoughts—give vent to over-
charged feelings, and forget unshared sorrows. As page
after page grew under her hand, she never thought it might
be a book at last. She had a hope that some eye might at
some time read the unpretending manuscript, and if *dawn*
came at last, she herself might read over its chapters of
sorrow, and add with sunshine gilding the hills of her life,
the concluding *finis*.

She never thought who would publish, sell or buy it—
with her it was only a manuscript. She thought not of sheltering it under the adorned and gilded cover of a book. She
had never known or dreamed or heard of one prophetic
glance of that influential and powerful individual, the publisher's reader, who sits in his sovereign chair, repeating
his favorite phrase, " 'Tis very well written, but not the
class of works we publish—we want something more thrilling ;" as with one wave of his powerful hand he banishes
into the dark realm of hopeless oblivion many a manuscript
freighted with winged hopes and glorious dreams of fame's
golden heights and immortal laurels ;—but she wrote on,
as the sea asks no echo to its moanings from the cold shore,
the stars hope for no thanks from the gloomy night, and the
flower seeks no reward from the crushing hand.

By accident, she became acquainted one day with a wise,
kind, polite old gentleman, Professor J——, a German, a
thorough classic and an accomplished Oriental scholar, an
extensive traveller, an excellent linguist, and a scientific
naturalist. He came to see her, and entertained and
charmed some of her loneliest hours. One day he showed
her his large and rare herbarium, in which he had preserved flowers, leaves and bulbs, which he had gathered in

Germany, France, Italy, Prussia, Poland, and some at the Crimea, Caucasus, and at Teflis.

He preserved the bulbs in his herbarium, just as he had found them, all but one, which he found in Teflis and which he cut open with a sharp knife and applied a hot iron to the inner surface of each part.

Four years after, when in St. Petersburgh, he examined his herbarium, and all those bulbs, once so perfect and symmetrical, were dried, shrivelled, musty and mouldy; while from the parts of the little Teflis bulb, to which he had applied the knife and the iron, little fresh leaves were peeping out. Its unscorched, unharmed peers, were moulding around it unblessed by no green resurrection, while through the sharp stab and the burning fire it had unfolded its germ of fragrant beauty. The quiet biding of the blade and the iron, like patient mortal suffering, had wrought out its unfolding glory.

The kind old gentleman took so much interest in Nepenthe that he told her some anecdotes about his interviews with Lord Byron in Venice in 1815, when he saw him swim four miles from St. Marc to Lido, and asked him if he were not afraid of the sharks ?

" Oh no !" said Lord Byron, as he was stepping into a gondola, " I am a fatalist—the sharks will not touch me until my time comes to die."

The professor lent Nepenthe some printed accounts of his travels to read, and at last encouraged her to show him something of her own.

She read him a little poem, written one night when she was alone and sad.

He sat still as she read, and at last, when she finished it, he broke out in his peculiar foreign, yet eloquent English :

" Why, Mademoiselle Stuart! With what high and mighty inspiration, is your mind endowed? Your thoughts, clear and beautiful, flow from your soul like a river. Men will read them and love them, and the world shall hear of you."

Poor Nepenthe was unused to praise. Nobody praised, flattered, complimented her. Sarcasm, suspicion, slight, insult were her daily food, her constant companions. But this man who had seen kings and princes, lived at courts, travelled with sages, whose intellect towered above the crowd around her, was too solemn, grave, dignified to flatter. His words inspired, cheered, thrilled, moved her. They sounded like a prophet's voice, speaking out from the sybil cave of destiny.

———

Long after the professor had gone, Nepenthe sat thinking, and these were her thoughts. "There are hearts in the world never pierced, never bruised, never stabbed, never scorched. They go through the world unscathed, untouched, unblighted, like dry, carefully kept bulbs in life's herbarium. But as years pass, they shrink and shrivel like those unscathed, unpierced bulbs in the professor's herbarium, growing older, mustier, and mouldier, never unfolding in fragrant beauty for any eye; while here and there is some lonely heart so rent by the sharp knife of trouble, so scorched and burned by sorrow's hottest furnace iron, that after years of calamity's heaviest pressures have passed, as you open the leaves of life, you'll find springing out of the broken, burning heart, some balmy leaves of fragrant sympathy, sweetly perfuming all life's surrounding pages."

———

"I will call my story Dawn," thought Nepenthe. "It may be from my poor, scorched, stabbed, burning, longing heart, it may come forth as a little germ unfolding into beauty, blooming in the sunshine and dew of young, bright eyes, and at last take deep and abiding root in the world's heart."

> " A flower of hope—float up to the light,
>   Its whitened umbels gleam through the night."

"Will one of its little leaves," thought she, "be preserved forever in Fame's great herbarium, so full of the illustrious classes and noble orders of soul-flowers."

Nepenthe sings in a low voice, as she looks out that night at the stars :

> "Up, high up in the Poet's mind
>   The Belfry bells are ringing,
>   The bells are ever swinging,
>   Swinging rhymes
>   In silver chimes,
>   Telling or past or future times,
>   But ever they tell of the golden climes,
>   Where, ever the bells are ringing."

CHAPTER XXVI.

CARLEYN'S CONCEIT.

"Enfin dans le cerveau si l'image est tracée,
Comment peut dans un corps s'imprimer la pensée ?
La finit ton œuvre, mortel audacieux,
Va mesurer la terre, interroger les cieux,
De l'immense univers regle l'ordre supreme,
Mais ne pretends jamais te connoitre toimême,
La s'ouvre sous tes yeux un abime sans fonds."
　　　　　　　　DE LILLE, L'IMAGINATION.

"THERE'S *one* thing I don't *like* about that Carleyn," said Miss Charity Gouge, "*he is so conceited.*"

"*Conceited !*" said Kate Howard. "I have never seen anything conceited in him. I am sure his manners are plain and unpretending."

"Yes ; but for all that, *he is* conceited. He knows he is a genius, and when a man knows that, it spoils him. If you should ask him pat and plump if he didn't think he could paint beautiful portraits, he'd say, ' Yes, I know I can.' *I* believe in not letting ' the left hand know what the right hand doeth.' "

"Yes," said Kate ; " but the right hand need not forget its cunning. Don't the poet *feel* that he is a poet ? Don't he feel the waves of emotion dashing on the shore of thought ? As his swelling soul careers over the ocean of beauty, does *he* not first catch the murmurs of liquid melody and *first* see the pearls beneath ? As he grasps the floating images of fragrant thought, and carves them into lyric forms, may *he* not value best their worth and cost ? If Pythagoras first found the proportions of musical notes from the sounds of hammers upon an anvil, each true poet knows the proportion of his exquisite melodies, as he catches the echo of the hammer of thought as it strikes the anvil of his sounding soul. On the walls of Carleyn's soul were stained, at its earliest creation, beautiful pictures. Long toiling through gathering thoughts and misty fancies, he has at last brushed away the dust of years, and with clear eye and cunning hand, reproduced these inborn images. After exploring these wondrous tracings and shadings, may he not modestly say, ' I have toiled, and brushed, and polished, and found at last this beautiful picture in my soul ?' "

" I *hate* this bragging," said Miss Charity. " Let another man praise thee, and not thine own lips ; a stranger, and not thine own mouth. Seest thou a man wise in his own conceit, there is more hope of a fool than of him."

" We give the miner credit for his golden findings," said Kate, " yet he who toils on alone, and strikes at last a vein of golden thought, as he catches its first sparkle and sees its earliest glow, can't he best weigh the hard-earned treasure ; if he coins rare images from the mint of thought, can't he have sense enough to see the stamp and know the value ? In the tower of each great soul is a mint for the coining of thought, vested with the royal prerogative of stamping its own coin with name and value. The soul's coronation time is when through its dim chaos of doubt it first cries out to its new-orbed thought, it is *my own*, and it is good—then God puts the laurel crown on the worshipping soul as it kneels in its inner court. Applause may or may not come afterwards from the outer court of the great congregation of thought worshippers.

This first joy flush is never vain, but tearful and meek in its triumph—in every giant soul's causeway is a basaltic touchstone, on which each pure thought leaves its genuine mark ; and these crusty jealous people who are always finding out and testing a great man's conceit—I always call them not touch-needles but touchy-needles. If I were a man I'd write one lecture about this conceit. I'd write it and deliver it too—if I had to pay myself a hundred dollars for the privilege. There hardly lives a great and gifted man who is not called conceited. As for me I have always found the greatest fools and dunces displaying the most unbearable self-conceit."

" Well," said Miss Charity in a spirited tone, " Carleyn has great ideas of what he can do, it don't take a person of any sagacity long to find that out, and true modesty," she added triumphantly, " is an element of true greatness—it is a great charm this perfect unconsciousness ; and I never can admire a great man without it. I have seen a great deal of the world, and I *know* I am correct."

" I haven't been as long in the world as you, Miss Charity," said Kate, " yet I have heard a great deal about this perfect unconsciousness, but I have never seen it. I have read in novels of radiantly beautiful women, who never knew they looked well, and irresistibly fascinating men, who unconsciously captivated every body, because they couldn't help it, but I don't meet any such men and women walking about. It is quite difficult for a person who owns a good looking-glass, and a good pair of ears, not to see and to hear about it, if he is handsome. We Americans must make such a fuss about every thing, fences and barns, and cars and curb-stones, book covers, medals and fans, even wagons and wayside rocks are plastered over with advertisements, of something new and wonderful. There's somebody's name on every thing. The chief aim of the people is to get their name up. Our almanacs—guides to infallible weather decisions, must be labelled ' guides to health '—which means a guide to some polychrestian physician, who cures every thing with some universal life invigorator. I don't despair yet of seeing some of the pure energy of vital action done up and for sale in boxes of salve, rolls of plaster, and bottles of lotion warranted to be made from a powdered philospher's stone, of purely vegetable origin, by a perpetually moving machine, circulating among all the crowned heads of Europe. Every thing is used as an advertising medium, but the sky over our heads—there are no caricatures up there yet —but if a balloon ever could get up so high some enterprising medicine vender would be for sending one of his posters up there, to fasten notices on some starry promontory, or suburban gates of some constellated city, to introduce among the bulls and bears of those shining streets, his valuable speculation, and benefit those upper circles by his philanthropic lotions, seeing that his sands of life have nearly run out.

" If a man praise any article to me, I begin to suspect that he has some of it in his pocket to sell.

" Once upon a time somebody gave me a whole bottle of Tricopherous, for which liberal gift I could see no occasion ; but some time thereafter the donor came round again wishing me to give my name to be inscribed on the outside of each bottle of Tricopherous in testimony of its virtues. I laughed till I cried at the thought of it—Kate Howard go ing round on a Tricopherous bottle ! I never wish to see

my name in print till I am married. But I do say that a
well conceived and carefully polished thought deserves the
acknowledgment of its original stamp far more than those
bottles of nondescript perfume marked *Parisienne, adoptee
par le monde elegant.* 13 *Rue D'Enghier.* 13, *Paris*, with
white kid caps and fancy ribbon neck-ties, marked sometimes 'Bouquet de Caroline,' they might better be 'Bouquet
de Jonathan,' or 'Pomade de Sallie,' for they have no memories of Outre Mer—and those sheets of cream-laid note paper, with 'Paris' carefully stamped in one corner, have
no gay Parisian associations, but authentic memories of their
native American rags. I have often wondered, as our Bridget says, how they can put such a deceitful countenance on
their fair faces; and even a gentleman, in the estimation of
many ladies, is not half finished or polished, or worth having, unless he has been to Europe, and come back with Paris
marked all over him—boots, hat, gloves and all—he must
eat, sleep, walk, talk, dress, and bow *a la Francaise*, and
dance well '*les Lanciers.*'

"I am glad there is something can circulate, even in
fashionable society, without full dress, white kids, and
French manners—and that is, a plain drab-covered book or
a poem. And no bars or bolts, or conventionalities shall
keep plain Jane Eyre from telling her thrilling tale of
Thornfield Hall, in stateliest mansion, to princely ears. You
might as well put gloves and slippers on a canary, advertise
a violet, recommend a mignionette, or puff a star through
the market, as try to puff a genuine thought through the
world. A star will shine—and a bright thought will burn
and shine somewhere, if only in one dark heart; that is a
glorious destiny, for when the heart beats up there, the
thought goes with it. Each great thought, as it comes from
the press of the soul, has an imported stamp—not of gay
Paris; but on each noble thought is imprinted in legible
type the stamp, HEAVEN; for every such good and perfect
gift cometh down from the Father of Light, from the city
beyond the sea of stars. It is a pity we couldn't get more
of the patterns of our thoughts from the royal family
above.

"But don't you want a moral to all this rhodomontade?
It is this. If a man's name can be appropriately attached to

everything, from a tin pan to a telescope, he can make a good picture, and know it, without being called conceited."

" Well," said Charity, " I'll never change the good name of Gouge till I find a man without any conceit in him."

" You'll have to hunt a while, Charity," said Kate, " before you find such a wise fool and brilliant dunce. You might as well expect to find the opposite magnetic poles of human nature at the same end of the life battery—and if you could find such a rare bird, he'd have to take *your* name —for the best part of him would be *Gouged* out of him.

" I wouldn't give a fig for a man unless he thought he could do something. A man can never accomplish anything until he feels there is something in him to begin with. Don't you suppose, Charity, that if a rock had a soul, it would know that it was a rock? if a star could think, wouldn't it know that it was a star ? if a flower could feel, wouldn't it be conscious that it was a flower ?—and every granite truth, starry thought, and flowery fancy, sees its faithful shadow in the reflecting fountain of its native soul. But here endeth my first lesson, for there comes Fred, and I always hide away my metaphysical patchbag when he's around, for he is a most unmerciful tease. He says no lady ever can carry on an argument in a logical manner : that they plunge right into a subject, and can't hold their breath long enough to get the pearls at the bottom : that the best of us are superficial, and never canvass both sides of a question, and half the time when we talk we don't know what we are driving at, and the best of our opinions are only echoes of our lover's, husband's, or brother's thoughts ; that we are very good in our way—that means, I suppose, that like birds in the air or fishes in the water, there's only one ele- ment adapted to our simple nature, and that is the domestic element.

" I wonder what we have eyes for, and what we have souls for, if we are to be cooped up in one set of cages, and never peek through or wander out, to see what is going on outside. For my part I like. to climb the spiritual fence, and see a few of the stars and smell a few of the flowers of truth, where man's free spirit is pasturing at large on the wide field of thought, and daily growing grander and might- ier. I get tired of thinking over the same old thoughts and eating the corn meal of common sense, and forever dwelling on the highly recommended yet stale subject of good house-keeping. To coop us in, and bar us out of the beautiful thought world, is compelling us to live on bran bread, while man feasts on angels' food and fathoms angels' themes."

Miss Charity yawned heavily, and then taking out her watch, exclaimed,

"Why, it is nearly four o'clock. I ought to be at the meeting of the managers this very moment, and they can't do anything without me."

As she went up to her room, Kate couldn't help saying to herself,

"When Charity talks about conceit, she'd better begin at home."

CHAPTER XXVII.

LOVE, JEALOUSY, AND RIVALRY.

> " I want a steward, butler, cooks ;
> A coachman, footman, grooms ;
>   A library of well-bound books,
> And picture-garnished rooms ;
>   Corregios, Magdalen, and Night,
> The matron of the chair,
>   Guido's fleet Coursers in their flight,
> And Claudes, at least a pair."—JOHN QUINCY ADAMS.

> " Les hommes seront toujours ce qu'il plaisa aux femmes."
> ROUSSEAU.

As Florence went out of the room—" Yes," said Mrs. Elliott, rocking back and forth in her drawing-room, " any woman not engaged, and not in love with some other man, can be obtained by any intelligent, good-looking man, if he have the right tact, address and perseverance, and is doing well in business. Most women know a dozen such they would accept, if they would offer themselves judiciously and romantically, by moonlight, or out by some grove. Florence and Carleyn may make a match yet, if she is prudent and cautious, and don't flirt with too many others. Carleyn is no flirt.

" Why don't *you* get up a flirtation with somebody ?" said she to Nepenthe, as she came in with her netting.

" I don't know how," said Nepenthe, quietly, " and if I

did, I wouldn't like to win or encourage the advances of a man I would not marry. I think these endearing expressions, coaxing tones, and languishing attitudes wrong, and very unpleasant in the recollection. I would rather have the love of one true-hearted man than see a dozen moustached and worshipful Apollos sighing at my feet. I would rather have only the *one* offer from the man I might marry than feel the pain of rejecting a hundred I could not accept. If a man really loves a woman, it must give her pain to say to him, No—and be a matter of regret to her afterwards "

" Very well got up sentences," said Florence, coming in just then, " and quite heroic. Talk about giving gentlemen pain, and breaking their hearts. Pshaw! Men's hearts don't break! Most any of them think they can have any woman for the asking—they are so full of conceit, they really believe that ladies will say, ' Yes sir, and thank you, too !' I like to take some of the conceit out of them. Yes, I enjoy it. I'd like the pleasure of refusing most all of them. Look at those young widowers, who have so adored their wives while living. They'll many of them marry in a little less than a year, some of them in even six months ; and if they marry then, they must allow some time previous for the preliminary love-making, engagement, &c. Who knows how soon they do *think* of it ? Do you remember what Mr. Hollow said, when somebody asked him why he married six months after his wife died ? He said he should not wear mourning for her so long as for a brother or sister, because she was no blood relation. But," she added, changing her tone, " when we see you playing the agreeable to a gentleman, sitting chatting so absorbed in the corner, we'll know *you* are in earnest."

" I would often rather talk with a gentleman than a lady," said Nepenthe, not noticing the insinuation implied in Florence's remark. " It is more natural for a lady to confide in some intelligent man, than in some other woman. Gentlemen pay more respectful attention. As they are out more in the world, if they are well informed, they give information on certain subjects with which we haven't the same opportunity to be familiar. Their minds are not as apt to be absorbed with the details of trifles, and for my part I think most of the agreeable men are married men."

" But you certainly wouldn't talk sense in society. It is

neither customary nor in good taste," said Florence. " You don't go into society to get or give information. There are lectures, libraries, churches enough to enlighten us. We go into society to be amused. During the whole of the fashionable sociables I attended last winter, we danced every evening all the evening. I never had but one conversation the whole winter, and that was with a gentleman from Boston, and it was purely accidental. It was waltz, promenade and polka, polka, promenade and waltz, all winter—and *this is society*."

" All do not go into society with the same motives," said Nepenthe, coloring slightly. " Some are 'lookers on in Venice.' I have been so little out of late, my ideas of society would probably be *outre*. I hardly know what is customary. Whatever is the tone of conversation, ladies often give it its caste, and gentlemen, while with them, try to talk to suit them. Gentlemen really like to give information. Each educated man, if he reads much, if he has travelled far, enjoys thinking and talking, on some one subject more than another. He likes to talk of that of which he likes to think. I believe almost everybody, rich or poor, ignorant or educated, knows something, from facts, observation, or experience, of which many others are ignorant. The charm of conversation is not so much in talking ourselves, and displaying our own powers, as to get others to talk, to draw upon their resources of knowledge. I can usually find, after talking a little with a gentleman, what he likes best, and I turn the conversation in that direction. He may be eloquent on that subject, though perhaps taciturn on every other. If a man thinks he is really imparting information, he will be natural and genial—he will like you better, and really think you more agreeable, though you only ask a few questions, and are a patient listener, and he does most all the talking."

" There is more in the way and manner than in the thought," said Florence, interrupting her; " men never like learned women to talk with. They care more for beauty, ease and style, than any great intellectual power, or wise conversation, full of tiresome, long words."

" I think," said Nepenthe, " if a gentleman have a horror of a literary woman, she need certainly display no pedantry before him. She can keep locked in reserve her best intellectual stores, and use with him only the common coin, the small change of conversation, talking of common things in a common sense way. In talking with ordinary people, on ordinary occasions, on ordinary subjects, it is as much out of place to use the largest and grandest words, as for a lady to wear her wedding dress and set of diamonds in travelling, or her opera cloak and hood at church. Those people who are always coming out everywhere with their words in studied full dress, are very tiresome and disagreeable. We begin to think that the display is so marked, that the original stock is small. I think on most any occasion, 'tis best not to use a long word where a small one will do. Conversation is like mosaic—small pieces are sometimes inlaid the best, and heighten the charm of the whole. Much of the German poetry, so expressive and beautiful, is composed principally of short, familiar words. We seldom think in long words. The best minister I ever heard was distinguished for his simplicity of language. He never used one syllable too many, or a word you could omit. He never piled up adjectives. His sermon would be a pure, clear stream of thought—his comparisons and images like flowers beside this stream. You could almost see their bright shadows and smell their fragrance. A flower is one of the simplest things of nature, yet the most beautiful ; and this clergyman always had a flower in his sermon. How often have I heard him allude simply and beautifully to heliotropes and violets, and the flowers never seemed *put in*, but springing up, and growing under his hand, a part of his elevated subject and elevated soul.

"An intelligent woman can sooner and surer find out what a man really is, than another man can. Men often make mistakes about each other. One man hides his heart from another, while often he frankly shows his gentler, warmer, kinder nature to a true woman. He may seem ice to a man, and sunshine to her. Every true man has some spot in his nature where tenderness steals in and flows out. A woman's hand, look or tone, may touch the valve of some secret hydrant, and raise the warm, gushing sympathies from the deep hidden conduit of man's rocky heart."

"Ladies who make some literary pretensions, are often jealous of those more beautiful than themselves," said Florence. "Woman is made to adorn man's life. There is a kind of style and manner men admire almost as much as beauty. I don't think there are as many hypocrites among men as women ; above all things I do despise a hypocrite," she added, with emphasis.

"Gentlemen have not as many yets, and buts, and ands," replied Nepenthe, not noticing Florence's last remark. "They have more magnanimity. Their true opinion and praise are less qualified, more outspoken. A lady, if speaking of another's superior beauty, will add, ' She has a good complexion, but her nose is too *retroussé*—she would be handsome, if her eyebrows were not too strongly marked ;' and she will add, ' She is not the style of person I at all admire ;' or, ' She has such a horrid walk, it spoils her appearance completely ; and then if her face is faultless, her features are too regular ;' or, ' She is deficient in style,' or ' Her hair is not stylishly arranged. She has too much *gaucherie* and *mauvais honte*—she is not well bred—I have seen her when she looked really homely.' Some ladies shake hands, or even kiss, and yet hate each other. I never want to kiss anybody for ceremony or custom, unless I really love them.

"Ladies will say, ' I am glad to see you—don't be in a hurry ;' and when the caller is gone, you will soon hear, ' I am glad she is gone—she made an everlasting call. I wonder what on earth sent her here to-day !' I don't think a man is as apt to be affable to bores as a woman often is. He will sometimes be too rude to those he dislikes, rather than too courteous and bland. I have known of gentlemen sending their wives into the parlor to entertain the tedious bores, while they slip out the back door, or escape through the front, on a plea of business, saying to themselves, ' Dear me, what do I want to see him for ?' I do think a man will speak and act more as he really feels, than most women, except those men who are always telling everybody they are delighted to see them, and treating every woman, young and old, as if they were making love to them. There are some such married men, who are always making each young girl they meet really feel that they would soon receive an offer from them, if they only had no wife."

"No woman ever gets by tact and after practice," said Florence, " that ease and elegance gained by birth and early associations with high-bred society. It is a great charm to

be always at ease, always self-possessed, never bashful,
never embarrassed. Very timid persons are apt to be awkward."

"I think that self-forgetfulness is the charm of character
and manner," said Nepenthe. "It is the custom of society
to make people all alike, smoothing down the salient points
of character, covering up and veneering over with the
rosewood of benevolence and mahogany of kindness the native structure of the heart. You can't guess what it is made
of, or if there be any heart left. We keep the heart so
draped and veiled by the curtains of elegance, bolted and
barred within the iron fence of custom, it gets no strength
and vigor by active free exercise. We see strangers only
with the heart in full dress. We conceal our true motives,
and often do not give the real true reason for our conduct.
Well, ' she is a person that says just what she thinks,' we
say of some one, as if it were an unusual and wonderful fact.

"We tell a friend who has a new bonnet that she looks
exceedingly well in it, just to make her feel comfortable;
but when she is out of hearing, we say that it is a shocking
hat; but I did not like to tell her so. I wouldn't be seen
in the street with such a hat I wish she would come out
for once with a decent bonnet, a real stylish bonnet."

"Well," said Florence, shaking her ringlets, "style is
everything. I could not be happy unless I could have everything in the highest style, house, servants, furniture. I
should be miserable in a plain, common house."

"There is no word in the dictionary like that word *style*
to city dwellers," said Nepenthe. "It is in every young
lady's mouth, stylish hat, stylish dress, stylish figure, stylish
air—it is all stylish; how different from the style we learn
about in the old rhetorics. If wealth be the magical word
inscribed upon man's livery, style is woman's spiritual coat
of arms; stylish, the highest commendation she can bestow
on manners, dress, equipage, aye—lover. Style makes a
splendid pageant of the holy bridal, and a costly show of the
solemn burial; stylishly they live, stylishly they love, stylishly are they buried. We refine away our ideas of comfort until water is purer from a golden cup, and roses
fresher blooming around some classic chiselled font, protected by marble nymph or dryad. In this age, I think we
are trying more to find the evil in things good, than the good

in things evil.   If Christ Himself, the All-Perfect One, were
to walk our crowded thoroughfare in his shining robes, some
opera-glass might be raised to spy, if possible, some dust on
His trailing garments or speck in their shadowy perfection.''

.   '' This talk about truthful conversation, small houses, simple dress and manners,'' said Florence, abruptly, '' sounds
very well in a lyceum lecture or in advice to young men.
But who likes to live in the only small house in a block ? to
be *the* person living in that small house ?   Who does not
prefer to have all the smiling domesticity he boasts of in
a fine large brown stone or marble front ? Most of the world
live, dress, and have houses as handsome as they can. These
are very prudent people who by years of toil have at last acquired ample means and an elegant style of living.   If you
live in a small house, they'll come in their carriage to see
you, and be glad you are beginning on so economical a plan,
and yet they'll look so patronizingly and condescendingly on
your one sofa, your one picture, which they carefully examine with a glass, informing you of the fresh arrival they have
just had of paintings and statuary from Italy.   They measure with their eye the value of your one marble-topped table,
and the color and quality of your one best silk dress, and go
away and say to their dear friends they found you quite comfortable, though living in a very humble way, for you make
no *pretentions* to *style*, they add, with a kind of pitying emphasis.

'' I really think there is a kind of vulgar air about people
who live in small houses ; they have such contracted ideas.
You can read economy and saving all over their simple
faces.   They are always making over dresses, turning carpets, and altering their old bonnets, eating with plated forks,
from granite ware, and drinking out of pressed glass goblets.
But, Nepenthe, you are too plebeian in your manners.   I
wish, while with us, you would keep a more proper distance
from our inferiors.''

'' My life has been too real,'' said Nepenthe, '' to keep any
freezing distance with any one.''

'' Well, well,'' said Florence, '' if you were once a beggar
yourself, 'tis no reason you should compromise us.   You
stop in the street and speak to every servant girl or laun-
dress we've ever had.   I believe you would bow as politely

to black Thomas, who brings our groceries, as to the Duke of Wellington himself."

"No matter how high I hold my poor head," said Nepenthe, "I must lay it at last on the breast of the same earth-mother as the humblest person I know. I can't see how a mortal woman, frail and doomed to die, and to be judged hereafter, solely by her trusting faith and deeds of kindness, can be proud, or conceited, or overbearing, or how she can be constantly light-hearted while her life, health, and future are all in the hands of One who can deprive her of life's pride at any moment."

"Well," interrupted Florence, haughtily, "these ideas would sound well in a book or sermon, but I think it beneath the dignity of any lady to be bowing and smiling to every passing Bridget or wandering Patrick. Such attentions make them independent, impudent, and intolerable."

"We can recognize any human being without being familiar with him," added Nepenthe, quietly. "If you were drowning in deep water, you would gladly be rescued by the hard hands of a faithful black servant. We may find faithfulness and gratitude among such persons, and they can often give us material aid. I prize as much as any gift I ever had, that beautifully chiselled lamb brought me by that poor sculptor out of gratitude for my visits to his sick child. The lamb is really valuable, and beautifully chiselled."

"You know very well," said Florence, "you invariably find ignorance wedded to poverty. For myself, I wish neither to touch or share the life or destiny of ignorant, low-bred, pauper humanity. I would hold up my spiritual skirts higher from the influence of this contagion than I would raise my delicate robes from the mud of Broadway some rainy day after a snow. I cannot relish anything common; my sympathies and tastes have been too highly educated. As for you, with your experiences, you may feel naturally no such distaste."

"If you should ever be," said Nepenthe, "in mental agony, bodily distress, or personal danger, you may find more sympathy, relief, and succor from some old nurse, faithful servant, or kind stranger, than from the formal, elegant attentions of a whole regiment of amateurs, beaux, belles, exquisites, leaders of ton. There may be no style in the shape or motives of the honest hands that bathe and bind up your wounded spirit or bruised limbs, no manner in the quiet, good souls with cheerful eyes that summon so quickly the warm water, hot flannel, fresh tea and clean linen. Proud as we are, how many days in our lives are we really comfortable? How many calm hours is the heart warmly tucked in and softly pillowed? If cold, we want fire; if hungry, food; if thirsty, water. So the heart has its hunger, chill and thirst; style can never warm and feed and cherish it; there must be warm hearts, gushing sympathies, and cordial hands. The heart wants comfort unmasked, uncostumed, simple comfort, dear comfort, which is never out of place, never out of date, never unwelcome, never an intruding stranger. In life's crowded car we want something besides hard apples and sweetened balls of painted pop-corn to keep us good-natured.

"Those who greet you so blandly, praise you so warmly while in the full bloom of beauty, and height of fortune, will be the last to cheer, sustain, and soothe, should your cheek pale, your step falter, or your heart despond. They will pass by you on the other side of fortune with their light step, ringing laugh, and say, 'How Florence Elliott has changed. She has lost all her beauty. I believe she.has been disappointed. How proud she once was! She must feel mortified.'

"I never see a living suffering woman, but I long to relieve her; or a tired, sobbing child, but I yearn to take it in my arms and soothe it; a hungry, haggard beggar, but I long to feed him; I would like so much to mend all the boy's broken toys, the man's broken fortunes, the woman's broken hopes, and the maiden's broken loves.

"Our poor young hungry hopes go wandering up and down, longing for rest and food. I often wish I could take all the worn and weary world in my arms and rock it to sleep. I wish I could sing some sweet lullaby in every heavy ear; I wish I could float some melody through the air, to hush each wailing heart, and pillow it somewhere at rest. I wish a troop of angels would come again and sing once more 'Peace on earth, good will to man.' I wish some other star could hover over, and lead our modern bewildered wise men to a peace-giving Christ.

"I wish everybody had a home. I wish every orphaned,

widowed and solitary heart could say at nightfall, I am going home—eyes are watching for me there.

"We must stoop to bathe the head of sorrow and wipe the human tear. The ladder whence angels descended touched the ground. No tree can kiss the clouds or bloom in heaven, whose roots are not clinging and clasping in the deep earth.

"If we stoop to raise up fallen humanity, what matter if our robes are soiled with the dust? We shall lie down in the earth at last.

"The poorest ragged wanderer in the world is as near the Great All Father as the radiant, crowned, and royal-robed sovereign of a proud kingdom. When we think of the fever, the passions, and the agony that can prostrate in one little hour the proudest and most beautiful form, how foolish seem these little assumptions of superiority!—all doomed at last to a narrow spot of earth, with no better final distinction than the corroding silver plate, or decaying rosewood.

"Kings and beggars, side by side, walking at last through the gate of dust, must rise cadets together, in immortal uniform, to walk through gates of pearl.

"Everybody likes kindness. Nobody is so high but that there is some one higher to give him attention or pleasant words. If blessed to receive attention, it is certainly blessed to give."

"Well, well," said Florence, "you come honestly enough by your sermonizing propensities—'tis a part of your glorious birthright. You may do all this out of policy. It is well for dependent people to be politic, I grant, but I am independent of such kindness. I desire no contamination with inferiors. I wish to be light hearted, and don't wish to be made gloomy or annoyed by other people's troubles."

"I often look on a young bright face," said Nepenthe, "where no trace of sorrow seems to linger, and wonder if a human heart ever attains its first score of years, and is thoroughly and constantly light-hearted—if no love hath mellowed, no grief hath softened, no sorrow chastened, no thought sobered. This one thought—it is appointed unto man once to die, will come to all, even while elated with happiness. The brightest life will end soon—may end now. Happy as you seem, Florence, I am quite sure that that only

is true happiness which is pleasant and thornless in the re-
trospect."

"God has set His private mark upon each individual
soul," added Nepenthe, in a low voice, after pausing a moment, "and we earthly appraisers must take care how we
underrate God's private mark of real value. Above the
heads we now scorn, angel hands may be holding some golden crown. Some soul we despise for its plebeian setting
and parvenu surroundings, may yet be transfigured in the
radiant robes of genius on the highest hill of fame. Some
passing ragpicker may yet doff his rags—his bent, worn hat
vanish into a crown, and his old hook into a sceptre of intellectual might.

"Nothing but sin can induce me ever to treat any human
being coldly. Nothing but sin, we say; yet sinless lips
once said, 'Neither do I condemn thee, go and sin no more.'
Every human being with whom we come in contact has a
right to our civility and kindness."

"Your remarks savor more of the kitchen than the drawing room," said Florence contemptuously; "they probably
take the hue of your early associations. Let each one take
care of their own set. I like a kind of hauteur in manners,
as if you felt above the common herd. But there is one
thing—I do believe it is wrong for a woman of low origin,
and of so much pretended principle, ever to attempt to captivate a highminded and honorable man."

Florence went out abruptly, her eyes saying a great deal
more than her lips, as she sailed majestically away; and
soon elegantly dressed, she went out to promenade Broadway.

As she went, Bridget looked out of the basement door,
watching the retreating velvet, satin and feathers; then she
went back to her kitchen, saying,

"Well, there's no mistake that I may never sin, Miss
Florence is good looking, magnificent good looking. I wonder why some people is made so magnificent good looking,
and more so homely, so magnificent homely. I wonder why
God couldn't have made us all good looking."

Bridget called everything she liked magnificent. It was
the only long word she ever used, and she thought it equally applicable to people and puddings, biscuits and bonnets.

"Well," soliloquized Mrs. Elliott, as she sat putting the

last touches on her new sofa cushion, "I have had this girl here about long enough. I think I have more than fulfilled all my obligations to Dr. Wendon, real and imaginary. There is nothing really pretty about her, and yet somehow people do like her, and men do take such strange freaks, particularly men of genius. I do get into such a fidget sometimes about that will. No matter how tight you tie Tabby in the bag, there's never any knowing when the cat's head may appear; and once give such a secret any airing, like Tabby, only let her see the road she came, and she 'll know well how to trace her way back again. So give a secret a little airing, and you never know where it may go; it may go back to head quarters. But I'd rather marry the girl off than send her away. I never set my heart on anything yet without accomplishing it, but I don't believe in intellectual women. I agree with Lessing in Emilia Galotti that I was reading this morning. *La femme doit rire, toujours rire ;* cela suffit a sa noble mission sur la terre cela suffit pour maintenir en joyeuse humeur l'auguste roi de la creation."

When Mrs. Elliott wished to say or think anything very wise, it was always said or thought in French. She prided herself upon this. She sat up late that night. She had in that evening's mail received a letter that gave her much uneasiness. She locked her door, and looked over old papers, and burned up several old and worn documents. She lay awake almost all night, and the text of that self-denial sermon kept ringing in her ears—Withhold not any good from him to whom it is due, when it is in the power of thine hand to do it.

CHAPTER XXVIII.

NEPENTHE REFUSES A SELF-MADE MAN AND WORTHY HUSBAND.

> " There's such a thing as dwelling
>   On the thoughts ourselves have nursed,
> And with scorn and courage telling
> The world to do its worst."　　CURRER BELL.

" You can't expect another such an offer, Nepenthe Stuart," said Mrs. Elliott, coolly, after wasting no little logic and rhetoric in vainly trying to persuade Nepenthe to accept of certain recent proposals of a very flattering and eligible nature, "of which," as she said most emphatically, "any girl in her senses might be proud,"—she ended her first series of arguments with this terrible prophecy, "you'll die an old maid."

"Well," said Nepenthe, "there's nothing disgraceful in that—nothing criminal."

"No," said Mrs. Elliott, "it is not a penal offence to remain unmarried, but you very well know old maids are universally let alone. The way they are sometimes treated in society is no better than actual solitary confinement. Young married couples seek their own companionship, young men and maidens get together by themselves, old people are too old to be their companions, children too noisy, old bachelors and widowers are hunting up young wives. What are these old maids, nurses, stocking-darners, corner-fillers, appendages, incumbrances, the world calls them. Their sayings and doings are much more criticised, even if their manners are circumspect, than those of the most weak-minded and ordinary women well-married. A husband is a shield to a woman ; a shield from criticism ; but an unmarried woman is very often the subject of remark. If she be vain or weak-minded, she is foolish ; if independent and outspoken, she is eccentric, or one of the strong-minded, so the world says, and if she lives as retired and sequestered as a nun, if she looks at a widower, or talks to a bachelor, if she sits within two feet of him in a large parlor, somebody will have it that she is after him. She is setting her cap, and some one will ill-naturedly say, though she is just his age, ' she looks old enough to be his mother,' and such trouble will be taken to find out exactly what her age really is from family Bibles, old nurses, or cotemporary school-mates, and all these estimates will often be summed up with the conclusion that though she looks, with her curls and youthful dress, only thirty, she's not a day under forty."

" A man may live alone for good and noble reasons," said Nepenthe, " and I have a far greater respect for a woman who will not marry because she does not love, than for a young girl who marries to avoid the odium of being called an old maid. There are women with the warmest and noblest of hearts living unmarried for the best of reasons.

Could their lives be written out, there would be some thrilling accounts of self-sacrifice and self-devotion.

"A woman may be lonely, and, at times, unhappy, unmarried, but if she be married to an uncongenial man, she is doubly miserable, twice as lonely, twice as unhappy as if living alone. She may have had forty offers, and yet somebody will ask, 'Why couldn't she marry?' while it will be said of the ugliest, crustiest, fussiest old bachelor, 'I wonder why he never married. It is very strange.'"

"But Mr. Nicholson is a benevolent man, certainly," said Mrs. Elliott. "I see his name on the list of all our prominent charities. Were you to marry him, you might be able to do very much good."

"Marry *him!*" said Nepenthe; "he would regret more the loss of a favorite horse than the death of his mother, who really suffered from his neglect. He is always offering his services, yet he would never take one step out of his comfortable path to save a hundred beggars from starvation. He'll smooth down his luxuriant whiskers as he exclaims, often audibly, more often mentally, '*no industrious person need starve.*' This prudent, sagacious idea checks effectually all his rising generosity. He comes to me with his new neck-tie, his patent-leathers, his costly bouquets, and wants me to be induced by these preliminary 'trifles' to promise to help him to offer up to his most worshipful self his daily matins and vespers.

"If he were never so handsome, wealthy and wonderful, I could never tolerate him if he were selfish. The highest order of goodness and of genius is never selfish. He always says with his eyes, when he comes out with his new suit, 'Don't I look well this evening, Miss Nepenthe? Who can resist such attractions? I have graduated with the highest honors of the best tailors in the city. I am finished and complete.' Were William Nicholson to robe me in ruby and wreath me with diamonds, and place me in a house of pearl, feed me on nectar and ambrosia, I would rather marry blindfold the first plough-boy I might meet. I would rather have a possibility of a heart than a certainty of unmitigated selfishness.

> "A guinea on his counter's brim
> A yellow guinea is to him,
>   That guinea he'll adore."

"Don't get excited, Nepenthe—there goes Mrs. Joshua Jenkins," said Mrs. Elliott, rising and going to the window. She was only three years ago a young lady, beautiful and accomplished, but poor—no better off than yourself. See what an elegant carriage, footman and livery—how splendidly she's dressed. I saw her the other day at Ball & Black's, and she was all diamonds, ermine and velvet. I am sure Joshua Jenkins makes an unexceptionable husband, yet I would much prefer Mr. Nicholson. Mr. Nicholson's money is invested in bond and mortgage, the best of all security—and Mr. Jenkins' is all in bank stock; and banks may fail. Then Mr. Nicholson can't be illiterate, for he is one of the Board of Education."

"It may be possible for him to be one of that highly respectable Board," said Nepenthe, "yet he does not write his name remarkably well. He always says conval'escent, voilent, and volumnious and tremengeous, and serup, and sperit; and I get so tired of hearing him say meetin' for meeting, and smilin', speakin', and larnin' and takin' of it; but I do not envy Mr. or Mrs. Joshua Jenkins. Nobody ever borrows money of him—he never loses a debt—he pays his servants low wages—insists on the utmost penny due him. He runs no risks. He never reads—he can't see the difference between Byron and Dr. Watts, but he keeps his thoughtful eye on the banks. His young wife was beautiful, he rich. There was a brief acquaintance, short engagement, and a splendid wedding. Now she has ermine, and velvet, and diamonds. Ermine is a beautiful fur. I should like to wear it—it suits my taste. I fancy it would be very becoming to me; and velvet is an elegant dress. I would like a very long velvet cloak, a black velvet dress, and a blue velvet and a violet-colored velvet waist; and I do admire the flash and gleam of a diamond. I wish I had a diamond ring. My hand has always looked lonesome to me without one. This life has so many dull, dark hours, I'd like to have something so pure and radiant always about me. There is such a celestial, transparent gleam in a diamond's light, my eyes seem to brighten as I look at one, and I feel the sparkle in my soul too. Yes, I like diamonds.

"But love is a softer ermine for the soul, a richer, more radiant jewel in the heart; and my heart would be so cold and ache if it couldn't be clasped in the embrace of a faith

warmer and richer than costliest velvet folds. I should
starve and freeze without love's little pearl set in my heart.
But Mrs. Joshua Jenkins' life must be dull. She has not
a single taste in common with her husband, and in society
she can't help being annoyed by his blunders. If he only
knew enough to keep still—but he will talk, and he over-
acts and overdoes everything. He says the flattest things
about nice days and pretty music. When I see them together, I think of a fair lily of the valley planted beside a
cabbage. I have heard it said in every wedding there is a
loss. There was a terrible loss in that wedding. Poor
woman! His money can't buy her happiness. His loves
are dogs, horses, wine and beafsteaks. Hers are music,
painting, books, and flowers. When she was so ill last season, some one suggested having some beautiful painting
hung on the wall near her bed, to divert her thoughts from
her sufferings ; so he brought home one afternoon the en-
graving of Mary Queen of Scots, signing the death-warrant
of Lady Jane Grey, and Peale's 'Court of Death.' These
were wonderfully calculated to relieve the gloom of the
sick-room.

"If I marry William Nicholson, Esq., five years to come
we'll be walking together, like Mr. and Mrs. Jenkins, like
two parallel lines, our heart-chords never meeting, though
stretching on side by side in the horizon of years."

"He is a self-made man," said Mrs. Elliott, dignifiedly ;
" that surely is in his favor, and he has attained a fine position among business men by his own unaided efforts."

"I'd rather he'd be a God-made man than a self-made
man," said Nepenthe. "Of all things I dislike this self-
styled, self-made man. Some of them are regular bores,
always taking such infinite pains to show you they know
something. They are great show-cases on the walls of society, just like the show-cases in the small fancy stores way
up town. Everything they have is stuck up in the windows
or in a glass box, always out on exhibition—gloves, collars,
caps, laces, hosiery, handkerchiefs, undersleeves, all arranged conspicuously to show the full dimensions and style
of each article, to attract the attention of passing pedes-
trians. If you enter the store, you'll find nothing, absolutely nothing that you want. It is all in the windows.
You can't even perhaps get a yard of narrow pink satin rib-

bon, or a paper of needles. They've 'had the articles, but are out now, will have them to-morrow, if you can wait.' So these self-styled self-made men are nothing but show-cases, or shop-windows in the structure of society, Hear them talk, you'd think they kept a variety store of know-ledge. They say, 'I didn't get it at an University, or College either.'

"They've a good many ideas at second-hand. They came across lots of knowledge in remnants and bundles. They haven't used their eyes for nothing. What a show they can make in conversation. It is astonishing. From head to foot they are knowledge all over. Their heads are like patch-bags—you can't find the piece of information you wish, unless you empty the whole bag. They've a good many remnants of knowledge, half a yard or so on this subject and on that, and they got 'em cheap too; and every opnion they advance they begin with 'To my mind.'

" When these self-made men get all rigged up in their second-hand ideas, they strut around like the countryman, exclaiming, 'See my new ideas—ain't they wonderful, don't they fit nice?' Then to finish their spiritual toilet, they put on a cap which covers head and ears, and the cap is Progress. This progress-cap caps the climax of everything they say or do. Every time you see or hear from them, they are over head and ears in progress. And first you know they are professed conductors in the car of knowledge, driving in advance of the tardy age. This progress cap is a kind of percussion-cap—it is always striking against something, particularly the crying evils of the times.

" When this self-made man first gets the idea in his head that this is an age of progress, how his eye twinkles, how he rubs his hands together—he feels as if he could write *such an essay*, and only let people know what an idea this progress is. He likes the word development, he puts it in everything he writes. He also puts in, ' We live in a wonderful age;' and if he quotes any poetry it is usually these lines :

> 'Full many a flower is born to blush unseen,
> And waste its sweetness on the desert air.'

And some how his manner implies that *he* is the flower that might have been wasted on the desert air, that *he* is the gem that was self-saved from the dark caves of ignorance and oblivion.

"He'll read some book all learned men study thoroughly at fifteen, and he'll talk about it at the table, as if nobody had ever heard of it before. If he happens to get hold of a work on geology, he'll talk of strata and formations every day for a week. If he hears a minister he likes, he says positively he is the greatest mind of the age. Next time he hears him, he says he is thought by all intelligent men to be the greatest mind of the age. He really thinks, this self-styled self-made man, that he has struck a vein of pure knowledge which these dull college plodders have dug for years, and never found any really valuable information. He knows just as much as those college exquisites, with Kappa Alpha's and Sigma Phi's dangling at their sides. How he secretly wishes he could wear some shining badge of his self-made-ship hanging at his side—an S. M., or something indicating his progress in knowledge.

"He says there's no use of digging and digging at the dry roots of these Latin and Greek grammars, making such a wonderful classic foundation—it is all waste time. Why he can build himself up in all necessary knowledge in one-fourth of the time, without having all this *cellar* and *sub-cellar* in the bottom of his head, which nobody ever looks into. It's a waste of brain capital—it is a dead investment, the paying such a premium for going through Greek and Latin grammars.

"For myself," said Nepenthe, "I would rather marry an excellent blacksmith than a tolerable lawyer, a stupid minister, a rich miser, and above all a self-styled self-made man."

"I have taken a deep interest in your welfare," said Mrs. Elliott, with some pathos in her voice. "I have seen very much of the world. I have taken some pains to bring this matter about, and I am very much surprised that you should hesitate a moment, or think of rejecting such a flattering offer as that of William Nicholson, Esq. His position and resources are certainly everything desirable, and he would really make you a most worthy husband."

"A worthy husband of all things is what I do not want," said Nepenthe. "All stupid people are called worthy, worthy, worthy. If all the men called worthy could be together in one picture gallery, what a smooth-haired, smooth-faced, smooth-lipped, long-eared, girl-faced set they would be."

"For a lady of your supposed sense," said Mrs. Elliott, dryly, "you have really some very strange notions of love and marriage. I always thought you had some queer streaks about you. You are certainly ungrateful. I have shown Mr. Nicholson much attention on your account. To me you owe your present position and standing in society. I have long wished to see you happily married, as I said before, to a worthy husband. I must add, in justice to Mr. Nicholson, that I think it a great condescension in him to offer himself to a portionless bride. There are other reasons I need not name why it is a still greater condescension in him to make this proposal at this time. The Nicholson family are one of the first in the country. You would be introduced in that set, and be always sure of an elegant home. I rather disliked Mr. Elliott when I married him, yet I think we got on together as happily as most married people do, and he left me well provided for. Should Mr. Nicholson die before you, he would leave you an ample fortune."

"I should hardly look forward to that event," interrupted Nepenthe, "judging from his present ample size and perfect health; indeed, I am afraid, should I marry him with my present feelings, should that melancholy event occur, I could hardly lament it as deeply as a bereaved, disconsolate and inconsolable widow is expected to."

"I regret that you treat my advice and consideration for your welfare so indifferently," said Mrs. Elliott, in an offended tone. "I could improve you very much if you would take a few of my suggestions. I see a great many things in you I could alter."

"I am not unmindful of any kindness shown me," said Nepenthe. "You have given me food when hungry, a comfortable bed to sleep upon when weary, a roof to shelter my aching head. If I wept for sorrow, you called me impatient; if I mourned a loss, you told me others have mourned heavier. When I burned my arm by saving you from the flames, you reminded me that others had lost both arms. I must needs be thankful that I had still two. If I lose one arm, it is no consolation that another poor sufferer has lost both. If my head is bruised, it is no consolation to me that

another woman is lying in the next street all **mangled and
helpless**, almost torn to pieces from some terrible accident.
A musical ear feels most keenly the least discord, while
another ear can imperturbably bear the most hideous jargon.
There are many people in this world who would clothe and
feed us, to whom we could never whisper a sorrow, or breathe
a hope. If we are keenly regretting some mistake we have
made, it is no comfort to have some one tell us we are weak,
foolish, injudicious, and ask us, ‘ What did you do that for ?
I could have told you better. I would have done very dif-
ferently.’ ”

“ We are getting away from the subject,” said Mrs. Elliott, coolly. “ Do you expect to marry an angel ? I should
like to know what your expectations are, and what you in-
tend to do with yourself.”

“ I want what every one wants,” said Nepenthe. “ I want
a friend. I long not for advice, counsel, opinion, criticism,
polite treatment. A lawyer, doctor, editor, if well paid,
can give me much of all these. I want something money
cannot buy. Money has great power. There is a pleasure
in being surrounded with elegancies, and being able to bestow gifts and favors. I am painfully sensitive by nature
to any defect in dress, furniture, living. I like draperied
windows, downy carpets, fine paintings and statuary, and I
do not like this endless pinching and screwing and stretching of things, to make them go as far as possible. I dislike
exceedingly scant dresses, shabby gloves, patched or sole-
less gaiters, ever-to-be darned stockings, dyed and turned
silks, black velvet bonnets done over for the tenth time,
with bits of withered lace and old drooping feathers, and
home-made undersleeves, of this highly commended wash-
illusion, which after once washing reminds one of real *illusion*. Those ironed-over bonnet strings, those imitation lace
collars, which once washed boast no more the soft subdued
look of real honiton, point or Valenciennes ; and then to
have but one best silk dress, which will always be either too
light for winter or too dark for summer ; and then if you
have one real fashionable dress, it makes all your other old
things—shawls, gloves, bonnets, look so faded and *pa*ᵥ*sé*, and
then, if to economize, one make it oneself, it may set like a
witch, and double or distort one’s tolerable native dimensions. It is written all over you, that you look as well as

you can—and the Irish chambermaid and porter will leave you to lift your own luggage and carry your own bundles up stairs, as they whisper to each other, with a careless toss of the head, ' O, she's not a lady—she's not nice-dressed !'

" I never was proud of costly dress, but I do feel just a little mortified, if shabbily attired.

" Then I have a longing to be able with my purse to bring out hidden talent, to elevate crushed and gifted humanity. I might be too proudly happy to have others looking to me for comfort, for help, for relief. I have often closed my eyes, and imagined what I would do if I were rich ; and I have, when I gazed on suffering, ragged humanity, or looked longingly on so many beautiful and precious objects, almost within my grasp, earnestly desired to be able to relieve the one and obtain the other. I do long to be able to be fed, housed and clad without begging, borrowing, or being under heavy obligations to any one. Yet much as I prize money for the liberty and power it gives, I will never sell *myself* for it. I would rather live on a sanded floor, have only a deal table, sleep on a hard bed, and wear my great grandmother's ' linsey woolsey ' dress, and have no friend to share my sorrows and feel my joys. . I must have a friend to love what I love, to worship what I worship, or be linked, by earthly tie, to no mortal man. I prefer my own companionship to that of one whose fine horses and full purse are his sole recommendations."

" But Mr. Nicholson has one congenial taste, he has a turn for poetry," said Mrs. Elliott. " I have heard him converse in quite a poetical strain."

" One evening," said Nepenthe, " when we walked down by the cliff, where we have such magnificent sunsets, I think he must have felt poetical, for I remarked, as he stood speechless, that it was a beautiful sunset.

" ' Yes, he replied. ' Do you know what it reminds me of ?'

" ' No," said I.

" ' It reminds me of the rose on the cheeks of beauty," said he, in a low, soft voice. Just then a cow came and looked over the fence, and mooed at us. ' Oh !' said he, ' isn't that a splendid cow ! I'd like to own such a fine creature as that. I have some cattle now in the country

which I'd like to show you, but I'd like to own that creature.'

"While he looked at the cow, I stood by the cliff and
looked at the sky and sea, bathed in a flood of sunset glory.
He turned suddenly, for the cow had gone, and asked me if
I thought he could jump from the cliff without breaking his
neck? I felt like telling him to try.

"He repeated to me one verse of his poetry once. He
said he considered it the best he ever wrote. I think it ran
thus :

<blockquote>
'Time goes on, he runs a race,
He hurries on, he rides apace;
Messengers Time doth send,
Eternity is Time without end.'
</blockquote>

I would like a man just as well if he didn't talk or write
poetry; but if he couldn't tell good verse from bad, or distinguish Byron from Watts, and was given to whipping up
such syllabub rhymes, I would prefer an incorrigible dunce,
who knew enough to speak when spoken to, and leave such
poets as William Nicholson, Esq. to marry his muse for all
me. He knows no difference between the flattest plati-
tudes, the tamest placidities, and the tinkle of fairy music.
He asked me one evening if I had seen any of Mr. Anon's
poetry—he thought that Anon made the best verses in the
language. He couldn't remember Mr. Anon's first name,
but he was sure it was Anon; and if he could find a well-
bound collection of Anon's poems, he would be happy to
present them to me.

"I told him I would give twenty dollars for a handsome
copy of Anon's poems, with his full name on the title page,
it would be such a rare book. At that time he took it into
his head that I was a great admirer of poetry, and all his
conversation had a poetical spice, flavor and turn; but as to
real taste, he would rather any time see a fine paving stone,
than look at Tintern Abbey or the Rock of Gibraltar."

"But you don't know all Mr. Nicholson's excellencies
yet. He has great firmness and decision of character," said
Mrs. Elliott.

"It doesn't take long to fathom a man when there is nothing in him," said Nepenthe. "His vacant brow wears the
sign, 'An apartment to let.' I know he has, as you say,
great firmness and decision of character. So has many a

mule you meet, carrying his heavy burden. He has the pertinacity, the positive nature of a man enough to carry his point, and have his own way, right or wrong; but he has neither moral sense, enlightened judgment, nor sober reason to control that will. I would as soon look up to and yield my will to your brown dog, or your gray cat, as to that of William Nicholson, Esq., sole possessor of one hundred thousand dollars, well invested; and either of the aforesaid animals would defend and help me quite as well in the path of rectitude and happiness, and comfort me better in affliction. Indeed I would prefer a respectable bark, or a comfortable purr, to his most eloquent strains of poetry."

" His manners are certainly gentlemanly," indignantly interrupted Mrs. Elliott.

" Mr. Nicholson has no delicacy of taste, no nobility of character," said Nepenthe, " and why he has chosen me I know not—probably for the same reason that he would prefer a brown house, or a white and black dog, to a gray one; about tall enough, about large enough, about poor enough, he says to himself, to suit my superior size, and to value my superior wealth.

" Were I his wife I should submit silently to things inconsistent and wrong, or resist his will and wishes when greatly opposed to my sense of right—and no true-hearted woman wishes to positively and frequently oppose the man she calls her husband."

" But you could influence him," said Mrs. Elliott : " you could gradually induce him to think as you do—there's everything in managing a husband."

" I don't wish to manage a husband—I have quite enough to do to manage myself," said Nepenthe. " I want a husband that will fit me, not one I have to make over. So far as I can see, this making husbands over is no very easy business: like bread worked over too much, they may get sour in the process. You can't manage them as you would a horse, with *bits* of advice and *bridles* of restraint.

" The lords of creation are apt to be quite sensitive on this point—and even a stupid, ignorant man may find out, as somebody will be sure to tell him, that he is the head of the house.

" I would rather be managed than manage—to look up to my husband, than to be always looking after his failings, enlightening his ignorance, improving his morals, and smoothing over his mistakes. I'd rather undertake to be the governess of forty children than of one man of Mr. Nicholson's formidable size and indomitable will."

" You are getting exceedingly nervous of late," said Mrs. Elliott, dignifiedly, " you should retire earlier, be more regular in your habits, and avoid the excitement of company. I dislike to see a young lady so excessively and disagreeably nervous—you should control yourself."

" Nervous !" said Nepenthe, " I wish the word were out of the world's calendar, it is so convenient. Men and women too call everything they can't comprehend, ' nervous.' What dictionary defines half of its allowed meanings ? ' Easily agitated, a colloquial use of the word,' says Webster : but not a groan is uttered, a sympathy expressed, impulse acted upon, anxiety endured, or accident befallen, but there'll be some cool mortals standing by, watching the style of the groan, the form of the sob, and to see how hard she takes it, as they shake their wise heads and exclaim emphatically, 'O, she's nervous—dreadful nervous.' If any one is quite ill, there'll be hundreds of people to say ' O, there's nothing the matter, it's one of her nervous spells ;' and if the nature of the disease baffles the doctor's knowledge and skill, he'll be sure to say to the attentive nurse, ' I think it is only a nervous difficulty, Madame.' And still human nature grieves on, and sometimes wails and dies after long continued pressure of agony. So long as its depths are stirred, its surface will be agitated.

" The great deep of a loving, suffering heart must at times be broken up, and tears must fall, sighs swell upwards, and sobs break forth. When the storm comes and the clouds gather, the deep billows of the soul must heave and swell, and subside, and he who stands on the shore of comfort with dry feet looking on, will mockingly say, ' How nervous !— did you ever see anybody so nervous ? You should control yourself.'

" Many a discouraged woman toils on with pale cheek and fading eye, while man says there's nothing the matter, only she's getting nervous—while from her heart, beating fainter and fainter, goes up to the Ear ever open on high, a silent testimony of patient, unrequited struggle, and uncheered, unappreciated toil.

"Who reproaches the ocean for its restless heaving, its roaring and wild dashing against the shore, and who shall hardly reproach, when deep answereth unto deep within the human heart, till its stirred sympathies dash wildly against the shore of life. As well call the tempestuous ocean nervous, as the impulsive, heaving heart."

"You *are* nervous," repeated Mrs. Elliott; "and what is very unfortunate for a person of nervous temperament, you must have read a great many novels. Pray where is the site of your love in a cottage, and who is the hero of your dreams? Is he to come from the greenwood, and you live together so comfortably on the balmy air? Air plants have sometimes no root. This airy home and airy lover of yours may never have root or foundation on mortal soil. Some singing minstrel or limping poet perhaps already claims the honor of your hand, and the first place in your so highly valuable and priceless heart."

"One has long since had place in my heart," said Nepenthe, coolly. "His words will never leave my soul—he has been domesticated by my heart's fireside a long time : I could hardly do without him. He was the first to tell me long ago, when in deep trouble to suffer and be strong. When I think of his peerless, consoling intellect, I am always reminded of footsteps of angels. My acquaintance with him has been one of the greatest pleasures of my life. He is a poet, a true poet ; his words are always beautiful and appropriate, whether he talks to me by the fireside in winter, or wanders with me by the seaside in summer : he has taught me the beautiful language of resignation, and I often feel when all alone ' a part of the self-same universal being' which is throbbing in his brain and heart."

"Where did you become acquainted with this paragon ?" said Mrs. Elliott sneeringly, "and what is his name ?"

"His name is Henry," said Nepenthe, "and I became acquainted with him at first at Dr. Wendon's. He introduced him to me one evening while in the library. He always chooses the poet's corner, and I must frankly acknowledge he is as near my beau ideal as any living man—that is, so far as I know him. Since that first introduction, after his pleasant prelude to our first pleasant interview, he was very often my companion. He pleased my understanding

as much as he captivated my fancy.   He has filled my soul
with dreams.

> " Dreams that the soul of youth engage
>   Ere Fancy hath been quelled ;
>   Old legends of the monkish page,
>   Traditions of the saint and sage,
>   Tales that have the rime of age,
>   And chronicles of Eld."

" Your head is full enough of such things now, without
his filling it any more," said Mrs. Elliott, really relieved to
find Nepenthe had some one in view.   " But his name is
Henry, you say—no very romantic name.   Pray what is the
other name of this beau ideal of yours ?"

" Henry Wadsworth Longfellow," said Nepenthe slowly
and distinctly.   " He is the hero of my imagination.   I hope
you may know him some day as well as I do—and long as
his name is, may his shadow never be less.   I owe a great
deal to him.   Come some time into my room, and I will
tell you something he says.   I should never get tired of him
though he said the same thing over to me every day.   I
found out from him that

> ' Life is real, life is earnest,'

—and each day I feel more deeply the force of his great
thought."

" You can marry whom and when you please," said Mrs.
Elliott, rising indignantly, " I shall give you no longer support or shelter.   Your foolishly indulgent patron and friend
is now on a foreign shore, and you may yet reap the bitter
reward of your ingratitude and folly."

Mrs. Elliott came back again with flashing eye, indignant
look, and elevated tone, to say, " You are hypocritical with
all your well-put-on amiability ; you havn't the least sense
of right, and are very headstrong."

Mrs. Elliott went out again, giving the door a most emphatic close, till every window in the house shook.

" I am not hypocritical," thought Nepenthe, as she walked back and forth in an excited manner.   " Why is it such
a terrible thing to have a way or a will of one's own.   The
flower raises or droops its head to suit its nature, the vine
clasps its tendrils in some native fashion.   Why can't each
heart, which has so many wild throbbings, and resistless
willings, have sometimes its way ?   Its inward bias, its at-

tractions are native and strong as the clasp of the vine's tendril.

"The heart needs no bruising, no breaking—only pure air and clear light, and it will struggle up and blossom into beauty. 'Headstrong!' 'headstrong!' I hate that word 'headstrong.' I wish some autocrat would define the boundary of that disputed territory, that 'unseen spiritual fence' between independent principle and stubborn obstinacy.

"Mrs. Elliott is one of those who always thinks her opinion correct principle, wholesome advice, and mine is stubborn obstinacy. How human nature gets pulled and hauled, and mauled and scolded, and driven like an ugly bear or a fiery horse—to gratify somebody's principle, or sense of right! That 'sense of right' has so many shapes and forms I begin to think it is a myth, or one of the lost senses. Mrs. Elliott might as well set the springs and wheels and complicated machinery of her clock in order, by going at it with hammer and tongs, as to take the feelings of the heart by storm. Oh, if the right hand could take the right key, and carefully wind at the keyhole of the heart, the secret spring of feeling would be moved; brain, will, nerve, and sense would act in harmony—the big wheels of thought would keep good time, and the busy hands move tirelessly around the circle of care. Then we wouldn't always be getting out of order, running down, or standing still. Bombard the castle of the will, stormed and starved and besieged, it is monarch still, and no sharp words shall tack down basting threads for the guiding of its lordly way over the carpet of destiny."

This was only a burst of indignation—it was not the outgushing of Nepenthe's true nature; like a tired child, she felt like sobbing herself to sleep in a mother's arms. She never could battle or contend; the effort was painful, the reaction depressing. The lancet and probe of reproof were never fit for her gentle nature—but the wine and oil of healing, and the balm and benediction of sympathy. Every great heart has a throb of its own, every great will has a will of its own.

Dispirited and sad after this long and tiresome interview with Mrs. Elliott, Nepenthe sits alone and thinks.

That roof had been to her no home but a shelter, and now she had no shelter. She took up a book from the table, accidentally left there that morning by Florence. It was Shirley. Nepenthe had never read it. She turns its pages carelessly over, and opens at last the chapter giving an account of the interview of Shirley Keeldar with Mr. Simpson, who tries to find who she loves. She is pleased to see any resemblance between her situation and the fortunate Shirley.

"Oh, if I were only rich!" she exclaimed, "I could be more independent. The heart is the same everywhere. Every human heart is human, but who shall conquer its love, or quell its hate? This secret of my love shall never escape me by any ordeal. It shall not be dragged out and burned at the stake of ridicule. I will hoard and hide it in the safe of my heart, and no burglar tongue or assassin hand shall force the lock. He who has the key alone shall open the safe, or the secret shall die with me; and in heaven, where kindred souls like stars cluster together, my soul may find its twin wanderer. Here this love can never go back in my heart and die.

'As if a rose should shut, and be a bud again.'"

Florence Elliott's love for Carleyn was becoming the ruling passion of her life. Madame Future had lain aside her veil and talked with her face to face.

Florence would once have spurned the idea of seeking or receiving such counsel; she went at first out of curiosity—now it had become a passion, the woman seemed really to enter heart and soul into her cherished plans.

It was an avowed opinion of Florence's, that it was no greater sin to express wrong than to feel wrong: she believed in expressing what she felt, if convenient. Her love and pride were both gratified in receiving attentions from the distinguished young Carleyn. She was becoming more and more beautiful since her first consultation with Madame Future, whose directions she implicitly followed. Through her, Florence had found out Carleyn's private tastes, likes, and dislikes.

He loved poetry, flowers, and simple dress, and these tastes she cultivated most assiduously—buying poetry, surrounding herself with rare flowers, and wearing them as her only ornament in her beautiful hair, and she dressed with the most elegant simplicity.

Many marvelled at the great change in her style of dress.
To Carleyn's dazzled eyes she seemed like a radiant vision.
How pleasant to have such a beautiful wife for a living
model !

She sat alone in her room one evening, after her return
from a party, and recalled his every look, word and tone, as
she thought, " How pleasant to have him watch my face, and
say, ' There, that's a beautiful expression—I'll put that
down ;' and then to find another beautiful expression, and
put that down—to have him trot all these expressions about
in his head, till at last he comes out with a beautiful finished portrait—to have my portrait sent to the Academy of
Design, as in the possession of the artist, Frank Carleyn—
No. 101—and go myself, and have admiring visitors ask
whose it was—and have some one tell them, ' It is the artist's beautiful wife'—'The artist's bride '—that sounds
well. Yes, I will be his wife," she said, " or "——and she
arose, walked back and forth in great excitement, and then
paused a moment before the mirror. " Thank God," she
exclaimed, " I *am* beautiful—my features are perfect, my
form symmetrical."

Madam Future, divested of sybillistic dress, manners,
tone, surroundings, dark curtains, obscure lights, colored
vials, charms, glasses—elaborately and elegantly arrayed,
sometimes goes into society. She loves solitude best, but it
suits well her purposes and plans to enter sometimes the
crowded salon, *musicale soirée* and reception. If she stoops
to mingle with the common throng, as she calls society, it is
to fathom some mystery in its secret net-work, to find out
some plot or counterplot, and thus gain some charm or coun-
ter-charm.

You might look in many a face, and meet no such eye as
Madam Future's. If it rested upon you, you felt as if under
the full blaze of a brilliant chandelier, as if every salient
point in your character were illuminated. Her look seemed
to fathom you—her eyes burned like consumeless fires. If
eyes fade that weep long, no tears had dimmed her eyes.
No, she never wept. The fount of tears had dried long
since. Every sorrow she had known, every disappointment
felt, had only formed some strange accretion round her
heart. That heart never melted to tears. Gathering years
of ossification, it turned to stone. As her tears froze away,

her revenge grew and burned and fed itself within her heart. She said she never in her whole life had been deceived but once.

The next evening after the party, Florence was guided by an unknown hand, through the dark, up many flights of stairs, into a circular room, where all the lights were extinguished. Looking through a long glass properly adjusted by Madam Future, she said, "I see a room—a clock on the mantel. I can plainly see the hand pointing to eight. There's a vase of flowers, and there are rare books on the table—and there is Carleyn reading, and Nepenthe Stuart sits at work by the table. She is knitting something—it looks like a chain. He stops reading, looks up and talks. Now he smiles—reads on again. She is looking up, and asks some question. They stand at the window together—he points upward.

"Yes," thought Florence, "I suppose he pays her some slight attentions out of pity, she tries so hard to interest him."

"Contrive," said Florence, "to whisper, or to have whispered these words into Carleyn's ear : ' Low family, doubtful origin.' Say also, ' She is engaged to Mr. Nicholson.' "

"Yes," said Madam Future, taking the piece of gold from Florence's hand, "there'll be a *bal masqué* on Wednesday evening—I'll be there—I can tell him something that will make him think."

Carleyn sat alone in his room, with a copy of Hyperion in his hand. He had borrowed it from Florence Elliott. Turning the pages carelessly, half a sheet of folded note paper fell out. There were on it a few verses written faintly with a pencil. They were in Florence Elliott's hand. He had heard her say one evening, that she had a careless habit of leaving things in books very often, much to her mortification afterwards. The verses were signed ' F. E.'

"Florence has deeper feeling and nobler conception than I have given her credit for," thought Mr. Carleyn, as he read the poetry carefully over. "Her few defects may be owing to early indulgence, and her great beauty ; and she loves flowers too. How beautifully she arranges them. I am always sure, if a person can write one good poem, he is capable of writing more, many more, if excited by any deep emotion or powerful feeling. If there is any pure gold of thought discovered in the soul, there must be a valuable mine somewhere in the spiritual strata."

Florence resolved to go to the great reception the next evening, charmingly dressed, and determined, if possible, to fasten the chain she was quite sure she was firmly rivetting. Never did she bestow such pains upon her toilet, never linger so long at the mirror. Never was her hair so artistically arranged. Never did her cheek bloom rosier, her eye flash brighter, never were her lips rubier, or her voice sweeter. There was not a touch to add, a charm to give, as she threw her snowy opera cloak over her fair shoulders, and went forth to the final conquest.

Madam Future, splendidly arrayed, went also. You could hardly know her, so transformed by elegant and fashionable dress. Her long, wavy hair, beautifully arranged, gave her at least a stylish appearance, as she moved with high bred ease among the crowd.

Any high-minded, ideal-loving man, to gaze on Florence Elliott's lovely exterior, would say, she is a lovely woman, a true soul and pure heart, must glow in such radiant eyes, and inspire such beautiful lips!

CHAPTER XXIX.

THE MUSIC BOOK OPEN AT THE WRONG PLACE.

"There should be no despair for you
    While nightly stars are burning;
While evening pours its silent dew,
    And sunshine gilds the morning.

"There should be no despair, though tears
    May flow down like a river;
Are not the best beloved of years ·
    Around your heart forever?"—EMILY BRONTE.

THE party given by Mrs. Norwood was attended by nearly two thousand persons. The entire house was thrown open for the entertainment of the guests. The first floor was devoted to dancing, the band being in the hall. In the picture gallery the panorama was kept moving in the evening. The upper floors were arranged for conversation, whist, &c. The basement to refreshments, billiards and bowling. The large number of carriages which thronged the streets made access to the house tedious and difficult. The whistle of the outside guard, as usual, announced arrivals, which caused the doors to open as the visitors approached.

They had all gone to the party at Mrs. Norwood's—fashionable belles, and exquisite beaux, matrons and maidens, were already promenading, chatting, dancing in those brilliant parlors.

It was a cool autumn night. The wind had a sound of winter, and the sky was dark and gloomy. Nepenthe sat alone in Mrs. Elliott's large parlor, looking drearily out through the half-open shutters. It was her birth-day night. A strange feeling of restlessness came over her, a disgust of books, of work, of solitude, a longing for social life. The measured ticking of the clock was poor relief to the undisturbed stillness reigning throughout the house. Nepenthe's usual quiet, contented manner, was gone. She paced restlessly back and forth upon the downy carpet.

"I am alone," she said bitterly. "I love music—I love society. How I would prize one heart that really loved me. O, if I only had a mother, a sister, or even one friend! Is life always to be a game in which I can take no part? How grateful I would be for the crumbs of happiness that fall from the bountiful table of others' lives. And now I have no home—I know not where to go to-morrow. And *I* am called *Nepenthe*—strange name for me, who am to drink the cup of loneliness and sorrow to the dregs."

Nepenthe walked to the window, and a few large drops of the rapidly gathering shower fell on the window-sill. She approached the piano and seated herself, to pour forth, half unconsciously, her murmuring in song—singing, as she turned over the leaves of the music book :

> "I feel like one who treads alone
> Some banquet hall deserted."

With eyes swimming with tears, she saw at the bottom of one of the pages, these words, sung so beautifully by Dempster :

> "Be still, sad heart, and cease repining ;
> Behind the cloud is the sun, still shining.
> Thy fate is the common fate of all,
> Into each life some rain must fall,
> Some days must be dark and dreary."

Nepenthe sang it all through, with exquisite pathos. She paused, almost choked with tears, as the rising wind seemed to whisper forth its wild chorus :

"My heart still clings to the mouldering past,
The hopes of youth fall thick in the blast,
And the days are dark and dreary."

Before her suddenly stood a vision—no, not a vision, but a tall manly form, and a pair of dark eyes were gazing at her with a surprised, embarrassed look.

"I thought you were at Mrs. Norwood's, Mr. Carleyn," said she, equally surprised and embarrassed, as she uttered the first thought that came in her head.

"I am going to Europe to-morrow," said he, after talking with her a few minutes.

"I wish you 'bon voyage,' said Nepenthe, after an awkward pause, with a few remarks upon the rapidly improving facilities for travelling, he left, intending to set sail the next day.

"He came hoping to find Florence at home, I presume," said Nepenthe, as she sat on the sofa with her face buried in her hands. "He may be absent two years, feasting upon beautiful sights, enchanted with bright eyes and graceful forms. He will forget me entirely. But how weak I am! He has never thought of me, while he is the only ideal of manly goodness I have known."

She had controlled herself so long, now she would give way to her feelings.

"If any one calls, say I am engaged," she said to Margaret, as she closed the door and shut herself in the parlor alone.

Margaret walked quietly out, and stood for a moment looking out of the front door, when Mr. Carleyn came up the steps again, saying,

"I left a small package in the parlor."

"Walk in, sir," said she, opening the door a little wider; "she is in there."

The little package had remained undisturbed on the corner of the sofa. He heard as he opened the door a suppressed sob, and the words, "I wish I had never been"——
The sentence was unfinished, as Nepenthe started up with tearful eyes and sad face.

"I beg pardon for intruding, but I came back for this little package," said Carleyn.

He seemed agitated, yet drew near the sofa and sat down. "I find you in some sudden sorrow," said he. "Propriety, perhaps, would induce me to withdraw silently; and yet, though I know not the cause of your sorrow, I know you are a woman, with a woman's heart. I came here to bid "——

As he said this, the door opened again, and in walked William Nicholson, Esq., with bland smile, new neck-tie, new suit of shining broadcloth, new patent leathers, and a boquet of such size, color and shape, as to remind one of a fresh cauliflower as it comes from the market.

Margaret went down into the kitchen, and told Bridget she was sure Mr. Nicholson had come courting this time, he was so fixed up—"and then he had such a big bunch of flowers."

Nepenthe was certainly surprised and sorry that on *this* particular evening he had done her this particular honor; and then the truth flashed upon her mind that Mrs. Elliott had probably concealed from him her recent positive refusal of his very flattering proposal.

Taking it for granted that such an offer would soon be gratefully accepted, he had the air and manner of an acknowledged lover—treating Carleyn as if *he* of course, in this interview, should have the advantage in claiming, and the preference in giving Nepenthe attention. Seeing the piano open, he asked for some music.

Nepenthe, perplexed, vexed, and distressed, was glad to play and sing to relieve her embarrassment. He wished her to sing "Thou, thou reign'st in this Bosom;" but she told him she couldn't sing it without the music.

While she was singing a sweet Scotch song, Margaret came in very unceremoniously with a basket of flowers, saying, "Here are the flowers Miss Florence wished you to arrange for the table to-morrow."

Putting them aside, Nepenthe sang a few songs, played a few difficult pieces, and then left the piano and commenced arranging the flowers—finding it extremely difficult to entertain two such visitors at the same time.

"When I see flowers," said Carleyn, "I am reminded of the first boquet I ever owned. I was a little boy then, and on a visit to my uncle in the city. He always indulged me in every wish, and on my birth-day offered to do anything to please me. We took a walk in Broadway. We went to a florist's, and he bought me a beautiful bouquet. There were a great many heliotropes and violets, mingled with other flowers. I was delighted with the flowers—and then I coaxed him to take me to see the hospital—the place he had so often visited. I often wondered what became of the little pale girl I saw there. She had dark brown hair, and large dark eyes. She was so thin and pale, she really looked unearthly, with her face lighted up with those large dark eyes."

"What did you do with the flowers?" said Nepenthe, without seeming to notice the last remark.

"I laid them on the little girl's pillow as I came away," said Carleyn. "Poor child, I knew she could have very few flowers in the hospital, and then, poor thing, I felt sorry for her. She was in the care of a cross-looking nurse. I know I wouldn't want such eyes to watch me if I were sick."

Nepenthe said nothing more, and Mr. Nicholson looked bewildered, as if the conversation had taken a strange turn. "I hope it will be fair to-morrow, Miss Nepenthe," said he, (he had never called her Miss Nepenthe before,) "and then we'll have a nice ride. I want you to see my new horses."

Nepenthe had lost all her quickness of thought, so she said nothing, *absolutely nothing* to this last remark.

Both gentlemen soon after left, and Florence and Mrs. Elliott came home about ten o'clock. Not finding Carleyn at the reception, Florence had no wish to stay.

That evening was the first time Nepenthe had sung or played since she came to Mrs. Elliott's, and Florence had no idea that she had any musical skill, taste or knowledge.

"How strange," thought Florence, as she came in the parlor, after Nepenthe had gone up to her room. "The piano is open, and here is a song I never sing—and it is a song Frank Carleyn was asking me to sing only the other day. I was going to learn it, and was practicing it before I went out; but I am quite sure I put it up, and that I left a waltz on the piano."

Ringing the bell violently, and summoning Margaret, she said, in an excited tone, "Margaret, has any one been here this evening?"

"No," said Margaret, frightened; "nobody but Mr. Carleyn. You know I always let him in. I thought he would wait until you came home."

" You know I told you to let no one in when I was out."

" I didn't know you were out at first, ma'am, and afterwards I looked up stairs and down, and then I knew you must be out."

" Well, what did he say ?"

" He said he would wait awhile, ma'am."

Florence Elliott was not a fine singer, though she played well ; and she knew the song upon the piano was one of his favorites.

" A little after he came in," said Margaret, " I heard the piano, and some one singing ; so I thought you must be at home."

" Are you sure, Margaret, that it was *my* piano ? Wasn't it the piano next door ? Are you sure no lady has been here ? Mary Hume comes sometimes and plays when I am gone, and she always sings these sweet songs. She touches the keys and hums a little, and often looks over the music ; but she glides in and glides out again, like a little fairy."

" There's been no one in the parlor this evening," said Margaret, " but Miss Stuart and Mr. Carleyn."

Somehow these names didn't sound pleasantly together in Florence's ears.

" Margaret," said she.

" Ma'am ?"

" Never let Mr. Carleyn in again when I am out."

" You have often told me, ma'am, when *he* called, to let him wait ; and I really thought at first you were in."

Florence walked back and forth, excited and angry. This was the first suspicion she had had of Nepenthe Stuart's ability to sing and play. " Pretty business," said she, " Nepenthe Stuart's singing and playing for Frank Carleyn. She is always out of the room when I am home, and he calls, and I always meant she should be. It is a complete ruse. The hypocrite ! Then to think I told him she sewed for us, intimating that she was a seamstress. He'll begin to think there's some mystery about this, and mystery will excite a man's curiosity any day. As for singing, I never knew she could sing."

" How came Nepenthe Stuart to be in the parlor ?" she said, an hour after, to her mother.

"I wished her to sit there," said Mrs. Elliott, "while we were gone. Since that silver was stolen the other evening, I feel a little uneasy if I go out and leave the parlors alone. The truth is, I am afraid that Bridget is not quite honest."

Florence Elliott had a new reason for disliking Nepenthe. No one, not even a child, should come between her and her plans. "Sing for *him*?—how *dared* she?"

Poor innocent Nepenthe! Once more, in angry tones, she heard Florence and her mother talking in French, and she was the subject of their harsh reproach. "How dared she sing and play, in my absence, for Carleyn?" she heard repeated in loud and angry tones.

"Did Miss Stuart remain long in the parlor after Mr. Carleyn came in?" she asked of Margaret the next day.

"I don't know, ma'am. I only went in once, to ask her to arrange those flowers you bade me tell her to fix to send to the fair to-morrow. I didn't know he was there then, or I shouldn't have gone in. She arranged them, and they are all ready for you, in the parlor."

"How provoking!" thought Florence again. "He is always complimenting me about my taste in arranging flowers. Now he'll think of course Nepenthe Stuart does it all. These men only want a few things to find out more. I'd have given a great deal not to have had him know about those flowers. He is so fond of flowers, and says so much about their artistic arrangement. Well as I know Frank Carleyn, he is so true himself he never suspects any one—but once show him a little cause, a little deceit, and he will suspect everything. Drop one stitch in the chain of such a man's confidence, and before you know it they all go, and the elastic cord will break, or shorten forever."

"I do love him," thought Nepenthe, as she turned uneasily on her pillow that night. "If he were dead, I could think of him calmly—but if he marries another, how can I be happy?—and I could be so happy with him. His looks and words are so dear to me, I never shall forget his pleasant voice when he said, before I sat beside him in the carriage, 'I shall be happy to take this young lady under my charge.' And then, *he* gave me those flowers at the hospital. He little thought I was the pale girl, and he has not forgotten me as I was then. Those flowers made me feel as if God was near me ; though I was shut up in tho hospital, without friends, as if He would clothe me, with my little weak faith, just as he did those beautiful heliotropes and violets. But distinguished, courted, flattered as he is, how do I dare to think of him ? I must hide my weak, foolish love. 'Tis not because he is a distinguished artist that I love him—'tis for himself alone. If he were only poor, I could go with him anywhere in the wide world, and cling to him through all. If he were poor and unknown, and I rich, he should know and feel, as I now feel, that our two souls are kindred souls. I can enter into his thoughts, his hopes. I know I could cheer him when sad, cling to him through all trouble and danger. But I should be too happy if I were his. It would be too glorious a dawn after my long night. God help me to forget, to banish him from my heart —to still this love. Yet love is a holy and beautiful feeling. If I were a man, and he a woman, I would woo and win him. I know I could—but I must forget—my heart is aching, and my heart will almost burst.

"*Forget*, did I say ? Do the stars forget to shine, the river to murmur, the wind to whisper, the ocean to heave ? I might have stifled this love once, but it is too late now. I have only to hide it, to cover it up as a beautiful ruin in my heart. I cannot crush love—it will rise again— or drown it with tears, or put it to eternal sleep. Love is a clairvoyant dreamer, a somnambulistic sleeper. But I have a shelter to seek to-morrow, and what have I to do with love ? Bread must be earned, and water must be sure."

Carleyn sat in his room that night, thinking. "Yes, she must be engaged to Nicholson. No man could be such a goose as to be so marked, pointed and demonstrative, only to a woman he loved, and who he knew loved him. But yet I could not see anything in her manner to him that evinced the least of that ardent affection I should want the woman I loved to feel for me. But the learned compute that seven hundred and seven millions of millions of vibrations have penetrated the eye, before the eye can distinguish the tints of a violet. What philosophy can calculate the vibrations of the heart before it can distinguish the colors of love ?"

CHAPTER XXX.

MR. NICHOLSON RESOLVES TO BE INTELLECTUAL.

"Christian faith is a grand cathedral with divinely pictured windows. Standing without, you see no glory, nor can possibly imagine any; standing within, every ray of light reveals a harmony of unspeakable splendors."—MARBLE FAUN.

"THE girl is intellectual; yes, intellectual, I believe they call it," said Mr. Nicholson to himself, as he sat in his luxuriously furnished room thinking about Nepenthe; "and she is rather serious-minded, too, I should judge. If I were going to buy or sell an article, I should know just how to go to work, but this is a kind of thing I have never done before, ask a woman to marry me, and I hope I shall never have to do it again. I shall lose all respect for her if she is such a fool as to refuse me; but then, young ladies don't always make the best choice. They don't always know what is for their good. I am rich and good-looking, fine-looking, I suppose, at least, I think so when I stand up by that slender, pale Carleyn. He has no color in his face, and he is not substantial-looking. I wonder if he is much of a man. I suppose he makes good pictures, but that is very light work for a man, very. I guess, after I'm married, I'll have him take a portrait of Nepenthe and me. I'd like to encourage him a little. He appears to me a very well meaning young man.

"I have no doubt I shall succeed in getting her in the end, but I want to make short and sure work of it. I suppose, if you want to get a woman to love you, you must try and like what she likes. I can slick myself up and walk in and out of a room gracefully, talk about the weather, &c., but that is not all. I must be intellectual; yes, I must be intellectual. I rather think that will take. I'll read the last serious and deep work there is out, the one that is the most popular, and go and talk about it with her."

Mr. Nicholson shuts himself up three hours and reads

Renan's " Life of Jesus," filling his head as full as possible with the main ideas and most striking things in the book. He goes round in the evening to make Nepenthe a call, and after talking about books generally and new ones in particular, he ventures some deep remarks on the subject of miracles, and clearing his throat with a slight wise kind of a cough, he begins with—

" Don't you think, Miss Nepenthe, that most of the miracles in the Bible were intended to be—to be—taken in a figurative sense ?"

" They've a way of figurating everything off now," said Nepenthe. " Maybe, it was only a figurative Eden, a figurative Adam, a figurative ' creation,' a figurative ' beginning,' and perhaps a figurative Deity after all ; and the book that my mother lived and died by may be only a figurative book. It may be a figurative comfort, a figurative trust after all. Isn't there anything real ? I never can forget the words of that hymn they used to sing in the dear old church at Northampton when I was a child—

> " ' Firm as a rock Thy truth shall stand,
> When rolling years shall cease to move.'

" Those words I used to hear many a sweet Sabbath morning from that clear-voiced village choir. They are as plain to me now as if they floated on my ear only yesterday. Watts may be the great millennial prophet poet laureate, at that last glad bright morning when a kneeling world shall bow—

> " ' Before Jehovah's awful throne,'

and—

> " ' Earth, with her ten thousand tongues,'

—shall sing to that dear Old Hundred this anthem of the universe."

" These miracles in the Bible," said Nepenthe, " are like those ' calendars of home, whose rubrics are colored by our hearts.' I read them when a little child in Paul's Life of Christ, Paul, who was so good an Oriental traveller and scholar. I cannot worship Renan's Christ because he has given him, with all his sweetness and superior nature, a Jesuit's cunning and craft in allowing him to pretend to work miracles in spite of his lofty nature, because, as he says, if he had died before he pretended to work miracles, he might have been dearer indeed to God, but his memory would never have been preserved among men.

"It seems to me, when we seek to 'look atter truth stars,' we must 'put out' such little reason 'candles' as this."

"Well," says Mr. Nicholson, quoting his author exactly, "'it is in the name of universal experience that we banish miracles from history.' I suppose, that is, they are contrary to the laws of nature. Many things in the Bible are contrary to the laws of nature."

"I'd like to know," said Nepenthe, "who dares to say he knows or has read half the laws of nature. There's ever so many volumes of them way up on the highest shelves of creation, and most of us never get tall enough to reach up to those books piled up on the top shelves, and in my opinion, the firm old Bible is the best ladder we can climb to get to any of them. Every time some new thought comes up, or a new expression of an old wonderful truth, somebody screams out, 'That's not so; that's contrary to the laws of nature,' because they have not found it in the few pages they have read of Creation's great code. Half of us have only learned the first large letters of nature, woven in with the big pictures in her first primer. We can't begin to read in easy readings yet.

"It will be a long time before we translate the deepest, finest, most intricate, passages in nature's eloquent pleadings, supplements, digests, her affirmed, recognized or unwritten, but beautiful and perfect laws—laws she promulgates many a day as she opens with a morning-glory for a text, and stands in the great blue pulpit above, and closes with a holy star for a benediction.

"I do not like Renan's Christ, because it is, in my opinion, contrary to the laws of human nature to represent an incomparable, unsurpassable, unrivalled, sublime type and model of humanity or human divinity living 'face to face with God,' perpetrating a grand series of striking, startling frauds.

"This is contrary to all our universal experience of mortal goodness and greatness. One exposed deception, one suspected fraud, imposition, hypocrisy or humbug, dethrones for us from its loftiest pedestal on the shrine of our reverent admiration, our most æsthetic and faultless earthly idol. A thing we can't tolerate, but rebuke with scorn in a servile inferior, we can't allow to stain and soil the glorious robe of the kingly, sovereign soul of the Prince of Peace. Nearer to men, dearer to God, is our sublimest ideal—not farther from God, dearer to men.

" We can't like this Jesuitical gleam, this sardonic light, playing around the pure, radiant aureola that halos the image of Christ in every little child's worshipping heart.

" Things men call miracles, marvels, impossibilities, incredibles, may be according to some profound laws of nature, which our poor mental spectacles have never read, studied, or even glanced at. I often hear ignorant boys and stupid men talk about the laws of nature, as if they had swallowed whole the immense immortal digest of ' Creation.' We'd better try to search more and grasp the heavy books on the topmost, celestial shelves, before we dare to say to a truth or thought clothed in a new, strange, startling dress, ' Go back to the tomb of doubt.' Let us wait till some learned judge cites, clearly and correctly, the exact statute, the infallible authority, before we excommunicate a bold, bright thought that comes to seek communion with our best thoughts and join the great congregation of martyr truths, whose once stifled cries have been long changed into words of sweetest music, thrilling the world's restless heart.

" If a man hasn't a whole thought in his head, if he is stupid, dumb, silly, blind, if he don't know anything, when a great soul towers up before him saying, ' This sublime thought has flashed upon my deep studies like a new star in the sky of my soul,' this imbecile fool will cry out, ' Hang the truth ; burn, starve, choke or drown it. That is contrary to the laws of nature.' You may so cage and shut out a bird from the light, that it can't sing, or so tie a vine that it can't grow upward or bloom. So you can so fence in a truth from the light and air that it can't grow or thrive—but the poorest apology, the most miserable dilapidated old cage in which to enclose a sublime truth is that old stiff wooden fence made of the laws of nature.

" I like to jump into the car of investigation and leave the old stage-coach of doubt behind, and say to the antiquated wiseacre who stands on reason's highest, muddiest bank watching for the old rumbling, ricketty coach of experience to come along, which has been driving, with its one lame horse of reason, every day for years from the ark to the flood and back, I'd say, ' We'll give you a very grey wig and gown, and elect you Lord Chief Justice of the Supreme Bench of the World's Fools.'

You take out of the Bible the living breath of inspiration, and it is like the Van Jayen in Spitzbergen, as Lord Dufferin. tells us—" like a river larger than the Thames, plunging down hundreds upon hundreds of feet; every wreath of spray and tumbling wave frozen in a moment stone-stiff—rigid as iron, awful, everlasting death-in-life, staring up at the sun and the stars in their courses, and never meeting the Norland winds and the washing waves with the thunder music of its waters.

" All the French cloud-wreaths woven around my mother's Bible will melt away at last in truth's clear sunshine. A soul must be bathed in sunshine to write that which can never be written correctly by mortal pen, the Life of Jesus. As well might we try to inlay in our heart's mosaic, sorrow's tears, or photograph for our albums the evening star.

" The meek, majestic life of Christ is the sweetest violet in the world's heart—its only real heart's-ease, and Renan's clear, graceful, graphic, picturesque, delicate, brilliant, tender hand, with his rich, life-like, tropical coloring of Oriental thought, would rob the most glorious of glorious lives, the fairest unfolding of the sacred heart, of the deathless living perfume of inspiration's sweetest violet.

" To give us a life of Christ without its transparent, pure, single, sublime motive, principle and aim, loftiest and truest —is to leave us beautiful violets in our garden, but take away the peerless perfume for which the violet is so dear.

" But almost all the clergymen buy Renan's book and read it too," said Mr. Nicholson, very much taken aback by Nepenthe's reception of his first intellectual remarks ; " and if they blame, they praise it too. It has, you must grant, a most perfect style."

Just then there was a loud quick ringing at Mrs. Elliott's front door, and soon a whole surprise party of fifty masque-raders rushed in and took possession of parlor, piano, library, chamber, dining room and kitchen. It was domino all over, up stairs and down.

This nocturnal assembly at last disrobed themselves of their long divers colored mantles, caps, and wide sleeves, and amused themselves until midnight with dancing, cha-

rades, and other diversions ; and Mr. Nicholson, very good
at dancing and charading, put off Renan's spiritual or intellectual domino, which he had been wearing all the evening,
which was altogether too long, large and wide for him—and
never put it on again, because he feared Miss Nepenthe
didn't like it.

As he stood by the table about twelve, eating some lemon
ice, jelly, and cake, Nepenthe thought, " Mr. Nicholson is
himself again."

CHAPTER XXXI.

DISCLOSURES.

> " The bleak wind of March
> Made her tremble and shiver,
> But not the dark arch
> Or the black flowing river ;
> Mad from life's history,
> Glad to death's mystery,
> Swift to be hurled—
> Anywhere, anywhere
> Out of the world."

It was a dark stormy night, dismally the wind howled, it
rained in torrents, when a loud knock was heard at Mrs.
Elliott's door, and then a succession of quick impulsive raps
as if some one were in eager, desperate haste.

" Sure ma'am, and no one would come to-night, and so
late !" exclaimed Jane, as she paused a moment before she
opened the door.

" Is Miss Stuart within ?" said a bare-footed beggarly-
looking boy. " I want her to come to —— street right
away."

" It is impossible for her to go out this stormy evening,"
said Mrs. Elliott. " If the case is urgent, she can come
early to-morrow morning."

" Oh, ma'am, but that will be too late," said the boy—
" let her come now, and here is a watch I will leave till I
return," and he held out a valuable gold timepiece ; " take
this, ma'am," said he, " till I come back with the lady, but
let her come now."

Almost afraid to follow her ragged conductor, yet impelled by some strange strong inclination, Nepenthe went on through the gloomy streets, and as she hurried along and passed under the street lamps, she saw moving swiftly by her, with downcast head and veiled face, a form like Mrs. Elliott's—and the lady, whoever she was, walked like Mrs. Elliott. At last Nepenthe reached a small house, and followed her silent but fleet-footed guide up the narrow staircase into a small chamber. Throwing aside her damp shawl and dripping umbrella, she was led by the boy to the bedside of a pale-faced emaciated woman, with long black hair, and large hollow eyes. The sheet was suddenly drawn over the face of the woman, and as suddenly thrust back.

"You are Nepenthe Stuart," said she, gazing at her with glaring eyes, "I should know the likeness anywhere—come here close to the bed," and taking a little dark-colored vial from under her pillow and swallowing a few drops, she said, "I have much to say, and these are my last words." Then holding up a small package, she said, "Here is something that belongs to you, but do not open it till you get home. Here is one letter directed to Mrs. Caroline Stuart, your mother : it was written long ago. I knew it would be written. I watched at the office. I took it out. It enclosed money. The money is still within it. The letter asks anxiously about your mother. I answered that she was dead. It also asked anxiously about a child. I answered the child is dead.. A fortune was ready for you then, but I had reasons of my own why no child of Caroline Stuart should receive one of those hated dollars. Had your mother received one of those letters before her death, it might have made her happy—it may be, she would have lived. I hated her. I hate you still, with those clear bright Stuart eyes ;" but she added, "The soul, if material, must change every twenty years, as the body does ; so then no one can be punished for crime committed twenty years ago, because he is not the same person—he has lost his identity. I have committed no crime since, though I have tried and failed. Had I carried out my designs, I would have had you long since beyond the reach of human voice or human knowledge. I—stood over you when asleep—I—"

, The woman struggled to speak again. She lay still, fell into a deep slumber, breathed fainter and fainter, gasped a few times, and died.

Nepenthe felt relieved when safe at home again. She could not get asleep till near midnight—and then, as the clock struck twelve, the old vision that once haunted her midnight dreams walked through her room again, and stood by her bedside, but now it was all clad in white, but still it had the same long, black, wavy hair.

It was morning at last, and Nepenthe awoke after one brief undisturbed morning nap, unrefreshed and sad.

The next afternoon, as Mr. Selwyn was walking up street, a ragged boy came up to him, saying,

"Are you a dominie, sir ? are you a dominie ?"

"Why do you ask me, my boy ?" said he kindly.

"There's a woman dead round here, and we want some one to say prayers."

Many of the clergymen had left the city dreading contagion from the epidemic, but Mr. Selwyn had no such fear. He followed the boy to a house where a pale corpse lay coffined. It was not quite the time of burial.

He sat down a moment by the window, and moved his chair near the table, when something lying on the edge of the table fell. It was a little box. It opened in falling, and there fell out a chain with a locket attached to it. It had an old-fashioned case. He took it up and looked at it. It was a correct likeness of himself, a miniature painted on ivory years ago.

"How came this here ?" he uttered in an involuntary whisper.

In the bottom of the jewel box lay a torn and folded paper, beginning, "In the name of God, Amen." It was a part of a copy of his own will, made more than twelve years ago. There was also another fragment carefully folded and lying on the table It was a part of an old letter written in a woman's hand, and it read thus :

"We lived together happily ; there was never one cloud to darken our path. One morning I stood at the door when he left the house. I shall never forget it. I kissed him good morning. He turned back and said, 'I'll be home early to-night, Lina.' He always called me Lina. I remember at night getting his slippers and dressing gown ready, and preparing his favorite supper. He liked violets always. I had a little bouquet of them on the table. The fire in the grate burned brightly. It was a cool day in October. He

came not at six—at seven. O God! he never came again.
I saw him no more. I heard nothing from him. He left
his place of business as usual.

"Twelve years have flown, and I have never heard a
word. Two months after he left, Nepenthe was born."

Some of the events of our lives are so wrapped up in
mystery that we try to forget them. This death and burial
of this strange woman haunted Mr. Selwyn's mind; he
could find no trace of her history.

Nepenthe Stuart's mind was also left agitated, perplexed
and harrassed. Why had this woman so persecuted her
dead mother? Why so watched and haunted her life?
She had never made an enemy by a harsh word or rash
deed; and yet, parallel with her existence, had ever been
the hatred of this implacable enemy.

All that could be found of the strange woman's recent
history were a few vague rumors that she had lived in that
place only three months; that she slept with two bolts at
her door; that she always had a box under her pillow at
night; that the day before her death she was walking about,
apparently as well as usual; that she died on the twenty-
fifth, and she had often said she would die on the twenty-
fifth.

The woman had no known relatives, so Mr. Selwyn's
anxious conjectures could never be cleared up, never be
quieted, never be silenced; and yet over the dead he read
slowly, solemnly, and humanely, " Earth to earth ; ashes to
ashes : dust to dust." So had turned long since his young
bright hopes to mocking dust.

The hand of his little clock on the mantel moved on to
four. Mr. Selwyn took home his likeness, feeling that he
had a right to it, as there was no other to claim it. As
he sat in his room writing, a man with an organ commenced
playing under his window, and at last little images came
dancing out as the man played, to the great delight of the
surrounding children.

As the organ played Mr. Selwyn wrote on in his old
journal : "So we turn away at the wheel of life, burden-
some, heavy as it is, almost weighing us down; yet some
sweet music may grind out of its very discord harmonious
trills of happiness, little chimes of joy-bells, some friendly
polka or some sympathetic waltz. They awake, thrill, and

depart, without our bidding and without our willing. We turn this heavy wheel of life, hoping to see something open and bring out little forms of happiness dancing as if to meet us—but there opens ever only darker dancing shadows and deeper revolving mysteries, till through all the stops and pipes and organ swells of the cathedral soul ascends its despairing miserere."

A heavy cloud was gathering overhead, and wrapping, as with a pall, the sky so bright only an hour before. Mr. Selwyn looked out, and he could see no blue sky; he sighed bitterly: "So is my life," thought he. "The blue sky of its early morning is all cloud-covered. I have one little vain hope left. Will it ever dawn? Will I ever see it realized?"

He involuntarily took up a book of poetry from the table before him, and read, as his eyes rested upon a page :—

> "The light of smile shall fill again
>   The lids that overflow with tears,
> And weary hours of woe and pain
>   Are promises of happier years.
>
> "There is a day of sunny rest,
>   For every dark and troubled night,
> And grief may bide an evening guest,
>   But joy shall come with early light."

Carleyn came in to see Selwyn early the next morning. The bed was undisturbed, the embroidered pillow frills were as smooth as when they came from the laundry the day before, the tulips were spread out as stiff and bright as when Margaret first folded over them the linen sheet according to Mrs. Edwards' very particular directions.

"I'm afraid you've been watching ghosts again," said Carleyn, kindly, as he glanced at the bed and then at his friend's sleepless, weary eyes; "you'll think youself mad, Selwyn."

"I never had such a night before, Carleyn," said he. "There are moments when the power of clear thinking and strong imagining comes over me; the weary body may long for rest, but the worn soul lies not down like a tired child to dreamless slumber, but walks forth along the coast of thought, where the ' tidal driftings of the heart come and go, and with clear eye looks off the battlements of reason, looks off and listens to catch the sounds that boom across the shore eternal, gazing back, defines each faintest outline of

the shadowy past, judges mercilessly some almost forgotten
sin or wrong, screams like a night bird over each hill-top of
memory, or wails like a ghost around the ruins of the heart.
We vainly lock up our sins and our sorrows in the eternal
safe, for there comes, at times, a fear they cannot be for-
given ; even though a divine substitute has been made, even
under the very shadow of the Redeemer's cross, they will be
our sins still. Through them we have suffered, we do suffer, and we fear we will suffer. Some nightly touch of the
clairvoyant soul, whose spirit-rapping must be heard on the
walls of the heart, will open the gate of tears, and the grief-
tide rushes in and overflows the last green leaf of comfort,
while whispered tones recall the dear lost face, the sweet,
silent voice. When the clairvoyant soul thus patrols, rap-
ping here and pausing there, the strongest hearted and
proudest man may tremble and weep. You have never had
to dig up and explore the tombs of the past, and pore over
the old half worn inscriptions of lost hopes, lost friends, lost
loves. May you never be a kneeler at the gate of sorrow, a
bent and bowed worshipper at the tomb of regret, a lone pilgrim in the desert of despair."

" I wonder what made that man walk so last night," said
Mrs. Edwards, as she sat in her front basement cutting out
a new kind of tulip. " If he only had such a toothache as I
had, he might walk ; but he seems well. If a man has money
enough, and health and clothes, I can't see what should keep
him out of his bed. I never knew a man before that would
grieve and keep awake and think all night as a woman will."
There was a bundle sent to Mr. Selwyn the next night.
Mrs. Edwards said that he was up later than she had known
him to be for weeks, and he was evidently reading some
writing. She had just looked once more through that convenient crack. As she sat, after breakfast, embroidering a
palm leaf in her muslin band, she said to Miss Kate Howard, " that Mr. Selwyn never looked so bright and so handsome. She did wonder what had got into the man. She
began to think that he was going to be married," but that
evening he astonished her with the intelligence that he was
going, next week—not to be married—but going to England.

CHAPTER XXXII.

DARKNESS WITHOUT ; LIGHT WITHIN.

> "Send kindly light amid th' encircling gloom,
>   And lead me on :
> The night is dark, and I am far from home;
>   Lead Thou me on ;
> Keep Thou my feet, I do not ask to see
> The distant scene ; one step's enough fo me."

MR. SELWYN is in England, and he hears, as he sits quietly in his room one pleasant morning, a manly voice singing—

> "I travel all the irksome night,
>   By ways to me unknown ;
> I travel like a bird in flight.
>   Onward and all alone."

He listens ; he hears nothing more, but soon the adjoining
door opens, and a gentleman walks out. He is not alone—one
other pair of feet keep pace with his as he goes through the
hall and descends the stairs.   Mr. Selwyn hears some one
say, " This way, doctor ; there are trunks piled up close by
the stairs at your right hand."   Mr. Selwyn looks out as the
street door closes and sees two gentlemen walking slowly on
the opposite side of the street.   One has a green shade over
his eyes, and carries a cane in his right hand, and he has the
arm of the other gentleman.

It is a beautiful morning, the windows are open, and the
air is still.   Mr. Selwyn hears one of the gentlemen say, as
they come to the crossing, " Here's a curb-stone, doctor ;
we'll walk slowly along here, for the men have been fixing
the road, and the stones are a little out of place."

" The rough path in life seems the safest for me," answered the other ; " 'tis on the smooth roads we are apt to
slip."

" He is a doctor, and is blind," thought Mr. Selwyn, as
they passed out of sight. " How hard to be blind such a
beautiful morning."

Just then there is a knock at his door. 'Tis a woman with a basket of clean linen.

"Is Dr. Wendon in ?" she says, setting down her basket.

"This is not his room," said Mr. Selwyn.

"Oh !" said the woman, "I have made a mistake ; but he had this room last month when I came. It may be that he has taken the next room. They told me I should find him on this side of the hall."

"I saw the gentleman in the next room go out a few moments since," said Mr. Selwyn.

"I ought to have come earlier. Mr. Leaden comes to take him out mornings about this time," said the woman, as she took up her basket and went down stairs.

"I don't believe that man was always blind," thought Mr. Selwyn. "He does not walk as if accustomed to walking in the dark. I am thankful, that in all my affliction, I can have, in loneliest hours, the companionship of books and nature."

In about an hour the gentlemen came back.

Dr. Wendon opens his door, while the other pair of feet descend the stairs again. Mr. Selwyn can hear him moving slowly around the room, as he puts his cane in the corner, opens and shuts his wardrobe door, and at last moves his chair slowly up to the window and draws a heavy sigh. By-and-by somebody opens his door without knocking and says, "I have come to read to you this morning, doctor. What will you have ? the morning paper or the last of Jane Eyre ?"

"I dreamed last night," said the doctor, "that I was at home with my mother, in the old farm-house. I thought I was a child sitting at her feet. She was reading to me out of the Bible. She put her hands on my head just as she used to do, and looking into my eyes, said, earnestly, ' *There's only one book*, Walter—there's only one book,'— and then she said, ' Thy word shall be a lamp unto my feet and a light unto my path,'—and she made me repeat it till I could say it correctly, and she said, ' Don't be so troubled, Walter,' as she opened the Bible again and read, ' Thou wilt keep him in perfect peace whose soul is stayed on Thee,'— and she taught me that, too. Then she read something more about the Lord's being an everlasting light. I wish I could remember it. I regret I did not read more of the Bible when I could.

"I had an elegant copy of the Scriptures lying on an embroidered crimson velvet mat, on a little table in the corner of my parlor; but after I had written in it the date of our marriage, and the advent of our little Violet, I seldom consulted its sacred oracles."

Mr. Leaden repeated slowly, "The sun shall be no more thy light by day, neither shall the moon give light unto thee; but the Lord shall be unto thee an everlasting light, and thy God thy glory." "Thy sun shall no more go down, nor thy moon withdraw itself, for the Lord shall be thy everlasting light, and the days of thy mourning shall be ended."

"The Bible, to me," said Dr. Wendon, "is like the well of Sychar, deep, and nothing to draw with. These promises are not mine."

"You have a claim to them all," said Mr. Leaden, kindly. No eclipse need hide your soul from this spiritual sunshine. 'These things have I spoken unto you, that in me ye might have peace.' 'Thy word is very sure, therefore thy servant loveth it.' 'These things have I spoken unto you, that my joy might remain in you, and that your joy might be full.' He has put you on the darkening waves, that you may follow the guiding light hung out astern. Only believe, and you shall hear a voice as you take a hand stretched out to you from out the dark, 'Peace I leave with you; my peace I give unto you: not as the world giveth, give I unto you.'"

"I once read in a book," said Dr. Wendon, "that there was no real trouble, so long as we can have God for our friend. I know no earthly philosophy can comfort or make me happy, afflicted as I am. If there is such a thing as peace, I would like to have it. As I stumble along my dark way, I wish I could walk and talk with God, and I would not be so perfectly desolate. I read in the Bible, when a child, about Paul and Silas singing praises in prison, and it seemed to me very strange. My soul is in a dark prison, and I cannot sing praises. I cannot see how God communes with man. It all seems dark and mysterious to me. Right before me I can feel

> 'The great world's altar stairs,
> That slope through darkness up to God.'

I cannot go forward without some hand to lead me."

Mr. Leaden was called away, and the doctor sat alone by the window till almost sundown; and at last his pent up heart burst forth in the words of that beautiful hymn :

> "'Though like a wanderer,
>   The sun gone down,
> Darkness be over me,
>   My rest a stone;
> Yet in my dreams I'd be
> Nearer, my God, to Thee,
>   Nearer to Thee.'

He struggled long with doubts of his own fitness and of God's willingness, as he walked back and forth during the long evening, and at last he knelt down and prayed like a tired child at a kind Father's feet, and this was his prayer :

> "'Just as I am—though tossed about
> With many a conflict, many a doubt,
> Fighting within, and fears without,
>   O Lamb of God, I come, I come!
>
> Just as I am—poor, wretched, blind,
> Light, riches, healing of the mind,
> Yea, all I need in Thee to find,
>   O Lamb of God, I come, I come!
>
> Just as I am—Thou wilt receive,
> Wilt welcome, pardon, cleanse, relieve,
> Because Thy promise I believe,
>   O Lamb of God, I come, I come!
>
> Just as I am—Thy love unknown
> Has broken every barrier down;
> Now to be Thine, yea, Thine alone,
>   O Lamb of God, I come, I come!'

Morning came at last, and as the sunshine fell on those sightless eyes, these words floated into the illumined casement of his soul, like a chime of heavenly music :

> "Immortal light, and joys unknown,
>   Are for the saints in darkness sown."

As he rises, and goes about his room, alone, as before, he sings with radiant face :

> "Thy will be done! I will not fear
>   The fate provided by Thy love;
> Though clouds and darkness shroud me here,
>   I know that all is bright above."

CHAPTER XXXIII.

PRUDENCE POTTER'S NEW DISCOVERIES.

"O dear! I am clear beat out. I wonder if there are any more stairs ?" exclaimed a sharp, impatient voice, as a straw bonnet with green ribbons, a brown shawl, a gray bag, and spectacles, were seen slowly ascending the fifth flight of Mrs. Edwards' stairs. "Well, well! what can't be cured must be endured ; but I guess my rheumatism won't be any better after this. I never thought I'd get up so high, but I'd climb twenty pairs of stairs before I'd pay six dollars a week for *my* board—but that mortgage money will all be lost if I don't stay and see about it.

"Here," said she, suddenly turning round and addressing the Bridget behind her, who had been showing her the way up stairs, "Here," said she, "just read what's on that card. I must have put my best spectacles in my other pocket. I was so flustered when I came off."

Bridget takes the card, and reads—

"Trap, Fogg & Craft,
Attorneys and Counsellors at Law."

"Trap, Fogg and Craft, is it? Well Mr. Fogg gave me the card, and he says it is a *stiddy*, respectable firm. Well, I must stay here until this business is done. If Priscilla's husband hadn't died until Spring, I might have stayed there, and saved paying all this board. It is a good plan to visit when you can, and save paying your hotel bill."

"Here is your room, ma'am," said Bridget, throwing wide open a door at one end of the hall ; and turning round, she went down stairs quickly, as if glad to get back to her bed-making on the second floor, where she could smell of the nice young gentleman's Lubin and soap, and try a little of his fragrant pomade, and see how his new pearl-backed stiff brush would feel on her auburn curls ; and examine the pictures in his last magazine, and chat a little at the window with yellow-haired blue-eyed Mike, who is trimming the grape vines in the garden opposite, and who has promised to marry her, if Margaret won't have him.

Miss Prudence stands up erect, and looks around, and then, as she folds up her shawl in the old folds, she says to herself, with the old smile on her face, " Never less alone than when alone."

When the bonnet and green ribbons are stowed away in the bandbox, and covered carefully with the clean pocket handkerchief, to keep out the city dust, and the shawl wrapped in a newspaper, and laid on a shelf in the closet, and she has put on her high-crowned cap, with a frill all around it, and her other spectacles, she stands in her door and looks cautiously round. " I wonder if there is any men folks up here ?" thought she, as she began walking around on tiptoe, and looking into the half-open doors of the rooms on that floor. They were all servants' rooms, except the room opposite hers, whose door, as she said, was " open on a crack."

With one of her comprehensive glances, she saw at once the sloping windows, the old Brussels carpet, the old-fashioned high square mahogany washstand, with a piece of its marble top broken off, the single bed, the cracked glass over the bureau, the trunk in the corner, with the initials, ' N. S.' in brass tacks, the rows of nails at the foot of the bed, with their well-mended, carefully preserved dresses. All the furniture had been costly when purchased, and once graced the more elegant rooms below. There was a large oil painting standing upon the floor, leaning against the wall, and on the easel near it, an unfinished copy of the same painting, with an ivory pallet beside it, with newly mixed colors.

Miss Prudence walks up and looks in the glass. She always puts on her cap with remarkable precision, but her cap is one-sided, her curls longer on one side, her sleeve drawn up. She stretches down the curls, draws down the sleeve, pulls the collar around, and draws down her mouth on one side, as she says, " Why, how did I get everything so cata-cornered ?" But the more she adjusted her collar, curls and dress, the more crooked she was getting. The glass was crooked. It had been purchased long ago, for its elegant frame, as many boarding-house mirrors are, without regard to their true reflections. In most of the glasses in that house, your dimensions were either elaborated or elongated, twisted, exaggerated, or distorted. People like to look as well as they can, and have at least a correct estimate of their outer selves.

On the bureau is a well-worn Bible, with the name "Nepenthe Stuart," written in a delicate hand on the blank leaf, and by its side is a vase filled with fresh violets; on the table is a basket just large enough for a neat little lady to carry about with her. That trunk is the identical trunk once placed by Carleyn in the bottom of his carriage. Prudence walked about quietly, and started suddenly as she looked at the bed, for there lay asleep the young occupant of the servants' room, with an unfinished drawing of a violet in her hand. The drawing was correct and artistic. In the folio beside her are many sketches, and among them, an exact copy of a certain lay figure always to be seen in a certain room at the School of Design, with which the young ladies have so much amusement.

Miss Prudence walks softly out as she sees the sleeping young lady, saying to herself, "Well, well! Here's somebody fiddling away her time;" and then she steals back into her room and shuts the door, taking out her unfinished pair of mixed stockings and knitting away. You could buy stockings all made at the stores for half the cost of that yarn, and yet she laments over the idleness and folly of the picture-making young lady in that room; while Nepenthe, who is really not very fond of copying, is to be paid twenty-five dollars each for two copies of the picture on the easel. But Prudence wishes she could manage for her, as she sighs and says, "What can't be cured must be endured."

"Well, well," says my aunt Lydia, to whom I have been reading my story thus far, "don't go on saying anything more, Minnie, about attic rooms—we all know how cheerless are those rooms in the top of city boarding-houses, with only apologies for windows; and you needn't tell about her pale face and large eyes. All the heroines in novels have pale faces and large eyes, growing up and thinking themselves so plain-looking, yet they turn out exceedingly handsome after all. And don't put in any more moralizing or fine sentences. People can always read enough of them in books that are written on purpose. I always skip them in a story. It is the plot we want, not beautiful writing, or long conversations, or elaborate disquisitions. But tell me how Nepenthe Stuart, as poor as you make her out to be, ever got away from the Elliott's, and into the School of Design; for you can't get any kind of a room in the city, unless you pay twelve shillings a week for it."

"Well, aunt Lydia, be patient, and I will tell you how the morning after Nepenthe sang and played for Carleyn, a letter came from the lawyer Douglass to her, informing her of a bequest of two hundred dollars from Miss Susan Simpson, deceased.

"With this money she resolved to seek the cheapest respectable quarters for lodging, and furnishing her own food, attend the School of Design, and learn some of the many arts taught in that noble institution; that when her little pile of dollars was gone, she could sustain herself, either at the School of Design, or by giving instruction in some private family.

"There is a benevolent lady who has given so much time and money to the institution, that her name will always be associated with it; and she has a specimen book, in which each pupil, after being a certain time at the institution, puts a specimen of that which she can do best. After Nepenthe had been there a few months, her specimen was really considered the most beautiful and perfect by all the appreciative eyes which looked over the pages of the specimen book."

Nepenthe's hired room was in the top of Mrs. Edwards' house. She went there the morning after Mr. Selwyn sailed for England. She lived on smoked beef, boiled rice, brown bread, crackers, boiled eggs, and all those nameless relishless articles upon which ladies with slender purses, without cooks and kitchens, usually subsist.

Neither the Elliott's nor Carleyn knew where she had vanished. Florence felt much relieved. She was once more the sole attraction and queen supreme of her elegant home. Had she heard of the sudden or tragical death of this innocent and friendless Nepenthe, not one real pang of regret would have disturbed her selfish heart.

It was not until Nepenthe Stuart's vacation in the summer that Frank Carleyn happened to see the specimen book, and then found out how and where she had spent her time tho last few months. Under the beautiful painting of a group of violets he read, in clear, distinct letters, Nepenthe Stuart. And one of the young ladies, having begged a copy of some verses of Nepenthe's about her first gift of flowers in the hospital, had shown it to several of her intimate friends. The verses were so beautiful that one of the numerous friends who boarded with Carleyn showed it to him, and he managed to copy them for himself; he' was delighted to find the name of that little pale girl at the hospital. The original copy of the verse was in the same handwriting of those beautiful lines he had found folded in the Hyperion belonging to Florence Elliott, to whose fair hand he had attributed the writing of the poetry. He understood it now —Nepenthe had written both. They were the same metre, the same style; but yet, there might be some mistake: Nepenthe and Florence might write a similar hand, or Nepenthe have copied them for Florence. Florence was too noble to stoop to such an imposition; he had condemned her rashly and wrongly. There are minds in themselves so noble and honorable it is hard to get them to believe that an apparently high-minded woman would stoop to an ignoble or mean action. He asked the young lady who first showed his friend those verses of Nepenthe Stuart's if she had any more of Miss Stuart's poetry.

"I have but one other piece," and she showed him an exact duplicate of the copy of verses he had found in the volume of Longfellow's Hyperion which he borrowed from Florence Elliott.

He sighed as he said to himself, "Mr. Nicholson will have a very sweet wife; she sings and plays with great expression, and she writes very beautiful poetry; and now I wonder who that tall, elegantly dressed, hollow eyed woman was I met at that reception. She seemed to know all about Nepenthe Stuart, for she spoke so positively of her being soon the wife of Mr. Nicholson. That woman must have been handsome once; her eyes are radiantly bright, yet fearfully hollow. Yet it is a queer place for Mr. Nicholson's expectant bride, in the School of Design. One would think *his* wife need to perfect herself no more in any branch of science or art. She knows a great deal too much for him already."

After this, Carleyn and Florence were often seen together. He was becoming one of the first artists in the city. He was young, good, gifted, handsome, graceful and accomplished. Everybody thought he was engaged to Florence Elliott, and many said what a beautiful wife for an artist. He could model his ideals from her.

Mrs. Elliott, though a very fine looking woman, began to look worn and worried ; something troubled her. She had frequent and long consultations with Mr. Trap, from which she came out with a heavier cloud on her brow than ever. She would sit by herself, silently thinking, for days, as if in a deep, troubled reverie. Ever since Nepenthe's mysterious disappearance, she had been anxious and uneasy ; while Florence, who neither knew nor shared her mother's troubles, was delighted that the girl was out of her sight. Mrs. Elliott would have given much to have found out where Nepenthe had gone.

CHAPTER XXXIV.

THE NEW PRIVATE IN COMPANY G.

"For when we may not do, then will we speken,
And in our ashen colde is fire yreken."—CHAUCER.

WHEN I see a head of beautiful curls, I am apt to think they adorn some plain face, for I have seen so many ordinary looking girls whose hair curls splendidly, as the schoolgirls say, but there never was any curl in Charity Gouge's hair ; nobody ever suspected such a thing, nor do I suppose that was the reason of her plainness. But she never tried to curl it ; she said " Let well enough alone," when Mr. Vole mischievously asked her one day " Why she never curled her hair." He always liked to see brown hair curled —wavy and brown ought always to go together.

But " something must be going to happen," Mr. Vole said, " for Miss Charity was really trying to educate some curls." True enough ; she had her hair done up in papers for three days, and that was the reason her meals were sent up to her room. Mr. Vole found it out some way.

" I wonder when we are to see those curls," said he to himself one evening. " Miss Charity must be going to 'have a companion.' " That was the phrase she always used when she spoke of any of her friends marrying.

Wednesday morning the curls were all right—thirty-two of them, long, smooth and glossy. She had brushed and combed, pomaded and fussed, twirled over her fingers, then rolled them over a stick ; they were real bona fide curls, and so she came down to the breakfast table. I thought Mr. Vole would nearly crush one of Kate Howard's little fairy feet—he kept stepping on her toes and looking so express- ively. " Good morning, Miss Gouge ; and how do you this morning ?" said he. " Have you been ill ? You look VERY *well* this morning."

Kate Howard was almost convulsed with laughter. She stuffed her kandkerchief in her mouth, and kept wiping her face with her napkin, and fidgetted in her chair, and tried to become absorbed in a dignified conversation with old Mrs. Vole, who sat the other side of her. Mr. Vole stepped on her toes again just as she was getting respectably straight, and whispered in a low tone, " I guess Miss Charity is go- ing to have her vignette taken."

Miss Charity went out quite soon after breakfast. Mr. Vole stood by the window with Kate Howard, who was scolding him for making her laugh so. She should have to change her seat at table. As Charity went out Mr. Vole said, " Miss Gouge always walks as if she was afraid she would be too late for the cars—or as if she had some im- portant business to transact immediately. Did you see that new green velvet waist ? and all that display of jewelry ? Won't she make a picture ? Did you ever see such a nose ? Thin at the top, as if there wasn't flesh enough to cover the bones, and the end is large and rather fleshy ; the olfactory commencement is dearth, and the end superfluity."

" She has such cold, clear, staring grey eyes," said Kate, " I feel, when she looks at me, as if I were being dissected, body and soul, as if I ought to be wicked, if I ain't."

" Yes," said Mr. Vole, " she has scalpel eyes, as if she could take you all apart and put you together again a great deal better than you were before. The mouth is cold, criti- cal, gossippy ; it always looks as if it wanted to say ' what's the news ?' and the chin is sharp enough to cut window glass with."

Mr. Vole was more than half right. Charity had gone to sit for her picture. She had made an appointment with the artist Curleyn. She wanted to be taken in a cloud, and yet she wanted the green waist to show. Perhaps Carleyn could compromise the matter, and show a little of the clouds and some of the green, too. Mr. Vole thought it too bad to Gouge out a cloud so.

Quite tired and out of breath, Miss Charity climbed the stairs and reached Carleyn's door. She paused a moment to adjust her curls, smooth down the folds of her green dress, and arrange the corners of her mouth and droop her eyelids a little ; then she knocked gently, but the response was only an ominous silence. Carleyn had actually gone ; the studio was closed.

If anybody said, did, or looked anything that Miss Charity didn't like, or with which she didn't agree, she called it insulting her. It was a queer construction of the word. "How did Mr. Carleyn dare to insult me so ?" said she, angrily, "as to go off without fulfilling his appointment."

If you would think Miss Charity's eyes sharp and critical when in a serene state, what would you think to see her angry ? They had a stab you, shoot you, knock you down look, and her voice was a combination of sharp steel and loud thunder. It was enough to make a quiet gentleman tremble and a timid woman shiver ; but she often said, "I don't want to be amiable. I don't like amiable people. Carleyn is treacherous and perfidious. With all his cat-like softness of manner, he is really a hypocrite," said she, indignantly.

How she wished there was somebody there she could scold ! She had flattered herself that her portrait would be hung in a conspicuous place at the next exhibition of the Academy of Design—perhaps in the very spot where this year had hung that wonderful Nepenthe, which had so bewitched everybody, and about which the critics never would get tired of talking. Then those curls—that three days' tribulation—were all for nothing !

Carleyn had gone, and so suddenly, that few knew where Some great emergency must have called him peremptorily from his beloved easel.

The next week, as Prudence Potter stood in the post-office, waiting for a stamp to put on her letter, a gentleman by her side dropped a letter he was just about to hand to the clerk to mail that morning. Prudence picked it up, and somehow managed to read the superscription—she had on her new spectacles—it read thus :

FRANK CARLEYN,

Company G, —— Regiment,

New York S. M.

CHAPTER XXXV.

AMONG THE MISSING.

" Theirs not to make reply,
Theirs not to reason why,
Theirs but to do and die,
Into the valley of Death
Rode the Six Hundred."

IT was just six months on the 15th, since Charity Gouge found Carleyn's studio closed.

On that evening, had you passed by Mrs. Edwards' boarding house about eight o'clock, you might have seen her standing at the door.

" I am so tired," said she, as she rang the bell, " I couldn't walk another step, but this has been one of the happiest days of my life. I havn't thought one moment since morning of Mr. Edwards or boarders either," as she sat down completely exhausted on her doorstep waiting for Bridget, who was unusually tardy in coming to the door.

" Bridget and Margaret are both out," said Miss Kate Howard, as she opened the door. " Why, Mrs. Edwards, how tired you look ! Come in and lie down on the sofa, and let me take your bonnet and shawl up stairs."

" I am tired," said Mrs. Edwards. " I never ate a mouthful of breakfast, I went off in such a hurry. I lay awake all last night thinking of those poor sick soldiers. There they were, more than two days on the bare floor without any beds or covering, and I don't know how many hours they went without food. But what could I do, with my hands full, and my boarders, and so many things to pay all the time, butter thirty cents a pound, and sugar so high, and nobody to take care of me if I get sick and helpless ? Prudence Potter says I had better let the soldiers alone, and let the rich people take care of them.   But I don't believe the world's going to be all taken care of by rich people, but I didn't know as I ought to go ; but just as plain as I can hear my clock strike, did those words come to me in the night over and over—that text of that self-denial sermon I heard once, ' Withhold not good from any one to whom it is due, when it is in the power of thine hand to do it,' and this morning I knew that I ought to go.

"As I said, I didn't eat a mouthful of breakfast.   You know I meant to take a great pail of boiled custard to those poor fellows.   I wouldn't make it of grocery milk, and I thought our milkman never would come, I never knew him so late.   I was in a great hurry to cool the custard, so I put the warm pail right on the ice.   I never was such a goose before, and of course the pail soon slipped off, and I lost almost all my custard in the bottom of the refrigerator.   I declare I could have had a good cry about it ; so I took the little milk I had left and made more custard, and only had three pints when I might have had at least three quarts.   I took some sandwiches made of those raised biscuits and that nice roast beef.

" I was glad I took that bag of lint, they needed it so much.

"All the time I get I mean to scrape lint, or knit stockings, but not of that horrid coarse yarn.   I should think it would take the skin off their feet, if they are like the feet of other men.   I am not going to make any more tulip quilts or embroider any more bands.   While these poor fellows suffer so, it isn't right to spend any time or money either on things we can do without.

"I went through all the wards and talked with nearly every man.   There were old and young—some educated and some ignorant ; some as fine looking and gentlemanly-looking men as you'd meet anywhere.

" I feel so sorry for some of them I don't think I can sleep to-night.   If I could only have given one of my biscuits to every man there.   As I had had no breakfast, I saved out one biscuit to eat myself about noon—but one poor half-starved looking man, with wistful eyes and emaciated hands, asked me if I couldn't give him a biscuit—so I gave it, and I havn't eaten anything.

"I took along some butter, and was glad of it, there were so many poor fellows at dinner time sitting up in their beds eating a piece of dry toast, without anything on it or with it. They havn't had any butter, and hardly any tea or fresh meat.

"Mother Government may be a very good and kind mother, and provide every thing, but somehow her boys don't get it.

"If one of those gentlemen were sick at home, they'd have to have every thing just so—the sheets just so white, smooth and clean, the room perfectly still, and every possible delicacy, care and attention given them. A man is three times the care of a woman when he is sick—and more depends upon good care, good nursing and good food, than upon medicine."

"It is too bad," said Kate, "when a man is sick, he can't be home and be taken care of."

"They won't let them go home," said Mrs. Edwards, "until they think they are going to die, and then they keep them drooping and dying about three weeks, waiting for some permission or some kind of paper to go to Washington and come back. By the time the paper is exactly right, the poor fellows are too far gone to be sent home. If they are sent, they die on the way, and it isn't the war that's killed them—it is the hospital."

"I believe after a while one of the privates won't be allowed to sneeze without sending to Washington for permission. I'd rather trust a brother of mine on the battle field, than have him languishing in a crowded, cheerless hospital. I met Charity Gouge to-day. She was in deep mourning, poor thing. Her only brother was killed in the battle of Fredericksburg. I did feel sorry for her, she almost worshipped her brother. He was a noble fellow, and there wasn't a bit of Gouge about him. The Gouges are a queer, miserly set. and nobody likes them.

"I don't think Charity can help being disagreeable. Poor thing, it will be some time before she wears those elegant green dresses."

"I wanted some milk porridge," continued Mrs. Edwards, "for those diarrhœa patients. They needed something beside dry toast and strong coffee—so I went out about noon to beg, borrow or buy a little milk. I walked all around the place, and after two hours' trying, got about two quarts. Nobody offered to let me make it at their houses, and all looked at me as if I was begging cold victuals or old clothes for myself.

" One wealthy lady, with three servants and an elegant house, told me I could probably make some at Mrs. McBride's.

" Mrs. McBride was an Irish woman who lived a little way off, and I could tell her Mrs. Exclusin told me to go there.

" I did go to Mrs. McBride's, and though she was an Irish woman, and poor, with no servant, and five small children, her heart was larger than Mrs. Exclusin's grand house. She gave me flour and salt, and cleaned her only little iron kettle for me to make it in.

" I never shall forget Mrs. McBride, and if one of her bright-eyed, rosy-cheeked boys ever lives to be in a hospital, I know he'll be taken care of. I am sure kindness to the sick is rewarded in this life, and," continued Mrs. Edwards, " the men couldn't have looked more delighted or grateful for a cup of nectar or ambrosia wreathed with diamonds and pearls, than they seemed with that one saucer of milk porridge. They ate like hungry children, though hardly strong enough to raise the spoon to their lips. If I could have had fifty quarts instead of two !

" If these men had staid at home they might earn enough to keep them in luxury. It is cruel to starve and stint them so. Some had six months' pay owing to them, and couldn't buy a pint of milk if they wanted it, for they hadn't a cent in their pockets. When they were near Carlisle, they paid a dollar or a dollar and a half for every loaf of bread they had, so it didn't take long at that rate to exhaust what little money they took with them into the army.

" As I was distributing peaches to the men who were allowed to eat them, one poor fellow who stood up near me, with a big shawl around his shoulder, held out his hand for a peach. As he took it, I saw gleaming out from under the shawl, a heavy iron chain binding his hands together. It frightened me a little. I didn't know but the man had been doing something criminal, till one of the men told me he had brain fever and was insane. Poor fellow ! he was the finest looking man there. Not letting him see that I noticed the

chains, which he evidently tried to conceal under the shawl,
I gave him another peach and stood still and let him talk.
He of course was allowed to say what he chose, not being
held responsible for his words, yet there was a good deal of
method in his madness.

"I gave the men little packages of loaf sugar to keep
by them and use in their tea when they had tea. I gave
him a package and turned to leave. I looked around and
saw him with the paper open in his hand, eating up the
sugar.

"Why," said I, "do you like sugar?"

"Yes, ma'am, and I havn't seen any in a year before.
They think we privates have no souls. The doctor says
I ought to have fresh meat every day, and I havn't had any
for a week. And this coffee—I can't drink coffee—it goes
to my head so—" Just then he coughed. "Last night I
caught cold, as there was a window pane out close by the
head of my bed, and when I was asleep it rained in, and the
sheets and bed got very wet. I'd rather die than be here
in this place and look at all these sick people; why," he
added in a whisper, "they are most all of them crazy.—
But do you know there's going to be a battle to-day?" and
he shivered, "the rebels are here, and I must go and shoot
them, but don't put me in the Chickahominy swamps again,
it makes me shake so."

"That man is going to rave, lead him out," said the orderly to two of the nurses. They were inexperienced young
men, members of the same regiment.

"Who is this insane man?" I asked.

"His name is Carleyn, and he has been unused to exertion or fatigue. I don't believe when he enlisted he was
strong enough to march with his knapsack as far as the ferry. Once, after having only one hard tack to eat, he march-
ed thirty-five miles in one day, and he fell exhausted three
times in that day's march."

"'I wish I had a lemon, my tongue is so dry,' said a
corpse-like looking man, on the cot bed just in front of where
I stood.'

"' Can't you give that man a lemon?" said I to the orderly, ' it won't hurt him—it may do him good.'

"' Nothing will do him good—the man is going to die, any-
how,' said the orderly.

"'Do give him one, sir,' said I, 'it may be of some com
fort to him.'

"'I will, to gratify you, madam,' he replied, in a civil,
but very cool tone, as he went off and came back with a lemon.

"The poor man looked so glad to get that one lemon. It
was the last attention his poor worn out body required.

"I looked back once more, to see the young boy, only
seventeen, on the cot just by the door. He was ill with
lung fever. My heart ached for him. I promised him some
chicken tea next time I came, as I put the three peaches I
had left in his hat by the side of the bed. He is my Ben-
jamin. Somebody ought to pet him, thought I, as I looked
at his clear, mild blue eye, and saw the patient smile on his
lips.

"Six months more, and some of those men were back to
their regiments, some had died. The poor man who was so
anxi us to have the lemon, died the next morning after I
saw him.

"But this hospital," added Mrs. Edwards, "isn't a type
of them all. It is one of those improvised hospitals, so deficient in comfort, system, and convenience."

Kate Howard reads in an evening paper a report from the
last battle field. Among the missing are the names—

RICHARD DOUGLASS,

FREDERICK HOWARD,

FRANK CARLEYN.

Among the six hundred who were sent on in advance to
make that perilous and almost hopeless attack, poor Frederick Howard was not missing, as the evening paper said.
In the Morning Herald he was reported killed. He was
Kate's only brother. Among the remnant of that noble company, he never came back.

> "Cannon to right of them,
> Cannon to left of them,
> Cannon behind them
> Volleyed and thundered;
> Stormed at with shot and shell,
> While horse and hero fell;
> They that had fought so well
> Came through the jaws of hell,
> All that was left of them,
> Left of six hundred.

When can their glory fade?
O the wild charge they made
All the world wondered!
Honor the charge they made,
Noble six hundred."

CHAPTER XXXVI.

BACONIAN PHILOSOPHY ILLUSTRATED IN A LITERAL WAY.

" The heart—the heart that's truly blest,
Is never all its own;
No ray of glory lights the breast
That beats for self alone.

And though it throb at gentlest touch,
Or sorrow's faintest call,
'Twere better it should ache too much,
Than never ache at all."

" Through passionate duty love flames higher,
As grass grows taller round a stone."—PATMORE.

WINTER and Spring passed slowly with Nepenthe, but midsummer came at last. There was a vacation in the School of Design, and she went in the country to spend a few weeks. She travelled over the same journey along which she once rode under Carleyn's protection. The mountains, the bridge, the river, Mrs. Titus' house, looked so familiar, and there was Levi Longman, as large as life, standing in front of Mrs. Titus' door. Hard, cold, cast-iron features like his, seldom change. There was no wear and tear of feeling or sympathies in *his* case. His broadcloth was of one long-established fit, bidding defiance to elegance or taste. Still he taught the young ideas in Titusville how to shoot, and to shoot up straight, without branching out in any centrifugal or fanciful direction. His circles of thought and instruction were *all* square—he couldn't make anything, either of solid reason or solid wood, without having a line and angle in it somewhere. He was a character. If you could see him walk only across the street, you would never forget that striding, straight-forward, angular walk. His motions were all angles. If there was a line of beauty, he always moved in right angles to it.

And there was Mrs. Titus, sitting in her little front window, looking out as usual for the coming stage.

Nepenthe soon became domesticated with a pleasant family, and was really attached to the children belonging to it. There was one, the youngest, pet and darling of the house-hold, always bringing her bunches of clover, dandelions, ribbon grass, cowslips and buttercups.

One day, as she sat sewing in her room, she heard the voices of some young girls talking merrily in the adjoining room. One of them had evidently been visiting the city, and her companions were asking her questions about the news and the fashions. It was a lively chat among light-hearted girls.

"Did you hear anything, Nellie," said one of the oldest, "about that young artist, Carleyn, who took Ernest Titus' portrait?"

"Hear anything! I guess I did. Every body was talking about him. But, girls, you needn't set your caps for him any longer. You had better let your minds get consolidated down, as Miss Prudence Potter used to say when we curled our hair for some party, or begged her to let us go off sleigh-riding with the boys. You must hang up your harps and walk on the bridge of sighs, for they say he is going to be married soon to Miss Elliott, a great belle in the city—Miss Florence Elliott.

"I saw her at the opera one night, in one of the private boxes. She had on an ermine opera cloak, a white hat and feathers. She was elegantly dressed, but somehow I shouldn't think of marrying her if I were a man. She looked so haughty and proud, as if the air ought to be sifted for her special breathing. But it is a generally understood thing. She is certainly very much in love with him. I went out a great deal while I was in the city. I was only there ten days, and Jane says she thinks I saw more and went around more in that time than she does in a whole year. People who live in the city think they can go around to see the stars and lions any time; so some of them go very seldom. But we country folks do up everything in a week, and it is pretty hard work, being out so late every night.

"I went to one wedding reception. Florence Elliott was there, dressed in white satin trimmed with point lace, with white natural flowers in her hair. There was a great crowd there. There were a thousand invitations. There were three ushers—every thing in style. I never saw such a profusion of flowers. There were flowers in every possible place, recesses, niches, or tables. I lost my aunt once in the crowd. As I was a stranger, I felt awkward, and stepped back in a recess behind some curtains to look at some flowers. Hearing low voices near, I looked around, and I could see Florence Elliott, and hear her talking very earnestly in the conservatory. She had some violets in her hand.. I heard a gentleman—I suppose it was Mr. Carleyn—say to her in a low tone, with earnest manner, 'I have come to urge you to fulfil the promise you half made me yesterday.' My aunt came for me just then, and introduced me to a Miss Kate Howard, a very lively young lady. But I am sure of one thing—Florence Elliott is completely fascinated with Carleyn. I passed her with the same gentleman once after that in the crowd, when he seemed to be inquiring about some absent person. I heard her say, ' I don't know where she is staying now. I believe she has left town. I suppose you know she is engaged to Mr. William Nicholson. I am sorry for her sake that she has such a very unhappy temper.. We took some interest in her, because she was poor. She will do very well to marry him. Nepenthe is a girl of quite good natural capabilities, considering her origin ;' and then, as she said this, she flirted her fan with such a queenly air, and coquettishly twirled her bouquet.

" I saw her once before, a year ago, at the Academy of Design. She was beautiful then—she is more beautiful now. Her complexion is clearer and brighter, her form more full, and her voice sweeter. It seems as if a beautiful soul must dwell in so fair a temple. But she'll never make Carleyn happy.

" When I was at school four years ago in the city, she was there too. I was one of the small fry, and of course of no account—but then I had my favorites among the big girls, as we used to call them. At school she was selfish, imperious, domineering, extremely overbearing to all those she thought not rich enough to move in her set. She had to be the leading one in all the charades, tableaux and private theatricals, or she would take no part. She was in a perfect rage once, because in one of the dramatic readings the part of Portia was not assigned to her. No man can ever change her. But where do we see a couple with both equally agreeable ? Refined men of real genius and real worth are apt to get haughty and unamiable wives. But it must be her beauty suits his artistic taste. I should think he of all men would admire a beautiful face."

Just then Mr. Titus came in with some large bundles in his arms.

"I saw an old New York paper to-day, Eliza," said he, to Mrs. Titus, "and I happened to read the marriages, and the very first one I read was Frank Carleyn's."

Mrs. Titus actually dropped the bread she was toasting, dropped it into the fire, as she exclaimed, "Are you sure, Timothy? And who has he married?"

"I think it was a Miss Ellet, or something like that."

"Ellet—no," said Mrs. Titus. "Wasn't it Elliott? The girls were talking to-day about his paying some attention to a Miss Elliott. It must be she."

"Perhaps it was," said Timothy, "but I think it was Ellet. Any how it was Carleyn—Frank Carleyn. I'm sure *his* name was plain enough; the lady I'm not so sure of—I never heard her name before."

"No matter what her other name was, she has a better one now, and I hope she deserves it," said Mrs. Titus; "she is a very happy woman to get him. I never shall forget how feeling he was when Ernest died. If he should go to housekeeping, wouldn't I like to send him some of my nice cream, and some of the big blackberries you get on the mountain, Timothy."

'And some of our nice Lawtons too," added Timothy.

"You must be mistaken, Nellie, about seeing Mr. Frank Carleyn at that reception in the city," said Kate Lamont. "I am sure Mr. Carleyn joined the army more than a year ago. He may have married Miss Elliott before he went, but he couldn't have been in the city when you were there, for it was just about that time I read his name in the Times among the 'missing,' and this morning there's a Frank Carleyn, company G, reported 'killed.' It may have been some other Carleyn you saw at the reception. I think there is a Mr. Charles Carleyn in the city. He may be a cousin of Frank's."

Nepenthe felt as if her soul had been stunned and paralyzed by some great earthquake. Her heart stood still. She couldn't move to close her door without being observed, so she sat still.

"O," said Mrs. Titus, "don't say Mr. Carleyn is killed. I won't believe it until I have to. If he had been a good for nothing drunkard, whom nobody wanted, and nobody needed, he'd gone through a dozen battles and come back alive, without having one hair of his useless head injured; but men whose lives are worth hundreds of others, a blessing to everybody, must always be among the missing or killed;" and Mrs. Titus could say no more, for she burst into a fit of sobbing.

Just then one of the little girls came in with a bunch of fresh flowers, and laid them on Nepenthe's lap—columbines, anemones, and evening primroses. "Desertion, forsaken, inconstancy," thought Nepenthe, as she took the flowers, whose language was only an echo of the language of her heart, which was beating violently.

"Do come and play with us, Miss Nepenthe," said the child, pulling her dress, "only just a little while," she eagerly added, as she saw Nepenthe about to shake her head and say, "Some other time."

"Do come, just this once!" said the child, and Nepenthe went out into the little shaded yard at the side of the house, where a group of children were playing under the apple trees :

> "I'm waiting for a partner,
> I'm waiting for a partner;
> So open the ring, and let her in,
> And kiss her when you get her in."

As Nepenthe joined the ring, the children went round and round in merry glee. Nepenthe's eyes were fixed on the ground. Her thoughts were at hard sober work, while she was playing with the light-hearted children. She did not notice that some one had slipped up from behind, and joined the ring, until she heard some one from the middle of the circle, in a familiar, manly voice, singing,

> "I'm waiting for a partner,
> I'm waiting for a partner;"

and in one moment Frank Carleyn seized and imprisoned both of her hands, and drew her within the circle, and kissed her, to the great delight of the children at seeing big people joining so heartily in their play. He looked pale, more shadowy and *spirituelle* than ever—but it was Carleyn still.

Just then a big wagon drove up to the door, and this was the signal for the little folks to pile in, as they were going off whortle-berrying. They all went but two little ones, who sat down on the door step to read over aloud the stories of the Man in the Bramble-bush, Blue Beard, and Jack the Giant Killer.

"Blue Beard," said Carleyn to Nepenthe, taking the book from the child and looking over the pictures, "was one of the first stories I read. After that, I can remember how we children huddled together around the hearth, listening at nightfall to tales of robbers, ghosts and murders, till we were afraid to stir, lest in some dark closet, or lonely chamber, we might meet a robber's eye, or see a murderer's hand. How the shadow of something on the wall of the dimly lighted chamber assumed dark and terrible shapes, and we drew the sheet close over our eyes and fell asleep, to dream of pale ghosts and midnight robbers. The self-same chill creeps over me still, at the thought of those bloody deeds we then in fancy witnessed. Blue Beard seems even now a half reality, and the hero of the bramble-bush, who performed in so brief a space the wondrous feat of losing and winning his eyes, is something in my fancy, even now, half real, half fabulous.

"It is strange how the thing we really believed true in our childhood, and we really saw in fancy, keeps still in our minds as a kind of fact. These first pictures of the youthful imagination were actually carved and stained on the walls of the heart, to which all after pictures seem fancy sketches, or like handbills posted up new every day, to be torn down to-morrow at leisure by sober reason. The early toy-books are the old masters, whose pictures longest hang in the gallery of the soul, and every holiday we brush off the dust of years, and find them bright still."

"Santa Claus will always seem to me like something real," said Nepenthe.

"Yes," said Carleyn, "he was an immortal, ever welcome hero in the land of my childhood. We exile him in after years from the land of facts, yet still is his portrait hung in *fast* colors by the heart's fire-side. Like the wandering Jew, We still see his imaginary form each Christmas morning, as we hear the rattle of miniature drums, and the clang of lilliputian trumpets. Sinbad the Sailor has started floating masts and swelling sails across the sea of many a young imagination."

"Yes," said Nepenthe, "and the Children of the Abbey has waked a good deal of romance in many a young girl's head ; and that illustrious Man of the Moon, so talked about in childhood, whose jagged eyebrows I actually saw when a child, is still a real picture in my mind. I often see him glaring ominously over my left shoulder, some lonely evenings."

"And poor unlucky Friday," said Carleyn, "is still to many, not *good*, but bad Friday—and I myself, I will own it, would a little rather commence a journey on some other day, although the journey I once took on a Friday in a thunder-storm, ended very pleasantly after all. I often think," said he, "I'd like to be a child again, and live once more in that realm lit up with Aladdin's lamp, so wondrous wise with mysteries and haunted by fairies, who kept our thoughts like little Micawbers, always waiting for something to turn up. But," said he, looking up at the western sky, "we are going to have a beautiful sunset. Let us take a ramble over the fields and then down the lane, where there is a fine echo, and in an hour or two we can see the sun set over the water. There are a great many bright things in the world for grown up people to enjoy. We have our ideals still."

"But we never find our ideals, say many practical experienced people," said Nepenthe.

"That is not true," said Carleyn. "I'll show you mine, some time."

They rambled half an hour, and at last they came to an old well, deep and moss-grown, under a beautiful chestnut tree.

"The philosopher says we can find truth at the bottom of a deep well," said Carleyn. "Look down, Miss Nepenthe, and see how deep this well is."

As she bent over and looked down the well, "See," said Carlyn, as he looked over her shoulder, "there—there is my ideal, reflected in the bottom of the well ; and my *ideal* is *truth itself*. I hope it will never vanish away and leave me, as children's ideals do."

He drew her away from the well, and they sat down under the tree. As he went on twining a wreath of oak leaves, he said, "There is another well of affection in the bottom

of my heart, where I see reflected the image of my ideal.
Whenever I look down into my heart, I see the shadow of
that beautiful image. I wish I could draw it"————

"Here they are! here they are! we've found them at
last," screamed a group of noisy children, hurrying to the
old well all out of breath, with baskets and pails full of berries.

"See, see, Miss Nepenthe, how many I've got," said the
foremost one ; "and these are for you," she added, handing
a cup made of two leaves filled with berries to Nepenthe ;
"and these are for you, Mr. Carleyn," said Mrs. Titus' orphan niece, handing him a basketful.

I wonder if the simple-hearted children really though!
Nepenthe's brimming eyes and blushing cheeks and brigh!
smiles were caused by her excessive joy at the sudden sight
of so many unexpected berries. Certainly her eyes never
had such light before ; the dawn of happiness was coming
to her soul ; she walked on home with Frank Carleyn and
the children, who were tired enough for once to walk as
slowly as older people.

The wreath of oak-leaves was twined around Nepenthe's
bloomer. That night, by moonlight, Carleyn showed Nepenthe the depths of his warm heart—he finished the sentence
so unceremoniously interrupted—he asked her at last the
one question in love's short catechism, and we leave her to
say what you, fair reader, would say under such exciting
circumstances, and the best wish we can make for you, fair
and gentle as you may be, is that some time some noble-
gifted and good man may ask you the same question Carleyn
did Nepenthe, that you may give the same short answer, and
have as sweet, bright dreams on your pillow that night, and
he find in your image ever after this ideal of truth, when he
looks into the clear depths of his manly heart.

Not until Nepenthe became his wife, did she reveal to
Frank how his image had so long been imprinted within her
heart, and that she was the little pale girl at the hospital,
on whose pillow, years ago, he had lain those beautiful flowers. And now to her, life seemed pillowed with flowers,
the air never before so fragrant. Little buds were opening
down in her heart, so fresh and green, after that sad shower
of hopeless tears, such a rainbow spanned her soul. And
that promise of Frank's, to love, cherish and protect, was a

sure pledge that while he lived the fountain of sorrow should never more quite overflow the springs of happiness. While she nestled quietly in the ark of his strong manly heart, she could outride with him life's roughest tempest and highest billow.

I forgot to tell you, reader, that Frank Carleyn had a cousin killed in battle, of the same name as himself, and a great many people thought for weeks it was our artist friend; but he was in the hospital for several weeks, very ill with that frightful brain fever, of which as yet he has said nothing to Nepenthe; and then, too, he was taken prisoner, after lying on the field wounded, two whole days, without food. It was there Kate Howard read his name in the evening paper:

"Private Frank Carleyn, missing."

CHAPTER XXXVII.

CARLEYN'S IDEAL.

> How wise in all she ought to know,
> How ignorant of all beside!
> > THE ANGEL OF THE HOUSE.

> If thou HAST something, bring thy goods, a fair return be thine,
> If thou ART something, bring thy soul and interchange with mine.
> > SCHILLER.

Is she rich, young, handsome, and highly connected?

"Important questions truly," said Carleyn.

"Were you appointed a committee of investigation, you might return with a decided negative to them all—and they are questions I cannot answer with monosyllables. I know, Mr. Selwyn, you are not actuated by mere idle curiosity, so I will answer you candidly. She is not rich; but when I think of her as poor, there comes to my mind that verse in the Bible which I used to hear repeated so often by an old minister—'rich in faith, heirs of the kingdom.' I almost reverence her simple rare beauty and affluent loveliness.

"She is young, but were she still younger or much older, my admiration and affection could not diminish. Her mind is stored with thoughts, her soul with feelings, rich, deep, exhaustless. No, she is not poor, so highly gifted by Nature with dower richer than Eastern princess; without her I am poor, but in her presence earth and air are clothed with radiant beauty. I have found my ideal wife at last, and in the loveliest of frames.

"I know not how she is connected, and care not to trace her history. I believe, in spite of dark whispers often repeated in my ears, that naught but pure and good ever claimed alliance with such as she. Without caring to investigate her earliest history, I am willing to stand by her side and share her destiny, without knowing the fate or history of any who may claim relationship to her.

"She is lovely, and gifted enough to move with honor and grace in any earthly circle. No position can elevate her. She will elevate every duty she performs, every position she fills; and she is fitted to shine hereafter among the spirits of the just made perfect in heaven.

"It shall be the aim of my life to make her happy. The trials through which she so early passed have given a sublimity and a sacredness to her character which makes me well nigh worship her. She is at an infinite remove from those gay butterfly creatures which haunt watering places and parties.

"I could not enshrine upon the altar of my heart an image so decked.

"The life we live is too brief to spend it with one who has no lofty principle, no truer aim or object in living, than to show and shine, dazzle and attract.

"Like a flower in a shaded, lone valley she was lovely and beautiful when alone, neglected and unsought—the only woman I have known in society whose aim was not sometimes, or all the time, effect."

"If," said Selwyn, "she is the picture hung up in your heart's studio so long ago, I long to see the lovely counterpart."

"I have not," said Carleyn, "wedded my heart to a hand, a foot, or an eye, but she seems all soul. I know not by what avenue she found the subterranean passage to my heart —before I knew it, I was surrounded by an influence I could not, would not resist. I have boasted of my insensibility, but the touch of that little hand thrills my soul, and makes a child, a happy child of me."

"Yes," said he, walking the floor, "I thought once, indeed Miss Elliott herself gave me the impression that Nepenthe was engaged to the wealthy Mr. Nicholson, and then I found out how much I really loved her, and how essential she was to my happiness; then I found out I could not live without her. Yes," said he, walking back and forth, "she will make me wiser, happier, better."

"How did you find out that Miss Stuart was not engaged to Mr. Nicholson?" said Mr. Selwyn, with some curiosity in his manner.

"Miss Elliott told me positively that she was," said Carleyn. "Of course I believed it; and to strengthen my belief in her engagement, some one, (I have no idea who) actually caused an opened love-letter, pretended to be written from Mr. Nicholson to Nepenthe to come accidentally in my way.

"I thought it strange, but supposed the letter a veritable document and authentic, as the writing was certainly like Miss Nepenthe's. But one day I heard Mr. Nicholson muttering angrily to himself something like this—that he should never be such a fool as to break his heart for one little woman if she didn't want him—he was sure there were as many good fish, &c. Then Mr. Vole told me afterwards, that Nicholson had been refused by somebody, he couldn't find out who, and he was really a little sore about it. He was still surprised that any sensible woman could refuse his great fortune and his well-dressed self. To him it was unaccountable. He at first thought the refusal only an evidence of diffidence, and renewed his offers; but he had to believe at last that even a portionless girl did not want him for her husband."

"Then you mean to marry her, and give up all the fine chances. There's Florence Elliott, a beauty and an heiress if rumor speak correctly—you have already a favorable place in her heart."

"Florence Elliott is beautiful, radiantly beautiful, but I never feel like clasping her to my heart, or confiding in her. I think of her as a wonderful fine painting, with its great 'sweep of hand and dash,' but not as a being I long to protect—not as a woman with a gentle, loving heart. I cannot agree with Pope—

> " If to her share some penal errors fall,
> Look to her face, and you'll forget them all."

Grace is in her step, but *not* ' heaven in her eye.' "

" It would be a good thing for you to marry a rich wife," said Selwyn.

" In my ideas of marriage," said Mr. Carleyn, " policy has never entered. I am glad I can support a wife. It is a pleasant thought that I can have one being dependent upon me alone for care, protection, and support.

" In entering the holy estate of matrimony no such sordid considerations should be thought of. There are many marriages in the world without love. I am romantic enough to marry for love, and I am vain enough to think she will marry me for myself—what I really am."

" How is it, Carleyn," said Selwyn, " that you never act at all conceited—never elated with the distinction you have gained as an artist, a distinction very flattering to a young man ?"

" My mother taught me," said Carleyn, " a long time ago, a maxim she had learned from an old book—' Do all the good you can in the world, and make as little noise about it as possible ;' and then I have in my own mind an ideal so much higher than any standard to which I have attained, that I have no feeling of vanity—no inclination to boast : and my heart is so far from reaching its standard of right, its standard of moral worth. I know and feel every day that it is a very good thing to be great, but it is a far greater thing to be good."

Carleyn writes in his journal that night this sentence— " Dim the blaze of science, hush the voice of song, veil the face of sculptured beauty, hide the loveliest embodiment of the artist's ideal, remove all the rarest, choicest, and costliest productions of genius, and the bereaved world would not be half so desolate as if deprived of goodness, lives pure and conscientious, principles of moral worth, deeds of every day piety—those silent invisible influences perfect and perennial, preserving pure and clear the turbulent fountains of life."

CHAPTER XXXVIII.

THE HEART AT MIDSUMMER—FROM THE LIFE.

Our great High Priest above, alone,
In temple of the heart hath throne;
At inmost holy shrine He bends,
In twain the mystic curtain rends.

WHAT a wonderful thing expression is! It makes some plain faces beautiful, some beautiful features ugly. Sometimes a worn and weary pallid face, lit by its strange glory, will wear a saintly, a martyr-like, an angelic glow.

"I don't like his expression," we say, as we meet some repellent face, with perhaps an Apollo cut of features, and gather up our spiritual garments, and hurry by, as if to escape some moral contagion, or flee some deadly malaria.

Have you ever had company, reader, when you couldn't make anybody talk, or sing, or dance, or play; till you start up at last, suddenly and desperately determined to get up something to entertain them, for there they all sit, with their clean collars and silk dresses, and don't stir or say a word. You try Copenhagen, and Proverbs, and Stage Coach, and at last, to get them thoroughly wide awake, you set them performing the very graceful original and astonishing evolutions of "Queen Dido is dead." After deciding conclusively by manual, cerebral and pedal logic how she *did* die, the collars and silk dresses begin to assume their stiff silence again, and some one, not you, for *you* are afraid to break the rich repose of your new mahogany and marble—some one starts blind man's buff. Chairs fly, bijouterie rattles, tables tremble, and you think you hear a faint sound of creaking rosewood. You at length cunningly manœuvre them into the more sensible and suggestive game of "What is my Thought like?" which brings out in mirthful flashes the profound erudition and metaphysical acumen of the gay circle around you, who can boast, many of them, of sixteen years of girlhood's thoughts.

When the girls are all gone, as you put the chairs up in their old places, all but one poor unfortunate, whose broken back you hide away in the extension, to await its morning's dose of Spalding's marvellous rheumatic glue, you extinguish the lights, and sit and think and wonder. What *is* thought like? Thought, Feeling, Expression! They make up life's world—they give us calm sleep, peaceful dreams, or frightful nightmare, and an aching pillow. They can make sweet bitter, and turn twilight's serene rest into midnight's turbulent tempest.

If I could only have caught and copied the expression on Carleyn's face, as he sat reading in his mother's Bible, this first verse that met his eye as he opened the book. It was marked by her pale hand with a pencil, only a few days before she died : " Withhold not good from any to whom it is due, when it is in the power of thine hand to do it." It was the text of that self-denial sermon he heard when a boy. It brought back a tide of golden memories. Go where he would, the words still whispered to him their clear, yet imperative echoes. As he read them slowly aloud, there came a look into his face, such as man's face seldom wears. It was a blending of will and purpose, regret, resignation, nobility, faith and enthusiasm in one single soul-ray—for expression is only a soul-ray. The face is like a window shutter in the dark, through which thought's prismatic colors gleam. Sometimes you almost see a faint violet purpling the east of the soul—though these mysterious soul-rays have their genuine heat and noble expansion, but no vision or color, yet visions colored with wondrous beauty—those beatific soul-beams—wake in us, as they gleam out from loving human faces.

I thought as I watched the stars last night, coming out one after another at evening's reception, our souls are like constellations instarred with thoughts, moving around the great Father-Soul, wearing their incadescent noonday glow as they turn towards, or eclipsed in midnight's shadow as they turn away from the full-orbed Central—or wandering out of their predestined path far from the sphere of true attraction—falling like once radiant aeriolites, heavy and cold and dark to the earth.

It is a beautiful proof of the immortality of the soul, that no imagery like that of stars and suns and skies and clouds fitly type its glory, or dimly shadow its beauty. Like the music of celestial spheres, these vibratory soul waves move with spheral harmony in one beautiful diatonic scale, with its deep, grave unisons, its multiplied octaves, its greater and lesser tones of melody, and so mysteriously alternating sweet sound and mute silence, break the profoundest hush of every soul.

You might search the records of the Church of the Ascension, where Carleyn had a pew for five years, and you wouldn't find his name ; but among that invisible congregation, the Church of the Ascension of Great Souls, his thoughts worshipped and communed. His was a heart for clinging and comfort, consolation and care taking ; one to whom you could frankly and fearlessly turn, when pushed aside by some rough soul, and thrust back into your shell like some despised snail, till you despairingly wished you were all crustacea, soul and all.

Some natures you meet, mine them never so deeply, are all strikes, faults, and fire-damps ; up-turn the whole soul-strata, and you'll find not a fragment that has a genial, genuine anthracite glow ; but Carleyn's soul, stir it, probe it, mine it as you would, there was the ring of the true metal, the gleam of the pure gold.

Have you never looked out of your window, reader, some balmy, still afternoon in April, when a shower had given the earth a deeper emerald, the sky a clearer sapphire, and the rose a more ruby glow ? So these words of wisdom from the lips of the preacher had fallen like April benedictions upon Carleyn's boyish soul. Duty's clouded sky had worn a clearer sapphire, faith's parched hillside path a deeper emerald, little withering ruby hope-buds had grown rubier, the skylark of happiness was soaring and singing in the still air of peace, life's once turbid river was winding along the banks of care, clear, overflowing and beautiful.

Carleyn sat and thought. If artist only could sketch and shade and finish a good man's noble and beautiful soul, how wonderful, rare and radiant the picture, taken after a midsummer shower of kindness ! The heart at midsummer, from the life ! Everybody with a heart would hurry to see it. Eyes classic and scholastic, æsthetic and rustic, would linger long and gaze upon it often. Goupil and Schaus, and Art's famed academics and most illustrious galleries, might strive for the first opportunity to exhibit it. All sovereigns gladly claim this new Columbus, long voyaging with the airy fleets of fancy, discovering and revealing at last this terra incognita, this long talked of first view of the heart. No diadem so impearled as to worthily crown the happy artist who could successfully execute this great picture. With wreaths of living emerald, the University of Time would confer upon him the immortal honors of the world's poet laureate.

Reader! lay aside your knitting, crocheting or embroidery—don't keep looking at that clock on the mantel, put off for to-day that calling, promenading, shopping, lay aside until to-morrow that new dress, whose elaborate braiding and endless fluting puzzle and weary you, and make your head and eyes ache so. You can wear that black silk one more Sunday, and besides it may rain, and if you are a modern genteel young lady, you never go to church when it rains. So far as I can judge from the looks of the pews, it isn't fashionable—few besides good old deacons go. As for our sable porters and weather-proof Bridgets, they go, but of course they are no patterns for us. But it is pleasant to-day, and don't sit with that frown on your brow, waiting for that trouble which you are *sure* is coming in to-day's express train of evils—don't stop to bundle up so warmly and nurse so persistently that little homely, hungry, noisy regret. It may die of itself if you let it alone. Lock the door, close the shutters, and say for once, you are not at home to Care; don't open the door, no matter how she thumps and pounds and rings and knocks.

Trouble will sometimes go away discouraged, if you keep perfectly quiet, and say not at home to her. Let Care go off for once without coming in. She'll go somewhere else. She has a long list of visits to make before night. Care is always calling around till dark, and sometimes she's out all night, disturbing people with her doleful serenades. I know, for she has kept me awake many a night. Leave this bread-and-butter world awhile, and come look with me at an old picture, which has hung in my soul for years.

Reader, you are the only person to whom I have ever tried to show it, and I suppose you'll never speak of it, or betray the confidence between us. It is among a collection of paintings strictly private. Sometimes it looks like a photograph, and then at other times I really think it is an original of the greatest of Masters. I found it, early one morning, as I was clearing away some of the rubbish in my soul's garret; and as I can never move it from where it hangs, just wait a moment, while I brush away the dust, let in the light, and unfold the canvas, and try to show it to you as it looks to me. If some famous artist could bring it out, it might make a sensation in the art world—but as for me, I have never handled a pallet or touched a brush in my life, and I'm too old to begin now. Yet I can sketch a little from nature rudely and crudely with the stump of an old pencil; but I can see if I can't create, and I have seen this picture in all kinds of lights. I have gazed at it by dawn-light and twilight, moonlight and starlight, dreamlight and daylight, real light and ideal light. I've been charmed with its shadowy profiles, its wreathed ignettes, its magnificent full lengths, with their clear, striking and graceful high, low, and mezzo reliefs. I can see them as plainly on a clear day, when there's no fog about me, as you can the green blinds and stone steps of that house across the way.

Don't say you can't waste time looking at it; you always read a story right through, and skip the poetizing and mor-alizing. That is not the way you take life, in one big su-gar pill, and all at once. Life has its epics, novel, exciting and brilliant; all the better for its calm quiet periods and semicolons of rest between. A book is a journey, with not all picturesque mountains, refreshing shade trees and glow-ing sunsets.

There's many a dusty road where you trudge along un-der reason's hot sun, in Thought's old gray overcoat, till you come at last through the cool trees to the green fields and flowers again; and see how life's story is coming out, and God's great book of nature has many a rough stony by-path between its cool green epics and fragrant episodes. You enjoy a good breakfast and an excellent dinner, but would you like to hear the dinner bell ringing all the day long, though a perpetual and never so delicious a repast were awaiting you below ?

Don't be in such a worry and fidget to get the first seat in the crowded car of life, that you may be the first to hurry over the ferry of thought, and ride up the great Broadway of excitement.   Better be last at a milliner's opening, than never attend a levee of soul.

Don't say it is too ideal or too transcendental—you have worked so long through busy Saturdays and toilsome Mondays, what if you should spend one whole day grouping and bouquetting soul-flowers, chasing butterfly fancies, or gathering sweetbriar thoughts.   You'll work better after a holiday in the pleasant groves of dream-land.   You won't meet with any flirtations or adventures, but you may sit and talk with cool refreshing thoughts, and wreath with fresh wild flowers some dear little orphan memory you'd almost forgotten.

I never look at anything beautiful but I long for some one to see it with me, whether it be sunset gold, or meadow green, or morning purple.

There is the heart's great Italy, frescoed with Transfigurations more glorious than Raphael's " holier Christs and veiled Madonnas," and beyond Reason's snowy Alps, where cold truths hang like icicles.   In the distance towers the great Mont Blanc of the soul, the savage and inaccessible Future, with its crags of ice and granite, along whose overhanging cliffs you can place one hand on perpetual immeasurable masses of great glacier griefs, and with the other pluck joy's sweet violets and resignation's beautiful rhododendron, the rose of the heart's Alps. You can look down on yesterday's ice-slides, and off at to-morrow's avalanchian scars and abysses, or turn and gaze far away into the tropical clime of soul, its beautiful conservatories, with sunny beds and fragrant borders of tube-roses and heliotropes, japonicas and orange blossoms, while Poesie sits weaving them like pearls in her coronet of song, round the oriole windows fadeless morning-glories twine, and at midnight's darkest hour faith's night-blooming Cereus unfolds her snowy petals, filling the air with her peerless perfume.

> In tropic clime of soul, that hidden land
> Through sorrow's evening late, night-blowing flowers expand,
> In trouble's deepest dark, faith's radiant Cereus glows
> With Fortune's orient morn, the starry petals close.

And the passion flower, " grand with imperial purple and rich with ethereal blue," blooms with its crown of thorns—and hard by are the green fields of contemplation, where hungry thoughts feed and refresh themselves, and patches near of cultured soil, where little growing cares and duties furnish daily food for the roving, restless soul ; and far away across the meadow of will, runs laughing along among the sober trees the little brook of impulse where wild water lilies grow ; and yonder is a square, closely-trimmed lawn where no stray child of fancy ever plays, and Regret's grim sentries patrol night and day, and keep Hope's frolicsome children off the tempting grass.

There is the Hall of Conscience, his register office—where Truth makes his impartial affidavits, and Justice records all the deeds of soul. Just in front of the Hall of Conscience is the fountain of tears, almost always playing with its wreaths of drooping spray; and near, half hidden by dark cypress and bending willow, is the soul's solitary chapel, and in its holiest of holies sometimes glows the radiant Shekinah, sure symbol and sacred shadowing of presence divine, and the oratorio where

> Thoughts like kneeling nuns behind the grate of time,
> In soul's high altar sing, the office pure, sublime.

There Faith chants her midnight mass for the repose of the unquiet soul, and crowds of worshipping feelings bow in meek, mute devotion, or rising sing their united Te Deum, their happy Gloria in Excelsis, and in the distance, towering above mountain and cloud, rises the stately dome of the soul's Valhalla—palace of immortality, with pillars, entablatures and arches gleaming with gold and glistening with pearls.   In its lofty royal observatory hang chandeliers of festooned stars, and there are perfect and complete quadrants and octants, achromatic and reflective, night and day telescopes, where without agitation and disturbance the soul takes her glorious observations, her unobstructed views of heaven ; while in Valhalla's halls calmly repose heroic thoughts, which once nobly fought and conquered in battles with cruel errors, in the long contests of ages ; and far off along the shore of destiny rolls Emotion's turbulent Atlantic, and yonder roars Passion's great Niagara, while at intervals bursts impetuously, from Doubt's immense volcanic chimneys, dense smoke, lurid flames, and overwhelming lava.

Once more, as the canvas unfolds, you'll see some starry

promontory of soul, and look off into the deeps of eternity behind, into the deeps of eternity beyond. Pause not to gaze at speculative meteoric dream, or fathom some metaphysical mist, lest a great, full-orbed truth pass the disc of the soul, unnoticed, unmarked, forever. See thoughts twinkle out from the misty via lactea of ages, and uncounted nebulæ of dim fancies flit in the dim ideal beyond.

As we gaze through the stained windows of our curtained souls into the depths of these trooping thoughts, who shall find their true parallax? Who measure the soul's proud perihelion to uncreated light? Who conjecture its farthest aphelion, its immense sweep through distant ages?

Look for a clock in the soul's cathedral tower that marks with hieroglyphic hand where truth begins, how far progresses, and where ends. Alas! the hands of the clock will point to the hour of midnight; it has not yet struck one truth sure, clear and loud, and the soul mournfully weeps in sympathy with the " throbbing stars," that it is so long, that like light from distant stars, truth's radiant rays are years coming to our visible horizon. Climb on tiptoe as we will, and peer through eternity's keyhole, we shall only approach, but never touch, the full-orbed truth.

Could artist find mountain-peak tall enough for studio close to the star-lit skylight above and there alone, :

> He patient kneels to art, and bathes in beauty's fount,
> Till face to face he talks on inspiration's mount,

there achieve this chef d'œuvre, the study of the heart from life, he might victoriously die, his name written in starlight above Michael Angelo, Correggio, Raphael or Murillo, his eagle fame nestling forever among the golden clouds of art's highest cyric.

CHAPTER XXXIX.

ASTROGNOSIA.

"Like the swell of some sweet tune,
  Morning rises into noon;
  May glides onward into June."

NEPENTHE STUART is quite busy a few weeks before the wedding—not in trying on elegant silks, heavy satins and embroidered muslins, laces and flounces, but her manuscript is really being published at last. Every evening she looks over several pages of her proof. There is a strange excitement in seeing anything of hers in print. She never knew how it would sound until she reads it aloud. She hides it hurriedly away when Frank comes, for she is keeping it a precious secret from him. She adds, changes, crosses out, corrects at night, and in the morning early she reviews and reads again, for by seven it goes to the stereotyper's.

This first child of her fancy is very dear to her; it is the creation of her own heart, weeping her own tears, smiling her own smiles, and breathing her own soul-life. As she thinks of it with real affection, and dreads the cutting steel of sharp criticism, she vainly wishes she had never launched such a little, inexperienced bark out on the stormy, capricious Atlantic of public opinion, in whose turbulent depths hide fearful sharks and devouring whales, watching for prey. She thinks dolefully of many a poor little book once carefully launched, and sailing off on the same perilous voyage, silent forever, through some sharp critic's sharpest thrust or heaviest broadside.

It may share the fate of many a light novel-craft, gaily trimmed and fully manned, floating down, and lost in the great Gulf Stream of Oblivion. But these reflections are too late now. Such clouds of fearful maybes always darken the sky, when our little hope-crafts sail silently away from our watching sight.

"It is too late," thought Nepenthe, "to put pussy back

in the bag. There's no tying her up tight now, to smother or drown her."

Once plumed her airy wing, if she find no green leaf of sympathy, the dove of fancy can return no more to the sheltering ark of her native heart. The world, with its opera glass always in its hand, is a poor home for a new book; and a freshman author must be fagged and drilled, and held under the pump of criticism, to have cold water poured on his breathing thoughts and burning words, by those wise sophomores who have had their eye-teeth cut long ago by some similar cooling and refreshing process; and thus they pay back the grudges of their novitiate.

But if Frank should read the book and like it, she will preserve her spiritual equanimity whatsoever blast the uncertain trumpet of fame may blow in her startled ears.

But at last, as she rolls up the sheets of her proof, and sends them away, she forgets for the time her little book—for the years of her lonely life have rolled away, and new, bright pages are unfolding in her history. It is the eve of her bridal. She reads over and over again in her happy heart, the beautiful dedication of her own life to her artist lover, as it is firmly bound and brightly clasped with his enduring affection.

Under the cover of his strong protection, she reads in fancy, in new letters, her new name, in the press of Time, waiting to be stamped with the signet ring and sealing kiss, ' Nepenthe Carleyn.'

The two volumes of their single lives will to-morrow be bound together. Not to be Volume first and Volume second, but ONE pleasant biography, illustrated with such beautiful engravings as love only carves.

" God grant," said Nepenthe fervently, " that each daily life-chapter may be begun with some sweet strain of melody and closed with some dewy benediction, that when on the last page of this precious Biography shall be written

' FINIS,'

we may sit down together on the banks of the river of the water of life, and review with pure pleasure the truthful, happy, and elevated pages of our short history—stereotyped in its eternal plates."

She stood by the window at nightfall, and looked out on God's great starlit roof, the only roof which had sheltered

her when there was no spot in the wide world where she
could repose securely at nightfall, sure of a home and shelter for the morrow.

Watched ceaselessly by no earthly eyes through all the
changes of her tearful childhood and lonely maidenhood, she
had ever been like a waif—sometimes at rest, then drifting
out alone on life's stormy tide. She looked out with brimming eyes upon the ever watchful, constant stars, which
shone long ago in the old windows at home—those dear,
faithful watchers were watching still. The only influences
which had followed her through life were the " sweet influences of the Pleiades." The only bands which had linked
her fragmentary life together, were " the golden bands of
Orion," the never failing light on her hidden path, the gentle light of stars.

Her faith had looked up more than those who have earthly loves and guides clinging ever around them.

On this eve of her bridal, the whole sky seemed giving a
grand joyful illumination, chanting one radiant bridal march
on its reachless range.

> " Where every jewelled planet sings
> Its clear eternal song
> Over the path our friends have gone."

She knew nothing of dactyl or spondee, metre or measure.
Without measuring or scanning from the De Profundis of
her full heart welled out these lines.

There was a mingling of sadness in the strain, for no
woman with a soul can launch out on an unknown sea, even
with a chosen guide, without a deep strange sadness, almost
a fear, to link her life and trust freely and forever with another's.

ASTROGNOSIA.

Strange, quiet, patient stars, ye've looked down on life's ill.
Through all the wrongs beneath, and kept your counsel still ;
Clear-eyed and bright, through nightly deeps patrol
Hiding your thoughts profound from human soul.

On in your calling bright, your mark is ever high,
Nothing shall cross your tramp, ye sentry of the sky ;
Tempest nor storm nor cloud shall check your stately beat,
Faithful each lonely hour your tireless bivouac keep,

Found ye in arsenal divine, in ages long agone,
Your evening chant, your nightly beat, your burnished armor worn ?
From living crystal river, hard by the Eternal throne,
Kindled your deathless flaming to light the ages on ;
For joy at earth's creation waved you those torches high,
And formed that glad procession to cheer the gloomy sky ?

Your lanterns o'er the restless waves of stormy life,
Show many a far-out ledge, on sorrow's surging sea,
Your quenchless lights burn steadfast through the dark,
To guide, from traitor rocks, some spirit's way-worn bark.

When trouble's icebergs, cold and grand,
Before dismantled spirits stand
Ye Pharoi of the fatherland,
Light safe along grim peril's strand.

Most blinded by the mist of fears, exiled on isle of time,
Through gathering showers of falling tears, we see but faintly shine,
These chandeliers in hall of Heaven, with starry festoons hung,
That guide o'er sapphire threshold, the spirit homesick long.

Within its curtained chamber my soul lies folded round ;
No coming comfort's footstep doth cross its threshold bound ;
Down to the tented spirit like angel from afar,
Steals through the misty twilight some watching, radiant star ;
And shines through falling tear-drops till sorrow's stone hath rolled
And through the open peace-door flit wings of sunset gold ;
The spirit sheds its grave clothes and walks again in life,
Serene as star ascended, looks down on mortal strife.

Come forth, each shrouded spirit ! all wrapped in mournful gloom,
In rocky cares and sorrows ye have a prison hewn :
In caverned wealth it hideth, and buried darkly lies;
It is not dead, but sleepeth ; it surely will arise.
Look up ! the stars are shining in yonder quiet skies,
From convent of St. Ego your monkish spirit hies.

Along the roof of nature, above old science's floor,
Our loftiest hopes like giants walk, as through enchanted door,
Ascend the tower eternal; where starry bells shall chime,
When on a world expiring shall fall the dirge of time.

Has failed, forever failed, all mortal rhyme,
To count the changes of a starry chime ;
Nor speech, nor language e'er was found
To translate pure such liquid sound

This bright vignette on nature's page,
Revered in verse through every age,
Electrotyped by Triune hand,
With hidden plates in silent land.

These lovely thoughts in nature's breast,
Have ne'er a mortal volume blessed ;
Too bright for poetry, too beautiful for song,
All the ideals fail, to paint the starry throng.

Art veils her face and kneels in reverent tears,
While puzzled science, knitting up the sleeve of years,
Drops all her stitches as she counts again ;
Sets up her decades, tries in vain,
With tangled speculations, baffled tries,
To ravel the long mystery of skies.

Like sentinels at intervals ye stand
Along the borders of that frontier land,
Where finite ends, and infinite is spanned,
And ever engineering on your golden track,
Fresh light on mortal path ye're sending back.

———

Dear face of friendly star ! you only smile good-night ;
Mid breaking hearthstone links and waning household light;
When loved ones tell us long and last adieu,
Your au revoir you whisper kind and true ;
Low through our lattice in some foreign clime,
Sing soft voices, auld lang syne.

———

Bright beads on strings of ages, the rosary of time,
Guarded by ancient Sages, as amulet sublime,

As on each virgin star they gazed, each pure and radiant face,
Rehearsing Pater Noster lines, perfection, beauty, grace ;
Who counts the starry chaplet, where'er on earth he be,
Must offer from his kneeling heart his Gloria Patri.

And we, another prayer send up, unto the Spirit, Son,
That we, like stars in duty's path, may shine unfailing on ;
And toiling up earth's cloudy heights may to our zenith rise,
And find our true celestial point, above in paradise ;
Trace back our longitude from earth, on Joy's meridian high,
Counting degress of happiness along the radiant sky.

Oh! could the starry ladder our yearning spirits climb,
And reach the topmost skylight where lamps eternal shine ;
In yonder great Valhalla put on our starry crown,
And join the bright procession that moves the ages on.

There come at times such longings to be what we are not,
We wish with sad despondings we had some brighter lot ;
Like thee, oh star unchanging, our loftiest endeavor,
Seems ever onward moving, yet standing still forever.

'Twill not be slumbering long ; in wider range
There'll be a waking soon ; we all shall change ;
These mantling folds of care shall backward roll,
Till beckoning stars call up to longing's goal.

We'll greet again bright stars when earth's dark nights are o'er,
And dawns the spirit's higher life on the immortal shore ;
Then morning stars shall sing once more, and shout for joy again,
As whiteclad souls through pearly gates pass up the golden plain.

CHAPTER XL.

MR. JOHN PRIDEFIT GOES TO THE WEDDING.

"We sit together, with the skies,
    The steadfast skies above us;
We look into each other's eyes,
    And how long will you love us?
The eyes grow dim with prophecy,
    The voices low and breathless,
Till death us part! O words, to be
    Our best for Love the deathless."

"How many bridesmaids? What did the bride have on? How did she appear? How long was her trail? What did the bridesmaids wear? Was she married with a ring? How many were at the reception? How many ushers were there?" All these questions asked Mrs. John Pridefit of her husband when he came home one evening, and told her he had stepped into Trinity Church and seen the artist Frank Carleyn, who took her uncle's portrait, married.

"Why didn't you come home for me, John?" said his disappointed wife. "I wanted to see the dresses so much. I like to know what people wear, and at such a time people look as well as they can."

"Because," said her husband gravely, "I only heard of it ten minutes beforehand, and I knew you couldn't dress in ten minutes."

"Did you go in that rig?" said she, looking at him with a dismayed expression.

"Certainly. I went with the dust of the desk on my coat sleeves. I have been in court nearly all day. Nobody looked at me, they all looked at the bride."

"Well," said Mrs. Pridefit, in a more good-humored tone, "What did the bride have on?—you haven't told me yet."

"She had on something white, I believe—something white."

"What is the reason, John," said his wife provoked, "you can never tell what a lady has on?"

"Well, well," said Mr. Pridefit, apologetically, "everything is ashes of roses now. If her dress was ashes of roses, it must have been the ashes of white roses; for I am sure it was something white. Almost any lady looks well in full bridal costume. Her charms are heightened, or defects softened, by attractive and airy dress; but the poor bridegrooms stand upon their own merits—they look about as God made them—no veil to adorn, no illusion before and behind and around. But this groom needed no help to make him look handsome—he is a fine-looking fellow, and the bride's face was like the face of an angel."

"Well, how many bridesmaids were there?"

"I can't say. I know there was one, and something white too she had on; but I must tell you something. We had cards two weeks ago to this reception. I was at home when they came, and to tell the truth, I lost six hundred dollars that day, so I forgot all about the reception cards."

Mr. Pridefit saw his wife looked more disappointed about the reception than the money, so he added in a husky voice, "To-day is the fourth anniversary of the death of our only child. O Eliza, Eliza! Life has been tame to me since that;"—and so it had. Under his pillow, night after night, had that little daguerreotype been hidden—the little lips kissed again and again; for never had John Pridefit loved any living-thing as he loved that little, laughing, open-hearted, affectionate child, and she only three years ago was drowned in a cistern, not far from her father's country residence.

But Mrs. Pridefit was Mrs. Pridefit still. Her heart still clung to "pomps and vanities;" she regretted even now she could not wear her light blue moiré antique at the artist's reception.

Little did she know that the artist's bride had once received so cold a reception from her hands and heart, when taken up half dead from that cistern, only ten years ago.

"Who gave away the bride?" said Mrs. Pridefit.

"When the clergyman said in his clear voice, 'Who giveth this woman to be married to this màn,' a fine-looking gentleman came out from the crowd, and gave her away. They say his name is Selwyn—he is a great friend of Carleyn's. The bride, I think, has no living relative, so this gentleman gave her away."

"That was strange," said Mrs. Pridefit. "Were there no relatives standing up with them? And where does this Selwyn live? Is he a stranger here? If it hadn't been for my neuralgia I would have found out myself."

"He has boarded some time at Mrs. Edwards', and is a particular friend of Carleyn's. That's all I know about it," said Mr. Pridefit.

"You never can get any news out of a man," said Mrs. Pridefit. But the next day she called on Charity Gouge, and she learned that some unknown friend had furnished the bride's trousseau, and sent her an elegant white satin wedding dress, with two flounces of point lace. At the head of the flounces was a wreath of tuberoses and geranium leaves. With the dress was a bridal veil of point lace also. The bride was said to be portionless; but she was dressed as richly as any wealthy bride, and her husband furnished nothing.

Miss Gouge thought there was some mystery about it. She had even gone so far as to question the dressmaker, but she either could or would reveal nothing, only that Mr. Selwyn ordered the carriage, and he was the last to say good-bye when they left for their wedding tour.

"Well," said Mrs. Pridefit, "when the bride repeated the words, 'With all my worldly goods I thee endow,' Mr. Carleyn must have felt *liberally endowed*. I was married in white silk; I have always been very sorry that I wasn't married in white satin."

While the carriage bore Carleyn and his wife off on their pleasant journey, in a little white-curtained and striped carpeted room in Titusville, sat one evening a rare couple—Levi Longman and Prudence Potter. Levi had concluded to buy a part of the lot belonging to Prudence, so he came one night to make the terms. He flavors his conversation with common sense, sober reason and cool judgment, as he sits in his high-backed chair, tipped against the wall.

When business matters are disposed of, in her laconic way, Prudence draws up her chair a little closer, and asks "How that blind doctor in the city recovered his sight?"

In his wisest manner, and most deliberate tone, Levi answered, "All the efforts of surgery and medicine, blisters, moxas, nux vomica, belladonna failed in his case—and then electricity was judiciously applied. I can't describe the

exact process, but it was in some way by employing elec-
tro-puncture, directing the electric aura against the eyes,
drawing it from them during the insulation of the patient,
taking small sparks from the eye-lids, or integument round
the orbits. I heard the doctors talk about passing down fine
needles through any of the branches of the frontal and superior maxillary nerves, and a slightly pricking sensation, indicating the nerve is pierced, a galvanic current is then
passed along the needles through the branch of the fifth
nerve."

Prudence looked puzzled, as if she didn't know any better
now than before she asked, but she only said, looking over
her spectacles at Levi, as she stopped her knitting, "*Don't
that beat all!*"

CHAPTER XLI.

THE RETURN—THE SURPRISE.

"Oh never again, while thy weal is my care,
  The dark sinfu' regions o' spaedom I'll dare.
  'Twere vain to expect thou wilt cost us nae tears,
In our toil-wearied way through the dim hoped.for years;
But aye we'll see in thee, as sweet and as dear
The Agnes awa' in the Agnes that's here."
  DAVID WINGATE.

"I have ordered the carriage to stop with me at a friend's
house on the way," said Selwyn to Carleyn, as he met him
and his bride at the depot on their return. They stopped
before the door of the most elegant house in that vicinity.
Carleyn was surprised, yet he chose to gratify Selwyn, who
looked unusually bright, and who seemed to feel perfectly
at home as he went with them into the large parlor, and
asked them to walk into the little.library out of the parlor,
for there they would find the owner of the establishment.

There was a beautiful portrait of a lady in a recess on
one side of the mantel, a lady apparently about thirty-five—
on the other was Carleyn's ideal Nepenthe, and as Nepenthe stood before it, her face radiant with the dawn of hap
piness, the resemblance was so striking, she herself could

see it. Now that her face wore its native sunshine, the picture might be taken for her portrait.

There was also a striking resemblance in the two portraits.

"That picture on the left side," said Selwyn, "was taken by Carleyn at my urgent request, a few months before your marriage. It was taken from a miniature painted on ivory some years ago. I intended it as a present for you. That vase on the little table is of exquisite workmanship, and was imported by me some years since. The violets in it came from the conservatory belonging to the owner of this house. On the outside of the vase I have had engraved the word Nepenthe in letters of gold."

That vase—that vase! Nepenthe held her hand over her eyes and thought. She had seen it in early childhood often filled with violets, and filled by her mother's hand. It was the most beautiful thing her childish eyes had ever seen. The past began to dawn upon her bewildered mind. That portrait! it seemed almost to speak as she gazed upon it.

"It is my mother's picture," said she at last. "Oh that those lips had language! Life has passed but roughly with me since I saw thee last."

Taking her arm gently within her own, Mr. Selwyn drew her before the mirror, and bade her look up, and see reflected there the owner of that elegant house, the lady who had recently come into possession of that valuable property.

"And here is the deed of the property, which I hand over to the rightful owner," said he, putting a paper duly signed, sealed and delivered into her hand.

As Nepenthe saw him bending affectionately over her, the truth dawned at last upon her mind. She clasped her arms around his neck, and exclaimed, "My father! my father!"

Poor tempest-tossed, bereaved, long desolate man, he held in his arms at last his Nepenthe. Henceforth he could forget much sorrow and misfortune.

"My child! my child! my Nepenthe!" he exclaimed.— "The bitter cup long drained is removed. My prayer is heard. My Lina's gentle hand hath held out to me through all this darkness, this cup of. joy to be my solace, while she quaffs her purer Nepenthe from the river of life."

CHAPTER XLII.

MYSTERY CLEARED UP.

"If in our daily course our mind
Be set to hallow all we find,
New treasures still of countless price
God will provide for sacrifice

"Old friends, old scenes will lovelier be,
As more of heaven in each we see;
Some softening gleam of love and prayer
Will dawn on every cross and care."

"Tell us about all your wanderings, dear father," said Nepenthe the next morning as she refilled the vase with fresh violets from her own conservatory.

"There was a claim of twenty thousand dollars due me in a distant city," said Mr. Stuart, (for he likes to be called by his last name now.) "I heard one day that the parties owing me were intending to make an assignment of all their property to certain preferred creditors. I sent a brief note to my wife, took that morning's express train, which left in half an hour, hoping by seeing the parties before their intended assignment, to induce them to prefer me, and liquidate my claim by paying in whole or in part. The note never reached my wife, nor did any succeeding letters. I was informed by letter, three weeks after my departure, of the death and burial of my wife and child. I was not at all well that day, and I had fallen down through a hatchway the day before. The severe blow caused by the accident, and the fearful news conveyed in the letter, caused an illness which terminated in brain fever. I was ill a long time, and unable to travel. For a time I lost all recollection of any events happening during the last four years.

"Of course my physician did not advise me to visit the scene of my loss with my feeble health and unsettled brain. After some months of medical treatment I was allowed to travel, and visit new scenes, if possible to regain my mental vigor and tone. But when I found out two years since, that she who I believed had died so soon after my departure, had lived and struggled on for years, thinking me faithless, and at last had drooped and died of a broken heart, my strength gave way. I was sorely tempted. My reason seemed shaken. I preached no more.

" I could not even bear the name of Professor Henry, the name the students gave me, as there was another Stuart in the University whom they called Professor John.

" I walked my room many a night, and wished I had never taken that fatal journey. I have been the victim of an almost fiendish revenge.

" A woman to whom I was engaged when a very young man, and whose fearfully violent temper, accidentally discovered, caused me to violate my contract, has persecuted me and mine with relentless fury. She intercepted all my letters. She wrote me, under an assumed name, that letter informing me of the death of my wife and child, when both were living and mourning my absence. She was a watcher at my wife's death-bed, a nurse at the hospital, a cook at Dr. Wendon's ; her hand cut with a knife the rope to which the pail was attached when you, Nepenthe, were almost drowned. Attired as a man, she attempted your life one evening—and to carry out her subsequent plans and mystify her movements, she assumed the name of Madam Future. Having a large telescope in the top of her house, by turning it in certain directions she could easily see the movements in many of the houses near.

" When Carleyn's windows were unshaded or unshuttered she could plainly see his face and features, and tell what he was about.

" The telescope itself was so concealed that Florence Elliott really thought it some magic glass. She whispered in Carleyn's ear many false statements concerning you, and your unknown father and dead mother—but she herself is dead now, and we will try and forget the irretrievable wrong she has done.

" One night I shall never forget. I had done some great service to a stranger. I came home in a calmer frame than usual, resolved to do my duty, and try and banish useless recollections. I found on my table a sealed note with these words—' Your wife did not die soon after you left, but lingered lonely years after, watching and waiting for your return, and died at last of a broken heart, believing you faithless. Your child is not dead, but is a homeless wanderer in the wide world, while you are enjoying wealth which can do you no good.'

" I read this cruel letter, and as I thought how her sensitive nature lingered out years of agony, I walked back and forth, almost maddened with grief. It seemed that my heart must break. I moaned, I sobbed, I wept, I shrieked. Suddenly I felt something give way within, as if my heart itself had burst. I put my hand on my heart—I could feel no motion—for years I felt none. I asked a physician's opinion. He said there was a sudden obstruction, and that any great excitement might cause insanity or death. He advised me to keep calm and quiet—so I preached no more. It would have been hard for me, with my wan face and worn heart, to bind up the broken-hearted, and preach deliverance to the captive ; to inspire faith and hope in desponding souls. So not caring whither I went, I travelled on. I spent two months in the northern part of Texas, travelling sometimes on horseback, sometimes on foot, often sleeping at night upon the prairies and in the groves. When the sky was clear and cloudless, I wandered about in search for water, cutting and breaking the limbs of trees, making a big fire by a fallen tree for a back log, baking and eating some corn bread, and boiling water for tea. After supper, we—for there were three companions with me—lay down on some blankets spread on the ground, with our travelling bags for our pillows, and with gentle zephyrs, wreaths of curling smoke, and flickering shadows dancing about us, we were lulled into quiet slumbers in spite of the owl's dismal music, barking of foxes, and howling of wolves, and all but myself awoke in the morning, refreshed and invigorated. But no sky seemed to me bright, no air balmy.

" In the sky of the soul, each cluster of blessings has its lost Pleiad, and you may count over your circle of loved ones, yet that one who is not, you cannot forget. Many a life-picture has its dark back-ground of clouds, of doubts, and of mysteries."

Mr. Stuart paused—and taking from his pocket a little package, opened an old yellow-looking partly torn letter.

" This," said he, with much emotion, " is the last page of

a letter written by my wife only one week before she died.
I can see the traces of tears in nearly every line, but the
style is hers, the handwriting hers, though evidently written with faltering pen and trembling hand." Mr. Stuart
reads :

" It is always November in the heart where such a mystery broods. The dead leaves are always falling, and the
shrieking winds are never weary. O, could we close gently the eyes of loved ones, and lay them tenderly away,
safely cloistered with the Great Father above—but not to
know when or how or where they are gone, to watch at morn
and evening for their coming, and yet they come not, tosses
the moaning soul on the billows of unrest, haunts the worn
spirit like a sleepless ghost, watching and wailing at every
turn to beckon and torture and scare the desolate soul.
These fearful minute guns on the wide sea of thought,
through the long lonely night boom and echo off the cold
shore of regret."

Mr. Stuart folded the letter, and said, in a low, sad tone :
" Poor Lina! she hardly suffered more than I. Many a
night for years I have called out in agony, as in a nightmare sleep, My child ! my child ! where is my child ?

" None have known my sorrow. I tried to outgrow sorrow, but some sorrow shadows lengthen as life's sun goes
down—they grow taller and darker, till no stretching the
drapery of oblivion, no lengthening the mantle of forgetfulness, can hide their skeleton limbs or heavy feet. Some
lost joys, like lost friends, may be first earth-covered, then
grass-grown ; but there are troubles that walk the desolate
shades of the heart like unappeased ghosts, ever and anon
muttering and staring through memory's half-open shutters,
while the words of remorse howl dismally around.

" You, Nepenthe, my child, are as fresh and beautiful a
gift, as if some Peri had lain you at my feet. You are the
one bright pearl cast up on the shore of my wrecked life.
Could sea-bird have wept out bright pearls in the hollow
wreathed chamber of the deep, surely this pearl of my heart
was wept into beauty in the hollow-wreathed chamber of
sorrow.

" The outer surface of society is clear, serene and sunny. With swelling sails and airy pennons, how gracefully
it floats along the conventional tide ; but away down in its

heart are under-currents, strong, rapid and powerful—there's no plateau laid along the depths of the heart where any joy cable, let down ever so deep, may lie long unbroken.

" So we braid the cable of our hopes, and have our great festal days over some new line of joy in the stream of life.

" Gay processions of sanguine thoughts, with bright banners and showy badges, and noisy huzzas, go marching up and down our applauding hearts. We pay out our joys off the bark of hope, and wait day after day for signals and responses. But there are no returns; there's a break somewhere, there come only a few faint signals, and the bell of the heart tolls out the day of failure.

" No mortal diver can fathom the depths of the heart; no plateau exists in the tide of human passion where any joy cable can be laid in a chain unbroken. Some voice whispers, it may succeed after all, and away up in the tower of humanity rings out another glad chime. Hope says we've found the error, and will correct it. But no; not till the whole life is taken up and laid over. So in the bottom of all our hearts lie buried many useless joy cables.

" You, Nepenthe, were entitled to property in England—property coming to your mother. We were married in England, but I had no marriage certificate. The clergyman who married us was a careless, dissipated man, and there was no such thing as our marriage certificate in existence; and I found it impossible to get the property, as the Duke of Wellington would not present my petition to the Queen. I walked up and down in despair, and gave up the hope of securing your rightful inheritance.

" But one day, as I came out of the Horse Guards into Charing Cross, I met the Colonial Secretary, who had just returned from Bermuda, and told him my trouble. ' I granted the marriage license, and will set matters right,' said he. Was it not strange that he, the only man in the world who could have helped me in the matter, should arrive that day in England, and meet me, just as I was making up my mind to return to America without securing the property?

" I have secured to you a fortune in your own right. This was the object of my recent visit to England. I meant that

Carleyn should marry you without fortune—for yourself—
and so I have kept until now the deed in my own hands."

Mr. Selwyn went out as he said this, and did not return
until late in the afternoon, and when he came back he looked very sad as he said,

" I was just called to see a beautiful young creature die,
in great agony, of over-doses of arsenic, the most distressing
and fatal of all mineral poison. With its rapid inflammation,
intense thirst, it executed its deadly purpose with alarming
rapidity, though the most counteracting remedies were
promptly resorted to. She was ill, and at first did not at-
tribute the illness to the right cause till too late.

" The mineral had inserted itself by corrosion beneath
the mucous coat of the stomach before any remedy could
be employed. Whites of eggs mixed with hydrated perox-
ide of vinegar were administered, followed by powerful and
long continued emetics. Every thing was tried, but all
failed.

" She had heightened her beauty, but she had rashly
increased the fatal dose, and rumor says that she loved to
passionate idolatry your husband, the distinguished artist—
and to captivate him she so heightened her natural charms
by this dangerous practice.

" She was dressed for some party when she was taken
so violently ill, and she is to be buried in the same dress.
She must have been brilliantly beautiful. I don't wonder as
she entered the church on Sabbath mornings, people turned
back to gaze at her."

Poor Mrs. Elliott, heart-broken and desolate, woe-begone
and horror-stricken, sat alone by her unburied dead those
two long, lonely days and nights, her soul clad in penitential
sackcloth, and sitting among the ashes of dead hopes. She
had given up principle, conscience, every thing, for this
lost idol.

The main wish of her heart had been the crowning of this
beautiful child queen of the heart and home of some distinguished, gifted man. Until the last, she had hoped to write
her name in that golden-clasped Bible, Florence Carleyn.

Never had she looked so radiantly beautiful as on that
fearful night when came that sudden, terrible agony.

" Oh," said the heart-broken mother, " the cup of bitterness I have pressed so long to other lips, I must drain to the dregs.

"If I had spent those precious hours I wasted in making her beautiful and accomplished, in the culture and ennobling of her immortal soul, I would not now mourn the death of my erring child. I shall go to her, but she will never return to me. O Florence! my child! my child! would God I had died for thee!"

For days the stricken mother wailed and shrieked and sobbed and mourned, yet shed no tears; and months after, if you passed through the Asylum at Utica, you might sometimes see a still beautiful woman looking out of the window, watching and waiting for Florence; sometimes quietly wreathing flowers for her hair, saying she would come soon, and then crushing them, and raving so wildly that all shrank from her in terror. It was one of those hopeless cases of insanity that sometimes linger for years, with no improvement, no relief, no change hut death.

She never seemed sane, but sometimes would sit gazing abstractedly in the distance, and repeating over the words, " Withhold not any good from him to whom it is due, when it is in the power of thine hand to do it." It was the only connected, coherent, rational sentence she ever uttered — That one memory seemed the one unbroken chord in the quivering lyre of her jarred and discordant soul.

That fortune she had lavished upon Florence belonged of right to Nepenthe Stuart. How and when it came into her hands was a secret known only to Madam Future and John Trap.

The former was dead, and the latter was too deeply implicated ever to reveal anything of the transaction. Yet from time to time, with no clue of their source, came sums of money to Nepenthe Carleyn, until all Mrs. Elliott had ever used of hers was paid. This arrangement may have been made by Mrs. Elliott the first day she sat down by her dead child, while remorse was keenest, and trembling reason still lingered on her throne.

I have often thought I never could feel sorry for John Trap, but I couldn't help it when I saw him the other morning. He could not stir his poor useless right hand and foot. He had a stroke of paralysis about a year ago, affecting the whole right side.

He was seized with it when he was foreclosing a mortgage, and he hasn't used the hand since.

I thought of a maimed lion as I looked at him one day as he sat trying to do up a package of letters in his left hand, muttering over to himself gloomily, " Withhold not any good from him to whom it is due." Something in one corner of the old newspaper with which he was wrapping up the letters attracted his attention.

He couldn't get up unaided and reach any of the books on the crowded shelves near him, so he read this article headed eleemosynary.

The article closed thus—" If thou comest to the evening of life and art old or infirm, all thy consolation will be, not how much money hast thou made, but how much good hast thou done, how many wrongs righted ? This is all the capital from which thou canst gain interest in the great bank of the everlasting Future."

John Trap groaned and muttered to himself again, "Withhold not good from him to whom it is due when it is in the power of thy hand to do it."

He looked at his helpless arm. " Poor hand," said he, " has lost its power ; the right hand has lost its cunning, it can do no more harm."

He looked up at his wife's portrait on the wall. " My poor Mary—she is rich now, and I am a poor beggar at the gate of Eternity. A better woman never, never lived. She tried hard enough to make an angel of me, but she could not, and it broke her heart," and tears long stifled, frozen tears, welled up in John Trap's eyes—" too late, too late," said he, moodily, gloomily, mournfully.

Reader ! I was at Greenwood yesterday, and saw a monument with this inscription, " Sacred to the memory of Mary, wife of John Trap,. who died January 1st, 1861, aged 28 years. Blessed are the dead which die in the Lord." If I could write another edition of Les Miserables, surpassing Victor Hugo's, even more tender, truthful and touching, and sell a million of copies, in the quiet Greenwood of its most pleasant thoughts I would erect the noblest monument to Mary, wife of John Trap, once numbered among those the world calls Les Miserables, but now the angels write her name among Les Heureux—the blessed.

If among the domes and spires of the celestial city, there

rises the dome of Valhalla, palace of immortality, where repose the souls of warriors slain in battle, surely Mary Trap's heroic soul rests there with a martyr's victor crown, and robed in radiant white. Alas! of how few of us can the angels ever write Blessed, until we enter into rest.

Blessed is the baptismal word with which the angels crown the soul as it comes up out of the river of death, and joins the white-robed church. " Blessed are the first drops of the life river that kiss the brow, as the transfigured soul puts on her radiant immortal.

> " All their tears are wiped away,
> All darkness turned to perfect day ;
> How blessed be the dead,
> How beautiful be they."

CHAPTER XLIII.

WHAT THE CRITICS SAY.

> " A perfect judge will read each work of wit,
> With the same spirit that its author writ."--POPE.

> " Who shall dispute what the reviewers say ?
> Their word's sufficient ; and to ask a reason
> In such a case as theirs, is downright treason."
> CHURCHILL.

> " Beasts of all kinds their fellows spare ;
> Bear lives at amity with bear."

THERE are many expensive bridal gifts on the table in Nepenthe's room, but there's one—the last, but not the least—on which her eyes will often rest. It is a little blue-covered book, with the word *Dawn* printed on its back. And Frank reads it aloud one evening. As he closes the book, he looks up to Nepenthe and says, archly, " If I had not fallen in love with you, Nepenthe, I should be in great danger of being captivated with the writer of this story. My boyish ideals were all authoresses."

" And mine were all artists," said Nepenthe, laughing ; " but you can't make me jealous, Frank," she added—and her whole face glowed with pleasure.

Mr. Stuart comes in the next Monday morning with a pa-

per in his hand and a very knowing look on his face. " Ah,
Frank," said he, " you wrote this review , I know you did."

" Yes, I did," said Frank, looking at Nepenthe mischievously ; " and I wish I knew who the authoress was. I might
be in danger of falling in love, for my boyish loves were all
authoresses."

Mr. Stuart takes Frank's arm and walks into the other
room. He says, as they stand before the portrait Dawn,
" There, Frank ; there is a pretty good picture of the unknown authoress ; and now I have introduced you," he
added, laughing, " I will leave you to cultivate her acquaintance."

A surprise never looks picturesque on paper, so we'll not
repeat Frank's comments and questions and Nepenthe's ex-
planations and answers. We will leave them a week, till
we see Frank coming in one day with a budget of fresh
newspapers. The morning, evening, daily and weekly papers, and we'll hear what the critics say.

" The Sunday Telegraph says," said Frank, " that you
have written a very good book, but it is of entirely a too religious a cast—a very serious fault," he added. " The
Morning Glory ends by saying that it is a charming story,
and its chief charm is its high moral tone, its elevated religious sentiment. You know how disturbed you were, Nepenthe, on account of that remark of Miss Charity Gouge's
about the book s being so full of ' chopped sentences.' Here
is a review, in the Metropolitan Day Book, which is a very
good offset to that. The critic says the style is simple and
elegant, and its language poetic and eloquent."

" Mrs. John Pridefit remarked," said Nepenthe, " that
the book was full of egregious grammatical blunders. She
evidently gave me credit for all the inaccuracies I put in the
mouths of my characters, and in ordinary conversation very
few persons speak with perfect grammatical accuracy."

" Don't break your heart, Nepenthe ; but the reviewer in
the Daily Wonder says your book is ' loosely put together,'
—but here is the Evening Guest, and the critic remarks
that ' the style is simple, concise, and natural.' The sharpest review you have had is from the Weekly Raven. The
editor says—' not knowing what else to do with your heroine, you set her school-teaching for her living, and this is a
stale resource for feeble authors.' I won't read all the

sharp things he says, but he evidently thinks it a great fault; but they say the editor is an Englishman, and down on all American books. But here is the American Violet, one of the ablest magazines in the country, and its reviewer says that this very school-keeping heroine is the chief charm of the book—so there's a heart's case for you, Nepenthe. There's also a very able review of a similar character in the Independent Truth Teller, and another very just criticism in the American Evangelist."

"What is there in real life," said Nepenthe, "for an educated poor young person to do for a living but teach? It is common in stories, but not more common than in life; but I wonder why I have had no reviews from the Morning Dew Drop and Evening Primrose. The editors are my personal friends."

"Oh! they have a grudge against your publishers," said Carleyn; "and they'll never notice any of their books. The editor of the Laughing Budget remarks that ' it is a bad taste to close with a death-scene,' but the Boston Puritan Evangel says ' the last chapter is a specimen of sublime and beautiful pathos throughout.' You see, Nepenthe," said Frank, "you've enough of all kinds of reviews to keep your spiritual equilibrium."

"No one," said Nepenthe, "can accuse me of writing a novel. I haven't written half the romance in my head. Of course it's a love story, for wouldn't anybody's life be tame and dull enough without a love story in it?

"But Miss Prudence Potter said she shouldn't have thought that Mrs. Carleyn, a professor, would have written so much of a novel," said Frank, "and the critic of the Courier, of whose keen eyes you were so afraid, says ' it is a charming domestic novel,' but Miss Charity Gouge says she never'll read it through, for she doesn't like women's writings."

"I am glad, Frank," said Nepenthe, " that my happiness does not depend upon the success or failure of my book."

Frank reads aloud one more review from the Christian Intelligencer. It is beautifully written, and in deep sympathy with the author. The writer evidently judges discriminatingly, and praises real beauties, enters into the spirit of the book, and Nepenthe feels, as she listens till the happy tears will come, that she would like to grasp the writer's hand, and thank her for her kind, sweet, sympathetic words.

"Here is my olive leaf at last," said Nepenthe. "It has fully rewarded me for opening my soul's window and sending forth the bird of fancy from the ark of my heart."

After sitting quietly a few moments thinking, Nepenthe said, "Frank, I could write a better review of my book than anyone else can. I could say the style and thought were good. The chief charm of the book is not in its plot, which is neither intricate nor intense. There are too many characters for a thrilling book. It might have more unity. The best plot is like a noble river, every image, flower, star, or fancy should be tributary to it, like the flowers along its borders, all adorning its bank or mirrored in its crystal waters; but I am so delighted, Frank, to think I have a review from you, and you had no idea whose book it was. Isn't it funny—a man reviewing his wife's book? and yet, for once, a husband's opinion was impartially given. What would I have done if you had said anything sharp? It would have been almost like the first cross word. I'm afraid I never could have recovered from such a shock. I feared you would think the plot meandered and zigzagged too much, and I do care what you think more than I do for the opinion of all the world beside."

"There's too much harmony between our souls," said Frank, "for me to find any great fault with any thought or fancy or feeling of yours. I felt a strange, peculiar interest in the author when I first read Dawn. She seemed to express my own thoughts better than I could myself, and that is as high praise as I can give any writer."

"Frank," said Nepenthe, "since I have seen this book in print, I've had a great deal better book come in my head. It is all plot, passion and pathos. I can see the plot right through, just as you can see all the way down this avenue in the evening, with its long rows of lamps on each side. So all along the new path of fancy, it seems as if I can see little lights hung on both sides from beginning to end, and my thoughts delight in roaming all through this illuminated plot. I seem to meet living people, and hear living voices talking to me, till I fall in love with my own hero and wake up very early in the morning to hear what he has to say to me."

"Is it a religious novel?" said Frank.

"I hate that phrase—religious novels," said Nepenthe. "They generally are a bottle of fiction's deodorized benzine, superior to any other article in market for removing moral spots and spiritual stains of every kind from Fancy's gay, grave or gossamer robe without altering the fine color or texture, and sometimes they take the whole color out of fiction, so you can't tell what color it is or was. A religious novel is often only another name for the tamest kind of trash—but I hope nobody will call Dawn a quiet book," she added, as Bridget came in just then with a paper, having in it another quite lengthy review, "for when 'all is quiet' on thought's Potomac, no victories are ever gained on fiction's broad, contested field, no laurels ever won, and my poor little book might have to go at last to wait at some dusty corner of Nassau street, and with faded, threadbare cover lie outside in the cold in Fame's cheerless Potter's Field, among those long rows of unwept, unhonored and unsung volumes over whose neglected heads you read in dingy letters, as you pass along, this dismal obituary notice :

"'ANY OF THESE BOOKS CAN BE HAD FOR 25 CENTS.'

"Frank, if my Dawn were one of those stately thought castles, from whose ivied windows you could look out on fiction's broad field and see a solitary horseman ride by, or some persecuted woman in white hunted and haunted by villains in black ; if I had made some dim, shadowy woods, where veiled ladies hide and ghosts hover in shrouds, it might be very popular—Mr. Caushus might, perhaps, sell three hundred thousand copies."

"Yes," said Frank ; "and you might have had some high-bred, haughty, heavenly hero emerge from those shadowy woods, hiding under his calm marble face boundless oceans of intensest passion, but bursting forth into wildest cataracts of emotion as some mysterious stranger crosses his path, holding in his coat pocket the dreadful secret and priceless safeguard of your hero's whole past life. You should have gifted this mighty, matchless, murderous man with tongue of ice and heart of fire, as his bloody deeds half frighten one's conscience to death, while his celestial, immaculate motives win the ceaseless admiration of the most spotless maiden's pious, profoundest soul."

" I have no trap-door in my garret, no dungeon in my cellar," said Nepenthe, " nor have I frescoed on the walls within any faithful copies or skilful reproductions of the great masters of fiction—but I have led my readers along the winding river of mortal life, and I hope they may find some little thought flower growing on its banks to lay away and keep in their hearts forever.

"I finished Hannah Thurston when you was out to-day, Frank. The book so bewitched me I couldn't leave it off until I had finished it. I don't believe one man in ten thousand could have so put off the shoes of conventionality and stolen so noiselessly into the inmost holy of a woman's heart, and given us those inimitable stereoscoptic views as Bayard Taylor has done. For a new traveller in the realm of fiction, he has made marvellous progress. You'd think he had lived and breathed there always.

" The hero Woodbury is just such an ideal real man as lives in many a woman's soul, but which few authors ever sketch. I almost wonder a man could so faithfully, gracefully and symmetrically portray such a real live hero. I wouldn't blame all the girls for falling in love and marrying - such a man as Woodbury, if they could find him. Then the book is so fragrant all through with a woody perfume,˙ you feel as if you were walking the—

" ' Secret shades
Of woody Ida's inmost grove.'

" The author has the good sense to find his heroine in the country, and keep her there. You almost breathe the odor of the new mown hay as you read, and you can see the wild flowers on Hannah's table. The author has studied nature reverently and honestly, and she has given him her most illustrious diploma in the university of fame."

CHAPTER XLIV.

COMPATIBILITY.

" So 'tis with us when fond hopes cherished long,
Upheld through storms of contradiction strong ;
To ripe fulfilment suddenly are grown,
And gates of Paradise are open thrown."—GOETHE.

" ONE thing is certain," said Kate Howard ; " Frank Carleyn and his wife will never separate for want of compatibility. Miss Prudence says the first question a girl should ask now-a-days of the man who makes her an offer is, ' Have you got compatibility ?' A great many matches are not made in Heaven. Mr. Vole says many of them are lucifer matches, made by the prince of the fallen angels."

" As Miss Potter says, we do hear a great deal about this compatibility. It really seems to be an acknowledged ground for separation. If our grandmothers who had unreasonable husbands, and our grandfathers who had vixenish wives, had only thought of this before, how much trouble they would have saved themselves. I don't believe I shall ever marry—so few of the gentlemen I know have this precious compatibility, and I would as soon try to domesticate myself in a snow-bank for life as with a man without it."

Kate has been reading " Prue and I " over again.—She's so delighted with it ; she says it is full of compatibility. She says she has a husband in Spain, and so long as he and she live so happily together, she is most afraid to think of any other husband. Her husband in Spain has such kind, urbane manners. He likes everything she likes, and he has none of those queer little fidgetty ways they say husbands do have—yet if she could find such a man as Prue's husband was, she'd marry him to-morrow, even if he were an old book-keeper in a white cravat, and she'd be willing to have him for the autocrat of her breakfast-table as long as she lived.

" Did you see the bride in church on Sunday ?" asked

Miss Charity Gouge, coming in suddenly and interrupting Kate's solitary soliloquy, as she seated herself by the register to warm her feet.   Charity is always warming her feet. If she can get into a kitchen, she will open the oven door of the cooking stove, and taking off both shoes, put her feet in the oven and toast them, as she says.   She is warming her feet the year round, except in the middle of August, and I sometimes think they are a little chilly then. All winter she wears two pair of stockings, and in very severe weather, two pair of shoes.   She says half the diseases are caused by too thinly covering the feet. Wherever she goes, visits, or calls, her first object seems to be to warm her feet.

"I saw the bride," said Kate, "but I was so taken up with watching Dr. Wendon, I forgot to see what she had on. I never saw such a look on a man's face before.

"Rev. Henry Selwyn Stuart, the bride's father, preached a beautiful and impressive sermon from the text, 'All things work together for good.'

"You know it was Easter Sunday, and the day of the Hebrew Passover.   It was just one year ago on Easter Sunday morning that Dr. Wendon thought he saw the dawn once more—so it was truly *his* Passover, for blindness passed away from the door of his spirit; it was *his* Easter morning too, for his long-entombed soul had its resurrection to light.

"As he looked over the hymn book with Mrs. Carleyn, I never heard a sweeter voice as he sung this verse of that beautiful hymn.   I could see tears in his eyes—I am sure there were tears in *mine*.

> "Walk in the light, and thou shalt own
>   Thy darkness passed away,
>   Because that light hath on thee shone
>   In which is perfect day."

"At the close of the services they sang again, and as Dr. Wendon stood up the cloud suddenly broke away, the sunlight streamed in through the window, and shone on his radiant face.   I could hear his rich manly voice in tremulous tones —

> "Now that the sun is gleaming bright,
>   Implore we, bending low,
>   That He, the uncreated light,
>   May guide us as we go."

"What will he do now?" asked Charity, in her practical way. "Will he make his home with his former protege, Mrs. Carleyu?"

"He is going next week on a mission to India," said Kate. "He heard a sermon a year ago from the text—'Come over and help us,' and he says that like a succession of alarum bells, breaking ever and anon on his ears, have sounded these words, 'Behold, I come quickly,'—he goes to wait with the weary night-watch for the breaking of the eastern sky"

Reader! you and I have some dear little hungry hope climbing the toilsome hills of our longing life; may it find at last some bright Easter morning its radiant dawn.

If you have patiently followed my story to its end, how I would like to look into your face as you lay the book away up in your soul's attic, where you lay away all stories read long ago. Yet much as I peer out into life's darkness to get a glimpse of you, I see you not, only in that weird dreamland where unseen friends nightly gather, and I fancy sing me to sleep.

Take this my prayer, that if soul-thirsty and weary, you may quaff life's purest Nepenthe. sweet with blessing and fragrant with balm. If we ever meet in the palace called Beautiful, above, I may look over your shoulder, and read your name among the names of earth's tired wayfarers.

THE END.